KATHERINE QUINN

THE
AZANTIAN
TRILOGY

CROWN
OF SALT AND
BONE

CROWN OF SALT AND BONE

KATHERINE QUINN

CITY OWL
PRESS

CROWN OF SALT AND BONE
The Azantian Trilogy, Book 3

CITY OWL PRESS
www.cityowlpress.com

Cover Design by MiblArt. All stock photos licensed appropriately.

Edited by Charissa Weaks.

For information on subsidiary rights, please contact the publisher at info@cityowlpress.com.

Hardback Edition ISBN: 978-1-64898-428-0
Paperback Edition ISBN: 978-1-64898-369-6
Digital Edition ISBN: 978-1-64898-370-2

Printed in the United States of America

Life isn't always full of color. Between the shades of gray, beauty and truth live. Don't be afraid to seek it.

PRAISE FOR KATHERINE QUINN

"Forbidden romance, whispers of hidden gods, and the mysteries of the roughest seas animate this adventure while leaving plenty of potential for future installments. Fans of the enemies-to-lovers trope will be pleased."
— *Publisher's Weekly*

"Quinn's writing style is lush and lyrical, her premise unique and spellbinding, the love story magical and full of heat. Readers will cheer for Margrete and Bash and gasp at the twists and turns."
— *Ashley R. King, Author of Painting the Lines and Forever After*

"A sweeping and extravagant fantasy weaving in romance and adventure that takes the reader in a voyage into a world they'll never want to leave."
— *E. E. Hornburg, Author of The Night's Chosen*

"My stomach is a riot of butterflies. This book is phenomenal and a new favorite with romance that is both HOT and sweet and just makes me yearn. And the end is so, so good. My heart is racing."
— *Desirée M. Niccoli, Author of Called to the Deep*

"The world building is phenomenal. The descriptions of the buildings, the castle, the ship on the ocean, everything is so vividly detailed you feel like you are there... You will be enthralled with this tale."
— *Beyond the Stars Book Blog*

"Filled with heart-wrenching twists and an addictive, sexy romance, *On These Wicked Shores* delivers a tantalizing escape into a dark and dangerous fantasy adventure where the lines between good and evil and love and hate blur. Readers will beg for more of Quinn's lush world."
— *Charissa Weaks, Author of The Witch Collector*

SOMEWHERE IN A DREAM
PROLOGUE

BASH ROLLED OVER IN BED AND TUGGED THE WARM BODY AT HIS SIDE closer.

Margrete let out a soft sigh, nuzzling his chest, her naked flesh warm and silky and utterly addicting.

He trailed a finger down her arm, unable to help himself. He *had* to feel her, to know she was real and not some cruel apparition. This time, she shivered, goosebumps rising wherever he touched. Her breathing audibly changed, her mind waking to greet the new day.

A new day where they once more woke in each other's arms.

Bash had never realized life could be filled with such happiness. It was foreign to him, an elusive emotion he believed he'd experienced before, not realizing just how empty his soul had been.

"You kept me up all night," Margrete groused, her voice thick with exhaustion. "Can we sleep in a little while longer?"

Bash smiled, wanting nothing more than to give in to her wishes. But there was work to be done on the island, a storm having demolished a few of the northern farms. Adrian and his men expected him in the main hall in an hour, and he had to prepare. Besides, they were still tracking the sea's beasts, their trail having gone cold weeks ago.

"Please," she said in a whisper, sensing his hesitation. She flipped onto her side beneath the covers and gazed up at him, her eyes bright despite the early hour. Mischievous.

Running a hand down the side of her cheek, he breathed in her scent and relished the simple moment. He'd faced victory and received praise. Felt his people's love...and their frustrations. And he'd gone his entire life being lifted on the shoulders of others.

But this—such a mundane thing, lying in bed with Margrete—was a moment that would become a precious memory. He suspected he'd return to such a time in the years to come, time when he'd look back and imagine the peace that embraced him now. After a lifetime of never knowing it, Margrete's affection was a gift. He still couldn't believe that she was his, and he was hers.

And he'd spend every damned day letting her know just how lucky he felt.

"What are you thinking about in that head of yours?" she mused, leaning forward to kiss his nose. "You've never been one for deep reflection. Does it hurt?" Her brow furrowed in mock concern, and she placed the back of her hand on his temple as if he had a fever.

"So cruel." He tapped her nose, and she wrinkled it, grinning wide.

"You're exceptionally easy to rile. And it's so much fun for me. I must find my entertainment somewhere. This beautiful island can be rather dull."

Bash tugged her flush against him, pressing her head against his madly beating heart. It belonged to her, after all.

"What will I do with you, princess?" He wove his fingers through her hair, gently massaging her scalp. She melted against him.

"I suppose you can keep me," she said dramatically. He could practically see her impish grin. His joy swelled.

"Oh, you'll never be rid of me," he promised. "How many times must I convince you? You're stuck with me now."

Because he loved her.

It had been a few weeks since the captain's attack, and neither of them had spoken the words. But with each passing day, Bash's love flourished. His heart was light and warm, and there was no denying what he felt.

He thought she mumbled something that sounded like "Good," but he couldn't be sure. Her breathing had evened out. She'd fallen back asleep.

Bash brushed a kiss to the top of her head.

Dawn beckoned, as did his work, but he allowed himself to stay in bed, indulging in the woman who'd saved his island and stolen not only his respect but his heart. Perhaps the day's work could wait a little longer.

A flash of silver light flickered across his vision. He blinked, frowning. *What the hell?*

Bash turned to where the light had been the brightest—the sea glass walls beside the door.

Another bolt flickered, and he jerked back.

The walls...they appeared as if they were *vibrating*. He rubbed at his eyes, trying to clear his sight, but the glass continued to quiver.

Shadows curled about the sides of their suite, flowing through the open windows and the balcony doors. He shot up in bed.

"Margrete, do you see—"

No one rested beside him, the sheets empty, her warm presence gone.

Panic rushed through his veins, his blood turning to ice.

Those peculiar shadows swarmed around him now, seeming to grow stronger, more determined. His alarm rendered him frozen, and he was helpless but to watch as they surged forward.

Bash opened his mouth to scream, but no sound came out.

Dense, black wisps churned and spun around his body, devouring their chambers and robbing him entirely of his sight. And just when he believed the shadows would choke the life from him, Bash blinked again...

He stood in the war room with Adrian, his friend's welcoming face cocked in question as if he awaited a response.

Like grains of sand slipping through his fingertips, Bash lost all memory of his morning with Margrete. Instead, he focused on Adrian and fell into their conversation with ease, speaking about the southern end of the island and the beasts they'd soon hunt.

Deep down he knew something was off, but it was as if his mouth and limbs moved without his consent. The passage of time didn't matter, and Bash suddenly felt too weary to make sense of it. There was only what lay before him, and it was pleasant and familiar.

Yet somewhere far away, a voice murmured across his thoughts, eager and persistent. It reminded him of Margrete's voice, but that couldn't be right, as this new voice was brimming with anguish.

Bash ignored the screams and honed in on Adrian's laughter. On his friend's thorough explanation for why they needed to construct another grand vessel.

Yet when the walls of the war room shook minutes later, Bash was deposited in yet another random moment of time. He didn't even struggle to decipher the change anymore. He simply fell into the bliss of routine until the world around him trembled, and he'd once again find himself back in Margrete's company, his worries melting away until he lost all sense of himself.

Whatever enchantment afflicted him, he didn't care. He was happy and loved and safe.

After some time, Bash paid no heed to the shadows that stole him. In fact, he welcomed their embrace and whatever magic they commanded.

Bash gave in.

CHAPTER ONE

MARGRETE

MARGRETE WAS FIRE AND LIGHT AND MALICE, AND NOTHING AND NO one would stop her from turning the world of the gods on its head.

Drenched in the cooling blood of her beloved king, she blasted open the portal to the Underworld, shattering the ground of Darius's wretched island and storming through a tunnel belonging to the divine.

Each wrathful step jolted her bones, a harsh stinging radiating down her spine. She inhaled the copper in the air, Bash's life essence clinging to her stiffened shirt, the potent scent fanning the flames of her rage, turning her into a living, breathing storm of heartbreak. Margrete barely sensed the humanity within, as if it shrank in on itself once Bash's soul departed her world. Though she supposed she couldn't even call herself human anymore. After completing the final trial on Surria's cursed island, a great shift had occurred, and now, nothing felt *right*.

She didn't feel right.

As if to confirm, her newly branded arm prickled. The gray swirls whirled across her forearm, the single black teardrop pulsating.

After she'd battled her father, her wave had appeared on her collarbone. Now, it seemed as if this new tattoo materialized after her fight for the immortality she didn't want. Or maybe it was borne from something else entirely...

She didn't ruminate upon the thought for long.

I'm going to kill them all, she thought as a silver door loomed ahead, intricate depictions of human life and other such absurdities etched into its thick metal. Light glimmered around its edges, luminescent in the dusky corridor. It had to be the door to the Underworld.

She shoved it open and barreled through. Nothing mattered.

Bash was dead. Darius had won. She was now a goddess.

Margrete repeated this about a thousand times to herself as she marched through a narrow passageway lined with opaque ivory sconces, blue flames seeming to reach out and lick at her skin.

She'd fought against evil and lost, but the war was nowhere near over.

The thing about loss was that sometimes it didn't hit you right away, not in its true form at least. Anger was a much easier ally, and it currently beat inside her head like a drum, drowning out her inner cries. Her unseen agony.

She could accept rage with open arms, because the alternative? Stopping her advance for just one moment would allow the burning tears to fall. The sheer weight of her loss would force her to her knees where she'd curl into a tight ball and wish the world away. She'd be useless, and while giving in was tempting—oh-so fucking tempting—she feared she wouldn't have the strength to rise again.

So, she didn't give in, and she didn't allow her tears to fall, and Margrete stormed ahead as if an army was hot on her trail.

The damp walkway went on forever, and with every thud of her boots upon the stones, her resolve strengthened, despair driving her.

"Margrete! Wait!"

The voice at her back reminded her of an annoying bell. As long as it didn't belong to Bay, she didn't much care who its owner was. Margrete didn't trust herself *not* to kill him for his part in Bash's death. He was the one who'd delivered the blade into her hands, and even if he'd ultimately saved her, she still felt anger. However unwarranted.

With the entrance to the realm of the dead growing closer, Margrete's magic opened its maw and exhaled, shuddering with anticipation. She relished how it whispered in her ears, a low melody that harmonized with her own breathing. It was almost like sharing a body with two souls, her power its own being, trapped in warm flesh.

Her name sounded again, and a hand fell on her shoulder. Such a frail, weak, *mortal* hand. Margrete never realized how breakable bones could be, but she knew without a doubt she could shatter the fingers on her shoulder without so much as a thought.

She spun around, annoyed by the interruption.

Mila. She reared back, her bright green eyes wide with uncharacteristic fear. She held up two placating hands.

"What?" Margrete snapped. She'd just lost the love of her life to some twisted game orchestrated by Darius, and dealing with Mila wasn't a priority.

"Calm down, Margrete," Mila begged, her lower lip trembling. Margrete cocked her head at that; Mila rarely showed any ounce of emotion at all. The Azantian rubbed at her stained shirt, which was ripped across the midsection, her right sleeve nearly shredded entirely. She'd put up a decent fight against Shade and her nymphs, not that Margrete doubted Mila's capability once her temper was incited.

But she was hesitant now.

Terrified.

"We shouldn't just rush into this." Mila gestured to the long, empty corridor of flickering blue light, gnawing at the inside of her cheek.

"Rush into it?" Margrete repeated, stepping closer. Heat danced in her belly and her breath grew hot. "Bash was just *killed*. I'm getting him back. The gods and their games can go screw themselves."

She made to turn around when the young woman brazenly grabbed her arm. Slowly, Margrete studied the dirtied fingers around her biceps before bringing her attention to Mila. Bold. Very bold of the sailor.

"First of all, we don't know where this tunnel leads, and second of all, your eyes are fucking *glowing*. Not to mention the air around you feels charged with...magic." Mila took a wise step back, allowing Margrete room to breathe, to seethe. "You're not thinking clearly, and when you're not thinking clearly, you're dangerous. More so now."

After she'd been given a gift she'd never wanted. No. It was a curse.

"As if you ever cared about me before," Margrete said, frost coating every word. Mila never liked her—she made that perfectly clear the day Margrete couldn't save Jace on the island. "From what I remember, you were begging me to command these powers before, and when I failed, you shunned me as if I'd allowed your friend to die on purpose."

Mila clenched her jaw, the freckles on her nose wrinkling as her nostrils flared. "I may not have liked you at first, Margrete, but that's only because..." Her focus shifted. "Well, to be quite honest, seeing you lose your shit was rather refreshing. It makes you seem like an actual person."

"Instead of?"

"Instead of some gratingly perfect specimen everyone loves and obsesses over all the damn time. I've heard your name spoken more times than I want to remember since you landed on Azantian. You may think me cynical for it, but I've found that when something looks too good to be true, it's because it usually is."

Mila didn't like her because she seemed too...perfect?

That was laughable.

Before Margrete could reply, more footsteps pounded, and Dani and Atlas sprinted into the light of the nearest sconce.

The former's head remained lowered, heavy with grief, as tears streaked Dani's face.

Shit. Now Margrete felt like an ass on top of it all. The churning fire that had fueled her moments before began to simmer.

Dani had lost her brother, Jacks. She let that thought sink in, grimacing when an image of Jonah washed across her mind. The young sailor had been so eager to join them, and he'd perished at Darius's hand in the most gruesome of ways.

She sucked in a deep breath, trying to clear the haze that worked to steal her empathy. Her humanity. It would've been so much easier to allow it control. At least then she wouldn't feel as though she were teetering on the edge of a cliff.

"Why did you follow me?" Margrete asked cautiously, addressing Atlas. She shoved Jonah and Jacks from her thoughts. While a dull and profound ache throbbed in her chest, they were wasting precious time.

The warrior lifted her chin. On a bad day, she was obnoxiously proud, but now, a cloud seemed to hover over her head, weighing down her shoulders and turning her eyes a dull shade of blue.

"I followed you because that's what my king would've wanted." Atlas's right eye twitched, showing her nerves, but she quickly regained control of her emotions and lifted to her full, towering height. "And *when* we get him back, he'll probably owe me more than a promotion."

Mila shook her head, her red hair grazing her cheeks. "Now's not the time for jokes, Atlas, which is surprising coming from you." She observed the blonde with both disdain and awe. Mila had a gift of expressing scorching emotions on a delicate face.

Atlas didn't drop Dani's hand, but she stepped closer to Mila, her hackles rising. "I'm doing my damned best, Mila. Am I supposed to pretend to be some hardened piece of stone that doesn't break or feel anything other than contempt?"

"How dare you—"

"Enough!" Margrete roared, her voice shaking the walls. The blue flames captured in the sconces wavered erratically.

Dani inched forward, eyes locked on Margrete. Dark curls tumbled into her face, her golden-brown skin smudged with grime from their fight in the arena. But even covered in dirt, there was something different about the woman, and not merely because of what she'd lost. Her blue eyes appeared to glimmer with purpose, and Margrete had to force herself to turn away from their intensity.

"I'm not wasting another moment," Margrete said, "but if you desire to do so, please stay behind and don't get in my way."

She continued deeper into the Underworld, knowing this passage had to end at some point. She'd walk forever if that's what it took.

A few seconds later, heavy footsteps pummeled the rocky earth, her reluctant companions trailing behind. The part of her that still felt mortal, that still felt like *her*, questioned why she wasn't demanding they turn around and head back to the human realm. They might not last long down here—if they ever made it to the Underworld—and they certainly weren't composed of the divinity Margrete now embraced.

She didn't question her role among the immortals anymore. All of it overwhelmed her, yes, but instead of fighting it and telling herself she *wasn't* a goddess, Margrete welcomed the change with open arms. If it helped her find her love, then she'd embrace it.

She'd become a living nightmare if she had to.

Silence ensued as they walked into the unknown, and after many long minutes, the tunnel widened. Another door stood erected in the center of a rounded stone antechamber, though this time, it had been fashioned of an opulent gold that shone with thousands of glimmering gems. Margrete considered its odd position in the middle of the room with skepticism.

She came to a sudden halt, and Atlas gently bumped into her shoulder. Margrete flinched at the contact, and the sailor wisely put distance between them. It appeared that everyone was frightened of her.

For a good reason. She frightened herself.

"We're getting him back. *Together*," Atlas said at her side. Her eyes were trained straight ahead, at the brilliant gold door. "Bash is my king, but more than that, I know he'd fight for me too. For us all if he could. But," she added, her voice stern, "I wouldn't just follow *anyone* into the depths of the Underworld."

They locked eyes. Atlas gleamed with sincerity, not an ounce of doubt marring her face. For a fraction of a heartbeat, Margrete didn't feel as if she were adrift, floating between realms. She gave the warrior a curt nod, her throat suddenly constricting.

"Once we go through that portal, there may be no turning back," Margrete warned, raising her voice and turning to address the other two women. "Now's your chance to turn back. Your *last* chance."

Silence ensued, but no protests sounded.

Surprisingly, Dani was the first to break the weighty quiet. She dropped Atlas's hand and squared her slight shoulders. Her damp cheeks had long ago dried, but the tear tracks still gleamed in the meager light of the enclosure.

"I fear nothing anymore," she murmured, her voice cracking. "I lost my twin, the other half of my soul, and if there's a chance to get him back, or even to say goodbye, I'll not waste it. I'm coming for Jacks. For my friend, Jonah. And for the island I love."

"And I want to shed the blood of the god responsible for the death of my father," Mila added. "The same one who orchestrated a twisted game that killed the man I might've found a partner in." Grant and Jace—two men whom the hardened sailor had given her heart to. "I won't rest until my father's blade is slick with Darius's divine blood."

Mila's lips curled up, baring her teeth. Margrete noted her hand rested on the blade in question, the one Grant must've given her.

Too bad the honor of killing Darius would be hers. Margrete wanted to be the one to watch as the light died from his seafoam eyes.

"It's settled," Atlas said. She motioned to the door. "We're all doing this, Margrete, and we'll follow you into the dark. Now it's up to you to lead us there."

Margrete whirled away from her companions. Three people who couldn't be any more unalike. And yet, she couldn't deny that having them in her arsenal would be an advantage. She thought of Bay for a pained moment, realizing he'd stayed behind. His hesitance after such betrayal hurt more than she expected.

The warriors before her would suffice.

Atlas was strength and grit and fortitude. Dani's presence reminded Margrete of the humanity she felt drifting further and further away. And Mila...she was that voice—that *loud* voice—in her ear, calling her out on her bullshit.

As much as she wanted to storm into the Underworld alone with her magic blazing, Margrete wasn't sure what she'd be up against. She scrutinized the trio, taking her time to drink in their determined features, to make sure their convictions held true. Not one of them showed a hint of uncertainty, and Margrete knew they meant every word.

"Fine. But stay close to me and keep quiet," Margrete said, shifting once more for the door. She ambled closer until three feet separated her from the golden slab and the gilded handle in the shape of...

A liander bloom.

The knob opening the portal to the Underworld resembled a sedative disguised by petals—the same flower she'd once used on Bash the night they shared their first kiss. Her heart clenched at the memory, but she swallowed it down with a grimace.

Her emotions would get the best of her if she didn't control them.

Lifting her hand, she brought it to the cool metal handle. It was ice beneath her skin, and the contact sent a charged current dancing up and down her arm. Her fingers tightened on the knob, and her breath wavered as a crushing weight settled onto her shoulders.

This was the moment of no return. A moment she'd either celebrate or curse.

Margrete pulled on the handle and opened the door that led to nowhere and possibly everywhere.

This time, her ensuing curse was echoed by the others.

CHAPTER TWO

MARGRETE

SHE HADN'T EXPECTED THE UNDERWORLD TO BE SO BRIGHT. NOT that she'd known what to expect.

Margrete pushed beyond the portal's threshold, looking up, up, *up*...

They had been delivered to a cliff overlooking a rocky valley, the pale stones sharp and unforgiving, all jutting out as if pointing at them with accusatory fingers. *Warning* them. Uneven stairs crept downward, the steep path cutting through the center of the rocky landscape. Far away, she heard dripping water, the steadying noise matching her heart rate. She followed the sound, spotting a slim waterfall in the far distance, its pure blue flowing down a crag and disappearing into a gorge.

It was infinite; an entire world imprisoned by towering rocks that rose on forever to kiss a cloudless sky...which shined with *three* suns. All differing colors, all intense, and equally breathtaking. One shone a pale, buttery yellow, the second a robin's egg blue, and the third a brilliant red. The last sun cast the realm in an eerie crimson glow, causing goosebumps to form up and down her arms.

Amber leaves sprouted haphazardly from the rugged terrain, the flora a warm shade of autumn. No fanciful flowers bloomed, but spindly sea-green reeds flourished around the pathway before them, leading them to a castle far grander than any built with mortal hands.

Gasps sounded from behind her, and Margrete realized she'd forgotten her companions entirely as she took everything in.

The palace—if the word did it justice—rested in the heart of the valley, with no end to its size. Brilliant lights poured from its core, the structure glimmering with hints of every color imaginable. It reminded her of a rainbow trapped inside a glass jar.

The neighboring stones of the ravine were dull in comparison to the lustrous palace, and if she squinted, she could make out what appeared to be crushed gems embedded in the rock, the facets sending blazes of light radiating across the Underworld.

From the rough landscape, the fortress rose high into the air, giving way to seven spires soaring higher than the eye could see...seven spires and what appeared to be seven levels, dense walls encircling each landing. Only when she lowered her head did she see the stream of vivid red surrounding the otherworldly palace, hugging its rugged shores.

Margrete peered over the side of the cliff and at the narrow stairs leading down. They were treacherous and steep, and just as dangerous as their destination.

Her eyes glided across the precarious path, the stairs leading to the palace, and to a bridge of enchanting blue and silver glass that ran across the red stream. Instantly, her mind went to Azantian and its glass bridges.

There could be no denying that the Underworld held similarities to the island. How it shone with transcendent light, its gems brilliant and unnatural. The way the air vibrated with raw energy that worked to both enliven and soothe.

Perhaps such similarities were due to Malum having created Azantian. He'd fashioned his island after the official home of the gods, and the longer she surveyed the palace, the more she found bits and pieces of Bash's realm shining before her.

It made her eyes burn with unshed tears.

"Holy gods," Atlas whispered behind her. "And here I thought we'd step into a fiery pit, or even some depthless lake brimming with souls."

"Those stories are from human myths," Mila said, distaste evident in her tone.

Margrete tuned them out. Gripping the sides of the tunnel, she focused on the crispness in the air, the slight chill. Her power sparked in her chest, warming her bones and causing her toes to curl in her boots. But even with the warmth, a hint of bitter adrenaline remained.

She noticed how her magic was akin to an untamed beast. Margrete recognized it as its own entity, and while she commanded it, she knew it belonged to something far greater than herself.

"Look for movement," she instructed coolly, fearing an onslaught of guards at any given moment. Then again, did the gods truly require soldiers to defend them?

Squinting, she made out hundreds of arched windows lining the rooms of the palace in the far distance. She hoped to spot a figure, anything really, that might give her an idea of its occupants. But the cavern itself was empty and soundless, all except for the gurgling of the distant waterfall and the blood-red stream. She wondered if it *was* blood.

Time to find out.

Margrete took the first step down the pathway. Each one after sent an intoxicating tingle up and down her frame, like the very ground held magic. It was a pull she felt, a *connection* to the palace, that quickened her movements.

It took at least half an hour to climb down. Margrete's limbs trembled as time passed, the grief she'd wrestled down before catching up and making it difficult to take in a full breath. Anger had been the force driving her, but now, stranded in silence, an ache took up residence in her chest. A hole that seemed to grow larger and larger with each new inhale. She felt as if she were floating and plummeting all at once, her mind unable to fixate upon one solid emotion. The dam was breaking, and so was she.

And the worst part was, she was entering into this new world not only broken, but without a plan as to how to fix things.

In order to get Bash's soul, she'd have to enter a realm of death, and somehow, make it out with her own soul intact. All of it suddenly felt hopeless.

She felt hopeless.

Margrete had always put on a good act when needed, but even with the buzz of her new power, she felt like a small child, locked in that same tower in Prias, just another soul that fate controlled.

She wanted her partner, her pirate. Her Bash. She wanted to be the strong woman she knew she could be, and she wanted him at her side, his hand in hers, a silent support.

She'd gotten a taste of what it was like to have everything she'd ever wanted, and she wasn't about to give it up. Not now. Not ever. She dug her nails into her palms, focusing on the sting, reminding herself to be harder. To be stronger.

A clang pierced the too-quiet air.

Margrete held out a hand, signaling the others to halt. The noise came from her left, the glass bridge leading to the palace a meager fifty feet away. Whimsical designs painted in lively reds and spirited yellows decorated a few of the scattered boulders, which rose well above their heads. They also provided a decent place for an enemy to hide.

The moment that thought crossed her mind, gray smoke streamed from behind the largest outcropping in the near distance. A lone figure stepped into the center of the path, their form shrouded by thin fog. Margrete grabbed Atlas's shirt, and with a nod to the others, quickly ducked behind the nearest rocks. They each dipped into a crouch, Mila the last to kneel.

But they were too late.

Without warning, a dagger rushed past Margrete's ear.

Many things ensued in the moments after, and they all happened in a blur. Atlas reached for her twin blades, her body moving in front of Dani protectively. Another dagger rushed through the air, seeming to arc as it soared, its murderous path an inch from Margrete's head. She ducked lower, the metal still singing in her ear.

But Mila. Her actions surprised Margrete the most.

A third knife came out of nowhere, whistling as it shifted directions, curving unnaturally toward her. Margrete's magic simmered, and she began to lift a hand in front of her when Mila jumped before her body like a shield.

As though time itself had been dipped in honey, Margrete fixated on the dagger, its lethal tip flying in the direction of Mila's pounding heart.

With mere inches to spare before the weapon stole the sailor's life, Margrete didn't react. At least, not with her hands or body. Her *mind* did.

One second the whirling blade hurtled in their direction, and the next Margrete demanded it to *stop*, a lone command that rang in her mind like a quake. The weapon quivered violently before freezing in midair...mere centimeters from Mila's face. It hummed with magic, and a soft, red glow highlighted the sharp edges of the dagger. A soft gasp left her companion's lips, and her shoulders sagged with tangible relief as her body slumped against Margrete's chest.

She snatched the blade, vibrations working up and down her arm. Gripping the hilt, she pushed Mila aside, feeling both thankful for her selfless act and infuriated. Surprise also mingled with those particular emotions, though she wasn't certain if Mila had acted so nobly because she *needed* Margrete or because the sailor genuinely cared.

"Show yourself!" Margrete demanded of their assailant, the weapon in one hand and her magic sparking uncontrollably from her other. It screamed for freedom, her palms burning even as the sensation of frigid waters seemed to glide down her body.

No more daggers sailed through the air, but the quiet was somehow worse.

"Come out!" she bellowed again, her lips curling up into a snarl. Maybe Darius had somehow beaten them to the gates. If he had, then Margrete was prepared to turn his own knife on him—and this time, make sure it found his black heart. She was immortal now, and only a god could kill another god.

This almost made her smile.

Thick tension saturated the air, and she lifted her palm, preparing to fire recklessly into one of the many crevices lining the pathway, when a thunderous voice called out.

"My sincerest apologies. I thought you were another, far less virtuous deity."

Margrete snapped her head up and to the right, finding the approaching figure of a man. Impossibly tall, he loomed above them on a jutted-out portion of stone, hovering like a wrathful demon.

It wasn't Darius, though that had to be whom he spoke of.

"Who are you?" she asked, her voice harder than steel. Her palm hovered in position, ready.

He laughed; the sound a melody of discordant notes that sent teasing shivers down her spine. The figure stepped off the crag with fluid grace, landing without a sound. The others scrambled behind her. Thankfully, they had some semblance of self-preservation.

Perhaps sensing their fear, the man casually shoved his hands deep into his fine black trousers, his walk dangerously carefree as he sauntered over. Darkness swirled about his face, but with every step it lessened, slithering away and back to the crevices from where they came.

When his features came into full view, Dani, who'd been quiet thus far, let out a surprised little yelp. Margrete barely contained her own.

Taller than she'd originally suspected—which should've been impossible—stood a man, his deep brown skin glowing in the valley's ethereal light. He was beautiful in a severe kind of way, every angle of him sharper than an Azantian blade, his gray-blue eyes of matching intensity. A crown of silver encircled his head, just above his black curls, the metal untouched and polished. Regal.

A god. A *king*.

She took in his every fine detail, noting his impeccably tailored black pants and matching jacket, silver threads working down its luxurious sleeves. He smiled, adjusting his cuffs, unbothered by the sight of four women glaring before him.

"My name is Halio, and this is my realm," he said, his smile widening. "And I take it you're the mortal who found herself turned into a goddess. Well, not just *any* mortal it appears." He stepped closer, and she tensed. "After all, I can sense *him* all over you. I assume he'll be here soon enough."

His realm. Margrete had been right. This *was* a king of sorts—the king of the dead.

From the corner of her vision, Atlas lifted her dagger. Margrete reached behind her, grasping the woman's arm and stilling her foolish movements. Her blade would do nothing against this being. He was the nameless God of Death.

Well, now *not* so nameless.

Margrete pushed away from her crew and boldly strode toward Halio. Nerves skittered down her spine, but she managed to fix her face into what she hoped to be a mask of apathy.

"It was Darius who forced me to undergo Surria's *trials*," she spat the word, "and it was him who made me into the being you see before you now. I wanted no part of this."

She waved her hands around the valley. Margrete wouldn't tell him of her *true* mission, that she was here for one thing and one thing alone. Bash's spirit. The God of Death probably wouldn't take too kindly to her stealing one of his souls.

All they needed was Bash's body, which she prayed his mother had found, and then they could return his soul to where it belonged. Nymeras were supposedly protective of their dead, and if she'd seen Margrete enter the Underworld, perhaps she held faith that Margrete would bring her son back. From the little Margrete had seen of the nymera in the arena, she hadn't been indifferent to her son being captured.

Darkness washed across Halio's gray eyes, and he cocked his head to the side, the act feline. Margrete felt as if he were looking right through her, judging and weighing her. Something about this being was peaceful and riotous all at once, and she couldn't discern which quality stood out more. Seconds passed, maybe a minute, but she didn't break eye contact.

When had she grown so careless? She stood before an immortal without an ounce of fear. Just righteous anger.

Halio broke the battle of wills first, a spark of what she could mistake as approval causing his irises to soften. "The others have heard of your arrival," he said, casting a glance over his shoulder and to the palace, a subtle smile tugging his lips "I'm sure they're...eager to meet you. They'll be surprised to see that you're more...daring than anticipated."

"I don't care to meet them."

The god scoffed, smoothing the wayward curls that escaped his crown. The motion was so very human-like that it took her aback. "I'm afraid you must. They've already gathered in the main foyer. It is customary to greet newly birthed gods, and we haven't had one of those in quite some time. I've come to fetch you personally. Traditions must be honored."

She hissed a vulgar curse. How could she trust that they wouldn't strike her down the second she entered the room?

Halio's massive frame remained unmoving, his face stone. He wasn't going to budge, and frankly, Margrete wished to get such *niceties* over with. She would anticipate the gods' attacks and prepare for the worst. But one thing was certain—none of the bastards would end her life before she did what she came here to do.

When she managed to leave the introduction unscathed and learn all she could from the deities, she'd search the Underworld and turn over every stone. Bash was here, and the way her heart thudded in her chest when she took in the palace, she knew he was inside, hidden behind its thick walls.

Halio's attention flicked to Atlas, Mila, and Dani, a lone and mischievous brow rising. He seemed to linger on Dani the longest, and his lips twitched at the side before he tore himself away. "Are you not going to introduce me to your human friends? So brave of them to dare come here in their state."

At the mention of her crew, Margrete's magic flooded to her palms, traces of water sizzling in the scorching blue flames that danced in her hands.

"No, I will not introduce them," she said, not offering Halio an ounce more. He didn't need to learn their names. If anything, he was here to spy on them and glean info before bringing it back to the other gods and goddesses.

Margrete bit her cheek hard enough to draw blood. She was arguing with *Death*, and the recklessness of it all only worked to add fuel to her magic.

"I was merely being polite. I already know their names," Halio said, winking. "Their souls all have places devoted to them in my realm when they pass." He chuckled as he waved his hand behind him, his laughter ringing in her ears. "I am the last god you should worry yourself with. I'm indifferent to the petty politics of this place, and frankly, I care not for you, but for *balance*. Which has been thoroughly disrupted."

Sincerity marked his words as clearly as the pounding of her heart in her ears. She studied him a beat longer, marking his relaxed stance, how a single dimple popped on one cheek as he appraised her in return.

He wouldn't harm them. At least, not now.

Halio grinned as if he knew she'd come to such a conclusion, but then his smile dipped.

"I must warn you, however, that this isn't a place for mortals. If they stay here too long, their bodies will wither and decay. They'll *die*," he stressed, eyes locked on the Azantians. "And I am not fond of ushering souls into the Underworld before their time."

Margrete clenched her fists. Not one more person would die under her watch. She wished she'd made them stay behind. It's what she *should* have done. What a good person would have insisted upon.

"We don't plan on staying long," Mila said, her pert nose wrinkling. "In fact, the less time spent here, the better. I, too, am not a fan of being ushered into the Underworld before my time. Besides, I'm not impressed by this place thus far."

Seriously? Mila turned being threatened by Death into a joke. She was twisted in a way Margrete could almost appreciate.

Apparently, Halio respected her boldness too. He let out a thunderous laugh and said, "I like this one. She'll make a lovely addition to my realm when her time *does* come."

"I'm thrilled," Mila remarked dryly, earning a roguish smirk from the god.

Regardless of Mila's indifference to the mortals' predicament, true fear slithered through Margrete's veins. She briefly locked eyes with

Dani, noticing her lips pulled down at the corners. She wasn't the only one on edge from Halio's warning.

"Ah..." Halio whirled toward the palace. "Enough talk about death. I say we get on with the festivities. I understand time is of the essence, little Azantians."

"He never clarified how long we have until we go..." Mila snapped her fingers, releasing a disgruntled huff. "I'd like to clear that up before the life is choked from me."

Maybe she was more worried than she'd let on.

"I believe he was vague on purpose. I get the sense that the gods take pleasure from our anxiety," Margrete said, starting after Halio. Logic told her not to follow the God of Death into a den full of vicious deities, but logic wasn't a weapon she brandished. That vanished when Bash took his final breath.

"Sick bastards," Atlas mumbled, but she was a step behind Margrete. "We all stay close and follow Margrete's lead. No one goes anywhere alone. And if anyone feels...*off*, we get the hell out of here. I'm not saying goodbye to any of you."

Mila grunted in assent, shifting her blades so they were within reach. Dani merely tilted her head, her sapphire eyes twinkling in the light of the red sun. She was eerily calm. In fact, this was the calmest Margrete had ever seen her.

Halio aimed for the wide, glass bridge overlooking the river of red. He didn't pause to place his full weight on its smooth surface, even though she hesitated, not trusting the near-translucent glass to hold. With her luck, she'd crack the entire thing with one step.

Her teeth ground together, and she held her breath, her foot hovering over the bridge. *Just do it,* she scolded. *If he sees you pause, he'll use it against you.*

Her interactions with gods had supported such assumptions, but Halio...he seemed different. Yet she wasn't foolish enough to believe he was a friend.

Slowly, she took that first step, sighing in relief when the glass held. Each one after came easier, though halfway across, she made the horrid mistake of looking down. *Blood.* She hadn't been wrong about what flowed below them. A breeze picked up and brought the pungent scent of copper to her nose, the smell causing her to gag. She wondered where it had come from. How many bodies it had taken to fill the river with such gore.

"Everything all right?" Halio asked, not deigning to turn. She swore his shoulders shook like he was suppressing a chuckle.

"Fine," she snapped. *I just get queasy when I walk over a river of blood, that's all.*

She most assuredly preferred Azantian's perilous bridges to this.

"Blood is the essence of all life," Halio said affectionately over his shoulder. "I find it rather beautiful."

Margrete scowled at the god's back. They certainly held different opinions.

She had to rein in the urge to sigh in relief when they landed on the other side. *See, easy,* she thought, her nose still wrinkling from the pungent odor.

Now came the hard part.

"This way," Halio instructed, motioning them all to a pair of open gates. While composed of the same jagged stone as the cavern, it was what lay between them that had her anxiety flaring.

In the very center, a rippling blue and yellow light shrouded the view of the palace. It shuddered as she neared, like gentle waves swelling before smoothing. She couldn't see anything other than the living colors moving inside the frame, and she immediately thought of the portal Bash had used on her chambers when she'd been his 'enemy'. That felt like a lifetime ago.

I'm coming for you, pirate. Her promise seemed to put the confidence back into her step, which had been waning since they'd arrived.

"After you." Halio tilted his head, his smile daring. "I find I'm eager to see how this all plays out. Such an emotion I haven't experienced in centuries. Mortals in the Underworld! A new goddess! Such fun."

"Glad to be of entertainment," Margrete griped. She wouldn't waste time when Bash was trapped gods knew where. Marching up to the portal, she held a hand in front of her—the same one bearing her new and highly undesired flame tattoo—and tested the churning mass of moving color. Ice shot down her fingers and raced across both arms. The portal rippled where she'd grazed it, but other than that, nothing ominous occurred.

Margrete sucked in a deep breath and walked through with open eyes. She wouldn't be caught unawares.

For a moment, everything went dull and gray, and a great pulse of energy wracked her frame. The sensation quickly passed when her feet landed safely on the other side.

For the second time in nearly as many minutes, Margrete lost her breath. The palace courtyard had to have been fashioned from dreams and exquisite magic. She tilted her head once again, seeing that all seven levels blazed with a sheen of color, from apple red to seafoam blue, and when the crimson sky touched the stones, the many hues of the palace sparkled like jewels.

It was...breathtaking.

"Not what you expected, eh?"

Margrete flinched. Halio was at her side, that vexing smirk plastered across his shrewd face. She hadn't even seen him move. She tore her gaze away, convincing herself it was to check on her friends, but really, it was because looking into the death god's eyes felt a lot like falling and never landing.

"This is where we go when we pass on?" Dani asked, her mouth gaping as she took in all the opulent splendor. Atlas's hand still clutched hers. "It's beautiful. A world dipped in color."

"Unfortunately, this isn't where mortals go," Halio answered somberly. "This is the home of the gods. The souls that have departed are kept...elsewhere." He glanced at Margrete as he muttered the final word. She wondered if he could read her traitorous mind. If he knew why she was truly here.

Once again, she pictured Bash's face—not as he appeared in those wretched final moments, but when he had the sun in his eyes and the sea breeze in his hair. She would do anything to make sure he was that happy and carefree again.

"I must warn you before we head in..." Halio moved until he stood in whispering distance. "The others felt the ripple that occurred after you completed the third trial. After you *changed*. They are desperate for a look at you. Be on your guard. And do *not* incite their tempers."

"You mean they sensed me after I was forced to become something I don't even want to be?"

All traces of Halio's smile fell. "Since you already possessed most of Malum's magic, that third trial, on an island crafted by a powerful goddess no less, catapulted you into the final phase of transformation. I'm sure Surria was the first to sense your rebirth and the absence of her son's residual power."

"Where's Malum now?" Was he in the Underworld where the rest of the souls were kept? Or here, in the palace with the gods?

"Malum is in the Far Beyond, unable to set foot on these lands. It's found in the deepest level of the Underworld, and it's nearly impossible for a soul to break free. Thank the gods." Halio's lips thinned, a look of disgust painting his handsome face.

The Far Beyond. She prayed Bash wasn't there or they'd be screwed.

"He wasn't a friend of yours?" Margrete asked, curious.

"Did my cheery tone give it away?" he asked with a mocking laugh. "While I am often the balance among my fellow gods, it doesn't mean I'm fond of them. Though, I suppose, they aren't supporters of mine either. No one particularly *likes* death, after all. A shame, because death is merely the final stage of life, a place where the soul rests."

Maybe it was the absurdity of it all or how her body didn't feel like it was her own, but suddenly, a flood of alarm trickled through the cracks of her armor. Here she stood, drenched in the dried blood of her lover, and she was about to enter the lion's den. The apparent home of the gods. Oh, and her friends might die at any moment.

She clenched her fists, resisting the urge to look their way.

"You look better that way, covered in blood," Halio murmured, inspecting her appearance. "You want them to fear you, to see that you're not some fragile mortal that fate mysteriously chose. It's better to be feared among the heartless. They know nothing but blood and rage, and you, my dear, are covered in both."

With those parting words, Halio abandoned her for the main entrance.

Had he been attempting to help her? He might've thrown a dagger at them, but he claimed it had been meant for Darius. What did they say about the enemy of my enemy?

She'd have to keep him close.

Holding her breath, Margrete walked through an arched entryway of ornate silver leaves, Halio already inside. It may have been beautiful, but she couldn't be easily deceived; she knew all too well that some of the most beautiful things hid the most rot.

A hand slid into hers, warm and small. Mila didn't say anything, but she walked by Margrete's side as they strode through the doors and into the palace of the Underworld.

"I'll give you a second to take it all in," Halio said once they'd made it to the other side and the fog had cleared. Pride brightened his face. "It's stunning, isn't it?"

Before she could do as he asked and appreciate her surroundings, a scream pierced the air.

CHAPTER THREE

MARGRETE

HALIO DIDN'T REACT HOW MARGRETE THOUGHT HE WOULD. HE *rolled* his eyes.

"That would be *them*," he said in response to the ear-splitting scream. "I'm assuming Brielle is at the heart of it."

Brielle, the Goddess of the Deep Woods and the Hunt.

Margrete didn't realize her palms were lifted in a fighting pose until she had to forcibly lower them. Since she'd come into her powers, they were difficult to turn off, and droplets of water splashed down onto the marble flooring. Steam rose from where they landed. It appeared that even in the Underworld, the sea insisted upon following her.

Halio peered at her hands with a knowing smirk, his gray eyes seeming to smile as well. "I'd keep those to yourself unless you prefer a more violent introduction, as entertaining as that would be."

A part of her wanted to drown them all, but she willed her magic to cool. It took just a thought, a stern one, but it begrudgingly listened, slowly slinking back to the depths as if it were sullen at being chastised.

Halio started for the direction of the scream when he abruptly paused, a single finger held up as if in thought. "Think of this main floor as neutral ground for all immortals. Every level above us belongs to a different god or goddess. They have their own courts, their own rules, but here, they can't break the accord of peace we signed."

That shriek didn't sound *peaceful*, but she nodded, and Halio continued. Hopefully, she wouldn't need to venture to their separate courts. She'd get Bash out of here and return to her sister, who was probably worried sick by now. Birdie was under Adrian's watchful eye, and Margrete had to believe he wouldn't let any harm come her way.

Of course, thinking about Adrian had her thinking about Bay.

He'd done the unthinkable...but he'd saved her life. As much as she understood his actions, her grief was like a fire she couldn't put out. She thrust Bay's image from her mind as easily as one would turn the page in a book.

She'd deal with him after she rescued Bash.

Glancing around the foyer, Margrete studied her new prison, distracting herself by noting each detail of the luxurious cage. Towering ivory columns lifted from the polished marble floor like colossal trees, rising to kiss a ceiling crafted from warm bronze. In the distance, she made out a grand staircase, and while the details were blurred, the metal of the banister shone brilliantly.

No furniture lined the space, but abundant tapestries surrounded them, the threads shining with the finest threads. Margrete squinted at one in particular. Fashioned with silver and black fibers, it depicted Charion on his steed, a fist held triumphantly in the air, a faceless army at his back. The God of War in his glory days. A vicious and cutthroat god she was about to meet.

Halio cleared his throat pointedly when she lagged behind, her crew just as stunned by the grand images of the immortals they'd only known through lore. Mila lingered on Brielle, staring at the muscular goddess with wide eyes speaking of admiration.

Keep calm, Margrete repeated to herself, her nerves rising the closer she drew to meeting the gods. But if she could survive this encounter and get out as quickly as possible, then she could explore the rest of this peculiar place and get Bash.

As much as she wanted to rip out a throat, playing it cool was the wiser move. She didn't know if she could win a fight against seven immortals. It was a risk she couldn't take.

Halio waved a hand at a set of double doors leading off the main foyer, and with a dramatic whoosh, they opened.

Atlas sidled up to her and squeezed her shoulder. "Show no fear. They deserve nothing from you, princess," she whispered before dropping her hand. Margrete smiled at the nickname, knowing Atlas spoke it as a reminder of who they fought for. She was selfishly thankful she hadn't come here alone. Margrete needed Atlas's steady voice.

"Show no fear," she repeated, holding her friend's stare. Atlas dipped her chin and assumed the mask of a soldier. A role she'd been born to play.

Margrete sucked in a breath and peered into an obscenely decadent throne room. Like all things here in this palace, this chamber had been fashioned from every piece of stone and metal found across the world. There were gold, silver, copper, marble, and delicate porcelain accents. Velvet chairs framed the edges of the space, beautiful strangers occupying their seats. And in the center, where a throne would have resided, was a single stand cradling a book.

Light flickered in through a rounded stained-glass window overhead, pouring a rainbow of color upon the closed cover of the ancient text. Worn from age, its forest-green jacket was frayed and torn, a golden lock tied around its casing.

Her heart stuttered as a song began to play in her mind, the music a whisper, its melody one she couldn't quite make out. The longer she stared at the book, the more her magic thrummed, raging to the surface like it wished to wrap itself around the pages. This far back, she couldn't distinguish details, but it called to her, unintelligible whispers hissing in her mind.

"Welcome," Halio bellowed, drawing her focus from the mysterious tome. The god ran a hand through his curls, his long fingers brushing against the crown banded around his brow. "I'm sure you all don't need an introduction, but I'll give you one nonetheless."

Margrete stiffened, biting her cheek hard enough to taste the tang of blood. As coolly as she could, she took in the details of the occupants filling the chamber, the stunning beings seated in their fine chairs. She'd been far too entranced by the book, but now that she saw them all, she couldn't look away if she tried.

"Let me introduce Margrete Wood, formerly of Prias." The six gods and goddesses lifted their gemlike eyes her way, scrutinizing her every inch. Those assembled appeared unfazed, as if there hadn't just been an ear-shattering scream that shook the palace walls. The only discernible thing out of place was the overturned chair in the far right corner of the room, its legs broken and the velvet cushion torn.

An argument clearly had broken out, and Margrete had the awful suspicion it had been about her.

A blonde covered in lush furs wrinkled her upturned nose, the leather band tied across her forehead moving in place as she furrowed her brow in apparent disdain.

Another woman, this one short and gifted with voluptuous curves, raised her raven-colored head, her irises the deepest shade of violet. Margrete's breath caught, the stranger's delicate beauty so overwhelming, her knees shook. The goddess cocked her face to the side and sniffed the air, a sensuous smile lifting her lips.

She jolted when a throat cleared, commanding all attention.

A man stepped forward, bright silver hair falling to his shoulders, his tanned skin a dark gold. He was beautiful, as they all were, but while he appeared young, there was a kind of ancient wisdom that weighed down his soft features and clouded his yellow, catlike eyes.

"Finally," he said, clasping his hands behind his back. Excitement danced in his depthless gaze, a knowing smile gracing thin lips. "We meet the infamous mortal-turned-goddess. A rarity I'm thrilled to see up close."

Scorn was absent from his voice, which surprised her, given how most of the others were sending daggers her way. No, she felt curiosity and a hint of awe bleed out of him in waves. For a moment, she smelled evergreen trees and felt the chill of winter glance across her exposed forearms.

"I am Themis, God of Knowledge and Justice." He bowed low, his long, yellow jacket dusting the floor. "And this is Brielle, Goddess of the Deep Woods and the Hunt." He pointed to the woman in furs. "And that is Calista, our beautiful Goddess of Love." She gave a stiff nod, her black hair shifting over her violet eyes. "And I see you've already met Halio, the esteemed ruler of this realm."

"Forget about me?"

This came from a giant of a man in the far corner, nearly bathed in shadows. His muscular frame was adorned in the purest golden armor, his bright red hair cut to his shoulders. The harsh features and pointed jawline made him appear like violence personified. Margrete immediately knew who sat before her.

"Charion," she grated out, finding her voice.

The man gave a taunting tilt of his head, his stare alight with depraved amusement. The God of War. The man who'd once loved Malum enough to shatter the bond between brothers.

And the god who'd want to kill her the most.

"I've heard many...interesting things about you. And your little band of mortals." His stare landed behind her to where her friends stood guard. "How quaint they all are. I hope they don't perish beneath the weight of the Underworld. That would be such a shame." Charion lifted from his seat, sauntering over to where her crew now flanked her, all their stances turning stiff.

"Oh, I mean no harm," Charion said, noting how Atlas's hand inched toward her blade. "I simply wanted a better look at the woman who's caused such a fuss." He lifted his hand as if he planned to touch Margrete's cheek, but when she glared, her fingers glowing with blue and white sparks, he wisely dropped his arm.

"Hmm," he mused, the delight in his eyes turning into something wicked. "So much power for such a youngling. I can taste it. So sweet. So fresh." He licked his lips. "Such a shame you stole it though."

"I stole nothing," she said, trying and failing to bite her tongue.

Charion tsked. "You stole more than—"

"Malum was weak, and we all knew it," the goddess Calista interrupted, sighing dramatically. "Get over your crush, Charion. It's been centuries."

The God of War didn't deign to glower at the goddess. No, he reserved his irate stare for Margrete alone.

"I wonder how powerful she really is," he murmured, giving her his back as he made for his chair. "I bet it's because Darius himself fashioned her from both his soul and the sea he covets." He laughed, the sound brittle. "It would be such a deadly combination. She could be more potent than a god merely being born, and far more difficult to kill."

As if Margrete needed a reminder she had a target on her back. She'd have to be on her guard—

The war god whirled around, sending a stream of flames across the space. It flooded from his palms, the torrent aimed directly at Margrete's heart.

Just as she had with Halio's dagger, Margrete didn't think, she acted.

Lifting her palm, her pulse racing with adrenaline, she released a shield of wavering blue and white light. A strangled cry left her lips as the foreign magic struck her barrier with an agonized crash, and her arms trembled while she fought to keep herself in place.

Charion's magic wasn't like any she'd experienced before, and the hand up holding her invisible shield began to burn and blister. Pain trickled down her arm and to her chest, seeming to wrap around her heart and give a painful squeeze. The anger that bubbled just below her surface canted its head, igniting in response to Charion's aggression.

Darius had never used such brute force on her, not even in the arena. Charion was out for blood.

"She seems rather adept. I'd say it was surprising, but my earlier assumptions appear to be correct," Charion remarked, hardly affected by the use of such violent magic.

Adept. Gods, she was barely holding on. Sweat banded across her brow, and her muscles ached from holding up the magical shield. Yet the more she collided with his power, the easier it was for her rage to bubble up and wash over her. The air grew saturated with the scent of smoke and steel and victory, and she nearly lost herself to the god's lure when

Bash's face hovered before her, his image jolting her from Charion's malevolent grip.

She bit back a yelp as her skin burned, her shield weakening. She cursed, gritting her teeth as she clumsily flung a burst of her own magic across the throne room toward Charion. The God of War lifted a hand at the last second, a shield of his own appearing.

He grimaced, fighting off her attempts. She knew her strength was fading, and that he'd break through within seconds.

"Give me everything you have, youngling," Charion taunted, all traces of amusement gone. "I can't wait for my fire to devour—"

"Enough!"

Every head in the room turned toward the new voice. A gust of wind blustered between Margrete and the war god's magic, sending it scattering into nothing but residual sparks.

She looked to the source of the voice.

A goddess, this one wearing all white, strolled into the room with the grace of an apex predator. Her bright blonde hair had been braided artfully down her back, and her sea blue eyes resembled a certain god's Margrete knew all too well. Her heart thundered as her shield fell, Charion dropping his own.

"Surria." Halio bowed his head. "May I present—"

"I know who this is," Surra said airily, her voice akin to the winds she commanded, light and whisper soft. "You're the woman who stole from *both* of my sons. Magic...and a heart. Some might call you greedy."

As if Margrete wanted anything from her sons.

"As I've said before, I stole nothing," she said, cold heat burning her insides. "I didn't ask for Malum's power, and I certainly didn't want Darius's heart."

She wanted his head.

Surria's lips pinched, and her skin grew wan. Margrete sensed the rage she repressed, could taste it on her tongue. The goddess wanted her gone. Wanted to kill her with her own hands, which were currently clenched at her sides, the knuckles white.

"Either way," Surria grated out, "you've made quite the impression on us all."

Margrete had the suspicion that wasn't a good thing.

"Darius should be standing here," Charion said, "not this imposter, and not her dying friends who are already infected with death!"

Dying friends. She focused on her crew, noting nothing out of the ordinary other than their widening eyes full of alarm.

Maybe he's lying, trying to get a rise out of us. But even as she insisted they were fine, instinct told her otherwise. They didn't belong here. Sooner or later, this palace would devour them.

"I'm not sure why you're being so civil," Charion directed to Surria. "We should just kill her now and be done with it!"

"You only want Darius here so you can kill him yourself," Surria said.

"He *would* deserve it," Charion answered, lowering into his seat and grabbing his glass from a nearby side table. He drowned the contents.

"Can we get through one meeting without bickering for once?" Brielle, who Margrete had all but forgotten, crossed her arms and glared at everyone present. Atlas, Dani, and Mila had wisely kept quiet. They were practically statues with how rigidly they held themselves. What surprised her most was Mila's silence. Maybe they *were* experiencing the effects of the Underworld. Her pulse soared as a pang of anxiety rushed through her.

"My apologies, Brielle," Charion said on a sigh, giving her a mockery of a bow. Brielle rolled her eyes, flinging her long, honey-colored braid over her shoulder. "I suppose I was never one for these gatherings to begin with." He moved toward the exit. "I'll leave you to entertain our beloved *guests.*"

He yanked open the double doors only to slam them on his way out. His anger shook the walls.

"You must be weary from your journey," Surria said, ignoring Charion's outburst. She cocked her head, observing Margrete's tattered clothing with contempt, sniffing the air for good measure. "Perhaps a bath before dinner?"

Margrete's entire frame was a mess, her limbs quivering from her encounter with Charion. But she couldn't allow Surria to see; she'd use it against her.

"I don't give two fucks about a bath," she said, earning a stunned gasp from Mila, whose hand found her shoulder, seemingly to hold her back. Margrete shook her off. "I want my king, and I want to be free of this place once and for all. You can keep this corrupt magic. I have no use for it."

Silence. They stared at her in dazed silence.

"You don't want it?" Brielle asked, frowning. "But why?"

Margrete sighed. "I just want what was taken from me. This power is no gift, and I would rid myself of its hold now, if such a thing is possible."

"She isn't lying," Themis observed, silently appraising her in the far corner, his thumb and forefinger at his jaw. He scrunched his brow, seemingly confused by what he saw.

"I'm afraid your request to retrieve your king is unfeasible," Halio said, his gentle tone pulling her away from the God of Justice. "Once a soul passes, they cannot be returned to the human world."

She still wore Bash's blood on her shirt, the material stiff, copper heady in the air. It was a reminder of her true purpose here. She didn't care if she had to battle every one of these bastards in order to get to her king, and she hadn't allowed herself to think of anything other than success. If she failed him...well, she wasn't sure what chaos her anger was capable of causing. Her wrath frightened her.

Her nails dug into her palms. "I won't stop until—"

"I'll see that she gets settled," Halio said before Margrete could finish her threat. Dense, gray clouds billowed out from his robes, and he shot her a scathing look that should've sent her to her knees.

He claimed it was unfeasible, but Margrete was used to battling the odds.

Halio bid the immortals farewell, though they didn't react. They simply went back to whatever heated discussion had captured them before she arrived. He ushered her and her crew beyond the doors, sealing the door shut behind them with a gust of wind.

"Well, they're charming," Mila huffed, her voice far from strong.

"If only you knew," Halio replied, bringing them beyond the throne room and to a magnificently gilded foyer, a set of marble stairs erected at its end. It went straight up before forking in two directions. "But I'd be careful. Trust no one and nothing." Halio met Margrete's stare, his thick, black brows scrunching. "Not even me."

Noted. Though she wasn't sure she'd been in danger of trusting him to begin with.

"After you." He waved at the staircase expectedly. The Azantians all circled her protectively as she stared upward.

Just do it, she argued with herself. But it was easier said than done. She had no clue what new horror lay in wait, and once she fully entered the Underworld, she worried she'd be trapped in its hold.

Halio cleared his throat. She'd been hesitating for too long. She couldn't allow him to see how frightfully close to the edge she was.

Margrete clenched her fists and made to begin the climb when she heard it.

A name.

She went as still as death, turning in the direction the voice hailed from. A darkened hallway sprouted off the main corridor, though shadows clung to the corners. An uneasy sensation took residence in her gut the longer she peered in its direction, the same sensation she'd experienced when she glimpsed that mysterious book in the throne room. The moving shadows coiled and danced along the edges of the hall, and she could have sworn she saw a figure of a man flickering in and out of sight.

Margrete.

Her name. It was her name that had sounded. And the voice that had whispered it? She would've known it anywhere. One corner of her lips curled up, reckless hope taking root in her chest.

Halio, who had remained a silent presence at her side, shifted into view, his once smiling eyes tapering. "Everything all right?" he asked, seeming to grow taller. She took him in, almost for the first time.

"Yes, I'm fine" she replied, a sob threatening to crack her composure. "Let's continue." Margrete resumed her pace, but with each step she felt the piercing stare of the god burning into the back of her head.

The truth was if that *had* been Bash's soul somehow speaking to her from beyond death, then yes, everything was fine.

Now she just had to find him.

CHAPTER FOUR

BASH

THERE WAS ONLY PEACE AND A BLISSFUL VOID THAT ROCKED BASH from side to side. His thoughts were ones of joy, of memories made on wild waves and golden sands. Memories of a brown-haired siren who had stolen his heart. Days where they'd talk about nothing but the mundane. The little things that brought them comfort, like decadent pastries, the rich sound of thunder, or books they couldn't get out of their heads.

Bash couldn't remember anything else but those frozen moments.

In this place where happiness lived, Bash let go of his anger, his darkness, his fears.

He just *was*.

But then the great emptiness rippled and the joyous scenes playing across his mind shook and dissolved to dust. They were swept away by the thudding of boots, washed away by the steady beating of a heart he knew better than his own. Its familiar pounding broke down the haze of serene nothingness.

Bash couldn't feel his limbs, couldn't sense *himself*...but he sensed *her*.

A new vision glided into place, framed by the deepest shades of night. He moved through an opulent palace in a body that wasn't his own. All around him, he took in splendor and luxury, and with every blink, that devout heartbeat calling to him grew louder. His phantom frame shuddered to a halt then, and he glimpsed a staircase of ivory marble.

And then he saw the love of his life. The woman who made his blood boil and his heart race. Every time he saw her, it was as if for the first time.

He was so far gone.

Margrete stood before the staircase, one dainty hand gliding across the smooth surface of the banister, her graceful chin lifted defiantly. Bash felt indignation roll off her in waves, her body rippling with an unfamiliar red aura that wavered in and out of sight. His princess wasn't one to be angry, not like this, not to the point where he could practically *taste* it.

She was the optimistic one, the one he'd go to when he had a bad day, and she'd force him to calm his temper as she embraced him. She'd run her fingers through his tangled hair and make sweet promises that tomorrow would be better. That they'd get into some sort of fun trouble later and replace the bad memories with good ones.

This wasn't the same woman he remembered.

Bash called out to her. Once. Twice.

Her nostrils flared as they did when she was tense, on alert. Slowly, she turned, the red fog around her body recoiling. The pounding became a roar now, and with sickening awareness, Bash realized it hadn't been *her* heart echoing in his ears. It was his.

Why did it feel so strange though? Like it fought and struggled to do something as simple as beat? And why couldn't he remember much of anything? The last thing he could recall was a night on Azantian surrounded by his closest friends and family, little Birdie perched in Margrete's lap as she told her a cherished fairytale from her own youth.

"Margrete!" Bash screamed her name. His heart thudded again, somewhat stronger. He tried to take a step but found he couldn't; he couldn't move his legs.

So many questions, so much confusion. It became overwhelming, suffocating. That numbing peace that had embraced him a heartbeat before vanished, and Bash held on tightly to the sight of Margrete, almost as if his life depended on her meeting his eyes and calling his name.

But her brow merely scrunched, and then she turned, taking the steps with deliberate force. Something about her gait was different, more confident. Still, she drifted away—away from him.

The pounding in his chest stopped. *Everything* stopped.

And then Bash fell, down, down, down, back into the murky pool of sweet memories and soothing darkness.

He pictured golden sands and a smile meant only for him, of fingers running through his hair, and a voice whispering that tomorrow would be better.

CHAPTER FIVE

MARGRETE

Bash. She'd seen Bash. Or, more specifically, she'd *heard* him.

Margrete's heart swelled dangerously. Wherever his soul was kept, he'd broken free—for her. She was absolutely certain of it. Call it foolish, but she held onto that lone scrap of hope like the stars that clung to the skies.

Gods, she wanted to turn back to that corridor and run and not stop running until she heard his deep, raspy voice again. The temptation called to her, urging her to venture past the shadows and into the obscurity the darkness had cloaked. But she couldn't. Margrete had to be smart, to watch her every move, and when the rest of the gods went their separate ways that night, she'd return.

And then she'd find a way into the realm of the dead.

"You seem uneasy," Halio remarked at her side, causing her to flinch. He'd escorted her to the third-floor landing where a single entryway lined with waves stood tall before them. The metal rippled, the slick water gleaming in the light of the sconces. Everything about this place seemed alive. Unexpected, given the location.

"I'm fine," Margrete lied. Anyone who looked at her face would know she was far from fine. Atlas snorted from behind them. Margrete shot her a warning glare.

Was Halio thinking of her outburst? She assumed he'd talk with her once they'd departed the throne room, bringing up her demand for Bash's soul, but the god had remained suspiciously quiet. Perhaps he was simply accustomed to being obeyed without question.

Or, he was watching her as closely as she was him.

"This portal leads to your court," Halio said, overlooking Margrete's blatant lie. "Well, it leads to the court of the God of the Sea. The others have similar portals, but you must be invited before you can pass through."

"So, Charion or Surria wouldn't be able to move through this portal?" she asked, hopeful.

"No," Halio confirmed, and she breathed out a sigh of relief. "I wouldn't permit them to enter if I were you. It's best to keep them as far from your court as possible. Surria especially. She's none too pleased with you, despite how she tamed Charion earlier."

Margrete shivered. She grasped that Surria was cunning and cruel— if Darius's tale was anything to go by. Regardless of how much she despised Darius, his mother had forced him to murder his lover, and she'd imprisoned her sons for years. She wasn't to be underestimated.

A *small* part of her might even feel bad for Darius.

Some villains were born, but most were made. Margrete had been raised by a monster, but she'd triumphed over his cruelty. Darius hadn't been so lucky, but then again, he had thousands of years on her.

Would *she* have turned out like him had they switched places? Or would—

"I will leave you here," Halio broke through her inner strife. "There will be a guide waiting for you on the other side. There are some souls that the Underworld embraces for itself, each distributed to a court that best suits their needs. But take in mind, you cannot choose who is selected to serve." He shot her a pointed look. She *had* been thinking of another option for Bash should they fail, and he'd just squandered it. "I may rule the realm of the dead, but I do not rule death itself."

So he hadn't forgotten.

Halio bowed low before reaching out to grasp her hand. His fingers were frozen as he wrapped them around her. "And remember, don't make deals with any of the immortals. You'll end up paying more than you bargained for in the end."

With that final warning, he aimed for the stairs, never once looking back. Margrete waited until he was well out of hearing distance before twisting to her companions.

"Did you hear anything down there? At the base of the stairs? A voice?" The words rushed out before she could stop them. Gods, she sounded as desperate as she felt. Where was her numbing rage from earlier? She yearned for it now. All of this felt too real, the chance of failure looming over her head like a storm cloud.

Mila and Dani shook their heads, and Atlas responded with a confused, "No."

"Did you?" Mila pressed, arching a red brow.

"It doesn't matter. Not now." Margrete would be wise to keep quiet until they found a semblance of privacy. As Mila went to protest, she held up a finger, glancing pointedly around the palace. Who knew where enemies could be lurking?

"I see," Mila whispered, far from pleased.

Margrete faced the portal leading to *her* court, and with a wave of her hand, gestured to her friends to follow.

As it had before, her skin buzzed as she stepped through, frost chilling her skin. Yet just as quickly as everything stilled, it surged back to life again on the other side, that first breath of air a force that rattled her lungs.

Gasping, Margrete took in the hallway where they'd been deposited. It stretched endlessly, dancing navy blue shadows swirling in the distance, blocking the view of whatever lay beyond sight. Margrete had expected to enter a grand court, but she preferred this.

Standing off to the side, head bowed, was a tiny wisp of a woman wearing blue silk, her blonde hair braided neatly down her back.

This had to be the guide Halio spoke of. The one Death chose to grace her court.

"Goddess"—the stranger murmured before dipping into a graceful bow—"my name is Dawn. I will be showing you to your chambers and assisting you with all of your everyday needs."

The woman before her couldn't have been a day over twenty. Her lips stretched into a warm smile, but her skin...it was two shades too pale, nearly tinged a sickly blue.

Dawn was dead. Taken by death to serve *her*. Margrete simply hadn't expected her to appear so *real*.

Mila sucked in a breath through her teeth at the sight of her milky blue eyes, the irises barely visible. "Gods. Halio wasn't lying. You're truly dead."

Leave it to the redhead to get right to the point. Margrete scowled, but Mila simply rolled her eyes in response, shrugging a shoulder for good measure. Atlas gawked, but she elbowed Mila, effectively quieting her.

Dawn chuckled, clearly not offended. "I'm not alive, you're right," she said. "I was chosen to serve this court, and I am beyond honored to be in your service. My mortal life was devoted to the sea, and the All-Knowing Death dictated I serve it in the afterlife. If you're ready, I'll show you the way to the royal suites."

"So you had no say?" Dani asked, her short legs working to keep pace. Animosity saturated her delicate voice.

Dawn shook her head. "None of us do. But it is believed that only the souls who found peace in life can serve in death. I lived and died at sea, and not a day went by when I didn't pray to the gods. Now, if you'll follow me..."

Dani fell behind, gnawing at her bottom lip. Margrete could tell the answer still bothered her, and the sailor kept her eyes on Dawn's back as she flickered in and out of existence, her body not quite solid.

She wasn't allowed a true death, and while she may claim it didn't bother her, the choice hadn't been hers to make.

Tension caused Margrete's movements to stiffen as she trailed their new guide down the hall. She wondered how many other dead courtiers and servants filled the courts, those chosen to serve. How did they manage such a feat, to exist here in the palace, while others were relegated to the Far Beyond? It would be a question she'd have to ask Halio.

Margrete peeked at Mila, once more analyzing her pallor. The woman's movements weren't nearly as energetic as usual. Had the Underworld already dug its claws into her?

If they didn't find Bash in the next couple of days, Margrete would demand that they leave. Even if she had to force them out.

Dawn directed them down the corridor of stunning cobalt, intricate pewter sconces positioned every ten feet, all hissing white, graceful flames. When they neared an arched doorway composed of sea glass, Dawn slowed to a halt, reaching for the handle. Margrete noted how her pale skin shimmered at the contact, her entire frame undulating.

Dawn could touch and move solid objects. Interesting.

With the door now sprung open, Margrete stepped inside the chambers, drinking in all the minute details of a room that was obviously meant for her. A king-sized bed with silken white sheets rested in the very center of the space. Surrounding the bed was a stream no more than three feet wide, a small footbridge connecting each side. The twisting stream led off to the balcony, where it flowed over the edge of the palace in a gentle whoosh.

Salt permeated the air, and a soothing sea breeze tickled her cheeks. Shutting her eyes, just for a moment, she felt as if she were aboard a ship. Back on the *Phaedra*. Her lids jolted open with a start.

"Amazing, isn't it?" Dawn asked with an awed sigh. She motioned toward a pitcher of water and the four cups placed neatly on a carved wooden table beside an open window, the sky beyond dark. "Drink, rest, and talk among yourselves. There are fresh clothes in the armoire and a bathing suite in the adjoining room."

"Thank you," Margrete managed, her throat tight. This was not at all how she'd planned on taking down the Underworld. In her mindlessness, she'd schemed to blow the entire realm to pieces, gods and all. But once here, both logic and cowardice caught up with her.

It was too big. There were too many enemies. Too many opponents to fight in a place she knew nothing about. Her friends could perish at any moment, and their deaths would rest on her shoulders. Margrete liked to think herself brave, and maybe sometimes she was. But now? Now she was rendered frozen with anxiety.

"I'll deliver dinner to your rooms shortly, goddess." Dawn bowed her head and left through the portal. The door snicked shut behind her.

"Anyone else feel like they're on a boat?" Mila asked, not hesitating to grab a glass and pour herself a drink. "I wish this was whiskey," she remarked dryly before guzzling the water with a grimace.

"It is peculiar," Dani admitted from her spot beside Atlas. Margrete noted their entwined hands. "I can't help but feel as if something about this room isn't right. I don't know how to explain it. Like...like it belongs to another. It's cold and unfeeling, if that makes sense."

Atlas gave her a concerned look, but Dani finally dropped her hand and walked deeper into the room, her lips pursed in thought. They all observed as Dani abruptly turned, her stare widening. Margrete could've sworn her eyes flashed silver, but when she blinked, her irises were back to a stunning blue.

"What is it?" Atlas asked, every muscle in her body tensing. She gripped her dagger hard enough for her knuckles to turn white.

Dani shook her head, her curls bouncing. "This...there's something in here that doesn't belong. And it's dark, yet it doesn't feel innately evil." She held a hand to her temple and rubbed in exasperation. "It sounds ridiculous, I know. *I* sound ridiculous. Hell, I don't know what's wrong with me lately."

"You've had these feelings before, Dani. Back when we were on the island, you felt the presence of the undead at the same time I did, if not before," Margrete whispered. Intuition such as Dani's couldn't be ignored. If they ever returned to Azantian, she'd ask Nerissa for her opinion. The seer would be able to help if Dani possessed similar gifts. They could be heightened due to her being surrounded by magic.

No one knew how seers and mortals with such capabilities were born, but she'd once read a myth that claimed souls like Dani's and Nerissa's stole a piece of magic with them before they were born into the human realm. She wondered if such a thing were true.

Dani blushed, averting her gaze shyly. "I didn't do anything to aid us though. I just get these odd feelings sometimes. My mother used to say I was like my grandmother in that respect, but she died before I could learn what she'd meant."

Perhaps she *was* a seer. They were rare, but not nonexistent.

Whether or not Dani had stolen magic before her birth, or such a gift had been passed down her family line, her ability could prove to be vital.

"We need a plan," Atlas broke the moment, her tone all business. "We certainly don't want to linger. We shouldn't even be here to begin with, and I'm not sure how our mortal bodies will react. Not that I feel off, but that doesn't mean the ill effects won't present themselves soon." She gnawed at her cheek. "Besides, those fucking gods were gawking at you like you're their next meal."

Mila snorted and inspected her hand. "I feel and look fine, so I'm betting we have *some* time before we go all spectral on you." She hardly acted frightened by the notion, but Margrete saw through her charade. "But Atlas is right on the other front. Charion looked like he wanted to flay you alive."

Margrete hadn't a doubt he *would* have had she not reacted in time. She dropped her gaze to her freshly tattooed hand, which had magicked the shield. The barrier had appeared without a thought, and she twirled her wrist in amazement. What else could she do? As if to answer, her tattoo briefly sparked an iridescent white. Was this the mark of a goddess? Or something else entirely?

"Charion isn't my concern," Margrete spoke at last, glancing up to Atlas. "I *heard* Bash."

Three pairs of eyes turned her way.

"I heard him call out my name when we were at the foot of the stairs," she continued. "There was that corridor off to the right, the one cloaked in shadows. I think that might be where the souls are kept."

It was a guess, but she didn't have much to work with, and she'd take any scrap offered.

"We need to search as soon as it quiets for the evening." Atlas walked to Margrete's side and gripped her shoulders. "If that *was* him, then we'll wait until everyone is asleep, or whatever gods do at night, and open that door. Halio said they all had their own courts, so we wait until they return."

"Let's say we miraculously find him. Then what?" Mila asked. "Does he have a body? Or..."

Margrete flinched. She hadn't considered that. Gods, what if he was just some incorporeal soul, a flickering form like Dawn? His bloodied body had been abandoned on the island, left in the hands of his mother.

"I think I saw that nymera hovering over him right before we followed you," Dani added, seeming to read Margrete's thoughts. "She seemed protective of his body, so there might be a chance she still has him."

Margrete hoped Bash's soul-sucking mother had kept him safe. They'd deal with *that* when the time came. For now, they had to break into the death god's sanctum. She would've laughed at the absurdity if she could.

"We should get changed." She grimaced at her bloodied shirt. "And be on your guard. We need to be ready to leave at a—"

Margrete stopped mid-sentence.

A song played, and not the song of the sea. Airy, light, and whimsical, it wasn't at all like the deeper and more seductive chords the waters churned.

"What is it?" Atlas asked.

Margrete shook her head in answer and shut her eyes. The melody... the longer she listened, the more she picked up on the hints of yearning and sadness, of hope and despair. Every note held its own weight, and with every chord change, a new story unfolded.

She ambled around the chambers, and if the song lessened, she changed course. When she approached a simple desk positioned beside one of the many curved windows, she halted. The song played so vividly in her head. Almost *too* clearly.

Yanking open the drawers, she searched without a sense of

purpose, going through stacks of blank notebooks and quills, bottles of ink, and loose parchments. A bronze sculpture of a conch shell weighed the side drawer, the piece resting beside a delicate mother-of-pearl comb.

"What are you looking for?" Mila jostled into her shoulder. "Your lack of rambling is worrisome." Margrete ignored her.

She advanced to the last and largest drawer. The wood creaked as she opened it, revealing an assortment of brightly colored gems and other useless baubles. Still, the song intensified, and Margrete shoved through the mess until something caught her attention.

A *coin*. Another blasted coin.

She tried to pick it up. It didn't budge.

Margrete leaned closer. On the face of the silver piece, four words had been etched into the surface, a single droplet falling from the final word. It reminded her of the teardrop from her new tattoo.

Like Calls to Like.

This space had once been the chambers belonging to either Malum or Darius, and now they were hers. If her touch hadn't affected the coin, then there was only one thing that might. The only thing stronger than touch...

Snatching her dagger, Margrete prepared to prick her finger when Atlas's hand curled around her arm.

"What in the hell are you doing?"

She sighed. "Trust me?" Atlas's green eyes narrowed, but she released her. Slowly.

Margrete nicked her pointer finger, watching as a bead of *blue* bubbled to the surface. Her blood wasn't mortal, she reminded herself, but the sight of the unusual color sent her heart plummeting into her stomach. She was hardly aware of the eyes searing into the back of her skull when she lowered her hand and pressed her finger against the falling droplet on the coin.

The pad of her finger sizzled, a stinging running up to her wrist, but she held on, her mouth dropping open as the metal proceeded to dissolve. But the silver wasn't the only thing to vanish.

The corners of the drawer began to char, like a match had been lit and fire ate away at the wood. Gasps filled the space, her own included.

Soon, the wooden plank turned into nothing but ash, revealing a false bottom.

"Shit." All attention briefly turned to Dani in surprise, but she merely lifted a shoulder in reply. If *she* was cursing now, they surely had to be in trouble.

Seated on a cushion of plush white silk was a rectangular box crafted of black pearl. Margrete lifted it from its hiding spot, her pricked finger already healing. A positive, it seemed, to being a goddess.

The box was surprisingly heavy in her hands, much heavier than she would've anticipated. Carefully, she placed it on the surface of the desk, her friends gathering around for a better look.

No one spoke as Margrete lifted the cumbersome lid. She set it aside, uncovering an elegant key, untamed waves etched into the head and spindly tentacles grasping around its sides. But it was what lay in the center of the handle that consumed her.

An orb. And within that orb, a drop of glowing silver liquid shifted back and forth.

The song in Margrete's head intensified, and when she wrapped her fingers around the key once more, the riotous melody became unbearable. Twisting the handle this way and that, she noted that it didn't appear to be water... It was much thicker, and it shimmered as if a thousand miniature stars had been captured inside.

"Margrete."

She brought the key inches from her face, transfixed, drawn to the potent magic she sensed. Shivers wracked her frame, her body growing numb. That song...it sounded so familiar. Like she'd heard it before. It made her feel lonely. Angry. *Powerful.*

"Margrete!"

Hands shook her shoulders and she gasped, nearly dropping the key. With trembling fingers, she placed the enchanted object on the desk, stepping back as if it might bite her.

Mila gripped her shoulder, concern washing across her face. The song that had called to Margrete fizzled out into nothing.

She blinked, realization striking.

Margrete knew exactly what the orb contained, and while she couldn't explain her certainty, it didn't matter. She *felt* it, and she suspected it had to do with the god who created her. After all, he'd been born from the very thing captured within the glass. Meaning, *her* soul had been born from it as well.

"Surria," she breathed the goddess's name. "We've found one of Surria's infamous tears."

And with it, the power to create a god.

CHAPTER SIX

DARIUS

DARIUS HADN'T BEEN TO THE UNDERWORLD FOR OVER FIVE thousand years. The last time he journeyed below, he'd been on the hunt for a certain precious relic his brother had *supposedly* sacrificed on the island. Malum was crafty, and Darius suspected he'd found a way to retrieve the lost item and hide it away somewhere safe.

If the object had equaled Wryn's life, then it had to have been worth everything to his brother, and Darius had wanted to sate his anger any way he could. But finding the lost artifact of the dead god wasn't a concern today.

"Why do you hide? Are you not a rightful god anymore?" The mortal, Bay, kept a wise distance away.

Smart man.

Shadows rose like reaching moss, swallowing the Underworld in a vacuum of darkness. Time moved differently here, and while it had been evening when they'd departed the island, it was just an hour after sunset now.

While nighttime prepared to reign, Darius insisted they keep to the outer walls of the palace. Paranoia had been a constant in his life, and Darius imagined he'd known its meaning before that of affection.

His mother once told him, "The only thing you can trust is that you will be betrayed. So be ready to spill blood when it inevitably happens."

Words every son longed to hear from their parent.

His mother prepared him to strike and to strike without thought. But now...now he was *thinking*.

And he loathed it.

"We're delaying until the gods have retired to their separate courts," he answered Bay's earlier question, not sure why he felt the need to explain the plan to the mortal under his control. The man couldn't *move* without his consent, and he should feel lucky he was even allowed to breathe. But perhaps it was that haunted look in his green eyes that tore at something deep within Darius. Bay suffered the kind of misery he'd been all too familiar with, and for once, he didn't feel the need to lash out. Strange, seeing as Bay's misery was, in essence, Darius's fault.

"Besides," Darius continued, clearing his throat, "it would be easy to storm through the portal and into the palace, but that would cause a riot, and Charion is likely all too eager for a bloodbath."

It would be an inconvenience Darius wasn't in the mood to deal with.

"Why are there seven levels?" Bay asked, his curiosity palpable despite his obvious shame. His guilt lingered like moldy perfume.

It was odd having someone to talk to. Even if that someone was Darius's prisoner.

"There are seven levels for the seven most powerful gods and goddesses. Brielle, Calista, Charion, Themis, myself, my *dearest* mother, and Halio, God of Death. It's rare they ever venture aboveground, so they're usually found here, holding their own court. They don't care for mortals or their problems. Too messy."

Darius idly wondered if Margrete had met the Sea Court yet, or if she'd been brought to her chambers through the side entrance. *His* old chambers.

Was she rummaging through his cherished collection of books? Had she noticed his favorite mortal paintings he'd placed throughout the suite? Or was she laying in his bed, beneath his sheets, resting?

The last thought sent heat flooding his blood. He quickly sucked in fresh air, shoving down that particularly appealing image.

Or she's in Malum's old rooms. Seeing as Malum had been sent to the Far Beyond, and Darius was yet to meet his demise, he suspected his court would place her there. He seethed at the idea, having much preferred her in his bed and smelling of him.

Thankfully, his new accomplice was a decent distraction with his incessant questions.

"I never imagined they'd spend their time here. I figured they would be somewhere above, floating in the heavens, just out of reach," Bay murmured, running a nervous hand through his short hair. He didn't dare look Darius's way. "I mean, can they even answer prayers locked down here?"

Fuck. This man knew *nothing.* It was almost laughable.

"The palace before you is far grander than anything your puny mortal brain could comprehend. Its beauty is unmatched. And as far as how the gods spend their time...most don't care to interact with humans unless they absolutely have to. That's something Margrete will soon learn." Their cruelty. Their indifference. They were cold creatures who liked to play games with each other, using the weak as their pawns.

Prayers ceased to reach the Underworld centuries ago. There had been a time when the gods cared to answer them, but immortals were fickle beasts and had grown apathetic after a few thousand decades of lounging about.

Darius had actually wanted to be better than that, once upon a time. He'd wished to change the mortals' small, trivial lives, and if they ended up worshiping him in the process, then all the better. He never claimed to be perfect. But his plans fell by the wayside when his brother took up arms against him, and then his own ruthless mother cursed them both. He'd learned long ago that one had to be strong to make it in his world.

Bay kept silent, but Darius noted how he continued to shift anxiously on his feet. The lad practically itched to run, but he knew better than to try, or perhaps he'd accepted his fate, believing he deserved the punishment. There were clouds in those eyes of his, and they grew darker by the second.

He ground his teeth, frustrated with the ridiculousness of the situation. In all his years he'd never felt so worn after a fight, not even with his brother. Maybe that was a testament to Margrete's strength. He smiled at the prospect.

Or maybe it has nothing to do with magic at all. The notion came to him, unbidden. *Maybe you're just hurt. Weak like Mother said. You always did let your emotions get the better of you.*

Darius clenched his jaw. It was easier than it should've been to swallow down the shame, fear, and heartache. He'd done it so many times before that it had become effortless.

While he worked to compose himself, he wondered what Margrete had endured since her arrival. She probably stepped through those doors and had been forced to meet his fellow immortals, and then she could've seen Halio's shadowy corridor and wondered where it led. Or maybe—

"It's possibly called to her already," Darius mused to himself, moving closer to the gateway.

The door that would lead to death's domain. It beckoned to all the immortals, its eerie melody one their magic couldn't ignore. Some claimed they heard the voices of their loved ones speak to them through the portal, while others said music and the rushing winds met their ears.

Brielle once told him that she'd heard howling wolves and the roaring of the wild. Calista, however, said there was nothing at all, but Darius knew the Goddess of Love often lied. She tricked many with her title alone, but she was one of the most ruthless deities he'd come across. Love could be just as violent as it was gentle.

Darius made out Bay's audible heartbeat, the pounding growing amplified. Did he fear seeing Margrete after what he'd done to their king? While Darius knew it was *his* doing, the way she'd glared at Bay after he murdered his friend and her lover told him that she'd place some of the blame on Bay as well.

Had his heart not been broken and then remolded into steel, he *might* have felt just the tiniest bit sorry for Bay.

"We must be patient to avoid as much unwanted spectacle as possible," Darius said, twisting to the blond warrior. He shoved off from the side of the palace walls. "We'll see your *princess* soon. Though you're to stay hidden in my chambers until I require your...use."

The gods might wish to *play* with him, but Darius needed Bay as insurance. He'd be no use to him dead. At least, that's why he told himself Bay was still breathing. Though Darius would have to make sure he didn't keep the man down here for too long. Mortals didn't last long in the Underworld if they possessed beating hearts. Their presence went against the natural order of things.

Not that he should care either way. Darius was getting soft.

He aimed his focus at the palace. Margrete was already behind those walls, and if he knew the immortals at all, they'd begun to devise ways to kill her off. He just had to make sure he was there before they did.

And maybe...he could be the hero she needed.

CHAPTER SEVEN

MARGRETE

THE PLAN WAS TO WAIT UNTIL MIDNIGHT.

Atlas propped her booted feet on the desk, her belly full from the feast the uniformed servants had brought in. All of them had glittered like Dawn—not alive, but not dead, just stuck somewhere in between.

While they'd been offered rooms of their own, Margrete insisted that Atlas, Dani, and Mila stay with her. They shouldn't be separated.

Dani curled up in a chair beside Atlas, a book of fables in her hand. Where she'd gotten it, Margrete didn't know. Either way, it didn't appear as if she were actually reading it; she hadn't turned the page in over twenty minutes. And Mila, she didn't lose an ounce of tension in her shoulders, her focus trained on the door from her position against the wall. She leaned back, her arms crossed, her signature glower firmly in place. Not once had she glanced away from the entry. She'd taken on the role of protector, whether they wished it or not.

Margrete wasn't as strong as the redheaded sailor, and sleep called to her, the onslaught of grief and loss and rage causing her lids to grow heavy. It might've been a mistake to lay on the bed while they waited for midnight, because soon, she fell into a deep slumber.

Her dream began on the very island they'd just left, but now she was alone in the arena—no dagger, no crew, and no Darius to contend with. In her ethereal state, Margrete drifted across the dirt floor of the ring, the moon shining down upon her like a blanket of eerie white.

Her anger simmered at the sight of this place. She wanted the sea to swallow it whole, and maybe, if she learned how to tame it, she'd make such a command.

Movement caught her eye. Margrete turned just as an obscure figure floated forward between the two gates.

It wasn't Darius she sensed. Rather, it was her king.

His newly blackened hair had been slicked back from his face, and those same nymera scales wound around his neck, but he was unmistakable.

Even in death, his body long since cold, the connection between them couldn't be severed. So Margrete ran. She ran until the shadows dispersed and Bash stood before her, and she didn't stop until she'd flung both arms around him. There wasn't another soul walking this earth that could make her heart race and soar and plummet all at the same time.

Bash didn't startle, and he barely moved as she climbed up his body and wrapped her legs around his torso. Her emotions were too much, too crushing, and she acted without pause or logic.

"Bash!" She grabbed at his face, cupping his cheeks. Deep down she knew this was a dream, and she understood that he wasn't truly here with her.

She didn't care.

In reply, Bash's lips twitched, but the rest of him remained frozen. It puzzled her.

"Bash, look at me!" She forced his unseeing eyes to her. He stared right through her, making no attempt to bring his arms around her body.

Margrete lowered to the ground in defeat. The man before her—pale as starlight, his lips tinged blue—felt *empty*. Her heart thudded in her ears and she shook him, trying to rouse some reaction out of him, *any* reaction. Still nothing.

She fumbled a step back. Selfishly, she'd believed she could have him in her dreams, even if it were all pretend. She'd been wrong.

"Gods, I miss you," she whispered sadly to the ghost of the king. He was like a shadow, an imitation of the man who held her heart. "You haven't even been gone a full day and I feel lost. You became a part of me so quickly, so effortlessly, that it feels wrong to be without you." The power in her chest pulsated as if asking, *What about me?* But power and love weren't the same.

She'd practically been alone all her life, aside from Birdie, but Bash was her partner. His arms, her safe place. Not everyone experienced such a precious love, and she'd lost it in the blink of an eye.

Margrete shut her lids then, unable to see the husk of him.

"I'm going to get you back," she vowed under her breath. "And when I do, I want to give you my answer to the question you asked in the cavern. I want you to know that it was always a yes, Bash." It had been inevitable, her falling in love with him. While she'd always found him handsome, it was the flicker of *life* in his eyes that had drawn her in and refused to let go. It *still* held her tight.

She would see that glimmer of life again, even if it killed her.

"I love—"

Fingers colder than a winter's breeze grazed her jaw, and her lids flashed open. Her dream had transported them from Surria's island to their chambers on Azantian.

Bash cradled her cheeks now, his dark irises still glassy, but beneath the cool surface, she could almost make out a hint of the spark she adored.

"I will find you," she promised, a single tear escaping. "I feel you now, your soul calling out to me in the Underworld." He cocked his head, a pinch forming between his brows, the lone flaw marring his stoic features.

"Why aren't you ready?" he asked. "Bay will scowl at you all night if we're late. You know he's planned Adrian's party for weeks."

Margrete stilled. Adrian's party was two *months* ago.

A slow smile formed on his full lips, and he sighed deeply as though exasperated. "I'm assuming you're nervous about Adrian's gift, but I promise he'll love it." Bash ran his fingers down her cheek. Goosebumps rose as she stared blankly, watching the trapped memory play out before her.

She'd gotten Adrian some beautiful leather notebooks and vibrant inks and quills. Bay had gone shopping with her and assured her he'd like it. But she'd wanted to impress him.

"You know," Bash began, grasping both of her hands and swallowing them in his. "I think you're stealing away my friends, princess. They're starting to like your company more than mine." He tsked his tongue, tugging her closer. "You're lucky I, too, am enchanted, or else I'd be jealous."

Margrete remembered this day well. He'd teased her minutes before they'd gone to dinner, which was a lavish affair, Adrian's closest friends all in attendance in the grand hall.

Bash touched his lips gently against hers, a whisper of a kiss. "We better hurry...but when we get back, I expect some time alone. I haven't seen you all day, and I've been dying to learn what you thought of the ending."

The ending of the book he'd lent her. It was a tale of lost love and new beginnings, and all the adventure she'd craved long ago. She had loved it.

Bash continued speaking, though no sound escaped him. The memory was vanishing, the world slipping away. Around her, the walls to their chambers quivered, darkness beginning to engulf them.

"We'll have many more memories like this one, Bash," she promised. "I'm coming for you—"

A hand on her shoulder jostled her. The island and Bash vanished.

The hazy light of her foreign chambers came into focus, wiping away all traces of the king. Atlas hovered above, perched beside her on the bed.

Margrete could still feel Bash's fingers on her cheek, could still sense his presence. It made her want to cry and scream all at once, and frustration bubbled in her chest.

"It's almost time," Atlas said, no trace of emotion weighing her tone. Margrete envied her. Ironic that even after she'd been gifted the powers of a goddess, fear could continue to rule her. Maybe that would never go away, and in truth, a part of her wished it never would. It meant she still held onto her old self. That she wasn't some apathetic creature like Surria.

She shuddered at the memory of herself after Bash's last exhale. She had been unrecognizable. Utterly frightening.

Margrete rose, doing her best to not look shaken. But her efforts were wasted when she heard *it*; that same music, that haunting melody that had played for her earlier.

The key. It sang to her now.

Mila and Dani joined Atlas, and they all watched curiously as she ambled over to the desk and removed the ornate box. The music swelled, and she suddenly couldn't bear the notion of leaving this room without it. Whatever the object truly was, it *belonged* to her, and she carefully took the key between her fingers and tucked it away in her trouser pocket.

Atlas shot her a questioning look but said nothing. The fact that she trusted Margrete sent both unease and confidence spiraling into her chest. Along with gratitude.

Margrete's eyes prickled as she faced some of the strongest women she'd ever encountered. "I'm not sure where our journey will take us, but understand this...I am grateful to have such fierce warriors at my side. Women who have felt loss and grief and battled demons on an island of myth and came out on the other side stronger. Together, we can find Bash and restore the balance of the seas and the very world itself."

It was an attempt at a grandiose speech, and she prayed she hadn't fumbled it.

Originally, she'd wanted to venture to the Underworld alone, but that would've been a mistake. Maybe it had been the mistake of all the gods to isolate themselves, and while it had been a tempting thought at the height of her grief, she needed their inner strength, their loyalty, and their courage, to remind her of what she fought for.

Justice.

Mila's throat bobbed, the only sign of emotion on her shrewd face, and Dani bashfully glanced at her boots, a smile subtly lifting one side of her mouth. As usual, Atlas grounded her, placing a heavy hand on her shoulder, her thumb rubbing circles onto her exposed skin.

"Listen for the ones we've lost. If they're here, we'll find them as well," she added, even knowing they didn't have bodies to return to. They also sought the souls of Grant, Jace, and Dani's brother, and getting the chance to say goodbye...she would fight for them to experience that as well.

Dani gave her a jerky nod, while Mila clenched her jaw and briefly glanced away, unwilling to show how deeply wounded her heart truly was.

"We fight for Azantian," Atlas said firmly. She paused until Margrete met her fierce stare. "And now, we fight for you. The Goddess of the Sea."

MARGRETE GUIDED HER CREW INTO THE CORRIDOR AND DOWN ITS winding length. Not a soul roamed the hall. She'd seen one member of the supposed Sea Court thus far, and Dawn hadn't shown herself since depositing them back into the royal suites.

She'd be a fool to think others weren't close by.

On silent feet, they tiptoed past the flickering sconces, their flames casting shadows of wraiths and monsters against the cobalt walls. They'd walked farther than when Dawn showed them to their chambers initially, or at least, it felt that way. And the more minutes that passed, the less certain Margrete became of the portal's location.

Finally, *finally*, a silver arch came into sight. The magic within the portal shimmered and danced, enticing them to journey through. She sighed, her anxiety dissipating like steam.

"Thank the gods," she said aloud, running a hand through her hair.

"Technically, you're thanking *yourself*," Mila tilted her head, one red brow arched. The redhead's skin appeared a tinge paler, nearly sickly in the low light. Margrete frowned. There could be no more denying it—the Underworld was wreaking havoc on their bodies, and it showed.

Sooner or later, this realm would reject them. They had to hurry. And fast.

The crew didn't need to be told to follow when Margrete glided past the magic of the portal and to the other side. Unfortunately, it wasn't the marble staircase they faced upon exit. No, before them stood the most breathtaking room Margrete had ever beheld, and she had borne witness to Azantian and its towering sea glass palace.

A chorus of voices echoed as a hundred or more wide-eyed stares captured her in their sights, the courtiers' crystal glasses laden with bubbling blue liquid sloshing in their cups as they jolted in surprise. Margrete stilled, mouth gaping as she took in the festive scene.

Shit. They certainly weren't on the ground floor.

The chamber had to be well over three stories in height and equally as wide. A single throne sat upon a dais of immobile silver waves, and topping its center rested a magnificent sapphire gem. A crown had been placed upon its velvety jade seat, an elegant circlet of pearls banding around the silver.

The frozen courtiers' finery swished against gleaming opal floors, the specks of blue and silvery white flakes catching the light of the over-hanging chandelier. Hundreds of white candles lit up the resplendent fixture, highlighting the lavish court and its patrons.

Margrete did what anyone would do when faced with an unwanted social setting—she went deathly still, pretending as if she could blend into the background if she refused to move.

No such luck.

"I think they're waiting on you to say something," Atlas muttered through her teeth, elbowing her gently in the ribs. Dani took her other side, sliding a comforting hand to her lower back and rubbing it in soothing circles. Her touch sent an odd burst of calm through her veins, and her next breaths came easier.

Dawn flew through the parting crowd, and Margrete had the urge to hug her. A familiar face, however new, was entirely welcomed. She plastered on a smile that was both fake and uneasy, and likely appeared frightening to small children and adults alike.

"Welcome, goddess," Dawn intoned, announcing her to the room. She dipped low into a formal curtsy, prompting the other courtiers to follow suit. All held that same lustrous sheen as Dawn, their unnatural beauty painful to look at for too long.

"I wasn't sure if you wished to meet your subjects tonight, but it seems you've had a change of heart." Dawn's smile was strained, and she purposely raised her voice for all to hear, pretending this had been planned. She wanted to embrace the ethereal woman even more so now.

Margrete peered around the room, both shocked by the onlookers gawking and confused as to how the hell she and her friends had ended up *here*.

Dawn lowered her voice to a whisper. "The portals are known to be... finicky." She smiled brightly, though it didn't meet her eyes. "It will take some time to glean the difference between them. If you were attempting to go somewhere else, that is," she added.

Then where was the portal leading to the main floor? To Bash?

A flood of alarm chilled her blood.

Her power sensed something. It coiled like a snake, pulsating within her chest, itching to slip out and explore. She ignored whatever Dawn was saying, something about drinks or music, and searched the crowd.

Her magic seemed to scream at her to move, to run, and she scanned the murmuring courtiers, searching for a sign. For *anything*.

Her attention landed on the throne. The crown. It called to her, and her fingers itched with the need to touch it, to place it upon her head. The force of its lure was so strong. It reminded her of the pull she'd felt for the key, which she now grasped inside her pocket, sighing as a flood of energy tickled her skin. The crown grew close, and she hadn't realized she'd moved until Atlas's hand seized her arm.

Her touch was like a current of electricity, the shock coaxing her back to reality. The courtiers' faces floated back into focus, though their murmurings weren't as hushed. It took everything in her not to look back to the throne and the alluring crown resting upon it.

"Mistress?" Dawn prompted, head cocked to the side in obvious concern.

She had a right to be concerned. Margrete's knees wobbled, her vision tilting slightly. It felt like time had stopped and all of the missing moments were rushing back at her at once.

"Uh, we were hoping to stretch our legs and must have gotten lost," Mila provided. While an obvious lie, Margrete thanked her for answering when she couldn't.

"Since you're already here, how about some introductions then?" Dawn twisted around and snapped her fingers to a band of musicians hidden away in the far corner. They rushed into action, immediately plucking at their instruments. A hauntingly somber voice began to sing in a language she knew belonged to the ancients. The woman the voice belonged to was equally as stunning, her deep brown skin radiant beneath the chandelier, her cheeks shimmering with iridescent blue powder. She bowed her head to Margrete in respect, but she never faltered, her raspy voice strong.

No one danced as the music played, and Margrete turned to Dawn.

"They're waiting for you to tell them to dance," Dawn whispered under her breath.

Of course. "Feel free to dance. Enjoy," Margrete grated out, her palms clammy with embarrassment. The command signified her new position and her power over a people she didn't wish to rule. At once, they obeyed, but it became terribly uncomfortable to watch as they pretended to go back to their whispered conversations. Their focus continuously drifted her way, and even as the gifted singer wove a tale of unrequited love, not one person swayed or glanced at the stage.

Margrete seethed even as her body shook, her very soul seeming to quiver with the need to ascend the throne. Yet she knew if she did, she might never leave it.

There'd be no saving Bash tonight, and now she had to escape this enchanted room and its too many eyes. She wanted nothing to do with all this attention. It made her skin itch.

Monsters she could handle.

Gods she could face.

But a room of fancy courtiers? She wanted to rush for the exit.

A servant approached and raised a silver platter before her, a delicate crystal glass resting upon its polished surface. With hesitant fingers, she wrapped them around the stem, holding the bubbling drink close to her chest. Maybe it would calm her frayed nerves.

"Now," Dawn said, "I believe the first person you should be introduced to would be your oldest court member. She's been here for well over—"

Margrete heard the whooshing of the arrow before she saw it.

Before she could lift her hand up and form a shield, thick arms banded around her waist and yanked her sideways. As she soared, a flaming arrow shot past where she'd just stood, its sharpened tip a fiery shade of blood red. The ground rushed up and she squeezed her eyes shut, anticipating the unforgiving impact.

It never came.

That same body that had whisked her out of harm's way now cradled her. She smelled salt and smoke, and when she turned her head to her savior, searing bile rose in her throat.

Darius.

His golden face hovered mere inches from her own, and his irises shone with a mixture of rage and adoration, the conflicting emotions causing her heart to stutter. Both of his arms surrounded her still, having cushioned her fall, but when she attempted to sit up, he surprisingly rose, sitting back on his haunches.

Once free of his intoxicating scent, Margrete noticed the bluish-black pool staining his once pristine white shirt. The arrow that had been meant for her had pierced his back, its tip sticking out of his chest where his blood flowed freely.

The god crumbled, both palms flat on the floor. A pained look distorted his features as a gasp of pain left his lips. "Margrete," he whispered her name. His eyes were creased, his chest rising and falling unevenly. He appeared on the verge of passing out.

He'd taken an arrow for her. Even after she'd denied him, after she chose Bash.

She shouldn't have been surprised. His entire mission thus far had been to gain her affection, but she hadn't expected him to risk his own life. And who the hell had shot that arrow? It wasn't mortal-made; she could smell the harsh perfume of divinity painting it.

Only a god could kill another god, she knew, and it seemed as though one had attempted to end her life tonight.

Dawn was shouting something at the incoming surge of stoic, armor-clad guards, and the chamber erupted into chaos. Margrete leaned over Darius, shocked at how close she'd come to an arrow in her skull.

"Why?" she asked. Her chest tightened with renewed outrage, but seeing him bleeding out surprisingly didn't bring her joy. How she wished it had.

Darius lifted a trembling hand, and she flinched. Immediately, he dropped it back to his side with an agonized hiss.

"I won't let you die," he murmured, his eyes fluttering. "You can hate me all you want, but I will always protect you. Even if you never protect me."

She held herself back from slapping him. "You *killed* Bash. Stole my happiness. If that is your idea of *protection*, then I don't want it." The reminder had been one she needed, and her shock dissipated. "I hope you die." Still, the words felt odd on her tongue, the meaning behind them causing her throat to constrict.

Darius let out a weak whimper, his weighted stare never once leaving her, not even as a healer approached and kneeled before him, checking on his wound. Before he was carried out of the room, he uttered one final thing in parting.

"I hope you dream of me, sweet Margrete. Maybe then, you'll remember why I refuse to lose you again."

CHAPTER EIGHT

DARIUS

DARIUS HAD SUSPECTED CHARION WOULD MAKE AN ATTEMPT ON Margrete's life the second she left the safety of the royal chambers. Still, he questioned how the war god had managed to slip away so effortlessly. He must've had help. Charion couldn't enter the Sea Court without an invitation, unless...

There were a few loopholes, namely, Surria. She had birthed Darius and Malum, and perhaps with *her* invitation, Charion had been able to enter. That was the only explanation, however implausible, that Darius could come up with.

Yesterday, after waiting until the gods had departed for their own courts, he'd snuck into the palace. His prisoner was quickly deposited into one of the many guest rooms in his court, and he'd magicked the door locked while Bay screamed creative obscenities and delicious threats of murder. Thankfully, his drink was spiked with a little sleeping sedative. It had taken ten minutes before silence ensued, the sailor knocked unconscious.

Darius should've killed him a long while ago, but he'd refrained. He didn't wish to ruminate over why.

Now, doted upon by healers and arranged on a bed of fine linens and furs, Darius glanced down at his slowly healing injury. Since it had been a weapon fashioned by a god, the wound wouldn't heal instantly, but Darius would likely be back on his feet after a restless night of sleep.

But it had been worth it—Darius had been a *hero*.

He'd saved Margrete, and the look of disbelief in her eyes hinted that there was hope. While he wished to be in his old chambers on the other side of the court, he told the servants to prepare the guest room two doors down from hers.

In the meantime, he'd permit Margrete space, time to process and perhaps dream of him, and then he'd approach her again.

Pain twisted his mind, but Darius comforted himself with the knowledge that Margrete was near and that he could protect her from the immortals. He'd sent two of his oldest and most loyal guards to monitor the hall outside her room. He wouldn't put it past Charion to send spies. The God of War must've discovered Margrete meant something to him, and he hungered to take her away just as Darius had taken away Malum.

You should've let her get hurt, his inner voice snarled. It was his plan, after all. And perhaps Darius had initially intended for her to bear witness to the cruelty of his siblings. But then he'd seen her—

And his mind wasn't his own.

Darius dismissed his servants and laid back, shutting his eyes. He imagined Margrete was doing the same, lying peacefully in her bed, sleep beckoning. A smile formed as he let his power loose, tendrils of nearly invisible magic snaking from his fingertips and across the expanse of his room. The luminescent magic slithered through the crack beneath his door and into the hallway, headed toward the woman who'd become his obsession.

Sweet dreams, darling, he thought, just before allowing sleep to pull him under. Tonight, they would both dream of a time before Darius had betrayed her and lost the most important thing in his life. Tonight marked the start of their rebirth.

CHAPTER NINE

MARGRETE

MARGRETE'S FAILURE GUTTED HER.

Her fingers burned with the need to expel her pent-up magic, and the fact that she couldn't control it made it all the more frustrating. Sometimes she swore she could hear it whisper across her mind, a separate entity that was bonded with her soul.

All gods appeared to have the same abilities, in some form or another, but each held a trace of the subject or creation they ruled over. Margrete's magic could be glacially cold, much like the sea could be. Other times she even conjured glimmering droplets that spiraled around her palms, the sparkling beads of seawater reminding her of gems.

It was all new, and without a guide, or someone to tutor her, she was floundering.

She didn't speak to her crew as they settled in various lounges and chairs back in her suite, scowls painting their faces. They all had purple bruises beneath their eyes like they hadn't slept in days, and their skin appeared dehydrated. Yet instead of their waning health, they focused on the failure of an evening.

Stubborn. All of them.

She knew she was one to talk.

Margrete looked at her hands, spotting a smear of blue-black blood. She grumbled a curse. Darius's act of heroism didn't fool her.

Be patient, Bash. I haven't given up on you. She prayed he could hear her, even now.

She changed into a simple silk shift and climbed beneath the covers. While she had offered to share the bed with Mila, the woman turned down the suggestion with an eye roll and said, "I've slept in worse places. And you snore."

Margrete suspected the true reason she stayed awake was to watch the door. Mila didn't trust easily. After tonight, Margrete couldn't blame her.

Her head fell to the pillow, and she closed her eyes.

It was difficult to let go and sleep without Bash's warm body at her back. Whenever insomnia dug its claws into her mind, he'd demand for her to roll over and then he'd rub her shoulders, loosening any lingering tension. She'd eventually fall asleep to the soothing ministrations, his steady breathing chasing away all restlessness.

Margrete sighed, about to fling off the covers and see if Mila was up for a midnight adventure through the palace, when a gentle blue light flashed across her eyes. It lasted only a second, but her head lolled to the side and her mind shut itself off as she fell under sleep's spell.

GENTLE FINGERS STROKED HER HAIR, A WHISPER OF A TOUCH. *Margrete's eyes were shut, but every other sense prickled with awareness. She smelled the deep smoke and salt in the air. Felt the thick, corded muscles of the thigh her head rested upon. Gods, she could even taste the fresh strawberry on her lips as though she'd just taken a bite.*

When she flinched, the fingers tangled in her hair stilled.

"What's wrong, darling?"

The voice held traces of sweet softness, and hidden below, concern.

She twisted her head, meeting the sea blue eyes of a god—but it wasn't her turning, not really. Margrete watched her body move without an ounce of control. Her hand reached for the nape of his neck, and she positioned herself on the plush chaise beneath them until she straddled Darius, her knees trapping his thighs.

"I'm worried about what happens when your mother demands you finish the trials." It was she who asked the question—the vibrations still felt in her throat—but like her movements, she had no influence over her actions. This new voice was raspier than her own, deeper, and inherently seductive.

Darius's stare burned molten as he assessed her, though something told her that she wasn't the target of his anger. He brought a hand to cup her cheek. The tender act did little to disguise the fury swimming in his irises, how they sparked when Surria's name tainted the air.

"My mother hasn't been patient these long months, that is true, but I won't let her hurt you." His left eye twitched, and the muscled arms around her waist grew taut. He held onto her as if she might float away.

Margrete sighed. "She doesn't care about what you want, and she has the power to destroy everything, whether you wish it or not." Her throat grew tight, and her eyes prickled with burning tears.

This is Wryn, she reminded herself. Not her.

Margrete was glimpsing a scene from a past life.

When she shifted closer, inky-black hair fell across her vision. Darius grasped one of the strands, studying it carefully as he spun it around his finger. He seemed captivated by the midnight color of it, how it wrapped around his golden skin before he allowed it to fall.

"Listen to me carefully," Darius began, unnervingly calm. He lifted his head, and she found herself powerless in the snare of his gaze. "You're too important to me to lose. I simply won't allow it."

As if he had any control over the actions of his mother. Or brother, for that matter.

His hand drifted to her chin, his fingers gentle yet firm. "I-I've never known such happiness," he stuttered, having trouble finding the right words. He swallowed hard enough for her to track the movement. "My immortal life has been filled with empty years, and only when I held you in my arms did time begin to carry any semblance of meaning."

Wryn. These words were meant for Wryn. And yet Margrete felt each and every one of them in her very core. A single tear slipped down her cheek, warm against her skin. Darius leaned forward, kissing it away with an aching rawness.

"No tears, Wryn," he said firmly. "Your fear and grief turn me murderous, and I'm tempted to leave now and find Surria myself." She shifted in his lap but didn't get far; his hold remained impenetrable. "But that would mean I'd have to leave you, and I wouldn't put it past Mother to trick me and attack you when I'm gone."

"I can take care of myself," Wryn argued, but there was no confidence in her tone.

Darius shook his head. "No. I might have used my soul to give you life, but you don't have my power. At least, not yet." He ran his hand through her hair and cradled the nape of her neck. "You are the humanity I never had, and while I wish you had something in which to defend yourself, I find myself selfishly glad you aren't stained with power. It corrupts."

"You're not corrupt."

"Oh, but I am, little one. I'm a monster in everyone else's eyes but yours."

It might've been the intensity of his focus or how tightly he held Wryn, but Margrete believed him, and her heart gave a painful twinge. Darius truly loved her, his creation, the woman he fashioned from his soul. He cherished Wryn, that much was clear.

"All I see is you, Darius," Wryn insisted. "And there's good in you yet. Even if you can't see it for yourself. You're lucky I'm here to remind you of it."

One corner of Darius's lips tugged up at the sides, something mischievous washing away the tension of before. "That's my Wryn," he said, sighing. "Always so optimistic." The hand curled around the back of her neck loosened, and the furrow between his brows smoothed. "Always my light."

Bash called her his light.

And now, she knew Darius had as well. Margrete didn't know what to make of the churning in her belly or how guilt suddenly tugged at her heart.

If she failed to save Bash, failed to reunite his soul with his body, would darkness consume him? What if she wasn't enough to protect him? Maybe that's what happened to Wryn, maybe she hadn't been enough light to drive Darius's demons away.

The god, ignorant of the thoughts swirling chaotically inside Margrete's head, twisted Wryn in his arms. Before she could blink, he had her flat on her back, hovering over her as his blond hair tickled her cheeks. With his arms caging her in on both sides, there was nowhere to go, nowhere to look but at him.

Margrete felt Wryn smile, and at the sight of it, warmth flared in Darius's eyes. There was no hesitation when he leaned down to place a demanding kiss on her lips.

If she had any control over her body, over this memory, Margrete would have moved. Or rather, she would've liked to believe she'd have moved. But even trapped in Wryn's ethereal body and inside this memory, the touch of Darius's lips was overwhelming.

Where Bash's embrace was home, the god's touch was a raging storm on the open waters—exhilarating and dangerous, and frighteningly addicting. But deep down, it was wholly and distinctly wrong.

He took his time, leisurely exploring her, tasting her, his tongue sweeping into her mouth and tangling with hers. A low moan left her lips, and his sweet caresses turned needy. Snaking an arm below her head, he brought her impossibly close, and for just a moment, Margrete forgot she wasn't Wryn at all.

Darius finally drew back for air, his lids hooded and a smile brightening his sharp features. Margrete had never seen him look this way, had never glimpsed the raw joy and vulnerability he openly displayed. She'd known only the immortal who wore a mask and felt hatred in his blood.

He brought his lips to her brow. "You have such power over me, Wryn." He spoke in a whisper, his breath tickling her skin. "Only you."

Margrete watched as he pushed away, bringing her body with him. When he settled back on the chaise, he positioned her to rest against his chest. Thunderous beating met her ear, the god's heart pounding savagely. It seemed so absurdly human.

Wryn must have shut her eyes then, because the next time she opened them, she was hovering above, no longer inside Wryn. She was a phantom, a ghost, and the scene that played out before her would've stolen her air had she possessed any.

Darius had Wryn positioned against the chaise, her arms gripping its velvety back as he drove into her from behind. His large hands encircled the entirety of her waist, guiding her every movement and letting her know who was in control.

"That's it," he praised when Wryn released a moan and reached back to grab hold of Darius's muscular thigh. His head dipped, his eyes molten as he watched where they joined, his impressive length sliding in and out at a leisurely pace.

Margrete felt the light call to her, the ending of the dream, and yet...she couldn't look away.

Darius wrapped Wryn's raven hair around his fist, pulling her head back and exposing her slender neck. "You're so beautiful when you take me," he rasped, kissing up and down her jaw, lowering to her neck where he sucked at the sensitive skin. "Now be a good girl and say the words."

He thrust harder, and Wryn struggled to keep herself stable. Not that it mattered—Darius had her exactly where he desired. At his mercy.

"I-I love you," she said, a smile lifting her lips. "Gods, do I love you."

Darius rumbled his approval before flipping her around and thrusting back into her in one swift move. "Now repeat it once more when I make you come."

Margrete finally willed the scene away, fighting to reach the light of consciousness. Lingering had felt like trespassing on sacred space, and yet the memory had once belonged to her. The startling realization was the final push she needed to yank herself from the dream.

She had hesitated for far too long, and that in itself was more horrifying than anything she'd seen.

CHAPTER TEN

MARGRETE

MARGRETE WOKE WITH A GASP.

She fisted the coverlet, her body drenched in sweat as if she'd had a nightmare. In a way, she had. Though it had been her fault in the end—she'd *chosen* to stay and watch those final moments play out.

Maybe she had needed to see the proof of their connection. Or she'd been too stunned to do anything at all.

The truth, she knew, was far more complicated than that.

Darius promised she'd begin to remember her former life, but she wished she wouldn't. It didn't matter who she'd once *been*. It mattered who she was now.

Unable to fall back asleep, and with the moon still shining through the arched window of her rooms, Margrete padded across the chamber to the ornate desk where she'd found the key. Atlas stirred in her chair, both her legs propped up on a glass table before her, Dani beside her, resting her head on Atlas's shoulder. Mila had finally given up her watch and was fast asleep, her head slumped forward with her back pressed against the wall.

Margrete took a seat before the desk and began searching, hoping to find something left behind by Malum or Darius—whomever this room once belonged to. Much to her dismay, there were no more hidden drawers or secret compartments. She gripped the edges of the desk, frustration bubbling to the surface.

If she didn't trust herself to *not* kill Darius, she'd corner him and demand answers.

The god had been so tender in her dream before—

Before he'd taken Wryn with the passion of a man in love. Heat seared her cheeks. She needed to rid herself of those images.

Screw Darius and the enigma he'd become. She still had one objective—to journey to where she'd heard Bash's voice.

And she no longer had the patience to wait.

Shoving away from the desk, she slipped on a simple robe and snuck past her exhausted friends. The key she'd found earlier weighed down the robe's pocket, bumping against her thigh with every step. She'd yet to allow the key out of her sight. Whenever she went to put it down, her ribcage squeezed as if in reproach. So she kept it safely on her person as she walked to the door and turned the handle.

Of course, when she opened the door, two guards who hadn't been there before greeted her, both lurching to attention. Were they there for protection or something sinister?

Margrete tested the theory.

"Where is the portal that brings me below, to the first floor?" She mimicked the way in which Surria had spoken, an air of haughtiness turning her tone cruel and cutting. The men exchanged hasty glances before the taller of the pair cleared his throat. She could've sworn the second one peered down the hall, as if seeking approval from an invisible source.

"They change locations every three hours, goddess. And at this late hour, the portal you're seeking would be in the library," the first guard stated, the timbre of his voice deep with warning.

An odd place for a door. Then again, it was odd enough that the doors *changed* places.

"Show me," she demanded, lifting a brow when he hesitated. But the man, who wore a deep blue tunic with a silver wave emblazoned on the front, shifted reluctantly on his feet before giving her a stern nod.

Margrete bit into her cheek. Barking orders made her feel like her father, but all of this was yet another game, and she'd play her role no matter how uncomfortable it made her.

"Follow me, goddess."

She had to refrain from rolling her eyes at the title, and instead trailed behind the guard as he navigated the elegant halls with movements so stiff, she feared he'd crack and tumble over. They made a few turns, passing scurrying uniformed servants and a couple of drunken courtiers obliviously kissing in an alcove.

From somewhere far away, she heard the sounds of a party, music and laughter floating to her ears. It seemed the festivities hadn't ended after the attempt on her life. So much for devotion.

The last hallway the guard led her down eventually opened to a grand antechamber, the gleaming marble flooring reflecting her scowling face. She appeared worried, haggard, and a tad unhinged.

Her normal look as of late.

Margrete studied the ten identical doors lining the circular space, all of them closed and all framed in obnoxious, opulent silver. No servants or courtiers were seen.

"This one," the guard grunted, motioning toward the third doorway. It had been constructed like all the rest, but a nearly imperceptible golden, crescent moon and a single teardrop had been painted right above the handle. She thanked him, her harsh tone a clear dismissal. He bowed and marched back down the passageway.

At least she wasn't a prisoner like she'd assumed.

Margrete pushed on the third door and slipped inside without a sound. Sure enough, the library she entered was as luxurious as one could imagine; two stories high with thousands of leather-bound books crowding the overpacked mahogany shelves. Sea glass tables and high-backed chairs of gold were arranged neatly in a semi-circle. But situated in the corner, right beside a pretentious portrait of Malum—his long, black hair and dark eyes staring straight into her soul—stood the portal in question.

Her heart skipped a beat, and excitement pulsed in her veins. Her crew should be here with her, but there wasn't time to waste and she suspected they were growing weaker, if the dark circles below their eyes and sallow skin were any indication.

Once the portal's foggy blue mist cleared and she landed on its other side, Margrete scanned the grand foyer of the main floor. There were no lingering guards stationed, which she found peculiar, but Halio had told her that this area was deemed neutral, so armed soldiers would likely go against the agreement.

The lone sound arose from the ticking of a clock stationed above the staircase's first landing, its steady rhythm matching the beating in her chest.

On the ground floor, close to the mysterious hall, Margrete's skin tingled. She could practically smell Bash's signature scent of pine and sea, and she yearned to race to the portal and—

And what?

Fuck. She hadn't thought it all through, and if this was some fantasy tale she was reading, she'd curse at the heroine and wonder why she hadn't planned better. Whenever Bash was concerned, Margrete's logic was nonexistent.

The key in her pocket pulsated, its energy much stronger than when she'd been in her own court. Was it calling to something close by? Drawn to a door in Halio's court as she was drawn to the shadows masking the entrance to the realm of the dead?

She peered to the corridor that would bring her to Bash. As if sensing her presence, the swirling onyx mist roared to life, causing her magic to thrum.

A warning. She understood this with every fiber of her being.

Ignoring the sensation of the misty shadows clawing at her exposed skin and twirling about her legs, Margrete scurried forward. She all but sprinted down the hall, her aim ahead, on her prize, which happened to be a locked door.

A *locked* door.

She reached into her pocket, her fingers brushing against the polished metal of the key. Was luck finally on her side?

Unlike the rest of the obnoxiously lavish entryways, this one was framed with nothing but dark, uneven stones, the curving handle fashioned in the shape of a cracked femur bone. The scent of mold and rot clung to the air, and a draft carrying the aroma of wild earth filled her nostrils. The combination had her skin itching.

Bash? she silently called, hoping she'd hear his voice as plainly as she had yesterday.

No one answered, which shouldn't have surprised her.

Margrete grasped the key and brought it to the lock. It didn't throb as strongly as before, but she held firm, slipping it inside. A thrill shot down her back when it slid in without resistance.

She turned the handle.

Resistance.

Margrete clutched the bone, her hands clammy and slick. Fruitlessly, she jerked the key, the handle, then shoved against the door—doing everything she could to thrust it open.

The key didn't belong to this portal, fate working once again to diminish her hope.

Something wrapped around her neck, *tight.*

Sputtering, she dropped her arm, the key plummeting to the floor with a resounding clatter. Grabbing at her neck, she found nothing there but air, and yet the pressure increased, cutting off her oxygen. Panic surged, and she tasted copper on her tongue.

"That door is forbidden, goddess."

She couldn't turn toward the deep voice, could do nothing as the rope of invisible power cut into her skin. Margrete fell to her knees, the impact eliciting a hiss.

"Why are you here?" the voice continued, anger lining every syllable.

As she couldn't breathe, let alone speak, all she could manage was a choked gasp.

"Ah, my apologies."

A moment later the noose loosened, and the burning surrounding her neck was soothed by a frosted wind. Margrete shoved to her feet and spun around. Black spots dotted her vision.

Halio. He stood before her, his hands thrust deep in his silver pockets, his gray stare narrowed in reproach.

"I-I heard something," she said, raising a hand to her neck. Gods, it still ached.

He tsked. "Don't lie to the God of Death, Margrete. It's insulting."

She wasn't lying, not really. She *had* heard a voice—Bash's. Instead of saying that, she ran her hands down her robe and met the god's incensed gaze. How was she supposed to get to Bash with the fucking God of Death standing in her way?

"That, my dear, is the portal to the dead. As I'm sure you've already figured out." His focus drifted to the floor, to where the key had fallen. Surprisingly, he made no move to pick it up. If anything, he seemed to inch back. "And entrance is forbidden to all except me."

She curled her hands into fists. "I heard—"

"I know what you heard!" Halio's voice rose and his nostrils flared, his earlier kindness a distant memory. "And it doesn't matter. The man you're seeking is dead and cannot be brought back, even by you."

Fuck. That.

She didn't come this far to be turned away.

"No." The word slipped out of her mouth before she could contain it.

"No?" Halio lifted a black brow. The circlet around his head pulsed with white light. He took a step closer, then another, until they were nearly nose to nose. "You do not tell *me* no. Not in my realm when I have been nothing but welcoming. Do whatever you wish in your own court, but the realm of the dead is mine."

Margrete searched his eyes for anything, for a sign of lenience, a sign that she could bargain with him. She'd give *anything*. Maybe her desperation shone on her face, because Halio's eyes softened, just the slightest.

"Please." This time, her voice cracked, and a strangled sob had her chest trembling. She'd done her best to shove aside her emotions, but in the face of defeat, they all came rushing to the surface. "I'll do whatever you ask. I'll give anything. *Anything!*"

Halio released an exasperated sigh. Taking a step back, he cocked his head and studied her, his silence worse than any harsh words.

Just when she thought she could take no more, he said, "Such a promise is a dangerous thing to make, youngling. If you were wise, you'd accept what fate has dealt you and move on. You aren't ready for what it would take to fulfill such a bargain. "

Margrete dug her nails into her palms. She'd long ago promised that fate would never rule her again. "I don't care. I came here for Bash and I won't leave until I save him." Her magic flared to life, and wisps of blue and white light seeped from her pores. Her glow landed across Halio's face, illuminating his impossibly handsome features. "Please," she begged again, before doing the very thing she promised she wouldn't do. She dropped to her knees and lifted her hands in a prayer. In submission.

There was no other noise but Halio's steady breathing, and she didn't dare steal a peek at him from below her lowered lashes. The anticipation of what surely would be his rejection robbed her of air, and she trembled beneath the thin covering of her silken robe.

Halio made a sound halfway between a grunt and a growl.

"Rise, Margrete. Never bow before another, not even Death itself. Not unless they deserve it." She canted her head and met his eyes. The gray in them sparked before shuttering to steel.

On unsteady feet, she rose, feeling both furious and a fool.

A pensive look contorted his features. "For too long the immortals have played with the humans as if their lives were games, things to be toyed with for their entertainment." His upper lip curled back. "And the Gods of the Sea were among the worst of them. It is their fault their monsters have been unleashed upon the mortal realm, causing chaos and death. Too many deaths than is preordained. And as you know, messing with destiny is a dangerous thing indeed."

"Why don't you and the other deities do anything about it?" she asked. "You all have power? Why not step in and save the humans?"

"Unlike the rest, I cannot leave these lands. But as far as the other gods, they simply don't care. When you live for too long, the things that once were important lose meaning, and besides, the seas don't affect them, so they don't act. Only Surria could've brought her sons into submission, but she likes to watch the anarchy unfold," Halio added with distaste. "She may wear white, but beneath such purity lies a cruelty that even I shudder at."

"I heard about what she made her sons undergo on the island." Margrete stepped closer. "She's a monster if it's true. To make her own son kill his love."

She may hate Darius, but no one was born evil. Evil was nurtured.

Halio cocked his head, his expression cooling. "Yes, well, that's how the original gods were crafted, goddess. They'd never been human, and therefore, they aren't familiar with the same empathy you carry."

Margrete felt *mostly* like herself. She was angrier, perhaps, and yes, she sensed her magic with a clarity that frightened her. But her empathy, her heart? That she knew to be intact. And it beat for a man who had stolen it the second she laid eyes upon him on the *Phaedra*.

"I don't care about being a goddess or having powers," she admitted. "I simply wish to get Bash and return to the mortal realm. Someone else can have *this*." She motioned to herself. "I don't want it."

The God of Death laughed. "I'm afraid it doesn't work that way."

She growled. "Well, then I will use whatever power I have and save him. I don't care what it takes. What crimes I have to commit. Who I have to *kill*." The last part should've terrified her, but it didn't. She meant every word.

Halio's irises sparkled once more. "I've found that those who do not want power are those best suited for it," he mused, beginning to circle her leisurely, his hands clasping behind his back. Biting her tongue, she waited until a minute had passed and he came to an abrupt halt in front of her.

"I will make a deal with you, Margrete of Prias," Halio said. "One soul for the price of thousands."

"Excuse me?" She inched closer, not understanding his meaning.

"Fourteen days," Halio intoned, his voice seeming to shake the walls surrounding them. "Fourteen days to right the wrongs of the previous sea gods and destroy their ravenous beasts, and your king will be given another chance at life."

Margrete nearly crumbled from relief. She opened her mouth to thank him, but he held up a hand, cutting her off.

"I'm far from done, goddess. You will bring Darius with you, unite your magic, and slay his creatures. He caused this mess, and he should help clean it up. Besides, he has a lesson to learn, and I'm keen on providing it."

"I don't need him," Margrete growled, but Halio shook his head.

"That is my condition. If you can get him to agree to the terms, then I will make this bargain with you."

Margrete's rage returned in full force, and wisps of blue glimmered from her fingertips, a glow seeping from her palms and streaming down the hall. She didn't need Darius to kill the monsters. If Bash's life laid on the line, she'd destroy them all within a day.

"And if you fail," Halio continued, undeterred by her unimpressive display, "then not only will your king be forced to return here, but so will every soul on the island of Azantian."

She froze. Time itself might as well have stopped entirely.

"What?" The word was a screech. "Why would you want that? I presumed you wished to right the wrongs of Darius and his brother, to mend fate!"

"I am," Halio said softly. "Malum had no right to create Azantian in the first place, and its people are more powerful than any human has a right to be. It goes against the natural order."

"Then why haven't you destroyed it already?" Margrete challenged.

"Because only a deal bound in the blood of a sea god could allow me to destroy it. Azantian belongs to the sea, and I cannot take what isn't mine."

Margrete's heart fell. *Azantian.* If she failed...

"Decide now, Margrete. Patience has never been one of my virtues."

First, she had to get Darius to agree to help them. Then, she had to kill the monsters that had escaped the island. Margrete suddenly felt the hopelessness suffocating her. She didn't know the exact number of beasts that had escaped, and she wasn't sure of how many nymeras survived after they were attacked on the island. She only knew of Bash's mother.

Margrete was struck with an impossible decision. She wanted to be selfish, to strike the bargain without pause and hold Bash in her arms. Yet she understood the lives that would end because of her if she didn't follow through on her end.

Once more, she thought of her favorite fantasy books. The hero wouldn't endanger the lives of those they cared for. They wouldn't be so selfish.

But she was nothing like them; she was *real.*

Margrete had already made up her mind when she opened the portal to the Underworld. She'd made up her mind the moment Bash took his final breath...

"I have a condition of my own," she said. "I want Bash's soul. I want him to accompany me during the two weeks."

Halio scoffed. "He'd be a soul without a body. A specter."

"He has a body," she countered. "It's on Surria's island." Or wherever his mother smuggled him to. She'd have to search the seas once they went above. Whatever the case, she'd find it.

"You're asking for too much," Halio growled, a muscle in his jaw feathering. "I pride myself on civility and charm, but on matters such as this, I'm typically not so lenient."

"Grant me this, and I will make the deal. If you think I will fail, then you will finally be able to wipe Azantian from the map."

Acid coated her tongue as she spoke, but she *had* to get him to agree.

Another minute passed. The God of Death looked caught between slicing her throat open and falling asleep. But finally, he said, "Then let's see if your heart is pure, or if your own selfishness will lead to your ruin. You have yourself a deal."

The pain began once the final word left his lips.

Her arm. She glanced down, watching as dark ink spread around her new flame tattoo. Swirling vines, prickled with thorns, wrapped around the gray flames, ancient lettering blossoming like deadly blooms along the climbing black.

"What have you done?" she asked through gritted teeth. Margrete held her arm out as she lifted her chin to Halio.

"A deal struck between gods is always bound by two things." He took a step closer. "Ink and blood."

She paused. That didn't explain how her new tattoo came to be on Surria's island. She'd made no bargain with another god other than the promise she'd made to herself. Margrete wished to ask, but the stinging searing her arm made speaking all but impossible.

Halio reached for the sheath hidden beneath his jacket and brought out a dagger. Margrete's lips parted, but it was too late. Halio slashed through the whirling design already etched onto her arm, creating a single, shallow cut. Dark blue beads bubbled to the surface when he sliced at his own forearm.

"Final chance to back down," the God of Death warned.

The tattoo spread until it wrapped around the single, black tear dripping from the flames. It sparked a brilliant white before settling back to onyx, and she hissed in pain, almost as if Halio's dagger had pierced that exact spot.

"I'm not backing down," she snarled, ignoring the pain, ignoring all logic and sense. "Make the deal. Now."

Halio nodded, but for once a hint of emotion crossed his face, something akin to remorse. Or hesitation. But he still raised his arm and pressed it against her wound, a cut that was rapidly healing.

The shadows flared an ominous black before skittering away, abandoning the hallway and the gods who'd struck a bargain that could end in unimaginable death.

She just risked *everything* for one man. Now, the doubts were creeping in, even though her heart beat with renewed purpose.

No. She wouldn't lose this game, because that's what it was. The gods liked to prey on the weak. But Margrete had never been weak, and she refused to lose this round. For the man who saved her soul, she would do just about anything.

Even damn the one place he was sworn to protect.

If she failed, she knew he'd never forgive her.

CHAPTER ELEVEN

MARGRETE

"Are you out of your mind? What the hell did you do?" Mila slammed her goblet on the marble table, her rage palpable as she studied the addition to Margrete's already macabre tattoo.

The fresh thorns were sharp and grotesque, the frozen flames trapped by the winding prison of spikes. Just as she was trapped by her deal with Death.

"I did what I had to do," Margrete answered coolly. She slipped into a white gown from her armoire, feeling all kinds of off-kilter.

"You didn't have to do anyth—"

"You do not question me," she said, despising the words, the cruelty she'd forced into them. "I made a deal with a god, and if we succeed, we get Bash back. For good."

Atlas lifted a brow from where she sat in the corner, skepticism written all over her hardened face. She was far from pleased. "And what exactly does this deal entail?"

Margrete sighed. She knew she *should* tell them, but Mila's temper might cause her to do something rash, and to be honest, Margrete was too much of a coward to share the entire truth—

That Azantian would perish if she failed. That the people and island she'd grown to love would be swallowed into the sea.

This was her secret, her burden, and if she was unsuccessful, she wanted to drown alone. Her friends shouldn't have to drown with her.

"I made a deal with Halio last night," she admitted carefully. "It's based on the condition Darius joins me, but I've been tasked with hunting and killing the monsters unleashed upon the human realm. We have fourteen days to kill them or...or Bash remains here forever." Again, she left out Azantian, her cheeks heating. She'd never felt so rotten, so vilely selfish.

Stop. You're doing this for Bash. Be stronger. Tougher, she thought. But was she? Or was she becoming exactly like the sea god she hated?

The lines had grown far too blurred.

"What aren't you saying?" The small, hesitant voice belonged to Dani. She entered the room on light feet, her curls a halo around her dainty face. Her stare was as penetrating as always, and Margrete shivered beneath it. The girl saw too much. Especially since coming here.

For just a second, the key in her pocket thrummed, pulsating with awareness. Dani, as if she sensed it too, glanced at Margrete's pocket. Her gaze lingered before she tore it away with pursed lips.

"You may join me or not, but either way, it is done." Margrete barreled past them all and headed straight for the door. She reached for the key, although this time, it didn't respond as it once had, merely bestowing her with a weak buzz.

Before she could yank open the door and storm out, a knock sounded.

"Come in," she ordered, taking a step back and attempting to regain her composure. It was practically nonexistent.

The door creaked open, revealing a shimmering Dawn. "I've been sent to relay this message, goddess. I'd humbly advise that you accept right away." A violet invitation lay in the center of her outstretched palm.

Margrete seized the paper, inspecting the intricate golden script.

You are cordially invited to the Court of Love for a ball to be held this evening as Calista's most honored guest.

Honored guest. She highly doubted that.

She was about to inform Dawn that she wouldn't be able to attend when a new plan took shape. Darius was back in the Underworld. He was here, and she *needed* him now. Surely, he'd have healed by now and would be invited to the ball, and if she played her cards right, she could convince him to agree to her request. He owed her much more than that.

As his name flitted across her mind, so did the memory of her dream from the previous night. Wrapped in his arms, his warm kisses trailing up and down her throat—

"Tell Calista we will be there," she instructed a surprised Dawn, whose full lips parted. She'd expected a fight. To her crew, Margrete said, "Prepare yourselves. Tonight we dine, we drink, and we set our plan into motion."

The portal to the Court of Love was located on the fifth-floor landing.

Dawn had arrived an hour earlier to help Margrete prepare, and she was thankful she had. The slinky, silver gown she wore had been paired expertly with matching heels, and her thick mane had been done up in an elegant twist of intricate braids, a style she certainly wouldn't have been able to achieve on her own. To top it off, Dawn had painted her face with the skilled hand of an artist, her lips a luscious red and her eyes dark and smoky with kohl.

Tonight, as she traveled through Calista's portal—Atlas, Dani, and Mila behind her—she wore her polished appearance like the mask it was. She'd played a role for most of her life. What was another night?

Several members of other courts filed into a circular antechamber from different portals, all of them radiant and wearing the color associated with their chosen god's house. Many added ornamental symbols to their gowns or jackets in the form of brooches or jewelry, such as Brielle's bow or Themis's scales.

Those belonging to Charion's court sported a violent red and orange, while Brielle's house donned shades of the wild earth; hues of greens, browns, and the occasional burst of triumphant yellow. The few in Halio's court, unsurprisingly, wore black, but the delicate laces and glossy silks were unmatched in quality.

Margrete suspected those in ivory, white, and light gray belonged to

Surria. She had the suspicion that the goddess regarded herself above the rest of the immortals, much like the never-ending skies she ruled. Her chosen shade of the purest snow was merely a pretty little lie used to cover up the wicked truth.

The ballroom they entered was something out of a sinful summer dream. Brilliant fuchsia fires roared to life, held aloft by the thirty or so silver stands stationed around the curved chamber. The walls were brushed in deep violet, and when Margrete squinted, she could almost make out some sort of unusual design...

Well then.

Yes. There were figures etched in a light pearlescent color on the walls, all of them in...compromising positions. Margrete's cheeks flushed when she stumbled upon a particularly indecent pose between lovers that argued against gravity itself.

Tilting her chin toward the ceiling—and avoiding the sensuous illustrations—she found weightless globes of light floating above. They bounced around the room like trapped stars, their soft glow casting a decadent warmth upon the hundreds of glowing souls gathered.

Indeed, there were too many to count. Immortal revelers held pink crystal glasses in their hands, laughing, chatting away. The dance floor was overflowing, and a violin played alongside a whimsical harp as patrons gleefully lost themselves to the theme of the evening—decadent greed.

"Holy gods...well, holy *you*," Mila whispered at her side. She ran her quivering palms down her floor-length, midnight-blue dress, an indecent slit running up her thigh. Damp spots from clammy hands were left in her wake, and Margrete's chest squeezed, knowing it had nothing to do with nerves, but everything to do with the toll her body had been placed under. Mila's face was paler than ever, and her shaky steps hadn't gone unnoticed either.

Atlas shifted in her tailored turquoise suit, which lacked an undershirt. The warrior looked better than Mila, and even a slightly pink hue shone on her cheeks. She only stopped adjusting her outfit when Dani gave her an appreciative smile, a red hue working its way down her own cheeks. The quiet beauty wore a simple knee-length gown of polished pewter, the material clinging to her generous curves and reminding her of the luminous silver jacket Halio had worn at dinner. Margrete was certain Atlas found her equally appealing. In fact, Dani's health seemed to be getting oddly better, her skin dewy, her eyes bright. It was peculiar, but Margrete wasn't complaining.

A servant approached wearing a knee-length, reddish-pink dress and a neat, white apron tied around her narrow waist. Margrete accepted the rose-tinted drink she offered, downing the contents before snagging one more before the woman left. She hadn't even considered poison—that's how anxious she felt. When she didn't immediately die, she took another generous sip from her second glass.

"Nervous?"

Margrete recognized Halio's deep voice before she turned. The death god wore a fitted black brocade jacket and matching trousers, his silver crown even more lustrous under the ethereal lighting.

"Not at all," she lied. "I will convince Darius easily enough." Another sip was taken. It tasted like strawberries, and the liquid burned pleasantly as it slid down her throat.

"I hope so, goddess," Halio said, brushing aside a loose black curl. "Your clock has already started."

She froze, the drink in her hands an inch before her lips. "I thought it began once we made our way to the mortal realm?"

Halio shook his head, his eyes creasing in what could be mistaken as concern. "No, it began once our blood joined as one."

Shit. Shit. Shit.

That meant she had to convince Darius *tonight* and leave as soon as possible. An entire day had been wasted. Her magic reared its head, and her fingers tingled as glowing blue droplets whirled around her hands.

Halio *had* told her not to trust him. She should've known he'd leave that part out.

"Bash will be permitted to leave the realm during the hunt as we agreed?" she clarified, panic and rage making the room spin. Halio nodded. "Good. Then where the hell is Darius?"

Enough with the small talk. Time was slipping through her fingers like sand. She gave the death god her back and scanned the crowd. Her magic reached out, searching, calling to Darius. If they were made from the same soul, surely she could find him.

Halio chuckled. "I'm sure he's just waiting to make his grand entrance. He wouldn't miss out on seeing you tonight." His tone held a suggestion she didn't particularly care for.

"I'm certainly not looking forward—"

Margrete stopped mid-rant, having turned to find Halio gone, vanished into the overflowing crowd. She groaned, resuming her scan of the ballroom. Moments later, her crew approached.

Fuck. Mila grimaced as she pushed forward, but she stumbled before quickly righting herself. She appeared even worse than minutes ago. Dani held onto Atlas's arm, and Margrete swore Atlas was leaning on the petite sailor, her gaze clouded.

She wanted to ask how they were doing, but Margrete suspected they'd fill her ears with lies. Rather than waste time her friends didn't have, she got down to the mission at hand.

"Keep an eye out for Darius. I'm going to search for him myself," she told them when they were within reach, studying the fresh drinks in each of their hands. Mila chugged hers without shame before waving down a servant for another. Well, she might be slowly dying, but Mila could outdrink a fish.

When they'd all separated to investigate, Margrete wandered around the room, smiling tightly when a few members of her court bowed. None looked her in the eyes, and she noticed how their frames quivered as if in fear. That told her everything she needed to know about how the immortals treated their court.

Another glass was presented to her, and she didn't hesitate to take it.

Mingling with the divine required heavy drinking.

"There you are."

Margrete halted, her cup poised at her lips. The sugary-sweet voice came from behind her, and she whirled around, plastering a fake smile on her lips.

Surria.

"What a pleasant surprise," Margrete said, her fingers tightening on the stem of her glass.

Smile, she reminded herself. *Let her think you're weak.*

The Goddess of the Wind and Sky wore a tulle white dress with a plunging neckline. Gleaming pearls were braided into her golden hair, which had been swept from her heart-shaped face and into a half updo. Margrete cursed how stunning she looked. No one *that* evil should possess such beauty.

"I've been waiting for you," the goddess said, her voice a haunting melody Margrete wanted to scrub from her memory. "We didn't have much time yesterday with all the commotion." She waved her delicate hands in the air. "But I've wanted to get you alone for some time now. Though this isn't as private an affair as I'd wished."

Margrete gritted her teeth. Her mouth strained with discomfort at keeping her lips from turning into a scowl.

"What do you want to talk about?"

Murder? Your villainous sons? Your unspeakable cruelty?

Surria's pale blue eyes scanned Margrete from head to toe. Her lips twisted at whatever she found.

"I made a mistake many years ago with my son," she began, lowering her voice in an almost conspiratorial whisper. "Darius was always the more...sentimental of the two, and I thought if I gave him a *push* he'd grow stronger. To become the leader I'd wanted him to be."

Margrete didn't want to sit here and listen to lies. So she didn't respond, instead choosing to lift a brow as if to say, *And?*

Surria leaned back, her appraisal never-ending. Margrete couldn't help but feel wanting in the woman's presence, and it made her skin crawl.

"Seeing as you enjoy niceties as much as I do, let me be blunt," Surria rasped, and Margrete's heart thundered. "I don't want you here. I *never* wanted you here. But my son has refused to forgive me, and he's all I have left now. All my hard work for one child. My single hope." She shot

Margrete a pointed glare, as if losing Malum was somehow her fault. "Therefore, I wish to...make amends."

Margrete couldn't bite back all of her laughter. It came out like a snort.

"Am I amusing you?" The goddess's pale eyes flashed silver. A blatant warning.

She cleared her throat, calming herself. "Um, no, it's just hard to believe you actually give a damn about your son after the stories I've heard. And if *I* may be blunt, I simply don't believe you."

She began to walk away—to find the man they spoke of now—when granite fingers curled tightly around her upper arm. Instantly, Margrete's power hissed in reproach, heat coiling in her belly.

Surria leaned in close, her cool breath tickling Margrete's ear. "You've lost someone you love, haven't you? Perhaps a great loss changes a person, does it not?" The grip on her arm turned bruising, and Margrete stifled a groan. "I can see how you've changed. From an innocent, and frankly, boring noblewoman to a vengeful little creature who doesn't even know the limits of her reach." Surria scoffed. "I'd be very careful if I were you. It's a slippery slope. Wouldn't want you to fall."

Those unforgiving fingers released her, and Margrete's skin burned where she'd been held. Surria's smile turned deviously calculating, her long skirts fluttering as she slid back into the crowd, her final words an ominous parting gift.

Margrete had felt herself change. Had felt herself slipping, becoming a person she hardly recognized, her greed overshadowing all else. But that didn't mean she'd completely lost herself, did it?

No. Surria was merely attempting to bait her, and she wouldn't fall for such trickery.

You're nothing like Darius, she insisted to herself. *You still* care—

But the truth was...she *didn't* know the lengths she'd go to. Hell, she'd already gambled Azantian, so maybe—

No. She ceased every and all thought of the duplicitous goddess. Margrete had to focus and find Darius. Once she got her grip on the bastard, she'd wallow and consider her fall from grace later.

With another generous sip of her drink, Margrete scanned the room once more, carefully storing away every detail of the lavish affair.

The love goddess's party was exactly as she expected.

People lounged on velvet couches, their limbs entangled as wine and other drinks flowed freely. All those present appeared similar to Dawn; able to touch and kiss and drink, their shimmering bodies seemingly solid and yet not.

With her second drink half-empty and a pleasant buzz settling in her belly, Margrete took off for a chamber tucked away from the main hall and the raucous sounds of music and laughter. This new room held thousands of roses, and red and pink petals littered the marble floors like fallen raindrops. It smelled divine, every inhale causing her head to grow dizzy from its heady scent.

When she swallowed her last sip, yet another glass appeared in her hands. Her brow furrowed. She didn't recall taking another. Still, she drank, growing addicted to the warmth and lightheadedness taking over and soothing her restless worries.

A little voice in the back of her head told her to watch how much she consumed, but that overpowering scent...it shoved aside that sensible voice and muffled it.

In this vast and lavish room of roses, Margrete almost forgot about her purpose for being present here tonight. She simply observed the patrons with a nearly hypnotic interest as they laughed and touched and kissed, and when she imagined Bash, it wasn't pain she felt.

He would've liked this, she thought, growing dizzier yet. Of course, he would've already forced her to the dance floor by now. Or he would've stolen her away to a more private space. Yes, he undoubtedly would've carted her away to a secret alcove and kissed her senseless, that wicked smirk on his lips as he whispered naughty promises in her ear.

Margrete sighed dreamily, collapsing onto the nearest velvet lounge.

With blurred vision, she spotted Calista across the way, moving among the partygoers with a wide grin on her ethereal face. Her luxurious magenta silk dress left little to the imagination, and a high slit ran up her bronzed thigh. Margrete unconsciously leaned forward, watching with rapt attention as the goddess greeted her guests and flowed about the space. Only when she vanished around a bend, did Margrete snap out of her haze.

The Goddess of Love. How the title deceived...

Margrete knew the difference between love and enchantment and obsession, and it certainly wasn't *love* she felt whenever she glanced at the woman.

The music changed notes, turning deeper, darker, and without Calista to distract her, she swayed in her seat, her head ringing with magic. From the corner of her eye, she noticed the whirl of hands, lips, and tongues. Margrete couldn't stop herself from gawking, even if she wanted to. This space felt primal, and heat that wasn't her magic coiled deep in her belly.

She raised her glass to her lips. It was nearly empty. Again.

A hand wrapped around her waist, and a body dropped onto the cushion beside her. She hardly flinched when his coldness seared against her side, and a delicious ache began to throb in her core.

"Hello, goddess," said one of the most handsome men she'd ever seen. Based on his smirking mouth, he likely knew it too, but with the addicting drink in her hand and the otherworldly music thrumming in her ears, she couldn't remember why she should care. Gods, everything had turned so delectably fuzzy, and so very, very quickly.

The stranger's pallid hand descended to her thigh, the material of her dress thin enough that she felt the coldness of his fingers.

Why did his touch feel so damned good? *It shouldn't*, Margrete thought, frowning. It didn't quite feel right, not warm or as solid as—

"I'd remove that hand if you wish to keep it."

The coldness on her thigh vanished in a heartbeat. "I-I...my apologies, my lord." The beautiful man stammered, rising to his feet and all but running out of the room like a fearful child who'd been chided.

Margrete lifted her gaze slowly, taking in a suit tailored from the deepest shade of blue. Up, up, up she traveled, until she drank in the face of the man who'd delivered the threat.

"Hello, darling." Darius smiled wide. "Did you miss me?"

CHAPTER TWELVE

BASH

Bash was laid out on the sand, spending the afternoon with his love. She was down by the shoreline, her sister shrieking as Margrete chased after. They made a mess of their clothing, water splashing everywhere as they raced into the surf. Margrete finally caught up to Birdie, swinging her in her arms as the girl grinned wide.

He could watch them for hours. Both had known little joy under the captain's roof, and to see how much Birdie had flourished beneath the Azantian sun in such a short amount of time had his lips matching theirs —a toothy grin stretching his cheeks.

As he watched them play, something odd tugged at his chest.

It felt like alarm, which shouldn't be possible given how content he'd been seconds before. But there it was, a surge of fear that raced down his spine and caused him to sit up straight. Margrete and her sister didn't seem to notice anything amiss, and he might've ignored the warning completely if not for one thing...

While the earlier scene continued to play, another vision took shape to its side.

It was like looking at a distorted reflection.

Margrete stood before a looming shadow of a man, his face obscured by darkness. She wore a strappy, silver gown he'd never seen her wear before, and her features were soft and nearly glazed over as if she had imbibed too much wine. Her painted lips moved as she spoke to an invisible companion, her shock evident in the way her eyes sharpened.

The vision wavered, but Bash clutched onto it, ignoring the much happier spectacle on his left. He couldn't look away from the phantom Margrete, how different she appeared. How ethereal.

The shadowy form moved closer to her, his hand reaching for her waist. She let him.

"Bash! Come in!"

He flinched, forcing his attention to the shore where Birdie had splashed a wave of water across her sister's shirt. She waved her hand, urging him to join.

His body hummed, torn between running to the shore, and attempting to hone in on the eerie vision playing out to the side. He knew it didn't belong here...though he didn't understand why. His jaw clenched, unease creeping back in.

"Bash!" Margrete yelled again, her voice more insistent. "Come here before I drag you in!"

He hissed as blazing light assaulted him. Squeezing his eyes shut, he sucked in the fresh sea breeze, willing away whatever momentary lapse of insanity he'd suffered. It couldn't have been real. Hell, it didn't even make sense.

When he opened his eyes, the world became right once more, and Bash jumped up from the sands, sprinting to sweep Margrete off her feet.

Still, he couldn't shake the sense of *wrongness*, and it followed him long after the shadows took him, delivering him to yet another scene where his heart had been full.

CHAPTER THIRTEEN

MARGRETE

"Darius."

Margrete spoke his name in a nearly unrecognizable voice. It was deep and low and raspy. *Seductive.*

He looked stunning before her, so very *pretty.* Why was she mad at him again? There was something she'd been upset about earlier, but now all she wished to do was grab the lapels of his jacket and yank him closer.

Darius's stare turned molten and his eye twitched. He didn't move an inch, didn't press himself against her like she wanted. Somewhere in the back of her mind, she recalled her dream, the sensuous way he'd taken Wryn. How his groans had filled the air when he was deep inside of her. Lost to his pleasure.

She shouldn't be thinking about him. Recalling that memory. *Blushing* from it.

Margrete drowned her confusion with another pull of the bubbling pink poison swishing in her cup.

"Damn it, little one," Darius said through clenched teeth, his control a thread ready to snap. "You shouldn't have wandered into this room. And you should not be smelling nearly as delectable as you do now. It's making it so very hard to be a gentleman." Displeasure rang in his tone, though she couldn't grasp why he was irritated. Everything was so damned beautiful. *He* was beautiful.

And this peculiar room and all its people, all the bodies moving as one and indulging in their baser instincts? It was paradise on earth. Or rather, a paradise in the Underworld.

The world was meant to be enjoyed, Margrete realized as the drink continued to heat her belly. She shouldn't waste time not acting out on her desires. Her blood boiled, her heart pulsed, and she felt feverish as the music switched to a livelier tune. All around, the patrons moved, clothing ripped from bodies, soft moans filling the air. Margrete was entranced by the sight of the pleasure happening before her eyes, and she yearned to be a part of such magic.

Slowly, she brought her eyes back to the sea god. His fists were clenched tight, his jaw tense. She appraised him, taking her time, and all the while she shoved down the warning bells in her head telling her to run.

"Come here," she cooed at Darius, her voice not her own. She giggled at the strange sound of it. "I want you to come closer." She had to *touch*. To feel. If she didn't, she knew she'd die. Simply perish on the spot. The drinks she'd consumed bestowed everything with such an otherworldly quality, and she swore the furniture she sat upon glimmered. The very fabric touching her body was too much, the sensations too overwhelming. Her hands reached for the straps of her dress, sighing when one slid down her shoulder.

She needed it off.

A firm hand wrapped around her wrist. "You need to come with me. *Now*," Darius demanded, his breathing stuttering. His stare on her lips. His eyes shining with need.

Margrete shook her head, confused. "But there's a party! Come, sit." She patted the empty space on the chaise. He didn't budge when she tried to pull him down beside her, his body immobile as granite. Darius merely observed the spot with a tangible hunger, but he didn't move. Why?

Laughter rose above the violin's notes, and Margrete spared another glance around her, noting the naked bodies tangling together, the moans she'd heard rising in pitch.

She felt too hot. Was she on fire? That had to be the most likely explanation. She grew hotter still when she looked upon Darius, and she wondered if his blond hair felt as silken as it appeared. Margrete ached to find out, her skin buzzing with foreign need.

Her mind felt intoxicatingly foggy in the best way possible, and when she thought about it, she realized she'd never felt this good before in her life. Like nothing else mattered but giving in to lust and warmth and stolen kisses.

Darius approached, slowly, as if she were some prey he aimed not to frighten. He smoothed down his luxurious blue jacket before dipping into a crouch. He placed both hands on either side of her thighs, and she shoved herself into his arms, a soft whimper leaving her lips at the feel of his skin. Darius growled, shifting out of the way.

Margrete inhaled his scent and lifted her hands to his hair, giving in to temptation. Her fingers slid through his silken waves, moving to the nape of his neck, and Darius squeezed his eyes shut as she gave the ends a gentle tug. Hmm, it was softer than she thought, which felt impossible.

Her focus dipped to the exposed area of his neck, his collarbones. Slowly, she let her hands drop, grazing his skin as her body tingled in response. He practically purred beneath her exploring fingers, the god frozen, under her spell.

He was so very warm, so smooth—

Darius abruptly grasped her wandering hands, a pained noise slipping free from between his parted lips. His stare fell to her own lips and lingered there for a beat too long.

She couldn't hear the music or people or the court anymore. There was only touch and feeling. Only the thrill of giving in.

Darius's grip on her hand tightened.

"This room is for those seeking more than simply drink and dance." His blue eyes hardened, and the longer she stared into the depths of him, the more he cleared, the less blurred the room became. "The drink in your hand didn't help, but these chambers have a certain *influence* on any who pass through those doors." He scrubbed a frustrated hand down his face, a low groan rumbling his chest. "Fuck, I must've changed if I'm convincing you *not* to touch me."

She cocked her head in confusion. How could a room affect her so? His words made no sense in her state, and she was disappointed he wasn't succumbing to her ravenous wishes.

Darius continued, though his nostrils flared. "While the selfish part of me would love nothing more than for you to stay, and for us to...chat, I find I cannot allow you to remain here."

Margrete pouted. But *here* felt so nice. The music and laughter and the delicious fire spreading through her veins.

Before she could argue, Darius gently wrapped his fingers around her arm and hauled her to her feet. Dizziness overcame her as she collided against the hard muscles of his chest, and she pressed her hands against his upper body to settle herself. Darius hissed at the contact, a slight tremble wracking his impossibly tall frame. She instinctively ran her fingers down his shirt, lowering to—

He snatched her wrist.

"I don't want you this way," he growled. "Not like this, not under Calista's influence." Darius kept his grip firm as he led them across the rose-petalled room, the spellbinding notes of the violin wavering with every step to the door. He didn't let go, not even after he hauled her beyond the double doors of the chamber, the main ballroom just on the other side.

A jolt ran through her body the moment she passed the threshold.

Like a cloak of dense fog lifting, her vision cleared, little by little. The pungent scent of roses left her lungs as she gulped in fresh air, that cloying perfume leaving her body with every panting exhale.

Sounds came rushing back, the melodious notes of the harp ringing too loudly in her ears. The gossiping and laughing courtiers flitted all around her in a blur, and her knees knocked together as gravity weighed on her shoulders.

She held a hand to her temple, eyes shuttering. "W-what...what just happened? Why do I feel so wrong?" She couldn't make sense of it. One second she was on fire, the next drenched in ice.

Blinking, she lifted her head and took in the god, who still held her arm. His eyes were creased with concern, his attention narrowed in on her with concentration. She sensed his thumb rubbing circles on her waist, his touch tender and sweet.

Margrete tensed.

The otherworldly lighting lost its magical glow, and the roaring fires burning throughout the room felt more ominous than welcoming. Her body, which had been loose and relaxed, became painfully tense. And her vision—she saw the world with a sudden, heartbreaking clarity.

Darius. The God of the Sea, her *enemy*. He wasn't capable of feeling concern. He was a monster, she knew this well. He'd killed Bash and...

Oh my gods. She'd invited him to sit with her and—

Horror had nausea rising in her belly. She was going to be sick.

"Let me go," she murmured, growing more lucid by the second.

That room, this place, this court. It was all infused with powerful magic. Of course, the Goddess of Love would have a chamber made for lust. Shameful heat rose to her cheeks as she sucked in air, trying and failing to compose herself.

Darius's eyes softened, and he released her, although he did so begrudgingly, lingering before dropping his arm. "I simply wanted to help. You weren't...yourself. I'd guess Calista enchanted that room especially for you tonight, hoping you'd wander in. The drinks certainly didn't help." A muscle in his jaw feathered. "She knows how you feel about your king, but she's infamous for enjoying the aftermath of a regretful night of abandon. The gods love nothing more than to play with their new toys and manipulate them however they please."

Margrete fumed, feeling altogether mortified. How easily she'd accepted the drinks, how easily she'd drifted into a trap. She grew livid. At *herself*.

"I know all about how gods like to manipulate," she said pointedly, glaring daggers at Darius. She prayed he didn't see through her discomfort. Margrete had thoroughly lost her senses, but she couldn't appear weak—even though she'd made a fool of herself. More than a fool. She'd embraced her greatest enemy with tenderness, and she'd wanted him desperately.

Yes. I'm definitely going to be sick.

"I haven't been manipulating you," Darius seethed. "I just had to resort to drastic measures to make you see the truth. I've never lied to you."

Margrete was livid, but the logical voice she'd shoved aside came rushing back, screaming at her to make nice. She remembered that she *needed* the asshole. Although she currently envisioned wrapping her hands around his neck and squeezing.

Whether she liked it or not, she had to be smart about her words.

"Thank you," she ground out. It was physically painful.

"My pleasure?" He said it like a question, and genuine confusion painted his face. He hadn't expected any kind of thanks from her. Rightfully so.

Then again, he could've very well taken advantage of her in her state. She all but begged him to touch her. Yet the god had refrained.

She didn't wish to think of him as decent. He wasn't.

Margrete scanned the main room, finding too many eyes on them, some of the patrons holding their hands before their mouths as they likely gossiped at the sight of her and Darius standing so closely together. She scowled back.

Let them think what they wished. Soon, they'd no longer be her concern.

It was time to finish this game. And *not* fall into any more traps.

"Is there somewhere we can talk? Privately? And preferably *not* in any more enchanted rooms," she asked. Being alone with him was the last thing she wanted—specifically because she desired to slit his throat—but with so many courtiers ogling them, it had to be done.

When a passing servant whirled by, Margrete placed her half-full glass on the tray. Obviously, she hadn't done a great job handling her own tonight. A lesson she learned well.

"A dance first, perhaps?" Darius tilted his head back to where couples swayed on the ballroom floor. "And then we can slink into some cozy alcove and continue our little chat—"

"No, I don't think so," she snapped.

"A dance, and then I will talk about whatever it is you want."

"This isn't some game, Darius," she spat, briefly forgetting she had to push down her rage. She'd lasted all of a minute. Bash's face flickered across her mind, and her chest ached, a great emptiness throbbing. "I need to speak with you *now*. Time is running out."

"Hmm, impatient to get me alone, are we? I'm surprised, seeing as I assumed the enchantment wore off. Not that I'm disappointed," Darius mused, cocking a blond brow. His eyes dropped to her arm, to where the barbed vines spun around her flames. He went rigid at the sight, and his nostrils flared. "Ahh, I see now. A reckless little bargain was made."

She forced herself to nod. It took everything in her not to punch him square in the jaw. "Which is why we need to speak."

He shut his lids and took in a steadying breath, as if calming his temper. "I leave you alone for *one* day, and you've already put your life in danger," he all but growled. "Who did you make the deal with, eh? Charion? Calista?"

"Halio."

"Fuck." Darius shifted on his feet and ran a hand through his tangled waves. Without another word, he grabbed her arm, leading her off the ballroom floor and to a winding hallway lined with brilliant rose quartz walls. She had to struggle to keep his pace, and he didn't slow until they neared an unsuspecting dusty pink door at the end of the corridor. Darius glanced behind him before reaching into his trouser pocket to retrieve a golden key. He inserted it in the lock and opened the door, hurriedly motioning her inside. When she shot him a wary look, he said, "I have keys to all the courts. One can never be too careful. You'll learn the tricks soon enough."

She wouldn't be here long enough to learn the tricks.

Instead of finding herself in some sinful bedroom where he'd try to seduce her—as she'd expected from him—Margrete stood surrounded by thousands of green leaves and potted flowers. Every color greeted her, the varying blooms climbing up the stone walls to the apex of the domed ceiling. A swirling fountain trickled in the center of the small room, granite flowers spouting water a shade of light pink.

She spun around. Darius leaned nonchalantly against the closed door. She noticed how he kept his distance.

"What did you promise?" His words were much gentler than before. "What did you offer of yourself to Halio?"

"I...need your help," she whispered, ignoring the details of her bargain with the death god. "Or more accurately, I need you to right a wrong *you* committed."

Play nice, she reminded herself, but her magic flared in her chest, heating her skin until a trickle of cold sweat slid down her back. Her temper was going to win out. Yes. She might very well kill him now.

"It must be dire if you're already asking for my aid. I would've thought you'd last a week before you lowered yourself to begging for my help." Darius shoved off the door and strode toward her with feline grace. "Tell me," he demanded, halting inches away. "What did you promise?"

Inwardly, she cursed. Maybe she should be honest and relinquish the details. She hardly trusted him, but it might coax him to trust her. Not that she'd ever trust him back. She could manipulate him as well as he'd done her. *Better* even.

She craned her neck to look him in the eyes. "We have to work together to slay the beasts that escaped the night of the attack. Halio gave us two weeks. And if we fail...he'll destroy Azantian."

"And if you succeed? What do you get in return?" he pressed, a muscle flickering in his jaw.

There was no hiding it. "I think you already know the answer to that."

Darius scrunched his nose in disgust and fumbled a step back. "*Still?* You're going to try and save your king after knowing the truth?" He motioned between them. "I'm sure you've had at least one or two memories come back by now, so I don't understand how you can look me in the eye and ask such a thing." He began to pace. "We were happy. So fucking happy. And we could be happy again, but this time, I have a plan to make sure my spiteful mother doesn't get in the way. A plan to make sure she never hurts you again." He went still. "I'll kill any of them if they touch you. I'll burn this entire realm to the ground."

Margrete scoffed at his outburst. "No need to start fires, but wasn't it *you* who killed me in the first place? A thousand years ago? You didn't have to bring Wryn to the arena, and you all but presented her like a gift to Surria to do with as she pleased."

Darius whirled on her then, his irises stormy. He raised his hands as if he wanted to grab her, but he wisely dropped his arms.

"You have no idea what you're talking about, Margrete."

"I love him." The admission wasn't meant to wound—she was simply stating facts—but the way Darius's chest heaved with effort, she knew he'd been struck.

"You *think* you love him."

She shook her head. "Darius, you remember a different woman. I'm not *Wryn*." Even as she spoke the words, they felt untrue. She surprised herself when she glided closer to him and grabbed his arm, ceasing his fidgeting. His heavy gaze fell to where she touched him. "I know you regret what you did to her, and if ever there was a time to make it right, now would be it. Help me."

Darius was a statue. He stared at her with the kind of desperation she hadn't seen him wear before, and if it were at all possible, she might've heard the last of his immortal heart shatter.

A minute passed before he spoke, and when he did, she almost wished he hadn't.

"You've already made a bargain with one god, so why not two?" he asked bitterly. Margrete didn't like where this was going. "I will help you under one condition, and one alone." His stare narrowed on her, and some of his earlier animosity returned. "Once we slay the beasts and your king is alive, I will allow you to live with him until his body withers and ages and is returned to the sea. But after that..." His hand drifted to her cheek. "I want you. All of you. For the rest of our immortal lives. I want you to *try*."

To try and love him.

Margrete felt made of stone. She hadn't considered what would happen *after* she rescued Bash. She would remain a goddess, living for eternity. And though it could take many years, Bash would eventually die. Whether from old age or injury, he was always going to die before her, leaving her alone. She may get lucky, and he may be chosen by Death to serve her court, but she doubted that—he was half-nymera, and according to Halio, a monster.

Grief saturated her heart, and a single tear escaped her defenses. Darius watched as it tracked down her cheek to the tip of her chin before he swiped his thumb across the droplet with infuriating tenderness.

What he asked of her—

"And what if I don't want to be a goddess anymore?" she asked, barely above a whisper.

Darius shook his head sadly. "You cannot return to what you were before. That would mean ripping yourself open, and I don't think you'd survive." He opened his mouth as if he wished to say more, but then he closed it, his stare hardening.

More crushing weight settled in her belly. There was no escaping this, no escaping her cruel fate. She was always going to lose Bash one way or another.

The thing Darius didn't understand was that while another version of herself might've loved him once, he had never loved her back. Not really. Love made it impossible to break the heart you'd been entrusted with, to so easily give in to the sway of others and accept their lies as truth. Love was a gut feeling that refused to be ignored. A truth that shone brightly in a sky of darkness and uncertainty. Margrete had experienced that kind of emotion, that *gift*, and she couldn't imagine living her life without her partner at her side. The rest of the world be damned.

And that was the difference. Maybe one day Darius would learn this truth, but it wouldn't be with her.

Darius broke through her thoughts. "Say yes and I will make certain that we fulfill Halio's deal. I will make sure the other gods do not harm you. I'll protect you...and your king." He forced out the final promise, his nostrils flaring. Still, he probably saw this agreement as a win. A lifetime was nothing for him, and he'd proven he was a patient man.

So then why wasn't her answer coming? Logically, she knew it was her best option, but this man had taken her king. Had all but forced Bay to drive a blade into his heart. Could she ever tie her life to his for mere decades of happiness?

Darius held his breath as he awaited her reply. The desperation was back, and his eyes sparkled with need. "Say yes," he murmured.

One word.

Margrete shut her eyes, unable to look at him as she spoke. Instead, she pictured Bash, his arms wrapped around her, his teasing smile. The way he looked at her as if she were his entire world.

The truth was that he was her world too. If the roles were reversed, she had to believe he'd do the same.

The word slipped past her lips, and with it, the final remnants of her freedom.

"Yes, Darius. I agree to your terms."

This time, pain lanced down her spine, and before her knees buckled from the sheer intensity of it, Darius swooped in to catch her. His broad hands spanned across the entirety of her waist, his fingers digging into her skin, his grip eager.

"Now we seal the deal."

Instead of slicing his palm, Darius slowly leaned in, capturing her lips.

They were plush and surprisingly warm, and the shock of them had her freezing in place. Darius didn't pause as he pressed himself deeper, scraping his teeth along her lower lip.

Copper exploded on her tongue. Blood.

His blood.

The kiss turned hesitant, almost leisurely. And against all she'd endured, against her better wishes, Margrete's cheeks heated at the feel of his mouth pressed to hers, and she was helpless when a soft sigh escaped, memories of her dream rushing back.

A groan rumbled up Darius's throat, deep and full of desire. Her uncontrolled reaction had spurred him on, and when he bit down on her bottom lip, hard enough to draw her own blood, a dark part of herself awoke. The part of herself that she feared.

As her life essence poured from the shallow wound and into Darius's mouth, mixing with his, the lingering pain along her spine vanished.

A surge of power rushed down her frame, and the fog that had enveloped her dissipated. Finding her balance, she pushed upright and shoved at his hard chest, her magic propelling him across the room.

Darius struck the wall with a resounding crack and crumbled to the floor.

Margrete swiped at her mouth, both confused and enraged. She shouldn't have liked his kiss as much as she had, and that's what frightened her the most.

Taking the rumpled sea god in, she found him unharmed. Unfortunately. No blood—aside from his lips—marred his skin, and he appeared infuriatingly relaxed, even going so far as to lean back against the wall and stretch, a wicked grin forming on his face.

"Next time," she said, her cheeks heating, "slice open your damned palm." Unable to look at him, she turned for the door, determined to maintain some shred of dignity.

His laughter trailed after her, and then, so did his footsteps.

CHAPTER FOURTEEN

MARGRETE

Margrete couldn't feel her legs as she strode from the room, Darius at her heels.

So disoriented, she didn't pull away when he reached for her hand to guide her back to the ballroom. The music was muffled, as was the raucous laughter of the guests. Faces flitted across her vision, their smiles distorted and unnatural.

Calista's beautiful face captured hers from across the sea of courtiers, a cruel smile on her lips. Margrete met her vehement stare and glowered before shoving forward, out of this wicked place.

She wondered how she hadn't seen it before—the twisted enchantment Calista had spun. It had all been orchestrated by the love goddess. This party...she knew it had been planned for her.

Still, she kept walking, allowing the man she despised the most to pull her through the bustling crowd to the portal leading to *their* court. Her skin buzzed as they slipped past the boundary, and when she tripped over her feet, Darius's grip around her waist tightened, catching her fall.

Guilt. Insurmountable guilt nipped at her insides, eating away at her until she feared she truly would shatter and break into a thousand pieces.

Not only had she done the unthinkable and gambled Azantian, but she'd made yet another bargain that would end in heartache.

She'd never felt so despicable.

"Margrete," Darius called her name. She didn't answer. "Margrete, look at me."

Fingers gripped her chin, forcing her gaze up. She could've sworn she saw a trace of remorse wrinkle his features, his usual cocky grin nowhere to be seen. Hell, he didn't even seem victorious. Darius would get what he desired in the end, even if he had to wait a few decades before Bash died from old age.

Margrete jerked to a halt seconds before bile in her throat rose. Twisting to the side, she emptied her stomach on the marble floor in front of her feet. Darius surprisingly didn't jump back, but he let out a hiss of surprise.

"Shhh," he coaxed, an unmistakable panic causing his voice to quiver. "L-let's get you back to your room. I think you drank too much of the elixir."

Or your kiss made me sick, she thought venomously.

Gods, she wished that was true. The damned part of her that was still bonded to Wryn certainly hadn't felt nausea at his embrace.

They began to move again, probably headed for her chambers—she hardly took note. The last hour continued to loop around and around in her head, torturing her. How could she tell Bash what she'd done? She might be able to save him in *this* life, but what about afterward? Margrete would spend her days as a goddess beside Darius, and Bash would return to the realm of the dead. *If* they succeeded.

And the pain radiating down her spine...she imagined there'd be a fresh tattoo inked on her flesh. She wondered if it were half as horrid as the one on her arm.

When they reached her chambers, Darius opened the door and helped her inside, the god silent and brooding as he scanned the room with obvious distaste. Margrete wondered if these were Malum's old rooms. Judging by the way his lips thinned and his eyes clouded with thought, she suspected they had to be.

"Bash is coming with us," she said softly, her voice raw. "Halio permitted his soul to leave the realm for our journey."

Darius made a low growling sound.

"It's lucky *our* bargain depends on our success." He moved her to a chaise before walking over to the desk and giving her his back.

"A bargain you decided needed to be sealed with a stolen kiss."

"Better than slicing open your palm," he challenged.

He was impossible to argue with, and there wasn't a point. What was done was done. "I'm sending word to Halio that you've agreed, and then we leave tomorrow," she said, forcing life back into her tone. Defiance. "But if you so much as glare at Bash, our deal is forfeit. And..." she added pointedly, "*never* touch me again."

Darius inhaled sharply. "Fine. Though I didn't feel much resistance on your part. In fact, quite the opposite." He rolled his eyes at her ensuing scowl. "Either way, my deepest apologies." He didn't sound sorry at all. "And about your king, don't worry. I can't touch him without a body. And if by some luck the nymera still has it, then I vow I won't touch him."

"I don't see how you can be this upset." She seethed, bolting to her feet. She stormed his way, suddenly angry that *he* was angry. Gods, *she* should be the one in a murderous rage. All things considered, she handled her fury much better than she would've preferred. Maybe it had to do with those damned memories coming back to her, or how, whether she wished it or not, being around Darius felt so familiar.

He whirled around, blond locks tumbling into his eyes. "I'm furious at *you*," he said, and she took an instinctive step back. Heat curled at her fingertips. "I'm furious that you don't seem to remember a thing about me, or our time together."

Margrete met his stare with a lethal one of her own. "I *do* remember. Some things, at least. I've had dreams and fleeting images, but it changes nothing! If you ever did love me, truly love me, you wouldn't have forced me to kill Bash to begin with! You wouldn't be standing here now demanding the rest of my immortal life!" Her breath rose and fell unevenly. "It makes me think you don't know the emotion at all, Darius, you only think you do."

His hands clenched tight and flares of white and blue sparked between his fists. "I loved you," he said, every word a punch, a wicked assault of will. "Do not sit there and tell me what I feel. You may not fully remember yet, but you *ruined* me, and if that's not what heartbreak is, then I don't know what is. My mother was the deceitful one, claiming Wryn was an illusion that she orchestrated to weaken me. Foolishly I gave in...but I should've been stronger, should've known better than to trust her accusations."

"You should have known better," she said. "If your bond was as deep as you claim, you should've saved her."

Time ceased to move right as Darius looked down at her, his temper barely controlled. She sensed the threat of him, her magic coiling inside of her chest in response to the danger disguised as beauty. Then he surprised her by stepping back.

She believed he'd go in for the kill, that she finally brought him to the breaking point. Instead, Darius froze in place, and what he said next stunned her beyond belief.

"You of all people know what it's like to feel unwanted by a parent. For centuries I did everything, *everything* Mother wanted, if only so she'd look at me the same way she did Malum. But it was never good enough. When she brought us to the island to begin the trials, I'd finally lost my control. Creating you had been an accident." He ran a trembling hand through his hair, casting his stare to the corner. "I didn't believe you were real then, that you weren't just some hallucination I'd conjured. It took weeks on that island before I started to believe what we shared wasn't some grand deception, and it took months before I allowed myself to fall in love with you.

"The night of the trials, I went into that arena prepared to tell Surria to fuck herself once and for all. But then she'd somehow captured you and brought you into the center of the arena. She played on my deepest fears, claiming *she* created you to wound me. She laughed, calling me weak for even believing that someone could love me." Darius walked over to the desk and laid both arms on top of its smooth surface. "But the second the dagger pierced your skin and my blade sliced through your heart, I *felt* the truth. The half of my soul I still owned screamed in agony. And when your eyes closed for that final time, I swore I, too, died."

Margrete didn't know what to say. The anguish in his voice couldn't be faked, and the way his shoulders trembled with grief told her the truth. She believed him.

It still didn't change anything.

"I-I'm sorry Surria did that to you," Margrete said, the words hollow. This man might've endured crushing heartache, but he still turned around and forced her to undergo the same pain he had. Darius hadn't learned from the mistakes of his past.

"So am I." Darius shoved off the desk and marched toward the door, not once looking in her direction. When he reached the threshold, he paused. "You rest. I'll send word to Halio now so he's prepared to retrieve *him*. We leave at sunrise."

With that, Darius left her alone in her chambers. Margrete squeezed her eyes shut.

She hated how she felt sorry for Darius, but she did. He'd made the error of trusting Surria all those many years ago, believing that Wryn didn't care for him, that she *couldn't,* all because of the vicious creature who raised him.

Before she went to bed that evening, Margrete snuck into the bathing suite and slid down the top of her dress. The glossy material fell down her shoulders, dropping to her hips and exposing her back.

She couldn't withhold her gasp.

The grisly tattoo she'd imagined was anything but—

Three white lilies were inked down her spine. The third and final bloom was wilted, two petals snapped from its center, frozen in midair on her skin.

Lilies.

They were a flower known well by mourners and the heartbroken.

Margrete slipped on the silky nightdress that had been provided and crept back into her chambers, her mind too full of all the things she couldn't change. She lay awake long after Atlas, Dani, and Mila stumbled drunkenly inside her chambers ten minutes later, aided by a clear-headed Dawn. Margrete feigned sleep.

It took another hour before she fell asleep, and even then Margrete's dreams were brimming with fields of lilies. And whenever she reached down to touch their velvety petals, they'd wither and die, turning into dust at her feet.

When she woke with a start that next morning, she understood what the third wilting lily on her back meant.

Or rather, *who* it represented.

Her.

CHAPTER FIFTEEN

MARGRETE

Halio was waiting for Margrete and her crew at dawn.

Darius had yet to show, but he would. This was his victory, after all.

Surria's key weighed down Margrete's trouser pocket, the metal humming softly beneath the thick cloth. Since she'd discovered it, she hadn't been able to part with the mysterious key, and sometimes she'd catch herself rubbing the cold silver with her thumb, the unnatural energy it emitted a balm to her frayed nerves. It reminded her of night, when the wind whispered through your hair and the world was cradled in a blanket of darkness.

It seemed excited to be here, on the main floor, and she recalled how it had reacted similarly the other night. She suspected that whatever the key opened lay nearby. If only she had the time to explore more of the death god's domain, but Bash was waiting for her.

"You ready, goddess?" Halio asked once everyone circled him. The Azantians openly scrutinized the death god, clearly not trusting his intentions. Neither did she.

True to his word, Darius had sent out a courier to Halio relaying that he'd agreed to aid her, and she'd received a confirmation note the next morning. Five words were written in a neat scrawl: *You know where to meet.*

"Yes, I'm ready," Margrete said, her pulse thundering in anticipation. She thought of nothing but Bash, and even the threat of Azantian's destruction was second to his safety, an afterthought. It should've bothered her more than it did.

Halio's lips descended to her ear, his deep timbre causing her to shudder. "You know, the veil between worlds is thinnest at midnight." She shot him a confused look, and he clarified, his cold breath tickling her sensitive flesh. "As a goddess, you aren't saddled with the chains most humans bear, and therefore, some rules don't apply to you."

She drew away. "I'm still not following."

He heaved a sigh as if it were obvious. She found the god maddening.

"You'll find out, goddess, but just keep the king close when the midnight hour nears." A smile—one so subtle she might've imagined it—graced his lips.

If he was saying what she believed he was, did that mean—

If she could *touch* her king, hold him in her arms, her heart might explode. Unlike Dawn and the other courtiers who'd been chosen to remain in their respective courts, Bash's soul had already been delivered to the realm of the dead. She hadn't the faith to think she'd be able to touch him on their journey above, but the possibility of it was enough to bring a cautious smile to her own lips.

"My apologies. I was running behind."

Darius sauntered down the hall, shadows licking at his towering frame. He dressed much like her—linen trousers and a thin button-down—although he wore a fitted forest-green jacket that brought out the blue in his eyes. They held a slight glow to them today, like he shone with a secret only he was privy to.

"Darius," Halio murmured coldly, dipping his chin. "Late as always." His stare remained hard, and she noted how his nostrils flared as the God of the Sea took his place at her side. Atlas dragged a quiet Dani behind her and Mila crossed her arms, her focus locked on Darius alone.

The look on the redhead's face could sear a man alive. Or, well, a god.

Darius, seeming to feel her trenchant glower, turned his head, a flash of silver sparking as he drank Mila in from boots to crown. His eyes narrowed at whatever he found.

Pride filled Margrete—Mila had done *something* to unsettle him.

"Let's begin," Halio said, forcing her attention back to the door. "Margrete? If you'll come stand beside me?"

Her fingers trembled as she did as instructed, anticipation pulsating all the way down to her feet. The scent of heady magic struck her height-ened senses, the door to the realm of the dead awakening. Her own power responded with a subtle jerk, the predator inside of her soul eager to pounce.

"Wait!"

The cry came from Dani, who shook off Atlas's hold. Falling to her knees before Halio, she said, "It's probably too late, but I have to ask." Her quivering voice softened the death god's harsh features, and he bestowed a somber nod, permitting her to proceed. "My brother," she rasped, "I need to know if he's all right. If he's happy." A tear splashed to the marble floor, and her head drooped between her shoulders as more fell.

Margrete had been so focused on herself, that she'd forgotten entirely about Jacks.

And Jonah.

And Grant.

"Please stand, dear child," Halio intoned, holding out a hand. Dani lifted her pointed chin and studied the warm offering. In the end, she accepted without fear, placing her tiny hand in his and allowing him to help her to her feet.

"You've come a long way, and not just because of your loyalty to your king." Halio grasped both of Dani's shoulders as silver shadows swirled around his frame. "If you seek your brother's well-being, I will grant you that wish. Your soul is the kind that wouldn't be able to rest without that knowledge, and you have so much work to do yet."

His words struck Margrete as odd. But her protectiveness got the better of her, and she said, "*Without* a deal, Halio. I don't want her to carry that burden."

"Only for her, and yes, without a deal," Halio assured softly, prompting Dani's tears to overflow, her eyes shimmering with both grief and hope. "Do I have your permission to enter your mind?" Again she gave him a curt nod, and Halio continued, "Then shut your eyes and allow me in when you sense my energy."

The silver shadows dancing around Halio's torso flared and sparkled as his grip on her tightened. Dani went ramrod straight, as immovable as a statue. Margrete didn't believe she even breathed. She had the urge to yank her from his hold, afraid he was hurting her, but she forced herself to stay rooted in place.

Halio's irises clouded over, turning a milky white. They all watched in awe—even Darius—as the god's deep-brown skin became saturated with pure, radiant silver. He looked far from the harbinger of death, and she unconsciously took a step closer, drawn by his ethereal beauty. All of her fear for Dani's life evaporated.

A minute passed before Halio abruptly released Dani, who fell to her knees with a gasp.

Her eyelids flashed open, the onslaught of fresh tears sliding down her cheeks. And then she...smiled. "Jacks," she murmured, overcome with emotion. "He's with Mom and Dad."

Chills raced down Margrete's spine and the hair on her arms stood at attention. The joy on the sailor's face would be enough to warm the iciest of hearts.

Mila stumbled forward, awe written all over her face. Margrete knew she wanted to ask about Jace and Grant, but her lips were sealed, trapped between her teeth as she forced herself back against the wall.

"He's happy," Dani whispered, her knees trembling as she rose. "I saw him on Azantian before Mom and Dad were taken from us. It was one of our fondest memories." Atlas dashed to her side and wrapped a strong arm around her torso, supporting her weight. She brushed aside loose curls, pressing her lips to the raven strands. "Thank you, thank you," Dani said to Halio, her gratitude brightening her features.

"His soul has found joy, and he knows only love." Halio's smile was genuine as he assessed Dani. He lingered on her for a heartbeat longer, that same curiosity Margrete had seen earlier resurfacing.

Reluctantly, the god tore his gaze from Dani and shifted it to Margrete.

"I'm ready," she said, understanding Halio's unspoken question. She was forever grateful Halio allowed her friend some peace, but they had to begin their journey. Besides, her companions didn't have much more time —they appeared just as sickly as the evening before, and she swore Atlas's skin was tinged in a more pronounced shade of blue. If they lingered any longer, they'd never be able to leave.

"Well, since you're the one calling his soul forth, it is *you* who will open the doorway. If Bash doesn't respond, there's not much I can do. It will be up to him whether or not he crosses the barrier between worlds. All I can tell you is that his soul is conflicted. Like Dani's brother, he is quite content."

Bash *would* come; she didn't doubt that for one second.

Halio idly flicked his wrist, and the door unlocked.

He hadn't taken her key, but his attention drifted to her pocket, to where she'd concealed it. Halio's strong reaction to it meant it held some importance.

Stepping beyond Halio, she grasped the handle and dragged it open further.

Everyone but the two gods behind her gasped.

Fuck me.

Mirrors. Mirrors as far as the eye could see glittered in a cavern that went on forever. There was no beginning or end to the space, and even when she squinted, the cavern continued on, endlessly. Each pool of silver glass glimmered in the dark space like a star in the midnight heavens, a life trapped within its cool surface.

"Not what you were expecting?" Halio asked, his cold breath warm against her cheek. She flinched.

"No," she answered honestly. "I was expecting something more...dour."

Pits of tar, raging flames, a pool of souls. She hadn't pictured a wondrous cavern of luminous, silver mirrors. It was beautiful, she hated to admit.

Halio grinned. "Each soul contained in those mirrors is at peace, reliving the greatest memories of their human lives. They exist in a dream of never-ending joy. The idea was my greatest and my proudest creation." He motioned her to stand in the center of the threshold. Her knees wobbled as she obeyed. "Now, close your eyes and think of your loved one's name. Call him forth. But be warned, you may not be answered. Some souls are too weary for the land of the living."

Margrete's lids fluttered closed as she took in a few steadying breaths. It was now or never, and she'd put everything on the line for this one moment. *Everything...*even her soul.

She imagined Bash's face, and then, she called out his name.

CHAPTER SIXTEEN

BASH

Bash floated.

It was another day where he woke with Margrete in his arms, and yet, while he revered such easy mornings, something felt *off*.

The sense of unease swelled. His head swam, his vision blurring. He didn't feel real, didn't feel solid. It was as if he were missing a piece of himself, but Bash forced himself to lean into the moment and cling to it for dear life.

Margrete was playing with his hair while he rested his head in her lap. She spoke animatedly about her plans to renovate the old orphanage, the one where Bay had grown up. He smiled, amazed by her ideas, by how much thought and energy she'd put into restoring the decrepit building on the western side of the island. She cared about his people to a degree that had his heart singing.

"Bash."

He lifted his head. Margrete's mouth was moving, but he couldn't hear her words. His brow furrowed as his name sounded again, her voice like a bell, though her lips hadn't formed his name.

Bash raised his hand and cupped her cheek, and she smiled, leaning into his touch, an impish smile appearing.

"Bash. Where are you?"

He dropped his arm. Her voice had sounded again in his mind, and suddenly, his chambers shuddered. The sea glass walls flickered with silver, iridescent light, and he blinked, trying to right the world, but it continued to waver in and out of focus.

"Follow my voice," Margrete instructed. Well, not the Margrete holding him, but the one in his head. "You need to find me."

Bash turned to the woman in his bed, his breathing turning hard. Something didn't feel quite right about her—her smile was too perfect, her eyes too bright. And the room around him? It was unfocused, muted beyond the bed he lay upon.

What the hell is happening?

"Margrete," he whispered under his breath, his panic beginning to flourish. He pictured her, and when she called out again, he grabbed hold of her ethereal voice. The one that sounded *true*.

Bash felt nothing as he fell into the delectable melody of it, the sweet timbre of her cadence. He detected a hint of sadness weighing down the syllables, though he didn't know why. He didn't want her to be sad, and it had him clutching her even tighter as if he could devour her fears or grief with his firm hold.

A furious breeze whipped at his face, and suddenly, Bash was *falling*. His body buzzed everywhere, his limbs prickling to the point where he could no longer feel them. He was alive and yet *not*, aware and drowning in darkness.

His eyes shot open.

Nothingness. He stared into a void of nothingness.

Bash couldn't move as the chasm of black ignited. One by one, tiny flickering lights began to form and blaze. He squinted, trying to make out a familiar shape, trying to remember how he'd gotten here. All he remembered was...

"Follow me," Margrete instructed, this time much louder and far more demanding.

The lights swelled and brightened until the void became a deep cavern brimming with an infinite number of shining mirrors. "What the fuck?" he muttered to himself, bringing a hand to his hair.

He paused halfway to his head.

His hand—it wasn't right. He looked down at his body and began patting it, his panic turning into outright terror.

Gods, he could see right *through* his flesh. And his fingertips. They were black, the short nails a matching shade.

Another rush of air struck him with violent intent. Before he could panic at his bizarre state and lack of memory, he held out his arms before his face, battling the force of that supernatural breeze. He had to try and fight it, whatever this dark magic was.

"Bash!" Margrete screamed, the pain lacing her tone killing him, making him forget he was currently slipping between what felt like time and space. He had to get to her, had to—

The winds stopped. *Everything* stopped.

Bash opened his eyes for the second time.

Instead of an abyss of darkness, Margrete stood before him— surrounded by Dani, Atlas, Mila, and the tallest man he'd ever seen, a circlet of silver at his brow. Bash rocked back and forth, unable to find proper footing, this new vision causing blood to rush to his head in the most unpleasant of ways.

Another figure stood off in the shadows of a long corridor, unmoving, but Bash didn't care. No, the world could burn to cinders for all he cared.

She was here.

And she was looking at him, a tear glistening in her eye, her lips parted as a relieved exhale whooshed free.

He formed her name, repeated it. His head spun. He swayed.

But Bash ran to her, somehow found the way to move and sprint in her direction.

Joy shone bright in those blue eyes he loved so much, and he nearly crumbled. There was no otherworldly light obscuring her features, nor did a hazy sheen cloak the corridor surrounding her. This was...real.

Her.

Bash lunged for her, uncaring that nothing made sense, that he couldn't recall where he'd been but seconds before. He opened his arms with unbridled hope, preparing to wrap her in his embrace and—

His arms went right through her.

Bash stumbled, falling backward. A shroud of black fog swirled as he spun around.

Margrete's lips parted, a rush of emotions flashing across her face in the span of seconds. Only when she turned to the towering man at her side did the fog clear. Bash tracked her gaze, taking in the sight of a strapping man whose grim features spoke volumes. The stranger shook his head from side to side, a somber expression clouding steel irises.

Bash thrust his hands out before him, his black-tipped fingers trembling. He was a sickly pale color, his skin nearly translucent.

He heard Margrete ask the stranger what was happening, but he couldn't make out the answer. A series of chilling images hit him like a bolt of lightning.

An island.

Scales and teeth and dark eyes.

A dagger piercing his heart.

Bash cursed. He wasn't *alive.*

"This is how he will remain until he recovers his body." That came from the seven-foot giant, who shot Margrete a look of warning. "He's not tangible like Dawn and the others, as they've been selected by death itself to serve the Underworld. Your king was not. If I were you, I'd give him some space to adjust."

Serve the Underworld? Bash frowned, his focus alternating between the man and Margrete, whose hands were radiating flashes of blue light. It reminded him of the ocean during a storm.

She ignored the stranger, turning toward him, inching closer. "Pirate?" she asked, voice trembling. "Is that really you?"

She reached for him, stopping just before her fingertips grazed his cheek.

All the air whooshed from his lungs as he tried and failed to lean into her palm. There was only coldness where her warmth should have existed.

"It's all right," she continued, trying to calm him. It seemed an impossible feat. But it wasn't his state that disgusted him. It was himself. His actions.

"I...I hurt you," he managed, his voice weak, unused.

Margrete stared up at him with water-lined eyes. She was so beautiful it hurt to look at her. Like staring into the sun. Bash forced his attention down, breaking their connection and shutting his eyes. His shame was monstrous, his guilt a tangible thing.

"We need to get his body. Then, we go after the beasts." The voice belonged to Atlas, the familiarity of it loosening some of Bash's tension, though he still felt immobile, trapped. "Once he's whole again, he'll have time to heal. He will return to his old self."

They needed to get his body.

He was dead. Had died on Surria's island. And just before he'd left the world, he had—

Fuck.

He'd stolen a soul and drank from a human. He recalled that insatiable hunger...and then there'd been a woman whose scent he'd wanted to devour. Her very soul.

That woman had been Margrete.

He pictured her tears slipping down her cheeks as he clawed at her face in that horrid arena, unable to stop the enchantment placed upon him. He'd been a shell, his soul trapped by a dark magic from which he couldn't break free.

And Margrete had barely fought him off. She must've had faith he would come back to himself. But he never did. He'd been too weak to find himself in the monster his mother had turned him into.

He'd let her down. Let himself down.

He must've swayed, because the scent of lavender invaded his nostrils. He opened his eyes, finding Margrete, her hand raised as if to grasp his arm and keep him aloft. She cursed at her forgetfulness, her inability to steady him.

Bash didn't deserve her comfort. He deserved *nothing.*

"Tell me what's actually going on," Bash finally gritted out, unable to meet Margrete's worried stare.

"Do you want me to stay away?" she asked softly, hurt lining every syllable. Nervous energy poured from her in waves.

"I-I need you to explain," he said coolly, without emotion. He was retreating into himself, the only way he knew how to survive this moment.

"I made a deal with Halio, the God of Death. He offered me a chance to...to bring you back," Margrete whispered. Bash felt lightheaded. "I did it so you'd return to me. A-after you *died*—" She could barely get out the word. "I accidentally opened a portal to the Underworld. All I saw was your face, and all I could hear was your dying breath."

He was helpless but to seek her now, the connection between them greater than any shame. The moment he landed on her, a rush of energy jolted into his frame as though he'd been struck by lightning. She must've felt that same electricity as him, for she stumbled in place. Though she never broke eye contact.

"I want to hold you so fucking badly."

Bash watched the column of her delicate throat bob with all the agonizing emotion she swallowed.

He ached in places he hadn't believed possible. But Bash didn't merit her sympathy. His previous actions didn't warrant such kindness and understanding. Bash shoved away a second after a wounded expression darkened her face. He felt like he'd been punched in the gut.

"I-I tried to kill you," he said, the tremble in his own hands growing. "I lunged at you and tried to steal your soul."

Gods, he could still feel the coldness of a blade piercing his heart, her face hovering above him like a beacon to life itself. And in that final moment, as death cradled him in its arms, he'd finally had the strength to free himself of the dark enchantment. The spell that had been placed on him to *hurt* her.

Bash had never been more of a failure.

The very woman he'd tried to murder—the same one he loved with every ounce of light he owned—brazenly stepped forward. The crew followed her lead, though they gazed upon him as though he were a stranger. Still, they trusted *her*, and something akin to pride swelled in the place where his beating heart should be. There was just emptiness and silence in his chest now.

"You were being commanded by otherworldly forces," Margrete argued, unwavering. Her mind had been made up, and Bash knew there'd be no changing it. She was impossibly stubborn at times, a trait he loved about her.

Just not now.

Now, he wanted to chase her away, so she'd be safe from him.

"I didn't fight it hard enough," he seethed. "If it hadn't been for..." he trailed off, searching for his old friend. "Where is Bay?"

Margrete's eyes narrowed into angry slits. "I'm not sure, but he's the one who—" She couldn't get the last word out, but he already knew what happened. Bay had done what the others weren't able to do, and for that, Bash would forever be thankful.

"Bay is right here."

The figure he'd seen looming in the shadows—the one he'd all but forgotten—stepped into the light. Bash's hackles rose as the promise of murder echoed in his ears.

Darius. The God of the Sea, and the man who'd orchestrated the events that led to his plunge into darkness.

Dressed in a fine green jacket hemmed with gilded threads, he looked the epitome of perfection, not a single hair out of place.

He'd change that.

With a growl, he lunged for Darius, just as feral and as wild as he'd been in the arena, although this time he wasn't being commanded by the nymera blood surging through his veins.

No. This was all him.

"You!" The bastard didn't move as Bash's fist drove straight through his torso. Not even a flinch. He growled, fury consuming him. If he could just get his hand to work, he'd squeeze the life from Darius, god or not. He pictured it, imagining the light draining from the immortal's face. While he understood he couldn't actually harm him, Bash sure as shit wanted to try.

"I see that you're angry," Darius said, smiling as though they were friends who'd merely had a spat. "That's why I brought you a surprise."

Darius shifted to the side before thrusting a cowed Bay into the light of a nearby sconce. His friend's blond hair had grown out, and a strand dipped into his green eyes, which were trained on his boots in shame. Shame he shouldn't be feeling. Instinctively, Bash opened his mouth to thank him, when Margrete lunged.

No one stopped her as she slapped Bay across the face. He made no sound, just accepted her hate, her frustrations. Painful seconds ticked by, Margrete's chest rising and falling erratically, her stare filled with a mixture of rage and sorrow. Bay stiffened, righting himself. When he slowly turned his attention to her, tears shimmered in his green eyes.

"I had to do it, Margrete. He was going to kill you."

Every inch of her seemed to buzz with a foreign power, and even in his incorporeal form, Bash could taste the violent energy in the air. It startled him, but he shouldn't have been surprised after all they'd been through. Tensions were running high.

Hell, Bash would've already murdered the God of the Sea if it had been possible. He'd continue to devise ways. He may be dead, but Bash wanted the prick dead alongside him.

"That wasn't your call," Margrete said, her voice softer, brimming with heartbreak. Though the steel in her eyes hadn't softened.

"He's right, Margrete," Bash rushed to say, and both their gazes slid in his direction. "He had to do it. And if anyone shoulders the blame, it's Darius. Don't forget that. He wanted to pit us all against one another on that island, and he succeeded."

The sea god scoffed. "I merely showed them what you were. Your true nature would've come out sooner or later. I simply help speed up the process." He rolled his eyes as if this conversation bored him.

Again, Bash soothed himself by picturing his hands around the god's throat.

Margrete turned her mounting temper on the god. "I'm going to kill you when this is all over." She inched forward as if to attack, when a hand wrapped around her arm. The crowned stranger—who most certainly had to be another member of the divine—shook his head. A silent conversation seemed to pass between them when she turned to glower.

For the first time, Bash saw the murky ink spreading across her smooth skin, vanishing below the blue silk shirt she wore. Yet another thing he'd have to ask about, preferably when they weren't in Darius's company. Though his head might explode if yet another revelation was exposed.

"You don't have time to fight, remember, youngling?" The man pulled Margrete gently away from Darius, who had the decency to look affronted. "You have thirteen days left to slay the sea beasts, Margrete, and when you do, you'll get everything you want." Her nostrils flared, but she begrudgingly nodded, and he released her arm. She didn't look Darius's way again. Or Bay's, for that matter, who seemed all but a ghost of his old self. If Bash was corporeal, he would've tugged his old friend in for a hug.

But he wasn't, and so Bash stood there feeling useless.

"Let's focus," Atlas said, drawing the attention away from Darius and Bay. "Like Margrete said before. We find Bash's body first, reunite his soul, and then we slay the other beasts along the way."

"Fine by me," Mila agreed. "Though the one who made this mess should do most of the cleaning up." She shot a searing look at Darius, who grinned back. This infuriated the sailor more, whose ears were tinged a brilliant red.

"Seeing as his mother is the only nymera I left alive, you should be thanking me for *cleaning up* that devilish lot of monsters," Darius retorted. "Her horde followed her onto the island, and they were taken out by Shade and her nymphs under my orders. Again, you're all welcome."

The nymeras...they were all but defeated? And his mother...

"What are you all talking about?" Bash finally asked. He felt as though he were trapped in a twisted dream. Maybe he was. "Can we circle back to the thirteen days we have to kill the monsters? What happens if we don't?"

What disastrous bargain had been made?

Margrete lifted her hand for the third time, reaching for his cheek, before huffing in frustration and dropping it. It would take some getting used to, this barrier between them. The ache in his chest throbbed. He wanted to drop to his knees and profess his love. To beg for her forgiveness.

Bash could feel Darius's eyes on him. He refused to give the bastard more of a show.

"We have thirteen days to wipe out all the sea's beasts, and then Halio—" Margrete nodded to the god beside her. "—will allow you to remain in your body and be granted a second chance at life. Once we find it, that is."

"Oh, and you have to work with me," Darius chimed in, still grinning wickedly. Bash curled his hand into a fist. He pictured his fist driving into the god's skull, the bloody image calming him in the midst of chaos.

"A word of caution," Halio said. "Once Bash returns to his body, those...urges he felt before he died will return. He came into his true form late in life due to his parents' unusual pairing. I've never known a human and nymera to breed. It might explain why it took so long for his other side to show itself, and I'm sure his mother's presence didn't help." Halio sucked in a sharp breath. "But now that he's transformed, his new impulses won't just go away once you rejoin his soul with his physical form. However human you still deem him to be."

That's why he hadn't changed before now. Just like her, he was a new type of being.

"Lovely," Mila mumbled, and Dani shot her a look of warning. The ring around her sapphire eyes appeared darker than before, more pronounced. Before he could study her more, she shifted in the other direction.

"Well, this certainly is going to be real fun."

Everyone turned to Darius, and when Mila sent him another scalding sneer, they all joined her. "Oh, stop being so angry. This *will* be fun. There's nothing like a good hunt!" Darius ignored them all and began walking backward. "The mortal realm awaits, and we have so many monsters to kill." He winked at Bash. "And besides, I'm sure you'd like to be in your body soon, so that the next time you try to punch me, you at least have a *chance* of hitting me."

Bash's nostrils flared, but Margrete blocked out the sea god and his childish taunts.

She canted her head and met his gaze, nothing but love shining through. After all he'd done, she continued to look at him as if he were a man deserving of her.

"You told me once that you'd follow me to the Underworld, pirate," she whispered, a despondent smile lifting one corner of her mouth. His old crew had given them a semblance of space, but he continued to feel their attention on him. Likely making sure he didn't hurt her again. "You should've known I'd do the same." He grimaced, and she added, "And don't give me that look. Once we get your body back, kill a few vicious beasts, *and* save the mortal realm, you'll be at my side." She was an inch away, and Bash could've sworn he felt her breath on his cheek. "We save each other, and even if I have to save you from yourself, I will. You're not leaving me again. I'm far too selfish, remember?"

Bash wanted to argue and tell her all the ways he wasn't worthy of redemption, but gods, did he want to lean down and kiss her full lips, relaying everything he felt inside his soul. He loved her, and love made him hopeful.

If there was a chance he could redeem himself and save the realm, be a hero in her eyes again, he'd do damn near anything.

But if he tried to hurt her... His focus aimed for Bay, and his friend, as if feeling eyes upon him, finally lifted his head. He'd done the right thing by plunging that dagger into his chest, even if Margrete didn't agree. Bash would make sure he'd do it again if, or more likely, *when* the time came. He dipped his chin at Bay, silently communicating his thanks. A single tear slipped down his friend's reddened cheek.

Bay understood what Bash asked. But Bash would do everything in his power to make sure it didn't come to that. He loved Bay like a brother, and he didn't want one more person he loved to get hurt because of him.

Feeling reassured, he allowed himself a moment without walls or barriers or fears. Peering into Margrete's eyes, he whispered his truths, even if he was unworthy.

"I love you, princess. I love you so damned much that I would've done anything to save you. Made any deal, no matter the risks." He thought of the imposing stranger. Of the bargain they spoke of. He heard her take in an audible breath of relief, even as her eyes darkened at his words. "You are my partner, my lover, my friend. And I'll follow you to the end of the world and back."

This woman owned him, and if he didn't try to make up for the pain he caused her, then there was nothing left to fight for. He was already dead, and while a part of himself thought it best to leave her in peace and allow her to find another love, jealousy reared its head. *He* wanted to provide her with happiness. The same way she did him.

Bash's flaws aside, his possessiveness, he'd never been one to roll over and accept defeat.

He was a king, a fighter, an *Azantian*. And he wouldn't give up on righting his greatest wrong. Bash wouldn't give up on saving the one thing in this world that mattered.

He would not fall so easily again.

CHAPTER SEVENTEEN

DARIUS

Halio brought them into a circular room located off the main hall.

Seven portals of simple stone surrounded them, each shining with the same brilliant silver.

The journey back to the mortal realm would be a whole lot easier than venturing to the Underworld. Namely, it wasn't necessary to shatter the earth to get there. Humans had no idea that whenever the earth trembled and split, it was simply a god returning to their home. Therefore, a portal was far, far less of a hassle. Unfortunately, they only worked one way—*out*.

Halio motioned to the door on the far right. "This will bring you to the island of Maribella. I have all the faith you can find your own way from here," Halio said in that deep voice of his, ever the pompous ass. It wasn't as if he hated Halio—in fact, he was the one he despised the least —but he possessed the sort of pretentious face that Darius often desired to punch.

Or maybe he simply felt that way about most people.

Darius fixed his features into a mask of boredom, but inside he plotted. He scrounged his memories of the city, already deciding on which port master would be easier to swindle. They needed a fast ship, especially if he and Margrete were forced to bring the mortals along...and the ghost that continued to thwart his plans. Though Darius supposed he'd be entertained for a bit, seeing as the king continued to try and do him hard, all acts resulting in pathetic failure.

Riling him up may be a delightful way to pass the time.

Maribella, while beautiful, could be deadly. Located north of Prias, it boasted one of the world's busiest and most notorious ports that connected the northeast to the rest of the southern regions. Pirates and all sorts of shady traders sold their wares there; in a city overflowing with crystal clear waterfalls and bright blooms of every shape and color. He found it ironic.

"It will be up to you how you choose to track the beasts, but you can at least acquire a ship at the port, which is a kindness I didn't have to allow," Halio said, avoiding looking at Darius. While the man annoyed him, the God of Death despised Darius. He chalked it up to Malum and his mistakes, and despising him was a side effect. But it was hard to hate someone who was dead. Yet another person blaming Darius for Malum's misdeeds.

Typical.

"Let's get this over with," Margrete said, making haste for the portal, eager to face sea beasts and save her pathetic king. Speaking of, the man she'd brought back from the realm of the dead could hardly be called a man at all. His body flickered with every step he took, and each time he reached out to touch Margrete, a pang of hurt contorted his features and he recoiled in shame. Darius counted six times that he repeated the action, and every time, his frustration grew more apparent. He could practically taste it in the air, which had grown colder since Bash's arrival.

He would almost feel sorry for him if he were capable.

Darius prepared to follow on Margrete's heels when the petite redhead stepped in front of him and Bay. His unwilling companion hadn't spoken a word since his confrontation with Margrete, and to say the tension was high would be an understatement.

"Stay back," she warned in a raspy voice, her chin-length red hair as fiery as the passion swirling in her irises. *Mila*, if Darius remembered correctly. He was surprised he'd taken the time to learn the pawn's name, especially since she hardly mattered. The woman tilted her sharp chin, subtly shoving aside her jacket to reveal her concealed dagger. He bit back his smile at the act.

"Did you want me all to yourself?" he taunted, turning his grin wolfish. He lowered his face until it was a mere few inches from hers. "I do like a woman who's well-armed."

She didn't even balk. No. Mila fashioned her own shrewd smile, the intensity of it sending shivers down his back. "I *do* want you all to myself," she cooed, and Darius frowned in reply.

"Oh?"

"I find it's easier to cut a man's throat without witnesses." She whipped out her blade and expertly flipped it, shoving the pointed tip against his heart. It began to beat faster. "You may be here to kill monsters, but if you so much as look at my king and future queen the wrong way, I'll slit your throat and bathe in your blood. It may not kill you, but I'll enjoy myself."

Darius stared down his nose at the woman, who stood no more than five and a half feet tall, lean and small-boned. He assumed it wouldn't take much to snap her neck.

How surprising. Darius typically hated surprises.

Slowly, he brought his lips to whisper in Mila's ear, smiling when she shuddered. "Don't worry about me, Red. This deal works well for me too." He pulled back just enough to watch confusion mar her delicate features. "Oh, and I would very much like to see you try..." He snatched her blade and whirled it on her, the sharpened tip aimed at the hollow of her throat. "Your threat has already proven empty. Your skills are rather disappointing."

He straightened to his full height, grinning like a fool as Mila's nostrils flared in frustration. Feisty thing. He'd have to keep an eye on her and make sure she didn't get in his way. Though his blood heated at the thought of a challenge. Darius did enjoy his games.

Margrete cleared her throat, stealing Darius's attention. "Thank you

again, Halio. We will return in two weeks' time. *Successful*," she empha-
sized. Darius noticed how her tattoo briefly flashed silver as if the bond
between her and the death god had fully snapped into place. He
wondered what tattoo had inked her body when they made their own
deal. Every bargain left a different mark, and during the early hours of
the morning, he'd indulged, imagining his very thorough search of her
body. In this dream, he'd slid the flimsy straps of her silk shift over her
shoulders, watching the fabric pool at her feet. He would take his time,
exploring every inch of her on his knees, kissing his way up her thighs,
her hips—

His future queen's attention locked on Bash, shattering the delectable
image he had of her in his mind. Darius curled his hands into fists as some
unspoken thing passed between them. Margrete would remember the
king's true self once they found his body and his nymera instincts took
control. Then, the nauseating love fest would be at an end.

Soon, he'd make all of her fantasies come true.

Atlas and Dani walked behind Margrete and the king as they passed
through the whirling blue and yellow barrier to Maribella. Mila, of
course, paused to glower at him one more time before slipping past. He
couldn't blame her wrath—she'd lost much on the island. If he possessed
a functioning heart, he might've even felt guilty.

"I suppose I owe you a thanks too," Darius said to Halio, who grunted
in reply. "Everything worked out rather nicely because of your bargain."

"You and your brother have done enough damage, and a mere thanks
would never be enough," Halio grumbled, for once showing his frustration plainly on his face. "Maybe this time you can actually *try* to be
better. You could've been one of the greats, Darius. You're not like
Malum, who pretended his heart was pure, or even like your mother, who
doesn't hide her desires. I've always seen that." Darius's victorious smile
dropped. "You have the chance to become your own person and do good
in this world."

He hadn't expected those words from Halio of all people. Perhaps he
hoped such prose would unsettle him. Darius didn't believe him for a
second.

Rolling his eyes, Darius's magic reached out and grasped Bay's wrist. The man's silence, which he'd originally preferred, was growing tiresome. He hardly put up a fight as Darius tugged him forward. The poor thing was utterly defeated, not even attempting to make contact with Bash, who had tried to find his eyes several times since their reunion, hoping to gain his attention.

"Don't worry, Halio," Darius said over his shoulder. "I still plan on rewriting history."

And making it bend to his will. Halio had been right though; Darius wasn't like his mother or Malum. He wanted power, yes, but he always had a logical reason. Sometimes his reasons were selfish, like secretly craving the adoration of the mortals, but at least his benevolence would benefit both parties.

"Come on then, traitor." Darius tugged Bay with him through the portal. There was a slight resistance, the sailor beginning to show his stubborn nature once again. But Darius brought them both through and into the maelstrom of magic and thunderous winds. Black clouds dotted with flecks of silver and gold sparkled, eclipsing the realm between worlds. He sighed, relishing the brief moments of reprieve, of utter silence. He almost missed it when a blazing burst of light forced his eyes into a squint.

All too soon, he'd returned to the real world.

Warmth coated his skin, and a coastal air gusted, filling his lungs with the freshness of the open waters. There weren't many things Darius loved, but the ocean breeze? That first inhale tugged at the strings of his cold, black heart.

Maribella had been described by many explorers as a paradise, the epitome of beauty. Luscious green trees with low-hanging fruits dotted the mountainous region, which overlooked the clearest waters on this side of the world. The beaches weren't gray or brown, but gold, much like those found on Azantian. In Darius's opinion, Maribella was far grander than the island of myth, though he might've been biased, seeing as it was his insipid brother's creation.

The gateway brought them to rest upon the dunes overlooking the trading town, the bustling port and its dozens of grand ships visible. The heat from the sands seeped through the leather of his boots, and while the mortals shifted uncomfortably, Darius embraced the slight pain.

He was pleased to see his future queen looking ready for battle, her searching gaze akin to that of a hawk. Though, upon closer inspection, he noticed that her irises appeared darker today, less vibrant than he recalled. Or maybe they'd always been that dark of a blue? Suddenly, Darius couldn't remember.

"Stop gawking," Mila snapped, bumping into his shoulder. He didn't budge, but he gave the woman his attention, which people typically wished to avoid. She locked eyes, unwavering.

Gods. Now *he* was the subject of an unwanted stalker.

"Just know that while you're watching *her*," she nodded to Margrete, "I'll be watching *you*." The new goddess now stood a mere three feet away from her king, both of them trembling, neither speaking a word. Darius rolled his eyes. Lovers who couldn't touch. How very cliché.

"You can watch me all you'd like, Red," Darius murmured, tearing away from the nauseating sight of the star-crossed pair. "But you should know I like the attention."

One corner of Mila's mouth quirked. "I suppose you would. It's the only way you feel worthy. Sad, really."

Before he could snap her neck, or at the very least, compose a witty comeback, Mila shot off for Atlas. She, too, was eyeing him with the wrath of a thousand storms.

Mila lifted on her tiptoes and whispered into her ear, causing the line between the warrior's brows to deepen.

Darius had expected this. For everyone to hate him. In fact, it would've been suspect if they hadn't. And yet...when Mila finally drew back from Atlas, she skewered him with a look he'd never experienced before, not even from Margrete.

It was an odd mixture of rage, challenge, and surprisingly enough, fascination.

He broke their contest of wills, telling himself she was below him. He didn't need to prove a damned thing to her.

"Any ideas on a starting point?" Dani asked, hiding behind her curls. She had looked more at ease in the Underworld than in the human world.

"I'd suspect Bash's...*mother*," Atlas practically spit out the word, "would've brought him back to where her horde had initially made their new home. Based on my readings, nymeras tend to prefer colder waters. I'd venture a guess that we need to head north." For the first time since he'd seen her, Atlas abandoned Dani and marched to her king's side. Bash, as if realizing eyes were upon him, begrudgingly turned from Margrete.

"Agreed. Good call," he mustered half-heartedly. "But the north is immense, and there are countless islands on which they can hide."

"We have two gods on our hands," Atlas said. "Meaning they could probably track them." She cocked her head at Darius, an expectant look contorting her face.

Margrete and Bash exchanged yet another silent conversation. The half-nymera's eyes were creased, his lips drawn into a thin line. As if understanding, Margrete shook her head, a small grin taking shape on her mouth. The king almost smiled in return.

A few more revolting seconds passed before she abruptly nodded confidently, then faced Darius. All the softness she'd directed at Bash vanished.

"Seeing as I'm new at this"—she waved about her form—"how about you get us started and do the honors? Show off all the immense skill you boast about." She was trying so hard to appear strong. The act nearly fooled him. Or maybe it truly had ceased to be an act.

"Well, it benefits both of us, so I'll happily comply," he said, grinning at the king. Bash's sickly skin flickered red, his chest heaving with his trapped fury. It was a shame he couldn't act on his anger; Darius would've welcomed a fight.

Did he know of the bargain he made with his beloved? He couldn't possibly know yet, seeing as that conversation would be a lengthy one.

Darius's chest warmed at the thought.

"I'll find the nymeras," he added when Margrete opened her mouth to speak, likely to deliver a crude word or threat. The faster they got the damned king his body back and killed the beasts, the faster they could seal the deal. Then he'd wait a short lifetime, and Margrete would rule at his side. He could be patient, but none of that would happen if they failed, so unfortunately, he'd have to be a team player in the meantime. The idea was sickening by itself.

"Now, watch and learn, Margrete."

Darius strode to where the waves grazed the shore, and instantly his chest heated and his heart rate slowed to a blissful crawl. This was coming home, back to the beginning of his life, where he was born and where he'd probably die. His mother might rule the skies, and his fellow gods presided over human emotion and even death itself, but Darius always believed he'd gotten the best kingdom. There was no end to his—it was infinite.

The waves lapped at his boots when he stepped into the waters, and a low humming began at the tips of his toes, working its way up his legs, his torso, his chest. All else could fade, if only for a little while, and he wouldn't care. But Darius had to focus on the mission.

Shutting his eyes, he drifted, falling headfirst into the waters at his feet. If he had to explain it to someone should they ask, he'd liken it to tumbling off a cliff without a net, not knowing when you'd strike the waters or if you'd make it out alive. Giving oneself to an untamable entity like the sea was much like that, and you could never be certain it wouldn't swallow you whole.

Darius loved the thrill of it.

He drifted and fell and lost himself, his lashes fluttering against his cheeks as a thousand images of the vast deep raced across his mind. His kingdom, so pure and beautiful; from the coral reefs to the beasts that called the great blue beyond their home. They didn't have the cunning or greed of humans. They just lived each moment on instinct alone.

In the northeast, he scented the great Collossious, currently devouring a ship full of men. He hastily pushed beyond the copper flooding the sea and continued his journey north. That particular beast would come later.

While physically tethered to the sands of Maribella, Darius's mind veered off the coast of Rydor, an unforgiving region where rocks replaced sand and the skies were forever cast in gray. Soft snow fluttered to land on top of the waves while he coasted over, though he couldn't feel the cold himself.

Soon, a hint of rot clogged his nostrils, the telltale scent of a nymera nearby, and he moved faster, only slowing when he came upon Rydor's crags. He blinked, and there she stood. *Minthe.* Atop the cliffs overlooking the dull waters of the north, she scanned the horizon as if searching for an answer to her plight. Or searching for Margrete.

Darius had suspected Minthe hoped Margrete would return her son's soul. That she would retrieve it from the Underworld to be delivered back into his mortal prison. Now, she was simply waiting to be found.

It was easy. Too easy.

The hair on the back of his neck rose, and Darius opened his eyes with a jolt.

"Where is she?" Mila asked, suddenly at his side. He hadn't felt her move. Hell, she was becoming a fly he couldn't swat away.

Margrete and her king joined on his left, the former standing as far away as possible. The venomous stare Bash trained his way could slice a man in half.

"Rydor," Darius said, forcing a shrewd smirk to grace his lips. "And I believe she's been waiting for you to deliver."

"She's going to take his soul and kill you." Dani pushed past Atlas and stepped front and center. "I have a feeling that the nymera"—she shot a look to Bash—"doesn't plan on letting us leave. She wants him, and I gather she feels we're a hindrance. Or rather, an enemy."

Minthe wasn't entirely wrong. Darius knew of her past, of how Bash's father fell in love with her and then stole her child from her arms. She had a right to despise them.

"Her name is Minthe," Bash said to his crew, his jaw taut. "And I wouldn't put it past her."

Darius lifted a shoulder. "She's cocky if she thinks she can defeat two gods at once."

Ignoring Darius entirely, Margrete spoke only to her king. "We can do this, pirate. And maybe we can convince her to...to see reason. To see that we aren't going to hurt her." That they weren't like his father, she meant.

In many ways, Darius understood Minthe. She'd trusted someone she loved, and then she was hurt for it.

Margrete lifted a hand, holding it an inch before the king's jaw. "And if she refuses to listen, then I won't allow her to take you from me for a second time. I'll kill her before that happens."

"You won't have to," Bash asserted. "I'll do the honors. However," he paused, indecision weighing his voice, "we *should* kill the monsters first. I don't *need* a body right now, and what if I rejoin and—"

"You're still you, and even with nymera blood in your veins, you *can* fight it. For me." Margrete lifted her chin. Bash sighed, his black eyes flashing.

"So trusting," he said softly. "But when the transition occurs, I don't want you anywhere near me in case I can't defeat the enchantment this time." Margrete prepared to protest, but now the king shot her a pointed look. She closed her mouth. "I need that promise from your lips, princess. I refuse to hurt you. I'd rather remain in the Underworld for eternity before I ever harm you again."

Something in Darius's chest twinged. He believed the king's admission, that he'd give up his life without a second thought. When he'd been presented with a similar choice, Darius hadn't been as...heroic.

"Fine," Margrete acquiesced. "But this time we all will be prepared, and *he* won't hold us back." She briefly glanced over her shoulder to Darius, whose plastered smile broadened.

"We should hurry and secure a vessel."

No one spoke as Bay emerged to stand before them all. He met Bash's stare and held it.

"I won't apologize for what I did, Bash," Bay said, and Margrete's nostrils flared. "I did it to save her from you, and I know you would've wanted that. However..." He fidgeted, shoving his hands deep into his pockets. "I do regret the act of killing my friend. My brother."

Bash eased around Margrete, getting as close as he could to Bay.

"Thank you." Bash dipped his chin. Mila grumbled something under her breath and shared a knowing look with Margrete, but they didn't speak. "I'll forever be thankful to you for what you did. Saving her. Protecting me from making the biggest mistake of my life. And I hold no ill will toward you. I never will."

"But he—"

Bash held up a hand, silencing Mila.

"He did what no one else had the heart to do, and he's still our friend." He looked at all of them, except Darius. He had a feeling their *talk* would come later. "Forgive Bay. He's still the best of us. A warrior with a golden heart. If you can't get over that, then you can return to Azantian. Alone."

Bay flushed, letting out an audible sigh. The Azantians lowered their heads, but Margrete turned to the sea, anger still roiling in her eyes. She forgave everyone so easily, and yet she couldn't forgive her closest friend. Darius knew deep down she didn't blame him, but it lessened the pain to target that rage somewhere.

"The Collossious is on the way," Darius added once a painful silence had fallen. These mortals and their emotions were growing too much to bear. "We could kill a few of the beasts before we head to Rydor."

Shockingly, the insipid king nodded in agreement.

"Then we should get ourselves a ship. Now." Bay dipped his chin, showing his king the respect he believed he deserved. Darius curled his fists. "And then, we finish what we started."

THANKS TO THE JEWELS MARGRETE AND HER CREW TOOK FROM THE Sea Court, they were able to procure a small vessel from one of the many merchants Darius pointed out. Atlas insisted on doing most of the talking, and judging from the heated shouts of the vendor, he hadn't been willing to sell his boat. She'd quickly changed his mind when she towered over him, lifting her jacket just enough to expose the blade she concealed.

Her negotiating skills were impressive.

Dani stayed behind with the king—who couldn't very well be seen in such a state by the townspeople—while Margrete, Mila, and Darius followed after Atlas. They'd have to sneak Bash aboard after dark, losing precious time.

Again, the king was proving to be utterly irksome.

The people of Maribella wore clothing similar to the Azantians, though their linens weren't nearly as revealing. Light colors, mostly blues, teals, greens, and yellows, decorated the town, and the wooden dwellings were painted similarly. Narrow avenues wound throughout, the stones a light shade of gray, flecks of silver spotting each step. It was a place where many settled down in, open clearings situated between lush woods and sprawling hills leaving plentiful space for new homes to be built.

Many of the quaint shops boasted their flag—two lines of yellow bordering a circle of blue, an outline of a falcon in flight positioned in the middle. Darius had always favored falcons, the creatures a symbol of victory and freedom.

Too bad they wouldn't be spending much time here.

With Atlas, Bay, and Mila distracted with the ship, Darius had taken a seat upon the docks, swinging his long legs over the side. The bottom of his boots skimmed the water, and he sighed, sensing the energy the sea gifted.

He felt her presence before he peeled open an eye.

Margrete took a seat at his side, adopting the same pose, though her polished boots barely reached the surface of the lapping waves. The sea was in a mood today, and Darius sensed that it ached to rage.

"Coming to deliver more threats?" he asked, still looking out to sea. Behind him, the sailors and dockmasters were shouting, the pounding of feet on the planks like thunderclaps. He never understood why sailors had to be so *loud*. If they only listened to the sea, it would tell them everything they needed to know, with no screaming necessary.

Margrete released a weary sigh. "No more threats," she said softly. "But I want to ask you a favor."

He finally twisted to face her. "And what would that be, darling? You know I'm forever eager to please you."

He'd envisioned pleasing her since the moment he saw her on Azantian. The nights he crept into her chambers and watched her, Darius had pictured getting down onto his knees and—

"Do not tell Bash about our deal."

Darius groaned, her asinine request chasing away his naughty daydream.

"Afraid it would hurt his feelings? I thought you two shared everything," he said bitingly. Obviously, they'd had secrets in the past, from what he'd observed, but there'd been a shift on the island, and he feared they'd finally overcome their communication troubles.

Margrete's eyes creased at the sides. "We do. Or, we vowed we would no longer keep things from one another. Even if we think it'll protect. But I'm not asking you to hide this for long. Just until I tell him myself, which I'll do tonight."

She rocked uncomfortably back and forth, pointing the tips of her boots toward the water. The waves rose, splashing the leather.

"I don't want you to goad him further. He's already suffering."

Suffering. The man didn't know the meaning.

Darius considered. While it would be great fun to rub in the fact that Margrete would be *his* after Bash's death, the genuine pleading displayed across her face had him pausing. If she were ever to trust him, he'd have to gain it first.

Damn it.

"You care too much," he said softly. He hadn't meant to say it out loud, but the words slipped free.

Margrete stilled. "I've always been like that," she replied, looking anywhere but at him. "But I only care about those who are deserving, and then I do so with everything that I am."

"You'll get hurt that way." Darius knew better than most.

"I'd rather get hurt feeling too much than go through life being an empty shell." She gnawed at the inside of her cheek. "If that makes me weak in your eyes, I hardly care."

He scoffed. "I never said you were weak." She was strong in her own right, even when she was mortal. That was what initially appealed to him —aside from what she carried in her soul.

"You didn't need to say it," she said, her tone turning hard. "You act the malevolent god, and you play that part well, but you aren't fooling me. You feel just as much as any human. If not more."

Darius gripped the wooden dock, his knuckles turning white. "I only feel for you, Margrete, and it is enough."

She swiveled his way, her stare fierce. "Then if you care, do what I ask."

Play nice with her king. It seemed impossible.

"I won't say anything," he forced himself to say. "But you better tell him quickly, because I can't guarantee that it won't come to light should he piss me off. Which he does rather often when he acts the hero. He's no more a monster than I."

"Regardless," she snapped, clearly losing her patience, "keep your promise. I don't think I can handle any more sorrow. I feel so close to drowning as it is."

A sliver of wetness lined her lower lids, and a pang of something foreign shot across his chest. The words were spoken with such grief, such genuine fear, that shame wrapped around his neck and tightened.

"Our secret is safe, darling."

Margrete gave him her back, ending the discussion. That ache in his chest grew, and he brought a hand to rest above his heart. If this is what humanity did to him, then he wasn't sure he wanted it at all.

Darius returned to the waves. The sea didn't confuse him. Didn't make him question himself. He stared until he was called onboard, and even then Darius lingered on the horizon. He yearned for the day when the sun would set and his heart would be free.

If they completed this task, that day would come soon.

Darius would accept nothing else—because like Margrete, he, too, felt on the precipice of drowning.

CHAPTER EIGHTEEN

MARGRETE

THEY SNUCK BASH'S INCORPOREAL FORM ONTO THE SHIP A HALF hour before midnight. The vessel Atlas procured—the *Mare Deus*—didn't hold a candle to the *Phaedra*, but it would suffice. There were two cabins, one furnished with two sets of bunk beds, and the other, while much smaller, held one cot, presumably the captain's quarters. A few hammocks swung in the stockroom beyond, and Margrete knew exactly where she'd force Darius to stay. She'd made a point to avoid his eyes whenever she felt his stare burn the back of her neck on Maribella's beach, but in all truth, his presence was difficult to ignore. Wisely, Darius kept his distance, especially after their conversation.

And Bay...well, Margrete wasn't ready to think about him right now. She loved him. And she understood why he did what he did. Yet she couldn't seem to explain that to her heart, which had erected barricades where he was concerned. Foolish, perhaps, but they remained up none-theless. Even at this hour, Bay put himself to work, mending what he could of the older vessel, his eyes catching hers every now and again as she got familiar with their new ship.

She missed her friend. He was the person she wanted to run to and confess her guilt. Bay had the ability to calm her fears and force a smile to her lips, usually by saying something highly inappropriate. But she swallowed down the urge to go to him and turned skyward. Above, storm clouds blew across the expanse of black, putting an end to the notion of setting out right away. Mila would be highly disappointed.

She'd taken it upon herself to watch over the sea god, her harsh scrutiny having compelled him to the railing, away from the others. Secretly, Margrete admired Mila's courage, and Margrete was impressed she hadn't already attempted to stab Darius.

Margrete grazed the key in her pocket, the soft vibrations working up her hand. She worried if Darius knew of its existence, he'd steal it right from under her. Besides, her magic reacted to the otherworldly object in a way that felt oddly pleasant. It was a comfort amid such turmoil.

A gust of wind struck her, carrying with it the scent of salt and the welcoming open waters. It filled her lungs and caused her heart to skip several beats, and she instinctively knew a storm was brewing in the east.

But it was the warmth flooding her chest that captured her focus. And it wasn't magic or the feeling of Darius's stare.

Bash had taken to the shadows, but she felt him without turning. There was much they needed to discuss, and she wasn't feeling exceptionally patient. The sooner she shared her darkest secret...well, *secrets*, the better. He may very well hate her after, and that was an outcome for which she had to be prepared.

Their reunion hadn't gone as she'd pictured. She had the irrational image of them embracing, of him whispering sweet words of comfort into her hair. Of her wrapping her arms around his neck so tightly, he'd have no choice but to lean down and press his lips to hers.

But that's obviously not what happened. That wasn't their reality. It wasn't some pretty, picturesque coming together of two souls who'd lost one another. Fear and doubt and shame had clouded it.

Margrete yearned for the dream.

Without bidding the others goodnight, Margrete turned to her king. With a pointed jerk of her head toward the steps leading down to the cabins, she took off, knowing he'd follow. She chose the captain's quarters, assuming they'd need all the privacy they could afford.

Once she'd shut the door behind them, she whirled on the King of Azantian.

He remained still, an unmovable statue. The only movement was the feathering of his jaw as he stared at her with both longing and fear.

She loathed the miles that seemed to spread between them.

Bash took a step forward. Then another.

She swallowed thickly, forcing herself to stay in place as he advanced. His movements were feline in nature, and his gaze had turned determined.

"Princess..." Bash stopped mere inches away, his scales glinting in the cabin's low light, a few poking free from the top of his collar and reaching for his neck. Cautiously, he lifted his hand and held it an inch away from her cheek.

An inch was a mile.

Margrete shut her eyes then, pretending she could feel his touch. What she felt instead was *him*—the way his presence overwhelmed her and calmed her at the same time.

Bash was the tranquility of the center of a storm. The world around them could be drowning, and she'd be here, in the safety of his presence.

With a stuttering breath, she opened her eyes.

Depthless pools of midnight locked on her, his unwavering attention causing her heart to flutter.

"If I could only touch you..." He canted his head, his lips dangerously close to her ear. "Even with everything that has happened, even after I..." He swallowed thickly, likely thinking of the island. "Even after all that, I'm helpless in your presence."

Margrete exhaled shakily as he drew back to study her. He took his time, his eyes idly scanning her form, lingering on her curves. Finally, his eyes landed on her arm.

"Your tattoo," he murmured. "It's beautiful, but when did you receive it? I could've sworn you spoke of *splitting* open the earth?"

She lifted her wrist, careful not to brush him in his state. "Ah yes. Apparently, there are consequences to ripping apart the world." She tried to force teasing into her voice. She failed.

Bash's irises darkened. "I don't know what to say, and I feel so much," he finally rasped, running a hand through his tangled black hair. He grabbed at his nape, tugging at the short strands. "I...I don't remember much, but I'm well aware that I hurt you. Finding my body and reconnecting—it feels dangerous. And I'd rather carve out my own heart than hurt you again. Well, if I still possessed a beating one." He released a soft laugh, though it was humorless.

"What happened is in the past. We're not living some fairytale, Bash. Those are for the young and naive."

He briefly shut his eyes. "In that arena, I was *gone*. There was only the beast and what *he* wanted. I had zero control, and even when I managed to find you, for that split second, I wasn't strong enough to beat the evil lurking in my blood."

"You're not evil—"

He lifted a hand, silencing her. "*It* was evil. I promise you that." He scrubbed a hand down his face. "I'm not perfect, by any means, and as much as I want to be a selfish bastard and demand we head to Minthe first, I think I need more time. I'm still...fuck, I still feel like I'm dreaming." He peered at his hand, flexing it, studying the fingers. They shimmered slightly with the movement.

She noticed how he was stepping further away. It killed her.

"What was it like? Being trapped like that?" she asked, her voice barely above a whisper. She ignored his demand to wait. They'd revisit that later.

Bash forced his attention on her. "I can't explain it to you, but how you smelled...gods, it was intoxicating, unlike anything I'd ever known. I desired nothing but to steal your life essence and make it my own."

"But I'm a full-fledged goddess now," she argued. "I'm sure it would take a lot more to steal my soul now. And besides, I understand what I'm getting myself into. I know what you might do when we find your body, and I have the strength to subdue you if need be."

"You better," he said firmly. He shook his head and glanced to the small porthole, to the sea beyond. "Perhaps you shouldn't have come for me."

She scoffed. "As if you wouldn't have done the same."

The barest hint of a smile lifted his lips, but it vanished just as quickly.

"I probably would've set fire to the Underworld within the first five minutes," he admitted with a brittle laugh. "I would've burned their entire palace down to embers and clawed my way to you with my bare hands."

Her heart fluttered in her chest. She'd planned on doing the same... until cornered by the God of Death himself.

"Gods save us all when you lose your temper, my king."

"Oh, if I return to my body in one piece and succeed in *not* killing you, then they all should be frightened," he whispered, straightening to his full, impressive height. He returned to her face, his potent stare a brand. "I may be a mortal, but the wrath I feel knows no bounds. I wanted to tear Darius apart piece by piece and then set fire to his broken limbs."

The grotesque imagery should've frightened her...but it didn't. The world wasn't black and white, separated by good and evil. Right now, she swam in shades of gray.

If they had to bloody their hands, then so be it.

"We'll take them down together," she promised, even as the tattoo on her back prickled, a constant reminder of *one* of the gods who owned her.

She had to find a way out of her bargain.

"You know..." she began, sidling up to him, inches away from his taut features. They softened upon her approach, the rigidness of his muscles smoothing. "I was worried you would take one look at me and not recognize me. I'm so filled with anger, it scares me. But I also..."

"Like it?" Bash finished for her. She nodded.

"It's intoxicating, this new power. And while I'd rid myself of its hold in a heartbeat, I also want to use it to right the wrongs of the gods. They don't deserve their thrones if all they do is perch upon them."

A shrewd look settled on his face. "I always knew you were formidable, with or without magic, princess. But I've never been more attracted to you than I am now." His hand was once again hovering over her cheek. "It's not your wrath that is appealing, but your cunning, your empathy. Your determination. I see not only the woman I fell in love with, but a righteous warrior."

Margrete sucked in a nervous breath. She'd been so worried Bash would see her as a monster, but here he stood, at her side and ready to fight for what they could have.

If he still wanted her after she told him her darkest secret. Her betrayal.

"You're my everything, Margrete Wood," Bash whispered, so close to her lips that she felt his cool breath—

Wait.

Margrete stilled. Realization struck her and then...she attacked.

Her hands dove into his hair, eliciting a shocked gasp from his parted lips. The strands were so silken, and she tugged on the ends, hard enough that his gasp turned into a growl.

"H-how?" Bash stuttered, his lips moving against hers. He was trembling, his long frame swaying as if getting accustomed to the punishing weight of gravity.

She slid her hands down his throat and over his chest, landing on his hips. She dug into them, her thumb pressing where that delicious V of his formed. "Midnight," she uttered. "Halio told me to keep you close to me when midnight struck. And close"—she arched into him, running her core against his hardening length—"I will keep you."

It appeared as though the God of Death had gifted her a small mercy. Who would have believed he'd be capable of such a thing? Trick or not, she'd take advantage. Her delirium knew no bounds, her selfish joy too compelling.

"Fuck." Bash seized her nape, his other hand winding around her torso. He held on tight, and his grip might've stung before, but he couldn't harm her. Now, she ached for the bite of his touch. "I never thought I'd be thankful for the death god."

Margrete reached for him again, and her magic, her beautiful, terrible magic, sent an eerie blue light dancing on the tips of her fingers. When her hands connected with his icy skin, her magic flickering where they connected, she released a tear. It slipped down her cheek and dripped onto her king's hand.

Bash must've felt the wetness, because he leaned back, concern marring his face. "Don't cry, princess," he begged, his voice cracking. He clutched her chin, his dark eyes searing into her soul. "Not when we're going to win and beat them all at their own games."

When he went to kiss her, Margrete inadvertently flinched. Bash paused a hair's breadth away from her lips.

"What is it? What's wrong?" he asked, his thumb rubbing soothing circles at the base of her scalp. How she wanted to let go entirely and lose herself in him...but she had to tell him first, had to admit *her* wrongdoings. Secrets had torn them apart before, but no more.

"I need to tell you something," she began, feeling dizzy and altogether unsteady. Bash slowly inched back, but he didn't let go. She was grateful he didn't.

"The bargain I made, it involves more than Halio." Bash ground his teeth, waiting, but he didn't interrupt. "Halio demanded I get Darius to agree to help slay the beasts, and the only reason he's here—"

"Is because he required something from you as well. A deal of his own." Bash shook his head, anger pouring across his face and hardening his features. "I thought so, even if I feared being right. That snake."

She shuddered in her king's embrace. "I had to, Bash. I couldn't bear not trying. I've never felt such contentment, such bliss, as when I was with you on Azantian. I couldn't simply give up."

Bash's left eye twitched. "What did he request?" The words were clipped.

"He agreed to help if I lived the rest of my immortal days out with him...after you—"

"After I die," Bash snarled. "I see. So he killed and tortured us all, and yet he still gets what he wants in the end. What the bastard thinks he's owed."

Bash went to pull away, but Margrete took his chin between her thumb and forefinger. "We needed him to complete Halio's bargain, but once we finish it..."

She let her words trail off. Bash knew her meaning well enough.

A spark lit his eyes, and his shoulders relaxed. Slightly. "We're going to kill him," he assured her, sounding more confident than she'd ever heard him. It bolstered her own faith. He took both her cheeks in his palms and pressed a kiss to her temple. "He'll never touch you, Margrete. This I promise. I'll make sure of it."

More shame ate at her. "There's more..."

This would be the hardest part. Like a coward, she'd waited as long as she could to confess. But she couldn't let them revert to *before*, when they hid from each other. They would either grow together or shatter. She prayed it would be the former.

"Halio only agreed because Azantian is also on the line."

Now Bash drew all the way back. True fear contorted his handsome face, and the way he regarded her...accusation clouding his irises, had her feeling faint. "What do you mean?" he asked.

"If we fail, then Azantian falls."

There. It was said. Margrete dropped her head, unable to look at Bash, unable to see what would surely be disappointment or rage. She already felt like a villain, and perhaps she was. Villains risked everything and everyone for what they wanted, regardless of the consequences.

A minute passed, and it was the longest minute of her life.

"Then we can't fail."

Four words. Four little words that had her lifting her head and taking in his determined stare. Bash's lips were drawn in a thin line, his eyes harder than stone, but he didn't look at her in disgust. She felt his anger... but for some reason, she sensed his understanding above all else. Even if he didn't *want* to understand.

"How?" she asked. "How are you not raging at me? I probably would in your shoes." Even if they did win and save the island, Margrete wasn't sure she'd ever forgive herself, and this was Bash's home on the line. A realm he'd sworn to protect.

And she had risked it all.

Bash dragged a finger beneath her eye, catching another tear before it fell. He pressed it to his lips. "Love makes fools of us all, Margrete. It makes us commit unforgivable acts..." He leaned forward, resting his brow against hers. "I'm not saying I forgive your decision entirely, but I *understand* it. I wish I could say I wouldn't have agreed to the same terms, but I'd be a liar. Sometimes I'm afraid of the acts I'd commit in your name." Bash moved to grip her waist, trapping her against him. "Perhaps I'm just as bad as Darius, because I would do anything for you. To have you forever as *mine* and mine alone. But unlike him, princess, I would never shackle you to me if you didn't wish it. And I would gladly stand by and watch as you ripped apart the immortals one by one." He pressed a kiss to her nose. "I'd bow at your feet and lick away the blood coating your skin." His fingers pressed deeper, his need growing. "For my queen should never be tainted by such filth."

Margrete shuddered, the image of Bash on his knees sending a jolt of fire through her.

"I *will* destroy our enemies," she promised. "I won't let them dictate any more of our lives."

Bash's stare turned molten. "I trust you'll rid the world of them. Azantian won't fall. And you will never belong to Darius. You belong to *no one* but yourself. That is *my* promise." Bash nuzzled her neck, his lips slowly gliding to the shell of her ear. He bit down, eliciting a whimper. "Show them all what you're capable of, princess. Show them why I bow to no one but you."

CHAPTER NINETEEN

BASH

Bash felt a myriad of emotions.

He had the innate need to lash out and destroy the gods—even if he didn't stand a chance.

But most of what swam beneath his skin was...understanding.

Margrete's bargain stung. She'd risked thousands of innocent lives for *him*. What tore him apart more was knowing he would've done the exact same.

Worse even.

"Do you despise me?" Margrete asked, her eyes closed. Remorse was written across her delicate features, causing her lips to quiver. She waited with bated breath for his answer. How this secret must have tormented her.

Something snapped deep inside of him. "I could never despise you," he said firmly. "While I'm...upset it came to risking Azantian, the true fault lies with Darius. He's the bastard who orchestrated all of this. Who wanted what he couldn't have."

If he wasn't so fucking entranced by her, he would find the god now that he could grip his neck. Or slice it. Bash clenched his fists, his teeth grinding together almost painfully as he held himself in place. He couldn't lose his temper and screw up the deal, or all of this would be for nothing.

"I'm still so sorry," Margrete whispered, finally opening her eyes. "I was half a soul without you, and when I made the deal I was selfish and rotten and entirely too greedy to do anything else but accept. I never imagined failing. I couldn't, or I would've broken apart."

"We won't fail then," he promised. There was no going back. The past was done.

It was time to move forward.

Bash brought his lips an inch above hers, her heated breath tickling his sensitive flesh. "We may not be the heroes of our own story, sweet Margrete, but we'll still triumph in the end, or so help the rest of the world when it experiences your wrath."

She let out a harsh chuckle. He felt the softness of her lips move against his. A whisper of a touch. "Only for you would I risk it all."

Bash cupped the side of her face. Gently, he slid his fingers into her silky hair before he gripped the strands, holding her still, exactly where he wanted her. "The future is ours," he murmured. And then he closed the minuscule gap between them and kissed her full lips.

Their kiss began soft, slow, and hesitant, like it was their very first. There was a newness to it that sent exhilarating tingles racing into his core, a shock of electricity that had him groaning into her mouth.

Margrete wrapped her arms around him and dragged him closer, melting into his hold even as she gripped him fiercely. Her nails dug into the back of his neck, and the slight sting had Bash's pulse soaring.

"Mine," he whispered against her, his other hand digging into her waist. She shivered at the word, from the sheer possessiveness of it.

"Only yours," she rasped.

He lost the little semblance of control he possessed. As did she.

Jumping up and into his arms, Margrete wound her legs around his torso, her heels digging into his backside. The pressure reminded him of what it meant to be alive, and it only fueled his eagerness to succeed. As he was adjusting to the sensation of having a physical body, if only for an hour, his touch was bruising, but she merely pressed herself deeper into his punishing hold, welcoming it.

Bash let go. He grasped the nape of her neck and ran his nose up the column of her throat, breathing in her scent until it was all he knew.

When she made a sweet sound caught somewhere between desperation and pain, Bash lifted her into his arms and moved her to the narrow bed. He laid her out on the white sheets before him, and leisurely, he took her in, how her hair fanned around her head like a halo, how she was so exceptionally breathtaking and yet so fierce.

A stunning creature he claimed as his own.

Bash whipped off his belt and let it clatter to the floor. Margrete's eyes grew hooded as she watched him yank off his shirt, and then his trousers. She drank in his bare skin with a need that fueled his beast.

At the thought of his inner monster, he stilled. His scales. Gingerly he brought his black-tipped fingers to his throat, grimacing when he grazed a sharp scale. What if he lost himself again? What if—

"Get over here, pirate," Margrete demanded tersely, understanding where his mind had drifted. The gentle light of the oil lamp cast shadows across her, making her glow a radiant yellow. "Your scales are your armor. Nothing more."

She didn't understand. She never would.

"I'm a goddess now, remember?" she added. "You can't hurt me."

She practically shimmered beneath him, her skin alight like she'd been dipped in gold. Bash edged closer, easing onto the small cot. "You better mean that, princess, because if I do hurt you, it'll haunt me long after my death."

"Good thing you're never going back to the Underworld," she stated confidently, reaching out to him. His hands closed into fists as he fought the urge to accept her embrace. But of course, she seized his hands and unfurled each black-tipped finger with ease.

"Use your claws, my king. I like them."

Those words were all it took to send him crawling over her body, his arms on either side of her face. She smiled a triumphant smile, a devilish sort of thing he found he liked far too much.

"Just a warning..." Bash lowered onto his elbows, bringing himself close enough to inhale her every breath. "You gave me your heart in Azantian, and I don't plan on returning it."

"Good. And yours is mine."

Now it was Bash's turn to grin. "Always." He lowered his head and ran his tongue from her collarbones to her pulse point, sucking when he felt her heartbeat thundering against his lips. He might've sucked too hard, bruising the skin purposely. He wanted to see his mark on her. Wanted Darius to see it.

He leaned back to admire his work before his attention drifted down her body. He shook his head. "These silly clothes"—he snapped a button off her shirt with one flick of his sharpened nail—"have to go."

When he moved for the next button, set to rip her shirt to shreds, Margrete stopped him with a firm hand on his chest.

"Deals with gods leave marks, and if I take off my blouse, you'll see something you don't like."

Ah. The flames and vines must've belonged to Halio. Which meant—

"Where?" he demanded, doing his best to not storm from the room and fulfill his fantasies of slicing the sea god's throat.

Hesitantly, Margrete began to sit up, and he moved out of the way. He watched as she unbuttoned her shirt and eased it off. Cautiously, she twisted around, baring her back.

Lilies. Three lilies fell down her spine.

Bash took a deep breath through his nose. Again, he was seconds away from leaving her to satiate the violence swimming in his icy blood.

But instead of allowing Darius to win, he gently touched her shoulder, coaxing her to turn back around. "It means nothing," he assured. "And it won't stop me from wanting you."

Besides, that damned tattoo would be gone soon enough. Bash would make certain of it.

Relief flooded her face, and her cheeks pinked. She leaned back onto her elbows, calmed by his answer. In the face of such perfection, Bash was helpless but to stare while she unfastened her trousers, her eyes on him as she worked.

He ran his hands along her luscious curves. "You're stunning. So beautiful. So *mine*."

Margrete's movements hurried, and when she was finally free of her trousers, he tossed them aside.

"Absolutely breathtaking," he whispered, pressing a kiss to her chest, right above her wildly thumping heart. He traveled to her breast, swirling his tongue around the peaked bud, and she let out a tortured whimper, arcing into him. Her legs parted around him, silently begging, and he smiled against her skin.

"I can't wait to watch you ruin them all," he murmured, lifting onto his elbows. "What a glorious sight that will be."

Her eyes narrowed as she brought her heels into his backside, pushing him closer. "*We* will ruin them," she vowed, reaching for his neck, her fingers glancing over his nymera scales. He tensed, but she yanked him back to her mouth, thrusting her hips upward, his cock rubbing against the slickness of her core.

He groaned at the feel of her, so wet and needy. Bash almost came undone before he had the chance to begin.

"We have less than an hour, Bash," she reminded. "I want to spend it in your arms, and I want you to show me how hard you're willing to fight." She slid her hand up her body, moving to her breast, to her hardened peak. His teeth ground together when she slid one hand down, down, down her body, grazing the apex of her thighs.

He pressed a kiss to the corner of her mouth. Another to her jaw, her chin. She groaned as he worshiped her, delicious shivers wracking her frame. Bash drew back to stare at her, his gaze roving leisurely across every inch of bare skin.

"I'd love nothing more than to show you how much I'll fight for us, princess." He grasped her chin, their gazes locked. "Even after my heart ceased to beat, it belonged only to you."

Gently, he lowered himself down her body, his mouth leaving cold kisses on her breasts, her stomach, her hips. She shuddered, her lids fluttering closed. Bash smiled as he ran his tongue up her core. Her eyes shot open, and a strangled sound escaped when brought her into his mouth, his tongue working her. Hands fisted his hair as he licked and sucked. He could drown in her taste.

Her hands tightened painfully in his strands, and Bash released a low growl of approval, sending vibrations running up her body. Grasping her thighs, he spread her wide as he took his time feasting. When he brought his teeth down, slowly dragging them, she fell, her eyes rolling into the back of her head as she called out his name. Bash grinned. His name on her lips, uttered as she fell over the edge, was his favorite sound.

As she came down from her high, Bash drifted to her lips, pressing a kiss to her mouth, allowing her to taste herself. The pleasure he'd wrung from her.

"Miss me, princess?" He thrust against her, his length teasing her entrance. She tried to reach between them and grasp him, but he snatched her hands and threaded his fingers through hers, bringing their entwined hands down beside her head. "If I didn't know any better I'd say you missed my cock more than me." He nipped at her bottom lip.

"Foolish man." She shook her head, a soft smile blossoming. "It's because I love you that I need you. You've utterly ruined me. You alone."

He pushed into her, those words breaking him in the best way. Her back bowed, and they both let out a groan. Fuck, she was heaven, delicious heaven.

"Look at me, Margrete," Bash commanded, beginning to move. "I want to savor this moment, and when you come, I want to see the pleasure that I give you."

He pulled back, only to drive forward once more, rocking his hips as his hands released her wrists and descended to her breasts. He latched onto a peaked bud, his tongue swirling around and around before clamping down. A cry bubbled up her throat, and she arched her chest into his mouth, craving more.

Margrete wasn't meek, and she certainly took control of her own pleasure, shifting her body and soundlessly demanding where he should move. Bash eagerly obliged.

"I love you," he rasped between kisses, his length hardening inside of her, nearing release. Her core throbbed, and he desperately needed to feel her break around him. She was so close.

"Say the words again," he ordered, panting, delirious, and out of breath.

"I love you," she vowed, gasping as he drove into her heat. "In this world and into the next."

"Yes," he praised, picking up the pace. Each jerk of his hips elicited a whimper from her lips, her eyes rolling back as he commanded her body, bringing her closer to bliss. Warmth flooded his veins when Margrete tightened around his cock, her walls squeezing him mercilessly. "I never want to let you go, my queen."

The second the title left his lips, Margrete's mouth parted, her walls clamping down on him, drawing out his own pleasure as she erupted. He felt her insides flutter as she gasped, her legs trembling violently.

Bash shuddered above her, thrusting two more times before he, too, found his release. He collapsed, keeping most of his weight on his forearms as he caught his breath and rode out the euphoria buzzing in his veins.

They remained this way, entangled as one, for quite some time. Bash ran his fingers through her hair and pressed kisses against her flushed skin. The outside world vanished, and he enjoyed the ounce of freedom they'd been gifted. Slipping an arm beneath her waist, he pulled her with him as he rolled to his back. Margrete's head fell onto his chest, right where he wanted her to be. Although she'd find no steady rhythm of his beating heart.

"You better continue being so optimistic," she threatened, though her voice was soft. Bash had done this in the past, held back when he believed he didn't deserve her, and she likely feared he'd do it again. Especially now.

What she didn't realize was that he could overcome anything with her light guiding him. He knew this now. Hell, he felt like he could conquer the seas, the very world if he so desired. Margrete was his north star, and he had every intention of coming home.

"I'll be at your side the entire time," he promised, nuzzling into her hair. "We fight together. From now until the end."

She propped herself onto her elbows, a hesitant smile forming. Hope, so fragile and warm, lifted him up, making the world appear brighter. She cupped his face, her touch a whisper of a thing.

"Oh, and *when* we win, princess, I expect you to answer my question. No more excuses. You realize I'm of the impatient sort."

He hadn't pushed her, but he craved an answer. Or more like, he'd break if he didn't receive one.

Margrete ran her fingers to his jaw and then grasped his chin. "You'll have to wait for that answer, pirate. *When* we win, you'll have it," she said, echoing his words.

He was grinning like a fool. "Your answer better be yes then. All this teasing is terrible for my tender heart."

She smacked him lightly across the chest. "You and your tender heart will have to wait."

Bash opened his mouth to argue, but she silenced him with a kiss. Godsdamn this woman and her wicked tongue.

He couldn't recall what on earth he planned on saying, nor did he care.

CHAPTER TWENTY

BASH

Bash woke up cold.

His eyes fluttered open and he sluggishly took in his surroundings.

The *Mare Deus*, not the *Phaedra*, he had to remind himself, a bitter feeling settling over him knowing he'd never sail his beloved ship again. It had been the first ship he'd commissioned as king, and now it was gone, its fractured pieces somewhere in the depths.

A wave of exhaustion seeped into his bones as he shifted in place on the cot, the sensation causing him to frown. He hadn't believed he *could* sleep given his state, but his mind was hazy and yearning for the oblivion of dreams.

Last night he'd spoken of fighting and triumph, but in the harsh light of day, his body no longer solid—

He was consumed with doubts, the sun peeking through the porthole and slanting across the planks of their cabin, wiping away all of the confidence the night had given him. He would've thought that a perk of being dead would be a lack of anxiety, but apparently, he asked for too much.

With a frustrated groan, Bash rolled over...

And brought his hand right through Margrete's chest.

"Shit," he hissed, retracting his arm. He inched back and lurched to his feet, moving away from the cot on unsteady feet. She hadn't even flinched, but he could still feel the icy emptiness, his fingers numb and buzzing. Staring down at her sleeping form, Bash fought to catch his breath.

You need to stay strong, he repeated, over and over again until it sank in. If he broke or showed an ounce of hesitation or weakness, Margrete may falter, and then his island would be destroyed.

Which couldn't happen.

Bash had been orphaned at a young age. He'd risen to the occasion, became a king, and fought for his people. And he'd done so by shoving down his emotions. Margrete's entrance into his life destroyed his ability to do so.

Creeping over to the porthole, he took in the blank canvas of blue waves, focusing on the sea and its ever-present song. The rush of the waves, the whooshing winds, the taste of salt in the air. He watched the waters until his vision became blurred and his anxiety lessened. He'd given up so much of himself over the years, but never again would he hide. While it may seem like he was all but ruined, Bash had something to fight for—his chance at happiness. Not his kingdom's or his people's, but *his.*

Waves crashed against the hull as if agreeing, the sea in a chaotic state today. But that's what he adored about it—how it could change from one minute to the next, from soft and sweet to a merciless entity of ruin. The waters were as unpredictable as life was, and in a way, it was one of the truest things he knew.

A sigh greeted his ears. He peered down upon Margrete, who was just rousing, her brow all scrunched up, her nose wrinkling. He smiled when she fisted the coverlet and yanked it to her chest, a deep rumble escaping her chest.

"Morning, princess," he said, enjoying her ensuing mumbles of annoyance. Pride filled him; he'd worn her out the night before.

Hell, if he had a tangible body, it would be sore from where she'd dug her fingers into his skin. His back would be riddled with the evidence of her passion, the red marks her nails undoubtedly would've left. Bash usually wore them with twisted pride.

She finally opened her eyes and ran a hand through her mess of brown hair. In the early light, the shade reminded him of the deep woods on his island, the color of the trees in the summer when the sun hit them just right. And her eyes, of course, were his favorite. His people held them in high esteem, believing a person's soul shone through. In hers, he saw the sea, his first love. The infinite depths that could steal a man's heart.

She was the most breathtaking creature he'd ever beheld, especially now, pliant and soft from sleep. In fact, the mornings were always his favorite, when her luscious body was tangled in his. All their barriers were down, and the tension of duty was absent.

That wasn't the case this morning.

Margrete smiled, seemingly lost in her own memories, but just as suddenly as it appeared, her grin vanished. Bash despised what replaced it—sorrow.

He couldn't have that.

Leaving the porthole, Bash hovered a foot away from the bed, his hands curling at his sides. It took everything to resist the urge to reach out and try to trace the side of her cheek. "Remember your vow," he whispered, leaning in as close as he dared. "Victory will be ours soon enough." When Margrete didn't respond, he continued, determined to return that smile he loved so damned much. "When all of this is over, you made a certain promise to me, and I, for one, have been picturing you wearing nothing but a crown. Such a wicked sight, I must say." His lips curved when she rolled her eyes—a sign of life.

"Your mind is filthy, pirate," she said, though he heard how her voice trembled, her chest starting to rise and fall quickly. It appeared that the prospect of being his queen was doing something to her, and Bash grinned with delight.

"It's entirely your fault," he argued, aching to press a kiss to her brow. "Besides, your mind is just as dirty as mine, my queen, if not more so."

His queen. It sounded so right. It sounded like the best damned thing he'd ever spoken.

Margrete lifted to her elbows, eyeing him in a way that was far from teasing.

"What is it?" he asked, suddenly feeling cold all over.

"You know very well," she said, swallowing thickly. "As much as I'd love to pretend everything will be all right, I physically can't. I should be up on deck by now, training, trying to learn as much as I can from him."

Him.

"I know," he admitted begrudgingly, his teeth grinding together. Naughty images of Margrete wearing only his crown vanished in a blink. Reality had a way of ruining a morning. "I hate that you have to spend one second in his presence." It pissed him off to a degree that should've frightened him, but Bash choked on his jealousy, trying to hide it from her as best he could. Judging by her heavy sigh, he knew he failed.

"Trust me," she asked, their eyes locking. Bash could practically taste the affection radiating from her every pore, how her one look could tilt his world and send him careening into a freefall.

"It's not you that I don't trust, princess."

A knock rattled the cabin door, shattering the moment.

Margrete blanched, her gaze shifting to the door. Bash already had a decent idea that the man they spoke of now stood on the other side, likely wearing his grating, cocky smirk.

"One second!" she called, her lips tugging down as stiffness entered her shoulders. She rose to grab her shirt, tugging it on with mechanical movements. Just as the hem fell to rest an inch below her bottom, the door flung open.

"I hope I'm not interrupting."

Darius strode into the cramped confines of the cabin, his seven-foot frame taking up too much room. Bash jumped to his feet and rushed before Margrete, doing his best to shield her half-naked state from the bastard's eyes.

"Oh, wipe that dour look off your face, king. I'm simply here to go over the plan." Darius heaved a dramatic sigh before boldly taking a seat on the edge of their cot. Bash felt a small amount of devilish pride knowing the god sat upon sheets they'd made love on the night before.

Yes. It definitely wasn't Bash's proudest moment.

"All right, fine," Margrete snapped, crossing her arms and covering her chest. Bash eased to the side, the muscles in his neck tensing painfully at the sight of her exposed body. Her golden thighs were a temptation, and Bash bit back a snarl when Darius's attention landed where the material ended, his eyes lighting up with want.

"Stop ogling me," Margrete snapped. She smoothed a hand down her shirt, shifting uncomfortably before the god. "What's your plan?" She tapped her bare foot on the planks, waiting with the patience of a viper ready to strike.

He couldn't have been more pleased.

"The Collossious is near." Darius still hadn't taken his focus off Margrete, and Bash clenched his fists even tighter when the god blatantly took in her form, scanning her from head to toe without shame.

"So we take it out first." She shrugged a lazy shoulder. "Fine by me. How do we locate it though?"

"With magic, of course." Darius lifted up, wiping at his fine jacket as if dust covered it. Maybe it did. He had spent the night in the hull, after all. "I think it's time for you and I to have a little lesson, don't you?"

Fuck. He wanted to pummel Darius's face until he was a mess of blue-black blood. It was *his* fault Azantian was at risk, not Margrete's.

Though a tiny part of Bash whispered otherwise. He shut down that voice quickly...before the other emotions he kept at bay swam to the surface.

Darius turned his attention to him, and as if he could read Bash's raging thoughts, he said, "She needs to learn if she's going to live. And something tells me you very much like her alive, king. You can despise me all you wish, but it doesn't matter. You humans certainly enjoy holding onto grudges."

"Grudges?" Margrete hissed, her own temper assuming control. "You *killed* him. He has every right to hate you as much as I do. If not more. The only reason you're here is because of Halio. I don't know why he forced us to bring you, but you're a means to an end, Darius. Nothing more."

"I'd be careful of what you say, *princess*," Darius warned. Bash hadn't moved from his spot beside her, but the god towered over them both, his glare intent on Margrete.

"I think the one who needs to be careful is *you*," she shot back, and Bash turned in time to see a cruel smile tilt her lips. "Let's not forget the end goal."

Bash went rigid, all happiness from this morning fading to ash at his feet. He wanted to tell Darius *his goal* was fruitless, but he had to play along. Even if it killed him.

"Besides, Halio forced you to help clean up your own mess," Margrete added. "And one wouldn't want to upset the God of Death."

Darius's jaw clenched as he considered, and finally, *finally*, he brought his stare to Bash. The way he assessed him like a speck of dirt had his hackles rising.

"I've been tasked by Halio to help, yes. But don't think that I can't change the game if I didn't wish to."

"This isn't a game," Bash snarled. He hadn't lasted too long keeping his temper at bay. "This is our lives. If you actually felt something, anything akin to human emotion, you'd understand that."

Darius inhaled sharply at that, but then he shook his head, a tangle of blond hair tumbling into his eyes. The blue in his irises looked darker today. Deadlier.

He swiveled toward Margrete, effectively dismissing him. "Meet me on deck in ten minutes. We'll hunt the Collossious together. Without *distractions*." With that, the god spun on his heel and left the room, leaving only the sounds of Margrete's rapid breathing.

"Bastard," she muttered. Her palms sparkled with blue, her skin shimmering with an iridescent sheen. Her magic saturated the space, the air electric.

"Shhh," Bash soothed, getting as close as he dared. Their noses were inches apart. "Use him. Then we attack and wipe him from this world." She couldn't lose sight of the end goal.

"Keep reminding me, pirate, because I swear I'm afraid I'm going to snap and kill him before we fulfill the bargain."

The laugh that left him was brittle. "Whenever that urge overwhelms you, come to me," he said. "You've been my rock for so long. I think it's well past my turn."

Her body visibly relaxed, the crease in her forehead smoothing. He noticed how her magic simmered before dying out entirely.

Margrete could wipe out half the world if she willed it, and she still had no idea how to control herself. But beneath the magic, he recognized the light no power could compare to.

He had to have faith—faith in *her*, not gods or magic. The alternative meant his fury would rise, and he worried where it would be directed once he returned to his mortal body.

"Go," he said. "Train and learn how to best him. Use him for his knowledge only to turn it on him later."

Bash hardly recognized his callous words, but Margrete nodded, her features fierce.

"I'll meet you on deck," Bash promised, knowing she had to dress. While she did so, he'd scope out the new ship...and the enemy lurking onboard.

Bash left before he made a fool of himself by trying to touch her again. He marched up the stairs and into the blustering breeze, the sea roiling on either side of the *Mare Deus*.

At the stern stood Darius, and as though he felt his presence, he twisted to stare.

Triumph brightened his gaze. Like he'd already won.

But Bash smiled. The god had no idea that he'd given his enemies the fuel they needed to consume him whole.

In less than two weeks, Bash would make sure he coated the waves with Darius's ashes.

CHAPTER TWENTY-ONE

MARGRETE

THE SITUATION WASN'T PLEASANT.

Neither Bash nor Darius wanted to be within punching distance of the other. Of course, Bash couldn't do much damage, but when they found Minthe and his body, that may be a different story.

After Margrete had ascended the stairs and made her way on deck, she marked the positions of each of her crew, needing to see them alive and well. Atlas was teaching Dani how to mend sails, and Bay was speaking with Mila in hushed tones as they worked to right their course at the wheel. She locked eyes with Bay, her heart plummeting when he gave her a hopeful smile.

Margrete turned away. She couldn't speak with him now. Not when she had to put on a mask of bravery. As if to embolden her, the key tucked in her pocket pulsated, and she swore she heard the faint whisperings of the song it had sung to her in the Underworld.

You've been through worse, she reminded herself, lifting her chin. Gods knew she'd faced odds and risen above, and she'd do so again.

Marching to the stern, she ignored the burning eyes searing into the back of her skull. She hadn't a doubt Bash stood guard from the shadows, studying every move Darius made. Her king had grown harder since they'd left Azantian in search of the beasts. As had she.

Margrete paused, halfway to Darius. Gods, she abhorred how she needed him. If they failed, Bash would never forgive her—even if he claimed he would have risked Azantian himself.

She knew Bash placed all the blame on the god before her now, probably so he wouldn't hate *her* for her choices.

What a mess she'd made.

"What are you doing over there?" Darius's smooth voice broke the onslaught of chaotic thoughts and doubts. She met his stare, which softened considerably when they swept down to her trembling hands.

She should've known better than to display such vulnerability, but she couldn't control her own body. Margrete was worse than Darius, worse than any monster they hunted. She was so selfish, risking thousands of lives for one man simply because her own heart had shattered.

"I—" Her throat swelled up and she choked on whatever lie she planned to spew. When the sea god approached, his lips weren't lifted in a cunning grin, and his brows were creased in what could be mistaken as genuine concern.

The ship lurched to the side, though Darius never stumbled as he drew close. He placed a hand on her shoulder, squeezing lightly, and it was only the panic raging inside of her that kept her from brushing him away.

Margrete opened her mouth in an attempt to form a coherent reply, but she froze as shadows shrouded Darius's face. Tilting her chin, she took in the rolling gray clouds that rushed across the endless blue sky, muting the rays of the sun. The waves picked up in response, thrashing wildly against the hull.

She swallowed thickly, trepidation marking her heart like a scar. Today would bring change, she knew, something *big* she felt deep within her bones.

"What's wrong?" Darius asked, his voice firm. He scanned her face, seeming to search for wounds he couldn't see. "You're too pale." His hands skimmed down her arms, the touch far from sensual.

"I'm all right, just tired," she said, surprised when her voice came out steady. "I didn't get much sleep last night."

Darius peered over her shoulder, his expression souring. She knew he looked at Bash.

"It seems as if he doesn't approve of our nearness," he mocked, lowering his arm. "I take it you told him the details of our bargain?"

"Yes," she said, leaving it at that. Darius didn't need to know they also planned on killing him before she could honor their accord.

"I see," he mused, and she noted the exact second his walls went up. He straightened his spine and rolled his shoulders back. "Well, enjoy yourselves while you're able."

The usual scorn in his voice was shockingly absent, and she found the presence of cold indifference in its place.

"We best get started. You won't do much good if you have no clue how to wield your magic." His gaze lingered on her, sweeping across her lips, her nose, her eyes. He held them the longest. "Although I sense what's roiling inside of you, and it's rather strong, which works in our favor," he whispered, lowering his voice even further. "But you need to focus and pay close attention to what I'm about to teach you. The Collossious is close. Closer than I originally believed. It's aiming to hunt us first and gain the upper hand." He tore his attention from her and brought them to the waves. "He's a nasty creature."

She didn't like speaking with him like this, as if they were comrades. Darius would always be the true enemy.

Overhead, the clouds flourished and the winds became violent, whipping at her cheeks with a rage she felt deep in her bones.

Margrete welcomed the sea and its anger as she faced the god who ruled it.

"Then let's get to work, Darius."

"No, NOT LIKE THAT."

Darius's command drifted to Margrete's ears, her lids closed while her magic searched, reaching out into the waters and below their depths. She swayed on her feet, trying to maintain control. He wanted her to find the beast herself, claiming it was time she learned the vastness of her abilities. She hadn't disagreed.

Delving into the waves and traveling so far from her physical body wasn't as instinctive as she'd thought, and the taste of copper coated her tongue. She must have bitten her cheek.

"This is *your* kingdom," Darius cooed in her ears. "Remember who's in control. The sea is a powerful entity and doesn't like to be tamed, but you can do it. You have all the tools you need, should you choose."

The sounds of the ship—the whistling wind, the thunderous crash of the waves, the shouts of the crew—were replaced by a dull droning that pulsed in her ears. Her body gave a violent jerk, a single spark of gold glinting behind her closed lids. That divine lightning guided her deeper into the navy waters, luring her to where the Collossious thrived.

She went stiff, adrenaline trickling down her back.

"I feel something," she mumbled, narrowing in on her prey. She was flying through the sea, moving impossibly fast, getting closer and closer to the beast.

A flash of an image flickered across her mind. She smiled then, heart thudding in victory. Miles away, and moving nearly as fast as her, was the monster that men had written stories about for centuries.

"Keep pushing," Darius instructed. "Hold onto that image and release the magic you're refusing to set free. Take a deep breath and then exhale, loosen your muscles." She opened her mouth to protest, when he said, "I know you're holding back. Every muscle in your body is rigid, weakened from keeping it inside. Give your power a shred of command, allow it to reign over your human nature. Think of it as a partner, a friend. Only then will you truly experience the force you've become."

With the sea god coaxing her, she did just that, her teeth grinding together as she concentrated on the lethal creature swimming toward their small ship at a speed that shouldn't have been possible. And gods, was it frightening.

She didn't know what she expected—perhaps something like the sea serpent they defeated on Azantian—but the Collossious wasn't anything she could've imagined. It was worse. Likely twice the size of the serpent, the sharklike creature advanced with agile grace, the flickering light of the sun above shining light on its horrid design. Its dorsal fin glinted like the sharpest blade, its body sleek and covered in gray scales that reminded her of steel. She bet they'd cut her skin with ease, and that was just its body.

Its jaw...

As it swished through the waves, Margrete made out its three rows of jagged teeth, each tooth the size of her hand.

"I see it," she whispered, eyes still shut. "How are we going to kill it?"

They had hours, if that, before it approached.

"The beast has a few weak spots. Right beneath its jaw lies one, and another, its softer underbelly. Though that would be far riskier."

Her palms heated, a rush of pure adrenaline coursing through her veins.

"Yes, just like that," Darius praised, sensing her power. "It takes great concentration to take aim, but in time it will become second nature."

She felt him moving around her until he was at her back, his solid frame pressing into her spine.

"Keep your eyes closed," he instructed. "Now breathe with me. Nice and slow, in and out. Think of your breathing as the stone that sharpens your blade. Your weapon. If you lose control of it, then your magic will run wild."

She could hardly take in a steady exhale. The feel of him—all of his hard muscles, his warm breath at her ear, his hands on her body—was making it impossible to find her calm. As much as she loathed it, the part of her that would always be Wryn would forever react to his presence.

"In and out," Darius murmured, his voice firm.

She growled a curse but did as he asked. Several minutes passed until his hands moved to her waist. But by then, a great marvel occurred.

Margrete was with the beast, in the waters while her physical body stood on the *Mare Deus*. A prickling feeling stretched down from her shoulders to her wrists and then her palms, and she felt a cool composure override her earlier panic. Just like that, she'd connected, and her breathing—just as Darius had insisted—had centered her.

In and out. She repeated this over and over, whenever she felt herself drifting, whenever her own thoughts poked through the focus of the mission.

"When you take aim, when we have it in our sights, you'll keep that same even breathing," Darius whispered. She heard only his voice. It was soft, a melody that fell across her body like silk. "The magic responds to you. How you react, your emotions."

Margrete jolted. The Collossious roared, its warning rattling her bones, making her lose any semblance of peace. It thrashed in the water, snapping its jaws, and all she could think of was how those teeth might clamp down upon her.

Her eyes shot open with a start.

Darius was no longer behind her. Not at her back, his hands on her waist—

His chest pressed into hers, his hands now cupping both of her cheeks. She was panting, an overwhelming rush of adrenaline causing her knees to grow weak.

"You're going to be fine," Darius murmured, lowering his head, daring to move even closer than he already was. She was too anxious to move. "I'll be right here. I'll guide you."

"I-it's coming fast," she gasped, feeling like she was drowning. "It sees us too."

He nodded somberly. "It senses you, Margrete. Fresh blood. An exciting kill."

Fear slithered down her spine.

"We have less than an hour, I'd say," Darius mused, both his thumbs rubbing her cheeks. She hated how soothing the movement was. How it brought her back from the brink of suffocating. "Once the Collossious finds worthy prey, it won't rest until it coats the waters with your blood. It's now up to you whether or not you let it win."

CHAPTER TWENTY-TWO

MARGRETE

An hour later, Margrete felt the Collossious before her magic reacted.

"It's near," she whispered frantically, still beside Darius at the stern. They'd continued to practice her breathing, and he'd guided her with a gentle voice.

"I wish I'd known it would divert its course when it felt you," Darius said, his voice thick with regret. He'd given her space, leaning against the rail, but he was inches away, close enough where she could feel his heat.

The waves rocked the *Mare Deus*, though she hardly paid them any heed. Her mind was too scattered, all their work seemingly worthless. Soon, she'd face one of the most fearsome beasts known to man, and she wasn't sure she was strong enough. Yes, she was a goddess, and yes, she had power—but Margrete didn't feel like a goddess at that moment. She only felt like herself, and that didn't seem good enough.

"You better not let a damned thing happen to her."

They turned at the same time. Bash strode to them, appearing the commanding king, even as he wavered in the low light of the day. The clouds overhead were growing dense, darkening enough to blot most of the sun's rays. The ship lurched violently to the side, though his strides never wavered.

"I thought we had more time," Darius answered, for once not delivering his words with biting scorn. "But I will not allow her to be harmed. You have my oath." He had to raise his voice above the churning sea, which was coming alive with frightful intent.

"The winds are picking up!" Mila shouted from above, hanging from the main mast. She almost fell as she made to climb down, the vessel pitching to the left. Margrete exhaled in relief when Mila dropped to the planks, screaming orders at the crew. Bay scrambled to right the sails as they whipped in the vicious breeze, and Atlas and Dani checked each knot.

Bash's attention landed on her, ignoring the god entirely.

"I have faith that you will return to me," he said softly, though no less firm. "We've been through worse. And we'll fight to see another day."

Whereas Darius's voice had soothed, Bash's worked to rile her spirit. Her faith in herself. Funny how just a voice alone could have such influence.

Just then, a wave barreled into the ship's side, and Margrete went flying into Darius's hard chest with an *oomph*. The god gripped her shoulders, righting her. From the corner of her eye, she noted how Bash's jaw feathered with rage.

But now wasn't the time for jealousy. Now was the time to kill.

Darius turned her around to face him. "Let our magic unite, let them be one." His fingers bit into her skin, the intensity swimming in his eyes stealing her air. "Release yourself. Now," he ordered, and damn her body, but it reacted.

His magic flowed into her, meeting her own power with a reverberating clash. It collided with enough force to weaken her knees, the feel of it glacial. His energy seeped well beyond her skin until it seemed to flow with her life essence, the blood in her veins turning to ice. Seconds passed and her body grew accustomed to the intrusion...until it didn't feel like an intrusion at all.

She felt...*whole.*

"*We* are the beast's master," Darius uttered, his silken voice wrapping around her. "Though it refuses to bow. That means we attack."

"And if it gets too close to the ship?" She couldn't risk the others getting hurt. They were sprinting around deck, securing the ship, readying for the vicious waves that might threaten to send them all overboard.

"You're not going to like what I suggest," Darius whispered, the warmth of his body pressing into her hip. She shuddered.

"Tell me," Margrete demanded. "I can handle it."

Darius swallowed hard before saying, "I suggest we dive in. We're stronger in the water."

Yeah, she didn't like that at all.

"Like hell are you diving in with that thing!" Bash grated out. She felt an ounce of guilt at having forgotten he remained by her side. "We can withstand it onboard. My crew has mastered every kind of weather and—"

"And your crew shipwrecked on my island," Darius snapped. "And that was just a storm, albeit a supernatural one. This, on the other hand" —he waved to the roiling waters—"is a sentient being who will stop at nothing until your friends rest in its belly."

Bash froze, a muscle in his jaw tensing. He wasn't at risk. He couldn't die twice. But his crew?

"We can do it," Mila chimed in, shoving into the argument, her fiery red hair framing her sun-kissed skin. Her nimble movements brought her into their circle, her legs accustomed to the tumultuous swaying of the ship. Margrete saw Darius glare at the sailor, his eyes narrowing. Mila met his stare with a lethal one of her own, each battling for supremacy.

"No, we *can't*," Dani shouted, ten feet away as she fixed a loose knot. She stumbled over. Tugging at her sleeves, her long, black curls whipping at her brown cheeks, she appeared nothing short of terrified. "I can't tell you why, but—" She stopped, blinking rapidly as though chasing a lost dream. "I just know we won't make it. The air tastes like death, but the water...the *water* doesn't."

Her words made no sense to Margrete, but she wasn't about to argue with the one person taking their side. Bay probably would've fought with them too if he wasn't busy somewhere else on the ship, or more accurately, watching them from some secluded spot, taking in their argument in that calculating way of his. He'd been observant and on edge since joining them, and while he made a point to steer clear of Margrete, he had a new purpose in his steps that had grown every time she spotted him.

Her old friend was coming back to himself, though secretly she worried that night on the island had scarred him in irrevocable ways. She cared more than she let on. Far, far more.

If she survived the Collossious, then maybe she'd speak with him. Her heart panged at the mere thought. Ironic how confronting Bay felt more dangerous than slaying a monster.

Margrete tuned the now arguing crew out. She captured Darius's gaze, the sky gray behind his hauntingly beautiful face. The god nodded stiffly, seeming to understand her before she spoke.

"We go in," she stated loudly enough for the others to hear.

"Agreed," Darius voiced, though it wasn't necessary. They'd already been on the same page.

Only Dani seemed pleased by this, the rest of the crew scowling. Bash the worst of them. He crossed his muscled arms and shot daggers at the sea god.

She drew as close as possible to his intangible frame. To him, she said, "I have to do this and you know it."

His nostrils flared, though he dropped his arms at his side.

"You *just* came into your new gifts. If you'd practiced before, if you had more experience, it would be different. You're practically jumping in with your eyes closed, and that's going to get you hurt. Or worse."

He had a point. But it didn't matter.

"I need you to trust me." She scanned his face, his shimmering skin a sickly pale gray.

Bash lifted his eyes, which stormed with rage. "You know I trust you," he said through gritted teeth.

Her eyes prickled as unshed tears threatened, but she merely clenched her now sparking fists and focused on the swelling adrenaline, how it bestowed her the strength she needed at this moment and the one to come.

"Margrete, it's getting closer!" Darius called, his tone impatient. She ignored him.

"I love you," she said to Bash, needing him to hear the words.

"We have to go. You lovebirds can resume this later." Darius's words came out in a growl. "We still need time to swim out far enough away so the beast doesn't capsize this poor excuse for a boat."

She silently cursed. He was right.

Bash briefly shut his lids, but when he opened them, they were burning with fire, with the fight he'd promised her last night.

"I love you, princess," he said, the taut muscles in his neck relaxing. "Now go and do the impossible. But if you get hurt—"

"Margrete!" Darius's cry rose above the winds, cutting off Bash's plea.

"I can do this," she said, drinking in Bash one last time. Before he could say another word, she whirled around and sprinted for the stern, her blood humming and pulse thudding in her ears. At the rail, she shut her eyes and delved into the otherworldly energy that was just as much a part of her as her heart.

"It's now or never," Darius murmured in the shell of her ear. She hadn't realized how close he'd moved. "But I'm going to need you to let me in your mind. Words cannot be spoken in the dark depths."

"How?" she asked, not realizing she'd managed to block him in the first place.

She jolted when he took her hand in his, her eyes fluttering open. Somewhere far behind them, a rumble of disapproval sounded. Overhead, the clouds grew dark with foreboding.

"My magic recognizes yours. It *is* yours." Darius's thumb rubbed gentle circles on her palm. "I know every instinct is telling you to push me away, but when you feel me knocking on the barriers of your mind, let me in. Allow your magic to embrace my own. I promise you'll understand when it happens. Trust me."

She wanted to laugh at that last line, but her heart thundered as heat rushed into her chest.

"And now"—Darius shucked off his boots and climbed onto the rail— "we need to jump."

He looked down at her, stretching out his hand.

She observed it for a second, maybe two, then yanked off her boots and grasped his offered hand. He curled his fingers around hers, tightening his grip just as he leaned in to whisper, "Time to jump."

Margrete screeched as she was yanked forward, the world a blur of blue. When she struck the churning surf, she realized Darius had never let go.

He shifted to her beneath the waters, his blond hair wafting about his ethereal face. The time had come to let him in, and he silently urged her to grant the access he craved. She felt his magic—could practically taste the cool salt and spice that would forever remind her of him—and Margrete hissed when their powers collided yet again.

Brilliant sparks flared and sputtered behind her eyes, and then there was an eruption of blue and yellow and gleaming silver.

She didn't resist, didn't put up a fight. With the sea god's hand in hers and the vicious threat on the horizon, Margrete willingly broke down her barriers and embraced Darius's familiar magic.

CHAPTER TWENTY-THREE

MARGRETE

TIME AND SPACE WERE ABSENT IN THE IN-BETWEEN REALM WHERE she and Darius collided. Without walls or flesh to separate them, hundreds of images struck like arrows, hundreds of different memories that she'd yet to see.

All of them were much the same, various scenes where she held Darius's hand, or the two of them laughing and sharing a meal. She'd never seen him laugh like that before, not in this lifetime—so free and unguarded. The images shifted, and then she glimpsed the world of night and passion, the pair of them tangled in one another, the sheets in a disarray. He moved inside of her with force, a strong arm wrapped around her waist as he wrought pleasure from her body beneath the light of the moon.

Margrete didn't know how much time had come and gone as her past came back to her, but now there was no longer a doubt—if there ever was —that she'd well and truly loved him. Or a version of herself had. But as much as Darius had changed over the last thousand years, so had Margrete's soul. They may be linked to one another, but the spark she'd felt in Wryn's memories remained absent.

She sucked in a mouthful of water, allowing it to pack into her lungs. With a stuttering exhale, she opened her eyes.

Darius's gaze seared into hers, his brows scrunched together, a deep crease forming. He twisted away from her, only to whisper, *Hold on,* across her mind.

Before she could ask, the sea god encircled her, his chest pressing firmly against her back. A burst of blue light erupted, illuminating the seas, and then they were shooting across the waters, his arms tight around her.

Margrete panted, breathing in the saltwater with ease—a change that had come easier as of late. In seconds, it felt as normal as inhaling fresh air. *Better* even. Her body relaxed as Darius's power propelled them farther from the bottom of the *Mare Deus.*

She was brought back to the hours before, when he was in a similar position, instructing her how to keep her calm, how to welcome her magic. And while she was hesitant to admit it, the ensuing rush felt exhilarating, like flying through the skies on a cloudless day. Unbidden, her lips turned up into a smile, and she sucked in the salty taste of the sea, her blood simmering with excitement.

This was the adventure she'd yearned for back in Prias, gazing out from her tower, trapped. She'd desired the thrill of the unknown, the surge of adrenaline that accompanied risk. Such a feeling meant she was alive, and she had felt so very numb for too many years.

Until Bash came along and turned her world upside-down in the best possible way.

In a moment the Collossious will come at us, Darius whispered. *I will attack its throat, and you will remain below, aiming for its soft underbelly should the need present itself. I don't want you to interfere unless you absolutely have to.* Being connected to him allowed her to feel a hint of whatever he did, and she was surprised that alarm mingled with his determination. *Only if I fail do you attack, understood?*

They'd begun to slow, and she sensed the shift in the waters as the monster neared. The stench of rot nearly had her gagging, but she gritted her teeth, resolute and emboldened by the promises she'd made.

I will do what I think is necessary, she shot back, unwilling to be a useless bystander. *We work together or not at all.*

Darius growled across her mind. *Let me lead, at least,* he conceded. *Watch what I do and try to mimic it. You did a fairly decent job back at the arena accessing your true power. You just have to work on your aim. Your magic is natural energy, but it can be hard to contain.* As if on cue, the blue light at her palms glowed brighter.

If she'd just imagined the Collossious bore Darius's face, then she wouldn't miss.

Thinking of me again?

Margrete startled.

I'm inside your mind, darling. His chuckle caressed her. *Though even when you aimed, you still missed me, so perhaps think of a better target.*

She grumbled a curse along with a few other equally vile obscenities aimed at his expense. Again, he simply laughed.

Darius brought them to a standstill, the current whipping their bodies back and forth, causing her hair to fall across her eyes. When he released her, a part of her felt empty, and she hated that.

She recalled a time when he told her that he'd never let her go, right after they'd spent the evening watching the stars dance across the universe, the waves whipping at the shores—

No. That wasn't *her* life.

Fuck, the lines were beginning to blur.

Focus, Darius chided, though there wasn't any bite. He seemed to sense the turmoil raging in her. *Swim lower. I'll distract him and attempt to slay him with my magic. Remember, the jaw and underbelly. Those are its vulnerable spots, but if that doesn't work...* He eyed her leather sheath, silently urging her to retrieve her blade. She did it without an argument. Her magic had failed her before, and she refused to be caught unawares again. Adrian's blade was a comfort.

We work together—

Her words were cut off when a surge of water tossed them both backward. She went tumbling, spinning aimlessly. She couldn't pinpoint where Darius had gone, but she had the good sense to shove below, kicking her feet until she reached as far as she dared.

Sure enough, a shadow blocked out the little sun that filtered through the waves. The imposing beast swam leisurely above, its gaping jaw unhinged and impatient to carve through flesh. Rows and rows of teeth were visible, even from the distance, and dread pooled in her belly.

It had appeared out of nowhere.

Of course, her damned magic continued to glow at her fingertips, and she hadn't a doubt the creature would discover her soon enough. Just as she started to swim deeper, another beacon of light illuminated the waves.

Twenty feet above her, both arms outstretched, Darius drifted, looking the part of the fallen, dark god. His eyes were closed, his breathing even, his body unusually still. He appeared as if he were sleeping, even as the Collossious barreled his way, snapping its jaws in its eagerness.

Slowly, pale yellow and blue light emanated from his tanned skin, flourishing into a mighty beacon.

The beast shifted course, aiming directly for him, its lifeless onyx eyes wide. As it neared, she took stock of its body, which was a thing of magnificent brutality. They'd been right when they likened its scales to metal. It reminded her of a suit of armor. Still, the weight it must carry never slowed it down.

Stay there, Darius murmured, unmoving. *I can feel you itching to strike. It's best to let your enemy think it has the upper hand.*

Lovely. She was getting a peek inside the mind of a psychopathic god.

Not a psychopath. Just calculating, he replied. She cursed again. Once they felled the animal, she'd erect a thousand walls between them.

Darius took in one final, deep inhale, the Collossious no more than a few yards away—

His lids snapped open and light exploded, igniting the underwater world with devastating color. Bringing his palms before him, he shot out a surge of raw energy, the force of which she sensed even safely out of reach.

The beast flew backward, whirling in circles until it righted itself. Its lifeless eyes tapered. Darius had done nothing but anger it, his aim having missed its mark.

She blinked. Darius had done something similar once before...

Memories of him protecting her from a smaller version of the Collossious struck her mind. They'd swam too deep one day, way beyond the island's reach, and she'd gotten trapped between pieces of coral—

You're losing yourself to the past again, Darius said, jolting her from her past. *Think of me all you want later, but now isn't the time.*

She growled just as the Collossious drove forward again, more determined than ever. Darius shot off another blast of pure, divine energy, but the beast swerved to the side at the last minute. Darius kept going, lifting his palms and aiming for its broad throat, the god's grunts sounding in her mind.

The sea churned around them, seeming to hear the god's struggle, the waves eager to be of aid. The riotous current abruptly shifted, moving to thrust the monster farther back, but the creature was far too strong.

No wonder sailors feared the legend of the Collossious. A *god* struggled to defeat it.

While Darius shot off more and more of his power with abandon, Margrete prepared herself. He'd commanded she stay put, but he wasn't succeeding, and they needed the creature's blood to stain the waters. She squinted at its underbelly, her brow creasing.

All she had to do was aim. That's it. Simple really.

Ha. As if she believed that for one moment.

Margrete slowed her breathing as Darius had taught her and kicked upward.

This time, when the beast drove at Darius, he reacted too slowly.

She watched in horror as he careened to the side, his mouth parted in shock. The creature didn't hesitate. As Darius spun out of control, his palms flashing with magic he couldn't aim, the shark unhinged its mighty jaw—

And clamped down on Darius's arm.

Blue blood trickled into the water, the color nearly black. Darius screamed in pain, and the shrillness of it sent her into action.

Any sense of calm evaporated as she kicked with all her strength, swimming upward, toward the light and the bleeding god. She knew he'd live, as gods could only be killed by other gods, but he *had* created it, and if his magic thrived in its veins, perhaps it could do more damage than she initially believed. There wasn't much time to doubt as she lifted her palms above her head and screamed into the void.

The Collossious shook Darius from side to side, its teeth embedded in his muscle. It assumed it had won, and she smelled its triumph. Its bloodlust.

Hold on, she thought, not sure if Darius could even hear her.

Darius screamed again, and something about his pain sliced at her core. For a moment in time, she was Wryn, and her lover, the man who held her heart, was being torn to bits by a monster. Fury seeped into her pores, her fingers on fire as she lifted to the Collossious's soft underbelly and released her pent-up wrath.

She clenched her teeth, hissing in pain as too much power flowed from her body all at once. While not trained in the ways of the gods, she understood she'd done something wrong, even if the energy she discharged struck the animal with brutal force.

The Collossious screeched as it released Darius, who slumped forward, clutching at his bleeding arm. Margrete didn't stop. Not even as she swam close enough to touch its razor-sharp sides.

The creature was ten times her height, if not more, but that also could be its weakness. Margrete smiled, a wicked rush of adrenaline barreling into her chest. The larger they were, the slower they moved.

The beast writhed, attempting to thwack her with its fins, its head jerking from side to side as it searched for its assailant.

Margrete let go—

Only to find that nothing but a fizzle came out.

Her power...it was gone.

You used too much all at once, came Darius's weakened voice. With the beast distracted, he'd been given the chance to heal. No longer did blue blood flow into the water, but she could tell by the way his mouth twisted that it still hurt like a bitch.

You could have told me that! she snapped, reaching for her blade.

I didn't think you could even access that much so quickly! It should be impossible.

Her fingers curled around Adrian's blade, and just before she could plunge the tip into its belly, the Collossious shifted. In a whirl of motion, it whipped around and faced her, its maw opened wide enough that she could make out every glistening tooth.

She might be a goddess, but she still felt fear, and right then, it weighed her every limb.

Margrete thought of Azantian, of its people. A people she'd fallen in love with. She pictured Adrian and Bay, arm in arm, and Birdie down by the shore. She even pictured Nerissa, the stoic seer bestowing her with a rare, warm smile.

She imagined the life she'd chosen, and the man she'd chosen to spend it with.

The grip on the blade tightened. The determination to live rose above her suffocating fear, and she forced her body to move. She brought her weapon up—

But it was too late. The beast was on her, its mouth turning, its many rows of teeth inches from her face...

Silver light sizzled in the water before those sharp teeth clamped down. She swiveled toward Darius, whose face was pinched with focus and pain. Yet he didn't stop his assault, allowing his energy to barrel into the head of the creature, and when it tilted from the force of it all, the god's magic aimed true.

The beast...it *shattered.*

Each shining scale ripped free from its body, the shards flying in every direction. Margrete shielded her face and curled in on herself, but pain radiated from her arms, her legs, her back. She tasted her blood in the waters now, and when she finally peeled open her eyes, she gasped.

Blue seeped free from her wounds, mingling with the waves like plumes of smoke.

Adrenaline surging, she frantically searched for the remaining parts of the monster, though she found none. Only the scales glimmered as they descended, the growing light of the sun casting its rays upon the metallic pieces like falling summer rain.

They'd done it.

Defeated the Collossious.

Margrete smiled despite the agony. If Darius had healed, so would she, and she'd withstood pain before.

Darius! she called out, not finding him floating nearby. *Where are you?*

No answer returned. Just silence.

Darius, this isn't funny. Show yourself.

Again nothing. Margrete shut her eyes and reached out, searching for his magic, looking for the familiar glow of his energy force.

Everything was hazy, the world a muted blue. She found no sight of him. No figure swimming her way. No triumphant smile.

Some more cursed memories assaulted her, but she shoved them away. She wasn't on some island swimming with her lover, and she wasn't searching for the man she cared for. Margrete wasn't Wryn and never would be again.

But she still needed Darius.

Margrete thrust forward, sucking down water frantically. It was as though he'd vanished along with the beast, gone forever. Yet she knew that couldn't be the case.

She'd just started off toward the *Mare Deus* when she saw it—a flash of gold.

Margrete jerked to a stop, her wounds healing enough to where the sudden movement didn't send her head spinning. The rays of the sun filtering through the waves cast light on the gold once more, a mere spark in the gloom.

Darius's sigil ring.

She cursed, diving down, down, down, her magic burnt out and unable to propel her faster. Next time she'd have to be more careful and not expel all of her magic. It was a lesson well learned. At least she could still breathe, which was a small mercy unto itself.

Swim up to me! she demanded, though Darius didn't reply.

Had he been knocked unconscious?

Margrete.

Her name sounded from everywhere at once. The voice belonged to Darius, though it was weaker than she'd ever heard it.

Gritting her teeth, she kicked faster, her heart racing when his body came into view. The god didn't move, his frame hunched over itself, letting his weight carry him downward. Something wasn't right.

Margrete grunted as she reached out and grasped the hand wearing the ring, her fingers tightening on his wrist and pulling him toward her. Weightlessly, he drifted, and she searched his face.

His eyes were half open, blood seeping from his mouth. And his chest...

A scale had lodged itself deep within his heart.

Don't leave me. Darius's plea sent chills down her back. *Please don't leave me alone again.*

A flash of pain seared her. Such a hurt had nothing to do with the battle or the toll it had taken on her body. No, this pain had everything to do with the soul bound to hers, and the agony that had filled Darius's words.

She gripped his hand, indecision causing her to still.

Darius didn't deserve her help, but she couldn't leave him when he was a condition of Halio's bargain. And to be honest, the part of herself that would always belong to Wryn refused to let go. He'd belonged to her at one point in her life, and there could be no changing that. Just as she couldn't change the past, she accepted that she'd forever *feel* for the god, even if she didn't wish to.

Margrete grimaced.

And then she made up her mind.

CHAPTER TWENTY-FOUR

DARIUS

DARIUS WOKE TO A WARM HAND ON HIS BARE CHEST.

Before he even opened his eyes, he snatched the wrist the hand belonged to, a small gasp sounding. A feminine gasp.

His eyes shot open.

"Let go," Mila demanded, scowling down at him as if he were nothing. As if he weren't a *god*. One corner of his mouth quirked.

"Not before you tell me what the hell you're doing and how I got here." Darius wearily scanned the cabin, the rows of bunk beds all empty. He lay on a lower bunk, a subtle hint of citrus clogging his senses.

His body ached everywhere, his magic a dulled thrum.

"Margrete got your arrogant ass to the ship, even though I would've left you to rot beneath the waves." She scoffed. "And as far as why you're *here* in this room, you were in pretty bad shape. While I protested, the others didn't want to shove you between some barrels in the hull. I decided to stay and make sure you didn't stain my sheets," she snapped, yanking on his hold.

Her bed.

That's where the citrus scent came from. "And you've been passed the fuck out for the last two hours. I didn't think gods fainted like noble ladies at court who'd overheard a curse word."

Now the other side of his mouth joined in, and he found himself indulging in a rare, full smile. Before she could snap at him again, Darius released her wrist, noticing she'd clutched a damp rag between her fingers. She was *cleaning* him.

A porcelain bowl stood on a stool beside her, the water stained with his blood. When he glanced down at his bare torso, he noticed she'd scrubbed off most of it, though a patch remained where one of the scales had pierced his chest. That must've been what knocked him on his ass. It appeared as if his assumptions had been correct—the monsters that he and Malum created weren't average beasts.

Which didn't exactly bode well for him and his confidence.

Mila ran a hand through her short, red hair, her expression remaining one of annoyance. She was glaring at him as though she expected him to speak, to thank her. Maybe he *should* thank her—but his lips stayed sealed.

Without a word, she tossed the bloodied rag into the bowl and began to stand. He should've just let her go, but Darius grasped her wrist once more, the movement surprising even himself. Electricity shot up his arm as they collided.

"Why?" he grated out, loathing that he was reduced to this state. Why would someone who seemed to hate him even more than Margrete take the time to wash him?

Their eyes locked, his blue meeting her lush green.

"It's what my father would've done," she forced out, and this time when she jerked away, he let her. Something shifted over her face, something sour, and she glared down at him. He practically choked on her anger.

"He died because of you," she breathed, her voice softer than a falling tear. But she didn't need to raise it—venom laced each word.

She referred to the island and the trials. Her father must've been one of the unlucky few who perished. Shade had reported something about a bridge burning up in the second trial. A man failed to make the leap of faith. That had to have been this woman's father.

If that were the case, then Darius definitely didn't understand why she would help him now. He effectively orchestrated her father's demise.

He usually wouldn't have cared, so the onslaught of shame shocked him.

"Some aren't strong enough to undergo the trials," Darius replied stiffly, though even to him, his words sounded hollow. He found himself eager for a response.

Mila shook her head. "For a god who has endured thousands and thousands of years of life, you've learned absolutely nothing, have you?" She marched to the door, her hand hovering over the knob. With her back to him, she added, "It is our weaknesses that can be the most precious. And while they have the power to kill us, they're also what makes life worth the struggle. My father—Grant, by the way—would've told me to show mercy, especially to someone undeserving of it. He would've told me that if I acted out on my rage, I would be no better than the subject of my temper."

Darius went utterly still.

She peered over her shoulder, and suddenly, he forgot how to inhale. This creature was all hard edges and rage, a mortal who had always known her own mind and freely spoke it. Even at her own risk. And here she stood, scolding a god, her pointed chin lifted proudly.

"I will never forgive you for what you did to Grant, or to my fallen friends, but I will say this..." She narrowed her eyes into slits. "I feel pity for you. Pity that you don't understand what it is to feel anything other than hatred. I'd say I hope you learn to release that anger, but I'm not sure you're deserving of that gift."

With that, she twisted the knob and left Darius alone.

SOMETIME LATER, THE CABIN DOOR OPENED ONCE MORE.

Darius felt no pain as he angled his head to see who approached. All of his wounds had healed, and his power had been replenished by deep rest. He should've told Margrete not to exert herself before they leaped overboard, but to be honest, he hadn't expected her to expel so much power in the first place. She was far too young a goddess to have been capable of such a feat.

Standing at the threshold, leaning against the post, stood Atlas.

He felt an odd pang of disappointment at the sight of her—he'd secretly expected someone else.

"Get out," she said. "You've healed, and if you want sleep, you'll find it out there. You hardly deserve to steal Mila's bed. She's been too good to you as it is." She cocked her head to where a few hammocks swung by the supplies.

Atlas wasn't wrong. Mila had been *kind*, in the only way the snarky redhead could be kind. Darius was still reeling over waking with her above him. He briefly wondered where she was now. Her biting words were a distraction, albeit a painful one.

"Any day now," Atlas grumbled, her muscled frame tense.

Darius sighed before lifting off the cot. The chill night air felt divine against his exposed chest, but he'd have to recover another shirt. He was a gentleman, after all, and going shirtless was hardly appropriate.

"Goodnight, warrior," he said, smiling as he brushed past Atlas. She would be the hardest to crack, but he didn't have a doubt he could do it if he applied himself. Not that he would. Atlas didn't interest him in the slightest. He found her dull, even if her loyalty to her king was impressive.

As he passed into the storage room, he spotted Bay sleeping in the hammock in the far corner. And hovering above him, his body, nothing but a flickering shadow, stood the Azantian king. He didn't tear his focus from his slumbering friend, and instead of rage dancing in his gaze, Darius found only affection. It utterly confused him.

Bay had essentially been the one to drive in the knife. To end his life. And yet the king hovered over him, watching his friend as he slept. Like a dark guardian.

"You and I need to talk," the king said quietly, not raising his eyes.

Darius groaned. All he wished to do was settle into his hammock before they encountered any more beasts. His magic told him they were near, and if they didn't come upon them tomorrow, they certainly would find them the day after.

Bash jerked his head to the stairs and walked away without another word. Darius begrudgingly followed, though he clenched his fists at how the king commanded him. *He* was the god, not the dead mortal. Maybe he'd have to remind him of that fact, and pushing his buttons brought Darius much pleasure.

"Where's Margrete?" Darius asked when they were on deck, alone with the moon and stars bearing witness from above.

"Resting," the king said tersely, his nostrils flaring. He marched over to the rail and gazed out to the sea. "She fell asleep shortly after she hauled your body over the side of the ship."

Mila hadn't lied then. Margrete truly had saved him. Well, not *saved*, but she didn't leave him there. He eventually would have woken, though he would have been pissed to find himself in the middle of the sea.

"The deal you made." Bash turned to him. He was getting right to the point then.

Darius shrugged a shoulder, a smirk on his lips. "What about it?"

"End it," he demanded. "You and I both know she made it under duress."

"A deal is still a deal. You saw her tattoo, I presume?"

In all honesty, Darius had been dying to see the mark he'd left on her, but he didn't press. She wouldn't have told him anyway, let alone *showed* him.

Bash was already pale, but Darius swore he went a shade lighter. "The lilies," he gritted out. "Yeah, I saw them."

Lilies. How interesting.

"Pretty, aren't they?" Darius goaded, knowing full well he was being a bastard to have implied he'd seen them with his own eyes. What could he say? The king brought out that side of him.

"They'll be gone soon enough," Bash nearly growled.

Darius swallowed down a cruel laugh. "Oh, young king. You understand nothing of such bargains. That tattoo will grace her skin for all eternity. Our lives are tied together now. Until my immortal heart stops, she will be bound to her word." Darius suddenly grew tired of their conversation. There was nothing more to discuss.

His foe sneered, his unmasked rage on open display. "I will spend the rest of my life, however long it may be, finding a way out of it. But if by some chance I fail, do you truly think she'll ever love you for forcing the choice on her?"

Darius suppressed a growl. "She will forget about you eventually. She was mine first."

The king went to raise his fist before he remembered he couldn't do a damned thing to cause Darius pain. With a snarl, he let his arm drop. "Do you even hear yourself? You *had her first?*" He scoffed. "A woman like her isn't something to be owned. Love isn't about ownership or control or manipulation." He started to turn away when he added, "A part of me feels pity for you, god. You think you know what true love is, but the only thing that has filled your heart was pride and possession. To have someone like her return your love freely...well, that's earned, and a gift you'll never be given."

Why was everyone claiming they pitied him? First the redhead and now the king.

Bash left Darius standing there dumbfounded. He'd never been at a loss for words, but he couldn't speak. Hell, he could scarcely breathe. He understood that Margrete's anger hadn't simply vanished, and he suspected it wouldn't for quite some time. Still, he remained confident that she'd learn to love him as she once had all those years ago. So why did the idea of forcing her cause his chest to tighten and his throat to constrict?

He was beginning to regret permitting his emotions free rein.

An hour passed as he tried to convince himself that the king spoke lies, but the longer he argued with himself, the less certain he became. Which was entirely absurd. Just when he planned to head back into the moldy hull and get some rest inside one of the fraying hammocks, a rustling sound greeted his ears. He peered back to the waves, making out the shape of two outstretched wings. The raven made no sound as it reached the vessel, finding a perch on the wooden banister. In its gnarled claw, it carried a single wooden arrow no more than a foot and a half in length.

"And who might you be?" he asked, though he already knew the answer.

Tied to its leg with a forest green ribbon, was a thick rolled-up piece of parchment. Carefully, he took the small arrow in his hold and undid the package. Darius then freed the bird, who took off with a mighty flap of its onyx wings.

A favor for a favor. The next time you see my face, I'll claim it, and I expect you to stand up and do right by your title.

The note was unsigned, but this could've come from one deity alone.

Brielle.

She had a knack for weapons, often creating the most lethal of defenses from her sprawling woods. Darius lifted the featherlight arrow and brought the tip to his nose. He sniffed.

Instantly, his magic recoiled, almost vanishing entirely.

Fuck.

This wasn't simply an arrow with a head sharper than any mortal blade...no, it was poisoned. Poisoned with something he didn't recognize, and Darius knew every toxin known to man.

The question he couldn't answer was why she gave it to him in the first place, and why she might one day require a favor.

Those unanswered questions didn't stop him from curling his fingers tightly around the gift. He wasn't one to turn down a favor, no matter what the cost.

CHAPTER TWENTY-FIVE

BASH

Bᴀꜱʜ ᴡᴀɴᴛᴇᴅ ᴛᴏ ʙʀᴇᴀᴋ Dᴀʀɪᴜꜱ ᴡɪᴛʜ ʜɪꜱ ʙᴀʀᴇ ʜᴀɴᴅꜱ.

It had been a constant desire of his to harm the god, but after their little chat, he'd come to the realization that Darius couldn't be reasoned with. Only actions would shatter his sneering façade.

He glided down the steps and to the cabin he shared with Margrete, hoping she was awake. She'd been exhausted after saving Darius, who'd bled all over the ship. The god hadn't deserved her sympathy. If only they could've left him in the middle of nowhere.

When Bash had seen the bluish-black blood trailing in her wake, he had believed it to be hers and he all but leaped over the ship's side. But what good could he do in his state? Margrete had been right—the sooner they found Minthe, the better.

Bay had been the one to ease her on deck, his arms wrapped around her protectively. For just a moment she'd leaned into him, nuzzling his chest. But then she drew away, sprawling on the planks where she caught her breath, adjusting to the fresh air. Before Bash could reach her, she'd collapsed, unconscious.

Atlas, along with a scowling Mila and Dani, lugged Darius to the larger cabin below, leaving Bay with Margrete. He'd scooped her up and into his arms, wetness lining his lower lids. Yet he never let one tear fall. He merely clutched her to his chest and soothed back her tangled hair before bringing her to bed and tucking the covers up to her chin.

She'd been asleep ever since, and Bash had only left her side to check on a sleeping Bay. When he'd felt Darius's presence, he confronted him without hesitation, practically begging him to release Margrete from his curse. It didn't matter that his pride had gone to shit; he would've gotten onto his knees before Darius if it meant he'd let her go. All right, perhaps not on his knees. Bash had his limits.

Margrete's door was left ajar, leaving ample room for him to slip through. He paused at the threshold, his temper still rearing its head. He didn't want her to see him this way.

Fucking Darius. Bash knew better than to allow his taunts to sink in, but he was still a man, and he couldn't help his jealousy.

"Bash?" Margrete's voice drifted over to him from where she lay beneath the blankets. "That you?"

He sighed. She was awake, and right on time. The midnight hour approached.

"How are you feeling?" he asked, ambling to the bed. A single torch lamp had been lit beside her, its russet-orange glow casting dark circles beneath her eyes.

Margrete lifted, scooting her knees close to her chest. She appeared so small, so frail. Bash clenched his hands. *Soon,* he thought. All he desired was to hold her tonight and rub her back, something he found she enjoyed when insomnia struck.

"I can't get these memories out of my head," she admitted softly, her head still lowered.

Bash hitched a breath. The memories of when she was with Darius.

"It's not your doing," he said. "And it's certainly not your fault."

She tilted her chin, gazing just beyond him. "I see this different side to him, and I know the person I'd been all those years ago had felt love."

Bash's gut wrenched painfully, but he remained silent.

"It had been real, I can't deny it, but I'm stuck somewhere between feeling sorry for him and hating him, and it's messing with my head." She clutched her temples, groaning.

Just then the air shifted and rippled, and midnight arrived with a fresh breeze that cooled Bash's skin. He shivered, his body becoming somewhat his once more.

Slowly, he sank to the bed. She flinched as the cot shifted beneath him, her eyes shooting up in surprise.

"I hadn't realized what time it was."

"It's all right, princess. Just talk to me."

Bash scooted closer, positioning himself so his back rested on the cabin wall. Gently, he draped her over him, her head resting on his chest.

"I'm right here," he murmured. "Nothing you can say will frighten me away."

She remained quiet for some time, and Bash's insecurities couldn't help but churn. Would she eventually be happier with the god? Had she risked too much—

"I believe that a soul can change and grow," she began. He went completely still. "And as Wryn, I'd known nothing. I'd been a new soul, and Darius had been the only other being I'd ever come in contact with. While love eventually bloomed, I'm no longer that woman who'd given her heart to him. I've become someone entirely different, and I don't say that in a negative way, even if there is much I'd change about myself."

Bash made a disapproving grunting sound, and she scoffed.

"What I feel for you goes beyond destiny or right or wrong. My soul recognized yours immediately, and while it took us time to realize it ourselves, I've never felt more at ease in the presence of another. So at home. Even when I returned to the island and to Darius, there was never a comparable sensation."

Bash ran his hands through her tangled curls, the scent of salt clinging to every strand. She sighed in contentment, melting against him.

"I understand if you're conflicted—"

"I'm not," she said firmly, angling her head up to meet his eyes. "I've never once doubted you or us. Ever." She lifted a hand to cup his cheek. "You're my greatest friend, Bash. The person I cannot wait to wake up next to and start every day with. And no other man could ever steal my heart the way you have. Nor do I want them to. It's yours."

Relief spread through him, warming his chilled skin.

"This will be our greatest challenge, princess," he whispered, stroking her cheek, his fingers trailing down to her jaw. "And you were right," he began, and she stilled. "I do need to return to my body, regardless of my fears. I want to finish this at your side."

Margrete relaxed, settling back down on his empty chest. She grasped his shirt, her tiny hand aglow with magic. Bash didn't believe she was aware of it.

Soon, her breathing evened out, and she fell back under sleep's spell. But Bash spent the next hour holding her body to his. She centered his tumultuous thoughts, bestowing him with blissful peace.

Bash wasn't sure when he fell asleep alongside her, but he dreamt of the days that would follow, imagining two thrones in a chamber full of sea glass and gold.

He pictured the ending and the beginning of a story he hoped he'd be alive to take part in.

CHAPTER TWENTY-SIX

MARGRETE

BASH HAD ALREADY LEFT THEIR CABIN BY THE TIME MARGRETE woke.

But she wasn't alone.

Standing beside the porthole stood the last person she expected—Dani.

"I know you're awake," she said in that airy voice of hers. Margrete smiled, pushing up from the cot and resting her back against the wall. She felt better than yesterday, her body and her magic replenished.

"What is it, Dani?" she asked. While happy to see the young woman, she was surprised by her visit. They weren't nearly as close as she and Atlas...or Bay. She planned to speak with him today, especially since memories were flooding back from yesterday after she'd hauled Darius on deck. In her confused state, she still recalled how Bay had held her and carried her to her cabin. Before he left, after tucking her in, he'd placed a tender kiss on her brow.

She had to let go of her anger or she'd lose one of the most important people in her life.

Dani shifted toward her with enviable grace, floating across the planks to plop down on the thin mattress.

"You still have the key in your possession, right?"

Margrete cocked her head in question. Right now, it was hidden in her jacket, which she kept on her at all times. Since they'd left the Underworld, it hadn't hummed with the same heady magic, leading her to believe whatever it unlocked belonged in the realm of the dead.

"Yes, I have it. But what does that have to do—"

"Good. Keep it close and don't let anyone get their hands on it." Dani's blue eyes turned hard. "I sensed it last night...calling out. I thought I heard it when we were in the Underworld, but it's since grown muffled. Even still, I grasped its power, lying dormant."

"It wasn't just me, then," Margrete mumbled. "I thought I was slowly losing my head."

"You're not," Dani said. "But I came to you this morning because of a dream I had last night..." Margrete leaned forward, eager for her words. Dani had to be a seer or something of that ilk—there was no more doubt. "I dreamt of a book covered in blood and reeking of death. That key was beside it."

So it didn't open the portal to the Underworld.

"And the tears trapped in the orb?" Margrete pressed.

"I can merely assume they're what we suspected."

"Lovely." Margrete sighed. But the mention of the book stood out to her. "Dani, do you remember the day we arrived in the Underworld? The chamber we were first brought into?" Dani dipped her chin. "Well, I saw a green tome there, right in the center of the hall, bound together by a golden lock. Maybe that's what the key opens."

In truth, the key could open any number of doors or boxes or treasures. But that book held importance. It wouldn't be displayed in the throne room if it didn't.

"I'll think on that," Dani murmured, the muscles in her neck growing taut. When Margrete raised a brow, she sighed. "I've been...practicing," she admitted, shyly lowering her chin. "If I focus on an object long enough now, I can usually see it in my dreams. I'll attempt the same tonight. It started on Azantian last summer. All of my visions did. But since Surria's island, they've become...intense." A rosy blush spread across her cheeks, and Margrete realized this was the longest conversation they'd ever had.

Carefully, Margrete clasped both of Dani's hands. "Thank you for sharing, and thank you for speaking to me about this. I imagine it must be scary for you, these new visions and dreams." The young woman lifted her head, and a hesitant smile curved her lips. "I want you to come to me again if you see anything else. *Anything* else. Such dreams are invaluable."

After everything she'd experienced on Azantian and thereafter, magic was the truth of her new world. And if Dani had the gift of sight, like Nerissa, it could be instrumental to their mission.

Dani squeezed her hands, surprising her.

"Just promise me one thing, Margrete. Don't forget who you are. It can be tempting to give in to all of this, I'm sure, but you'll find nothing but darkness in such depths of power. Remember what you're fighting for."

With that, Dani rose and gave a slight bow. She slipped from the cabin, leaving Margrete to wonder just how obvious her transformation had become. Because she *had* changed, and it was no longer easy to ignore the voices inside of her, yearning for power. *Begging* for supremacy. Her skin itched at the notion of holding it in her palms again. And that wasn't a good thing.

Margrete had stepped off that invisible cliff, and now, she prayed she'd land among the waves.

A DAY PASSED BEFORE DARIUS APPROACHED MARGRETE. ODDLY enough, he'd steered clear. Until now.

"There's a beast headed our way," Darius said without prelude.

Margrete had just dressed and left in search of Bay, but once again, it appeared as if their conversation would have to wait. Bay had made a point to make himself scarce.

"Which one?" she asked, halting before the steps leading above deck.

Darius leaned against the wall, arms crossed, outwardly looking at ease and unaffected. Margrete saw right through him. Something dour weighed on his mind, and his usual mask bore many cracks today.

"I sensed a pack of three, but there's another closer. It must've sniffed us out. Well, you and me, to be exact. I hardly would expect them to change course for a mortal."

"They see us as the enemy? Even if *you* created them?"

Darius shoved off from the wall. "Of course we're the enemy. My brother and I may have given them life, but we are the only beings with a chance at destroying them. They're much cleverer than one might assume."

"I so adore fighting monsters with a brain. As if we need another challenge," Margrete bristled. "Well, which creature is it?" She waved her hands impatiently. "You never answered my question."

Darius brushed past her, headed for the stairs. She grimaced but was left no choice except to follow.

Once on deck, every eye of the crew drifted their way. Bash had been in deep conversation with Atlas, but upon Margrete's arrival, he snapped to attention. His stare seared into Darius with a venomous hatred before settling on her and softening.

Darius raised his voice so the others would hear above the winds.

"The Eliam is coming." No one spoke or appeared to recognize the name. "It's fashioned after the squid, although it's even larger than the Collossious, and its ink is exceptionally deadly. Meaning," he turned to Margrete, "I wouldn't suggest jumping into the water this time."

"Yay," Mila sighed, striding over with purpose. Margrete noted how Darius's gaze lingered on the sailor for a beat too long, his lips pressed together into a cruel grimace. "Well, go on then," Mila demanded. "Tell us the plan, almighty ones."

Margrete hadn't seen Bash move, and chills raced down her spine when his deep voice whispered into her ear.

"We should get the mortals off the ship and away from the battle," he said, his worry making his tone darken. "If you can't go into the sea, then the creature could very well capsize us and poison the waters."

"You are terrible at whispering, my king." Atlas cocked her head, her Azantian hearing picking up every word. Bash groaned. "We aren't leaving the ship. We'll stay and help in any way we can, regardless of us being *mere* mortals."

"We're Azantians," Bay's proclamation rang in the air as he walked up the stairs behind them, his boots striking the wood with a renewed purpose. Margrete twisted around, her pulse racing. She took an involuntary step forward before forcing herself to still.

"We have no clue how our bodies would react if we fell into the water," Bay continued with all the calm of the warrior he was. Atlas righted her posture, and Mila tilted her chin. Even Dani's face brightened at the sight of him.

They respected Bay. His steady voice had been missing in their lives when they needed it the most. Her grudge was to blame.

"Forgive him, princess," Bash murmured, this time too quietly for the crew to hear. Margrete swallowed thickly. "He protected what I cherish most in this world, and for that, I will owe him more than my life."

With Bash at her side, the promise of victory on the horizon, Margrete grimaced and then...looked deeply into Bay's eyes.

They were somber yet shrewd, and he stared back at her as if the entire world should crumble if she glanced away. The ice around her heart cracked, and she felt every ounce of shame radiate off her friend, silently begging for her forgiveness.

Enough was enough.

Margrete mouthed two words. Two words that she meant with every fiber of her being.

It's okay.

And it was. Or it *would* be.

Bay released an audible sigh, and his shoulders rolled back, the weight that had been placed upon them easing. She swore color returned to his cheeks, and he sucked in a deep breath as if for the first time in days.

Atlas rested her hand on his shoulder. "I agree with Bay," she said forcefully, directing a somber grin his way. "Let's hunt this monster down and show it what Azantians are made of."

CHAPTER TWENTY-SEVEN

BASH

Margrete was losing the battle—she was forgiving Bay. Slowly.

Bash couldn't have been happier as he watched the pair exchange a heartfelt look, relaying everything they weren't ready to say aloud.

At a time like this, he'd have slipped his arms around her waist and kissed her temple. He would've rubbed her back or stroked her hair—anything to soothe her frayed nerves. Because she still remained on edge, regardless of what transpired with Bay and their wordless conversation.

Of course, Bash could do nothing but hover. Absolutely useless.

"We have ten minutes, I'd say," Darius announced, his eyes flickering out to the waves. "Prepare as well as you can." To Margrete, he added, "Let's prepare in our own way. You have much to learn about controlling your magic. Namely, *not* releasing it all at once like yesterday."

Margrete glared, but she gave him a curt nod. "I'll meet you by the stern."

Darius sauntered away, but not before shooting a cocky grin at Mila, who had both hands on her hips. If anyone had the guts to stand up to Darius—besides Margrete—it would be Mila. Bash hadn't missed the way the sea god paid her extra attention, seeming to go out of his way to piss her off. To deliver her an arrogant wink or a pretentious smirk. It riled Mila up, and Darius, for some reason, took immense pleasure in that.

Margrete eased as close to Bash as she could. Sometimes he still felt solid, whole. If not for the way his skin shimmered and flickered, or the grating tingles shooting up his frame at all times, he might've believed he was alive once more.

"I saw that, with Bay," he whispered to Margrete. An inch separated them, but it might as well have been a hundred.

She rolled her eyes, trying to look stern. She failed miserably.

"I'm working on the forgiving part. It hasn't come easily," she admitted. "I still love him, I just keep picturing his hands covered in your blood whenever I look at him—"

Shouts rented the air, cutting her off. Margrete whirled around at the same time Darius called her name.

"Quit flirting and get over here!" he yelled. "I hate to admit when I'm wrong but...yes, I was horribly wrong. This one travels much quicker than I anticipated!" His voice had become muffled by the waves, which were churning wildly, building with every second. "Quick lesson, Margrete. When you release your magic, do it *slowly*."

"That didn't help at all!" she screamed back, but she was already sprinting to peer over the railing.

The surf crashed against the sides of the ship, and in the distance Bash made out the flash of gleaming snow-white skin breaching the surface.

The Eliam had arrived.

"Fuck me," Mila said, rushing to the railing, dagger in hand. Bay sprinted below deck, a whirl of blond hair and limbs, and Dani proudly faced the approaching beast with no hint of emotion on her face.

A beast that was slowly slithering out of the waves.

Giant tentacles whipped into the air, slim but deadly. They rose higher and higher, and Bash's heart would've stopped if he owned a working one.

A bulbous head surfaced, a pair of garnet eyes gleaming in the rays of the sun. If Bash was as naive as he'd been before Surria's island, he might've believed such a creature could be bested. Especially by a ship full of Azantian sailors and warriors.

He knew better now.

The creature swam at a leisurely pace, its speed reducing to a crawl. Those eerie eyes narrowed in on their small vessel, and Bash could've sworn a spark of excitement flashed across its bloody irises.

"Margrete!" Darius grasped her shoulders, and even in such chaos, Bash gritted his teeth in annoyance. He needed to cease touching her before he lost his damned mind.

"Can you sense its poison?" Darius asked raggedly, and she nodded. "It's grown even more potent over the years." The god ran a nervous hand through his hair. For once it wasn't all meticulously combed in place.

Yet as much as he adored watching the egotistical god fall apart, it didn't make Bash feel better about their situation. If Darius was anxious, then they truly were in trouble.

"It doesn't look nearly as bad as the Collossious," Atlas observed mechanically, assessing the target in her typical detached way.

"I highly disagree," Dani replied, pupils dilated in terror. "Looks can be deceiving."

Bay reappeared from below deck. He carried with him a handful of spears, the rest of his body strapped with smaller blades.

He tossed the Azantians a spear each, his grip tightening on his own until his knuckles shone white.

"It's going to capsize us first, and then deliver its poison." Darius lifted his palms, his magic unfurling, wisps of blue emanating from his hands. "The problem is its skin...it's made of the toughest material I could create, and even my own magic hardly affects it. It would've taken Malum and I both at our best to destroy it."

"*You* were foolish enough to create this one?" Margrete asked, snarling. "But of course you did."

"Strike for its heart. It's located in its belly, which lies just before its tentacles," Darius instructed, ignoring the scowls sent his way. "The skin surrounding it isn't nearly as resilient. A thankful construction error on my part due to time constraints."

The creature dipped beneath the sea, vanishing entirely.

Bash watched as Bay hopped onto the rail, spear in hand while he scanned the surf. His brave friend scoured the swells, sweat banding across his brow.

Silence. Torturous silence ensued.

Suddenly, Bay sent a blade flying—

Directly into the Eliam's belly.

Three white tentacles reared into the air, the beast screeching. Bash grinned, proud that Bay had struck close to its supposed heart. But the moment of pride didn't last long.

The creature thrust forward. It swam toward them, its arms outstretched, preparing to enfold the smaller boat in its grip and shatter them all. Bash's hands itched with the need for a weapon of his own, to do anything but watch as his friends took aim and unleashed their spears.

They all fell short, the sharpened tips landing inches away from their target.

As Bay scrambled below for their reserves, Margrete discharged a burst of magic, her palms ablaze with violent energy. Deep cobalt and yellow flared, her light competing with that of the sun. Loose strands whipped at her enraged face, her lips thinned in determination.

Darius joined her at her side, his own powers surging toward the advancing foe.

The creature didn't even pause. It took every hit they delivered and continued its movements, its slippery tentacles reaching for them, those bloody eyes focused on its prey.

Why weren't their combined powers working? Bash knew what Margrete was capable of and had witnessed it with his own eyes. And with Darius? This shouldn't have been as difficult as he'd believed.

The beast let loose a shrill noise that scraped across his insides. It was nearly on them, its sinewy arms feet from the *Mare Deus*—

A bolt of lightning struck.

It crashed down from a cloudless sky, colliding into the beast's impenetrable body with a chilling *crack*. Steam fizzled as the monster flailed, its arms lowering while black ink pooled around it, darkening the once blue waters. Even in his form, Bash could clearly smell the bitterness in the air, its released poison. Goosebumps rose as he looked up...

The outline of a woman hovered above, a halo of golden hair floating around her blurred face. Another bolt radiated from her body, hitting the thrashing Eliam, the smell of its burnt hide permeating the breeze.

Darius cursed. "I'd rather we faced the Eliam than *her*," he muttered beneath his breath.

The woman in the skies descended, dropping down gracefully, her frame held aloft by a gust of fragrant wind that battled with the stench of death.

Margrete lowered her hands, though they continued to pulse with light. She eased backward, closer to Bash, standing just before him as if in protection.

Perhaps he'd need it.

Because the woman in the sky was none other than Surria herself.

CHAPTER TWENTY-EIGHT

MARGRETE

THE GODDESS OF THE WIND AND SKY DESCENDED FROM HER REALM like a feather, her elegant limbs gracefully connecting with the wooden planks of the *Mare Deus*.

Her assistance—while needed—grated on Margrete. She'd come down like a savior, offering the extra magic they required to slay the Eliam. The question was why.

Margrete couldn't help but steal a look at Darius. His stare narrowed on his mother, his features cool, but it was the way he curled his right hand that gained her attention. As if feeling her, Darius went still, compelling his hand to remain open, forcing himself into the role of the unbothered god he pretended to be.

"Mother," Darius said, a too-bright smile on his face. "How lovely it is you've decided to help us on our little mission."

Today, Surria wore a white silk button-up, although her trousers were a crisp, dark blue. Her hair fell to her shoulders, her winds ceasing. She raised a thin, white-blonde brow at her son.

"I was just checking in when I heard the most awful commotion." She swept her eyes across the gathered Azantians. "It seems you're lucky

I showed up when I did. Though I am slightly disappointed you couldn't defeat your own creation, Darius. I thought you were stronger than that."

Surria shook her head, and Margrete noted how strained Darius's smile had become. His lips twitched with effort.

"Thank you, goddess," Bay stepped forward, ever the diplomat. His smile didn't even appear feigned. Gods, he was good. "We're so very grateful for your help. And you're right, you were just in time." Bay waited a beat before rising.

"Ah, a reasonable man," Surria said, beaming. "Glad to see not all mortals are so foolish and simple-minded."

Bay's teeth were on display now, and he scoffed playfully as if they were old friends sharing gossip. "Can we offer you anything, goddess?" he asked tightly.

Surria waved an idle hand. "I was planning on staying for dinner, but these conditions simply won't do. I would've pictured Darius on a much finer vessel than this...relic." With a flick of her delicate wrist, she brought about a gust of wind. It pushed against the sails, catapulting the ship forward. Margrete stumbled in place, nearly faceplanting. Goddess or not, grace wasn't in her arsenal.

"She seems like a delight," Bash whispered as Surria slipped her arm through her son's, leading him away for what appeared to be a not-so-pleasant chat.

"Surria is here for a reason," Margrete hissed. Bay joined them, falling into place at her side. It felt right to have him there, and slowly, more of her walls crumbled. "I don't think she actually wants us to fulfill Halio's bargain. She sees me as a distraction."

"Well, she certainly lent us a hand, regardless of her motives," Bash said, looking out to the waves. The Eliam had been terrifying. If they'd struggled to beat it, then how would they successfully slay more? She didn't wish to ruminate on that dour thought for too long.

Bay let out a deep breath. "About that...I already sent a missive back in Maribella," he admitted. "I figured we might need a hand."

She knew exactly where he'd sent it. To Azantian and Adrian.

Instantly she thought of home, of the island, of Birdie. She hoped her sister wasn't wracked with worry.

"Good," Bash said, relieved. "But I want my body back before I greet my men."

It didn't take much to glean he was embarrassed by his state, and Margrete found she understood his concerns. It would be bad enough if they glimpsed his transformed appearance, but to be nothing more than a wavering image? Bash would lose all credibility, and panic could ensue. If it hadn't already.

"I told Adrian where we were headed, so hopefully he knows where to find us should we not be able to send out another message." Slowly, Bay brought his sharp green eyes to Margrete. "In the meantime, you should work with Darius and hone your skills. As much as we all would rather plot his demise."

He was reaching out, offering her his hand.

All she had to do was take it.

Margrete swallowed thickly. "Perfect," she said, the word tasting odd on her tongue. Awkward and stiff.

But they both understood it would take time to get back to the way things were.

Bay's lips curved. He turned on his heel and slipped beside Atlas, likely to relay his orders.

"Thank you, princess," Bash spoke into her ear. "You *almost* convinced me."

She sighed. "It's getting better if that helps anything, but—"

The winds shifted abruptly once more, sending Margrete careening forward. Bash cursed, instinctively moving to grasp her arm. His hand went through her, as expected. But then warm fingers wrapped around her, tugging her back upright. She found her savior behind her, his eyes stormy and remarkably melancholy. The blue in Darius's irises had grown muted in a manner of minutes, the turquoise blotted out entirely, and the speckles of gold she'd seen were now absent.

"Careful, darling," he said, his voice missing its usual playful lilt. "Don't want you to tumble overboard before we reach Zandar."

"Zandar?" She'd never heard of such a place.

Darius nodded solemnly, ignoring Bash's icy glare. "Surria's home in the sky. It means *twilight* in the old tongue."

"I thought the gods usually stayed below?" Bash asked through his teeth, his hand shifting to his empty sheath.

"As if my mother is just any god."

APPARENTLY, ZANDAR MET THEM HALFWAY.

As the *Mare Deus* raced across the swells, propelled by Surria's winds, the island in the sky she'd created emerged from the clouds. They were given no explanation when the goddess lifted her hands in the air, her palms closing into tight fists. The forceful breeze ceased.

"Ah, home away from home." Surria sighed, smiling shrewdly at Margrete. There was something in that stare that reeked of foul intentions, no matter how warm her tone had sounded.

"Holy gods," Mila gasped, drawing her attention from Surria and back to the sky.

Bash hovered beside Margrete as fluffy white clouds sailed forth, blotting out the midday sun. Squinting, she made out just the barest hint of a fortress, or what appeared to be a fortress. There were high walls and austere angles, and nothing about it felt as if it belonged against the backdrop of whimsical blue. It certainly didn't feel like a home. It felt like a prison.

Before Margrete questioned how exactly they all would *get* to Zandar, powerful winds lifted her from the planks. She hung a foot in the air...as did every member of their crew, Bash included. She opened her mouth to scream when Surria thrust her arms forward—

She went flying, they all did, carried on winds reeking of potent magic, the scent of honeysuckle faint in the air.

Margrete gasped, floundering as she tried and failed to right herself. Yet no matter how hard she struggled, this magic battled with hers, not recognizing its energy; it was far from her experience with

Darius. She peered over at him now, the god an unfeeling statue as he was lifted.

Bash hissed in alarm, but he handled their ascent better than she did —as did the other Azantians, for that matter. Dani screeched, Mila had her blade out and ready, whipping it at harmless clouds, and Atlas and Bay had managed to grasp one another in their arms. She noticed how tightly Atlas clutched Bay, and she worried when he turned a shade paler.

Be on your guard.

The warning whispered across her mind, the voice more of an ominous growl. *Damn it.* She'd foolishly forgotten to rebuild the barriers keeping Darius out of her head. The problem was she wasn't sure how she'd blocked him to begin with.

Why is she truly here? she asked, Zandar approaching fast.

A sigh sounded, and then, *She's probably going to attempt to kill you tonight.*

Are you fucking serious? Margrete couldn't help the scowl she shot him, uncaring if watchful eyes noted her every move. *Why are we going with her then? Why allow it?*

One thing you'll discover about my mother is that she never offers a choice. His somber tone grew impossibly bleak. *The best thing we can do is play along and defend ourselves should the need arise. Which it will. And whatever you do, do not find yourself alone with her.*

Darius hadn't even glanced her way, but she tasted his despair as if it were her own. She blamed it on their bond. Or maybe she was beginning to see him more as a person and less as an unfeeling bastard. Margrete hadn't accepted any other explanation for his cruelty, but the image of her father replayed over and over again in her thoughts.

Abuse such as she'd experienced would've surely warped her mind over time. And Darius had struggled against his mother for an unspeakable number of years. He'd learned it from her, and such cruelty, Margrete believed, was taught. The question was, did Darius deserve a chance at redemption?

She hastily brought her stare to Bash, who rose beside her. His attention was trained on her, his gaze penetrating. A deep frown marred his brow.

He reached out a hand, even if they couldn't touch, allowing it to rest between them. She understood his meaning well. Margrete swallowed thickly and gave him a pained smile. She mouthed three words, ones he returned.

Bash's arm dropped to his sides when they reached the first cloud. Margrete gasped as she was placed upon its surface, her lips parting in a scream. When she didn't immediately fall through, she forced her mouth closed, swallowing her fear. It seemed to burn all the way down her throat.

The others collided onto the silken platform, though they let out a range of sounds, from sighs to piercing shrieks. The latter had come from Atlas, which shocked her.

Darius touched down with unnerving grace, appearing nothing short of bored.

"Welcome," Surria intoned from somewhere above. Margrete lifted a palm to her head and squinted against the harsh sun, finding a pair of imposing gates opened to the goddess's domain.

Surria dropped soundlessly before them. "Now, if you'll follow me," she chirped happily. *Too* happily.

Margrete exchanged worried glances with Bash, who clenched his jaw so hard, she feared he'd crack it, even in his ethereal form. Up here his body appeared less solid, and she realized in horror that she could see clearly through him when the clouds shifted.

"You can do this. And with Darius here, he won't allow anything to happen to us," he whispered as they trailed across the sky. They rose at an incline, bringing them to a solid wall of gray stone veined with silver, the gates blocking the entrance to the inner courtyard, and a pair of heavy-looking pewter doors that led inside.

"She could turn on her own son," Margrete argued. "But it's more than that. I don't feel strong enough." She allowed the crew to drift farther ahead. "I couldn't even kill the enlarged squid."

She was a joke and a failure, and the prospect of them facing any more beasts caused her to lose a shred of her hope.

Bash bristled. "Do you have any idea how ridiculous you sound right now?" She twisted to him. "You are the spark that ignites the flame. The diamond that shatters steel. You are insufferable and stunning, and absolutely the most powerful creature I've ever beheld." Bash's brows rose in exasperation. "You have no idea how I see you. How *others* see you. You are clueless, and that needs to end, right here and now, before we enter those gates and face whatever danger lurks beyond. But do not, for one *single* heartbeat, doubt that you are capable of being that single spark that sets fire to the entire world. Because you, Margrete Wood, are, and have *always* been, a force no human or god could triumph over."

Margrete lost the ability to breathe. The look in her king's eyes burned fiercely, and a pleasant heat crept through her body, surrounding her fearful heart and encasing it in a barrier of the hope she'd lost, and the hope he'd just now returned to her.

She had never loved him more.

"Is that how you truly see me?" she asked in a whisper.

"If you even have to ask me after that brilliant speech I just gave you, then I can't say anything else to persuade you." A subtle smile curled his lips, and she melted, as she always did. Damn him and that lone dimple. It would be her downfall.

"Hurry up!"

Margrete tore herself from Bash as Surria called her name from the gates, beckoning her and the Azantian king with a poised flick of her wrist.

Before she closed the distance, Margrete looked at Bash one final time.

"The only opinion I value is yours, because if that is how you see me, you'd be stunned by just how magnificent I find you, pirate. I may be the spark, but you are the oil that gives my fire life."

She turned before he could reply and marched toward the Goddess of the Wind and Sky. With the shrewd eyes of death and a venomous smile masquerading as innocence, Margrete stormed directly through the doors to the kingdom in the heavens.

CHAPTER TWENTY-NINE

DARIUS

HOME.

Well, his childhood home.

After Mother created him and Malum, she decreed they were too young and ignorant to go off on their own. She'd brought them here, to Zandar, her little floating palace of torture. Here, Malum and Darius stayed, confined in these halls, forced to undergo their mother's tutelage. From dusk 'til dawn she imparted her "wisdom," insisting they learn the cruel truth of the world before venturing into it. It had taken Darius centuries, but eventually, he learned it had all been about control—controlling *him.* Surria never desired children—she'd wanted soldiers.

It took him and his brother five hundred years to break free.

And now, Darius had returned.

They entered a courtyard of austere white stones and slick white walls—nothing like the courtyard of color and light of the Underworld. Darius loathed the color white and made a conscious effort to avoid it. White typically symbolized hope, but hope was a lie.

The incorporeal king was pathetic in his attempts to guard Margrete, who reluctantly walked behind Surria. Darius had caught her and Bash exchanging knowing glances on more than one occasion, and sometimes, Margrete would subtly shake her head or offer him a crooked smile.

They had that *way* about them. They could speak a language crafted with only their eyes. Darius was surprised when he wasn't immediately disgusted by the sight. Instead, he found his attention narrowing in on the imposing walls that climbed around them all, too on edge to *not* inspect his prison.

His throat constricted.

Relax, he scolded, furious that after all these years he was allowing the goddess to get to him. He had removed her claws long ago, and regressing wasn't an option.

Margrete went stiff as a board in front of him, her hands slightly trembling. He couldn't tell if it was from nerves or rage, but in the end, she forced one foot in front of the other. Darius swore at one point, she was about to glance his way before deciding against it.

He inwardly cursed. Had she *heard* him just then, thinking of his childhood? Could she sense his apprehension, his doubts, and the fears he thought he'd buried? He checked his barriers and found them to be intact. But when she *finally* snuck a peek, those haunting blue eyes locking on his, he had a suspicion that she'd gotten through.

Fuck.

Surria waved open the twin doors leading to her empty palace. She preferred it that way, claiming, "Why would I want imbeciles at my beck and call when I can do it better?" What she truly meant was that she'd force her sons to answer her calls and make *them* attend to her every whim. She'd promptly returned to the Underworld once he and Malum left, turning her sights to new pawns she could play with—her fellow gods.

"Sorry for the lack of preparation," Surria began, studying the grand foyer of white marble—and little else. This place felt more like a stony box than a true home. "If you'll join me in the sitting room, I'll summon a few helpers of mine for assistance with tonight's meal."

Helpers.

Shit. Darius suspected what his mother's game was now. Her helpers were often *his*. And a certain red-haired nymph had left him high and dry when Margrete shattered the island. Would Surria dare bring Shade here? While a useful spy, Shade was too often unpredictable and left Darius's skin itching whenever he encountered the nymph. Not that she hadn't tried to seduce him over the years. She was a cunning thing and probably saw him as a tool to be used.

Darius promised he'd belong to no one again. Unless that someone was Margrete. His missing half. The one person who had the chance of earning his trust. Who wouldn't betray him.

He glanced at his mother while the crew glided through another set of doors to the sitting room. Surria caught his eyes and held them, and anyone who didn't know any better might believe the grin she bestowed him was a loving one.

Darius saw straight through the perfect veneer. Her canines poked into her red-painted lips, the shade remarkably similar to human blood. He recognized how she cocked her head, assessing his every move, and he knew that her crinkled eyes held scrutiny rather than joy.

This was going to be a long evening indeed.

This was yet another dinner from his childhood. Another silent-filled night where his mother's scrutiny hid behind beautifully crafted smiles.

Around the massive dining table that had been built to seat well over two dozen sat the Azantians, Margrete, her ghost king—who'd been situated down the table from her—and of course, Darius. At the head, Surria had taken her place, a dainty napkin resting in the center of her lap. Manners were, after all, invaluable to her above all else.

"So, Margrete," Surria mused, "tell me why my son isn't good enough for you."

Darius briefly squeezed his eyes shut. If she believed she was helping him, she was sorely mistaken.

Margrete, to her credit, showed nothing. Although her king barely held on to his composure. His nostrils flared, and he shot the goddess a warning look that would have seared any mortal alive. Darius wondered how he might react if he was whole, if he'd be foolish enough to go toe to toe with a goddess over a scathing comment directed his lover's way. Love, he knew, often made one foolish. Darius was no exception.

Margrete leaned forward in her seat of honor beside Surria, a cruel smile tilting her lips. "Don't mock me with such a question when you know the answer all too well."

Surria chuckled. "She has claws," she said, approval in her voice. "But past misdeeds aside, why stay with this"—she motioned to Bash, who bared his teeth in warning—"when you know damn well it won't last. You'll live for eternity, and he'll die soon. Why not just skip to the part where you forgive a worried mother and the son who would give up anything for you?"

Bay slammed his glass of wine down onto the empty table. Dinner may not have been served, but it appeared as if they were getting right to the main course of the evening.

"Why did you invite us here?" Bay asked, forgoing his earlier amiable demeanor entirely. At his side, Atlas hummed her agreement, but Dani... she stared at Surria with a question burning in eyes that had grown clouded with sparkling silver.

Odd, Darius thought. He barely took note of the younger woman, but perhaps he should keep his eye on her after all.

"Because she probably wants to kill us all," Mila answered. She shoved up from her seat, resting her hands on the table. "So go on then, get on with it. I'm bored of all these pleasantries." No trace of fear etched her face, and if he looked closely enough, he might've sworn she was excited by the challenge.

Darius *almost* smiled.

Surria raised her crystal glass to her perfectly painted lips and took a long drink. The glass was empty when she lowered it to the table. All the while, Mila glowered, holding steady as his mother tested her patience.

"I plan on no such thing, young one," Surria said, eyeing Mila with blatant distaste. "But you may have just changed my mind."

Inside, something pinched Darius's chest. Mila didn't lower back to her seat. She stood *taller*. He cringed, considering what lay ahead, understanding that Surria would make good on her promise and torture Mila any way she pleased. Suddenly, Darius was a child once again, looking at his mother across this same table, begging her not to kill the mortal boy he'd befriended on an excursion to the mainland.

He'd finally found a friend in a small seaside town off the coast of Maribella. Mickail had been his name. When his mother said he could invite him up to their palace, Darius had been overjoyed.

That night, when Mickail's lifeless body had been slumped over the entrée of pheasant and seared vegetables, his life had changed. That was when he realized love was a weakness. That it might very well destroy him.

And now, that night felt as though it were happening all over again.

He. Couldn't. Breathe.

"If you even think about touching her..." Margrete glanced toward a grim-faced Mila, "I'll drown you in your own home." She stood so quickly, that her chair almost toppled to the ground. Bash sprang to his feet, both joining their outspoken friend. "And I'll enjoy every minute of it."

Surria leaned back in her seat and heaved a dramatic sigh. "So exceptionally intense tonight. I was merely teasing, something Darius never understood. The poor thing was always so very sensitive. Sit, sit back down, and don't allow one woman's ramblings to ruin an evening."

Silence passed, and Darius sat there frozen, a helpless little boy who did nothing to stop his mother from unleashing her temper.

Pathetic.

The double doors to the dining room swung open. "Ah, there's the food!" Surria clapped, childlike laughter following. She motioned to the cloaked servants to place plates of what appeared to be freshly caught lobster on the table. "Oh, and one more table setting, if you will. We have another guest joining us."

Bash and Margrete exchanged glances. As did Atlas and Dani.

Only Mila stared directly at Surria, unflinching in her silent accusation. Her pointed chin lifted, her bright red hair a flame surrounding her shrewd gaze.

Both goddess and Azantian maintained eye contact, neither succumbing to the other's will. Darius's airway grew less constricted, and as he focused on Mila instead of Surria, the invisible fingers around his throat slipped away.

Mila faced death without batting a lash. He felt both shock and a surprising sensation of fear grip him. Before either of the women could slit the other's throat, the doors opened a second time.

"Our guest," Surria said through her teeth, though she didn't break from Mila. The sailor was the first to glance away, and just so she could assess the newest threat.

"Fuck me," Darius cursed, grabbing his wine glass and chugging it dry. He motioned for an invisible servant to replenish it, and then he chugged that one too.

"Happy to see me, eh?" Calista swept into the room as if she walked on air. Maybe she did. She always walked over everyone else, so why not the elements that weren't hers to command? Like his mother, she'd taken far too much pleasure in her power over others, hurting any who crossed her for the simple pleasure of exerting her dominance.

"Can't you tell by my reaction that I'm thrilled?" Darius rolled his eyes, feeling childlike and altogether juvenile. "Pray tell, what are you doing here?" Because she sure as hell wasn't here to socialize. The Goddess of Love never left the Underworld without an agenda.

Calista smirked her full, pink lips. "I'd never turn down an invitation from Surria." She took the vacant seat beside Dani, who stiffened, her small fingers gripping the table. "And this lobster looks so very delicious."

"Mother," Darius scowled, turning his wrath for the first time to the true monster in the room. "What are you planning?"

"Nothing," she said, feigning shock. She lifted a hand to her chest, putting on a saccharine performance that often preceded bloodshed. "Now, the rest of you sit back down and eat before the food gets cold." She snapped her fingers in the air. "Oh, and music please!"

Rustling sounded and then a violin's sensuous timbre saturated the air. It reminded him all too much of the night he'd found Margrete at Calista's party, and if he didn't know any better, the melody was similar as well...

He opened his mouth to speak but...*couldn't*. No words came out but a pleasant humming, and before he could stop it, a smile lifted his lips against his will.

In fact, all the guests held smiles, even Margrete, who had obeyed his mother and taken her seat. Mila slipped into her own a heartbeat later.

Bash remained unaffected, though he frowned at the actions of his crew. The dead were impervious to Calista's charms.

As an immortal, Darius fought it, and he'd win, but Margrete hadn't the years of practice. She would fall under Calista's influence like the others. He wished he'd have taken the time to show her how to block the gifts of other immortals, but she hardly wanted to kill the beasts alongside him, let alone speak with him for a prolonged period of time.

Pressing his nails into the flesh of his palm, Darius channeled his magic, speaking to it like a lover, whisper-soft and sweet. It rose, its soothing warmth cascading into the emptiness of his chest. It settled the voices in his head and muffled the eerie violin's charms.

"Cease this immediately," he grated through his teeth, staring daggers at Calista.

She sighed, her violet irises alight with mischief. "I came to fulfill a favor, and I'm doing it. It's too bad this isn't yours to cash in upon or I would stop." She crossed her arms against her deep magenta gown, her golden skin shimmering in the light of the sconces.

Gods and their damned *favors*.

"Mother..." Darius turned to Surria. She ignored him, choosing to get up from her seat and approach a glassy-eyed Margrete. He could tell she battled to clear her senses but was ultimately failing.

Darius was out of his chair and flying across the room. He stood in front of Margrete, a wall before his mother. A wall she'd likely break and take immense joy in doing so. Hurting him filled her otherwise boring days with amusement.

Some people were just cruel because they liked the sensation of it.

Surria may possess actual magic, but her vice of choice was inflicting pain.

From his periphery, he glimpsed Bash, shifting to Margrete's other side, his phantom body quivering with rage. But Darius couldn't focus on the king at the moment.

"Move. I have some...questions for our newest arrival." Surria scanned him from boots to crown, her nose wrinkling in frustration.

"No." Darius clenched his jaw, his hands trembling at his sides. He told himself it was anger that made them shake, but he knew better. "Stop this."

"I'm merely giving you what you want," she said. "And perhaps once she's yours, you'll get over this ridiculous feud between us. It's really rather tiresome, and we could accomplish so much together. Think of it... We could rule over the Underworld, no more Halio to contend with. You'd be free to do as you please."

"I don't want anything to do with you," he snapped. "*Nothing* will change that."

Surria rolled her eyes, ignoring him as she looked over his shoulder. "Margrete," Surria called, beaming. She flicked a dainty wrist in the air, and winds carried Darius to the side like a harmless bird caught in a gale, holding him to the wall. Surria advanced, even as Bash dove in front of her, and she walked through him like smoke. His mother lifted her other hand, the one not retraining Darius in place, and brought forth another gust of wind. She might not be able to hold Bash, but she could *silence* him. Her magic spun around and around his flickering form, muffling his pleas, his mouth open in soundless horror. Darius read Margrete's name on his lips.

"Calista, if you'll please have Margrete explain how she feels about my son, I'd very much appreciate it. Maybe help...solve some of her misconceptions as well. I'd like to speed this process up, if possible."

Darius struggled under Surria's influence, the room taking on a hazy glow. While Calista stood and made for Margrete, he turned his sights to the crew.

Atlas, under the Goddess of Love's spell, drew closer to Dani. With her expression lax, her eyes clouded, Atlas pressed her lips against hers. Dani responded with a bold eagerness that wasn't at all like her, weaving her fingers into Atlas's hair and yanking her close. Bay began to sing to himself with a lopsided smile, twisting to Mila as he spoke of his lover's name.

The redhead's eyes were glazed as she listened to Bay, but then she brought her attention to Darius. Heat flared, bright and full of lust. She stood, ignoring Bay entirely, and made to walk straight for Darius, her hips swinging to the poisonous violin and its enchantment.

Even though it wasn't real, the sight of her caused him to go slack. While Mila wasn't glaring or making threats—which he usually found amusing—watching her look at him with such burning need made his pulse soar.

Calista's magic only amplified what the person felt, which meant... Mila found him attractive. Even if she battled with the sensation. Even if she hated herself for it. Darius didn't know what to do with this information, but he didn't feel disgust. Far from it.

"No," Surria scolded, waving a hand and thrusting Mila back into her chair. "Sit."

Calista smirked as she passed an imprisoned Mila, who regarded Darius as if he were the only person in the room.

Not real, Darius reminded himself for the tenth time. Mila would never look at him like that, and he could never dream of a world where someone as sharp as her would soften for him.

Darius grunted against his mother's wind, advancing a measly inch. He was just as strong as Surria, he *knew* this, but...but he was getting in his own way. Too distraught to focus properly.

Distantly, he heard Calista speaking to Margrete in low tones.

"All of it was real," she promised, and Margrete's eyes glowed. "He loves you so very much. You've forgiven all those who have wronged you before, and Darius never meant to hurt you." Calista reached out and trailed a delicate finger down Margrete's cheek. She shivered at the contact.

"No, he didn't mean it," Margrete echoed. "I feel his remorse even now. It breaks my heart. Sometimes I recall what we shared, and it makes me wonder if it could be the same way again. How it was between us on the island. It was so nice. So easy. And..." she paused, scrunching her brow as she searched for the words, "he makes me feel so alive." Margrete gave him her attention, and while she beheld him with the same softness that Mila had seconds before, Darius didn't feel triumph...

He felt the burning fire of rage.

"I don't want to earn her love back like this!" he screamed, shaking the walls of the dining room.

His mother laughed. "You *killed* her lover, sweet boy. That's so much worse than what I'm doing."

The grating quality of her voice had Darius breaking free, roaring as he commanded his own magic to form a shield. Instantly, he stormed her way, her body humming with energy, with the might of the sea. "Tell Calista to release them all. Now."

Nose to nose with his mother, Darius didn't feel the usual trepidation. He wasn't taken back to all the times she'd looked at him in disdain, hating that he never lived up to his brother. That he never became the powerful and ruthless child she'd envisioned.

Her mask slipped ever so slightly. "I tried for ages to rid you of the sliver of humanity you carried, but maybe unlike Malum, you need it to *grow*." She placed a hand on his arm, and it took everything in him not to shove her off.

"I don't want this," he said, avoiding the adoration filling Margrete's stare. He could feel it burn his flesh.

Yes, he'd wanted that look on her face for so long, and directed at him and him alone. But it wasn't real. How could he relish in it when it was false? That was no victory at all.

Darius stumbled back, the movement jostling something tucked into his jacket.

Brielle's arrow.

It was so slight, smaller than normal, but what coated its sharp point...

Could render a god useless.

"I'll give you one last chance, Mother," he warned, slowly reaching into his trouser pocket and wrapping his fingers around the thin wood. "Tell Calista to stop."

"But she can't." Surria gave him a feline grin. "I promised her one of my tears. We struck a bargain and sealed it in blood, and unless she completes her end, she won't collect."

As if to confirm, Calista's violet eyes flashed, growing even more determined. Soft light emanated from her skin as she ran her hand down Margrete's arm, murmuring words even Darius couldn't hear.

Bash continued to pound against the wall of wind, trapped and useless. When he met Darius's eyes, he stilled, dropping his hands. He mouthed one single word.

Please.

A shock of energy raced down Darius's spine. Time slowed to a crawl. The rushing in his ears muffled all sounds. There were seconds to make a decision, to allow Calista to fulfill his greatest wish...or to listen to the nagging voice inside of his head. A voice that told him this was *wrong.*

Darius was so close to getting what he wanted, but as he scanned the table, watching the crew in their drunken haze, his insufferable morals screamed out—

The arrow was flying through the air in the next heartbeat.

A spine-tingling squelch echoed.

Calista glanced down to her chest, lips parted, eyes wide.

"What have you done?" Surria screeched, freeing Bash as she turned her focus to her son. "I was helping you! You never forgave me for that insipid creation of yours, and now I'm righting a wrong! You should be grateful."

Calista slumped to the ground, her body landing in a graceful heap. Her lids fluttered dramatically before shutting, but when they did, the violin's song came to an abrupt stop. The spell that had befallen the crew dissipated, the room no longer warm and gold and full of warmth.

Bash sprinted to Margrete's side, his hands on her face—slipping *through* her face. She blinked rapidly, glancing around as though she didn't know where she was or how she'd gotten to that point. Bash spoke her name, continuously attempting to breach the worlds and touch her.

His desperation, his fierce love, struck a nerve inside of Darius...though it wasn't annoyance or even jealousy.

"Darius..." Bay broke the silence, stumbling to him, "g-get us out of h-here."

The man had all but crawled to him for help. Begged him, their *enemy*, to save them.

Darius turned toward his mother, who looked ready to set fire to her own palace.

"It's been a lovely evening, Mother, but let's never do this again."

Darius cocked his head at the crew, urging them to follow. Mila grasped Margrete's arm, yanking her through the room and beyond the doors. Atlas stumbled, holding tight to a surprisingly clear-eyed Dani, and Bay stayed at Darius's side, a grateful look on his face. He didn't say a word as he dipped his chin at him, but a great shift occurred.

It wasn't love he felt from Bay...but something even more precious.

Trust.

CHAPTER THIRTY

MARGRETE

THEY SPRINTED OUT OF THAT HELLSCAPE OF A DINING ROOM.

Bash didn't leave her side as the crew trailed after Darius, who shouted for them to run faster. The God of the Sea thrust open the palace doors and rushed through the courtyard. Surria's screams sounded at their backs, but no one bothered to turn around and waste precious seconds. Seconds that could give the goddess the upper hand.

Calista was dead. Killed by Darius. Margrete could hardly wrap her mind around it.

As she all but slipped down the pathway fashioned from clouds and magic, Margrete cursed herself for succumbing to Calista's influence. She'd heard the resonating timbre of the violin and lost herself in the sensuous tremor of the goddess's power. She'd fought at first, she really, really did, but gods damn it, she was exhausted.

It was a poor excuse.

"Hurry!" Darius snapped over his shoulder, Bay on his heels. Margrete was shocked Bay kept so close to the god who'd imprisoned him. Nevertheless, the Azantian matched Darius's every footfall, and they came to an abrupt halt at the same time, standing at the edge of the final cloud. Bay's trust wasn't easily earned, and the fact he'd trusted the sea god to help them now made Margrete question absolutely everything.

Darius lifted his hands, the taste of salt landing on the tip of her tongue. Walking to the edge, she gathered her own powers before peering down over the side of the clouds. Blue light whirled below.

"What are you doing?" Margrete asked, having to raise her voice above the onslaught of the new breeze.

"I may not be able to command the wind like my mother, but I can use other methods to get us out of here."

Darius clenched his jaw as the blue light drew nearer. Water arced into the air, headed directly toward where they hovered.

He was bringing the sea to them.

Clever.

Margrete channeled that now familiar energy and aimed her palms toward the waves the god had manipulated, her magic assisting his. Darius shot her a thankful look before returning to his work. Together, they lifted the massive wave to the skies, positioning the platform of moving water before them.

"Get on!" Darius commanded, a single bead of sweat trickling down his forehead.

"Like hell am I jumping onto *water*," Mila screeched, her alarm warranted. "We'll fall right through."

"As if I don't know how water works," Darius snapped back, earning a grimace from Mila. "Obviously, I'm a fucking god, and I promise you won't fall."

Margrete rarely heard Darius curse, and his tone was far from teasing. Exerting that much effort was straining him, and she realized he held most of the weight. She shifted, coaxing more magic forth, hoping to ease the burden. It slipped from her like tears, each drop adding to the wave's stability.

A crackling of lightning struck the skies. Surria's attention had likely left Calista, and now her full ire would be felt.

"I'll go first," Bay offered quickly, stepping off the ledge and onto the glowing platform of seawater. Fear throttled her as she watched him step onto the gleaming surface...

But he didn't fall.

"I'm fine." Bay hurriedly motioned to himself. "Now hurry up!" He waved his hands at Atlas, who hesitated for a fraction of a heartbeat before grabbing Dani's hand. Together they vaulted off the side and next to Bay. The water held.

"Mila..." Darius warned when she lingered, her face contorted in fear. "Trust me."

Mila's expression grew sharper than any blade. "As if that will ever happen," she hissed.

"If you won't trust me, then trust your friends," he countered, meaning the Azantians hovering safely. "You can rage at me once we're safely on the *Mare Deus*."

Mila scrunched her face, and Margrete realized she was likely thinking about Grant. The Leap of Faith. He hadn't been able to jump... and now she found herself at a similar crossroads.

Darius moved to her side, reaching for her.

"What are you do—"

Mila was cut off as Darius wrapped an arm around her waist, pulling her to his chest. He glanced down, his face softening at whatever he found. "Hold on," he whispered into her hair, and Margrete saw the slight tremor that worked through her frame. Darius bent down and scooped Mila into his arms, and before she could open her mouth and protest, he leaped to safety. She didn't scream, but she clutched the back of his neck, her fingers digging into his skin. Darius hesitated before he placed her down, and when he did, it was with surprising care. He tore his gaze from the redhead, whose glassy eyes were glued to his back.

"Your turn," Darius commanded, motioning for Margrete and Bash.

Her king shifted, his body barely a shimmer in the night. "Princess, I don't know if I physically can—"

"Yes, you can," Darius said to Bash. "My magic will hold you in your state."

Another bolt struck, this one closer, the sizzle of electricity burning her nostrils.

Bash's jaw feathered, but he nodded at the god. "I'm right behind you," he told Margrete, ushering her ahead of him. She didn't waste a moment, landing on the moving platform. She whirled around just as Bash made the jump. True to his word, Darius's magic held him, though she noticed how beads of sweat fell from his brow, dripping down his cheeks and to his thinned lips.

Darius grunted with the effort of holding them all aloft, and his face pinched as Surria released a spine-chilling scream.

"Come on!" Margrete snapped, urging him on. She didn't know what he was waiting for.

The god moved slowly, groaning as if in pain. He was barely holding on, and his skin had turned a sickly white.

Margrete brought her own power out to play.

Intuition and fear guided her as she reached out and commanded the water to steady, to become dense. Her searing palms blazed in the too-dark night, Darius's magic matching her own. As she shouldered some of the responsibility, the crease between his brows softened.

Bring us north, he commanded, his voice hoarse and weak.

That alone should've sent alarm bells ringing in her head, but she listened, feigning confidence while thrusting them toward the ship they'd abandoned, using her hands to pinpoint their destination.

Soaring through the heavens was not something she ever imagined a goddess of a sea would do, but then again, she knew nothing of her new world.

I think my mother drugged my drink, Darius admitted, speaking into her mind. *I feel...weak.*

That didn't surprise her.

I'm assuming she did so to aid Calista's *efforts, however futile they were.* Margrete snarled at the mention of her name. She wanted to burn Calista to the ground for even attempting to steal her free will.

Calista is dead, Darius said. *She died when that arrow pierced her heart. You can thank Brielle for that gift. Although I'm not sure of her motives.*

Good. I'm glad she's dead. No one should force another's love. It's sick. Calista's death saved Margrete from killing the goddess herself.

Aiming with one hand, her other working in circular motions, she coaxed the wave to move them, the platform they stood on slowly descending. Bash hovered at her side, an uneasy look marring his handsome features. He hadn't stopped staring at her since her admission at the table—

You're a natural, Darius said, helping her direct them down at a gradual descent. *I didn't even have to teach you a thing.* A brittle laugh sounded. *You're better at following your instincts than I ever was.*

Margrete remained silent until she spotted the *Mare Deus* floating like a hopeful beacon.

Thank you for getting us out of there.

Darius sighed. *I told you I'd never let her hurt you—*

But you could've had everything you wanted if you allowed her to continue. I was no match, and Calista's power had been too great. I would've done anything at that moment.

And there it was. The question that plagued her since they ran. Why *hadn't* Darius allowed Calista to inflict some sort of heinous love curse? This was the second time he'd spurned Calista's "help." First, during her party, and now, during Surria's disastrous dinner.

Darius's frustration could be clearly felt as they fell from the sky, plummeting quickly now. Mila shrieked, moving to wrap her arms around Bay, practically climbing him like a tree.

I...I don't want it like that. Not forced, Darius murmured. *What I felt with you...with the old you, was a love given freely, and it didn't feel right to steal it.*

Margrete didn't say that Darius *was* stealing her love...even if he'd collect in the decades to come. He *was* forcing her to choose him, even if he didn't quite understand that himself.

Only the gasps and panting of the crew were heard when they

reached the ship, everyone trembling with adrenaline and nerves. Everyone besides Bash.

He stepped off the platform after her, a towering shadow at her back. But his dark eyes were clouded and full of mystery, and she didn't like how his lips curved downward in defeat.

At last, Darius lowered himself onto the planks, and with an exhausted groan, he waved away the watery platform.

"I doubt she'll follow, but we should keep alert," Darius said. "The waters will alert me if she comes, but to be safe, there should be someone on watch every hour."

"Agreed," Mila said, taking the lead. "I'll take the first shift. That bitch won't control me again."

Darius's attention lingered on her as he nodded soberly. He began to head to the steps leading to his hammock when Bay grasped his arm.

"Thank you," Bay said, barely above a whisper. Her friend leaned close to Darius's ear, speaking too softly for Margrete to hear. But whatever he'd uttered made the god's ears turn a subtle shade of red, and this time, a soft smile bloomed.

"Get some rest," Bash said to them all. "Tomorrow we get to Rydor and get my body back. I'm tired of watching from the sidelines, and a king fights beside his crew."

Atlas dipped her chin in respect, and Mila gave him a crooked grin. Dani merely observed him, a curious look gracing her lovely features. Margrete wondered what went through that head of hers—and she'd ask. Tomorrow.

Mila sauntered to the stern and watched the horizon. Margrete had no doubt she'd keep a keen eye out for intruders.

She turned to Bash. "We need to speak."

THEY HAD AN HOUR UNTIL MIDNIGHT. AN HOUR BEFORE SHE COULD use her hands to cup his cheeks and force him to look at her. An hour before she could press her lips to his and speak without words...

But that had always been Margrete's initial reaction. Touch.

She'd been deprived of it since she was a child, and perhaps, deep down, it was the truest form of her emotions. But she'd come to recognize that words were needed, and more than that, you couldn't always solve an issue by drowning out the noise of the world with body heat.

Margrete shut the door after Bash entered their cabin. Tonight had been...well, it had been fucking awful. They'd all suspected Surria was up to something, and when Calista sauntered into the dining room, Margrete knew the goddess had planned a horrific evening for them. And while Surria's duplicity wasn't a shock, it was how *she* reacted that stunned her. Because, while under Calista's influence, a small part of her came to an understanding she hadn't wished to accept.

"Margrete?"

She flinched at the sound of Bash's voice in her ear. She hadn't realized he was right behind her, waiting for her to begin. Margrete sucked in a deep breath and turned.

"I'm sorry about tonight," she began, noting how his eyes darkened.

"You have nothing to apologize for," he said, his tone too cool, too unfeeling. Bash tried to be brave before her now, acting as if her words— even while influenced—hadn't wounded him.

"You know, there's a feeling I get when I'm around you..." She wandered to the porthole, giving him her back while she gazed out to the moonlit waves. "I think I always felt it. Like I'd known you my entire life." She smiled, thinking about their first weeks, how she convinced herself she wanted nothing to do with him. It had been an act, and a poor one at that. "The first time we spoke, you told me your people believed the eyes carried the truths of one's soul...and while you found sadness in mine, I couldn't help but see something else in yours. While I didn't understand what it was at first, I do now."

She spun around and began walking toward him, slowly, taking in his rigid posture.

"There are fantasies, Bash, and then there are realities that are even more beautiful. What I discovered in your eyes, what I saw as *your* truth, was a selflessness that shocked me. Because not many are truly selfless, not to the extent that they'd be willing to give up their own happiness. But there you were, a king who would've destroyed himself for his people, and the more I saw of that man, the more my heart became full."

Bash inhaled sharply, his stare unwavering. "But that's not a reason to love me, is it, princess?"

She shook her head. "You're not understanding me at all. You were the most beautiful soul I'd ever seen. The purest, even in a world of greed. I fell so deeply in love with your soul. And because of who you are, I became the best version of myself. Which is the woman *you* fell in love with.

"Do not, for one second, doubt that my heart beats with yours, or that we weren't bonded from the very moment I laid eyes upon you. I was already gone by then. I was already yours."

Bash inched closer. "I know your soul loved him as well, a long time before. And while I'm confident in what we have, I also have my doubts and insecurities. I can't help but feel a jealousy that steals away any and all logic." He ran a hand through his hair. "I hate that I feel that way, but how can I ignore that you're literally the other *half* of his soul? You were made for him—"

"The soul I was given is *mine*," she said firmly. "My origins don't matter. Only my future does. And you, Sebastian, are the future of *my* choice."

Bash lifted a hand to hover beside her cheek. Wetness lined his lower lids, but he didn't shed a tear. He simply beamed at her like she was his sun and he was helpless but to revolve around her.

He appeared raw before her, so painfully exposed. "Sometimes I just want to rip Darius's throat out with my bare hands when he's near you... or touches you, for that matter. It makes me furious to know he had any hand in creating the woman I love, and while I understand the history will always be there, it doesn't make it easier." He glanced at his boots, his nostrils flaring slightly. "I wish I was a better man who didn't feel such rage, who didn't question what we have, but maybe it's the changes I've gone through, how I have become someone else...it makes me worry that we're being pulled away, in two separate directions."

Margrete understood this. If the roles had been reversed, she might not be as civil as Bash. Even at the thought of it—if Bash had once loved another with such intensity—her insides heated and her magic reacted in turn. Light blazed from her palms, tickling her fingers and brightening the poorly lit room with power.

"I look forward to the day when all of this is done and we bend fate to our will. When we're back home and surrounded by all our loved ones. By Adrian and Bay, Birdie and Nerissa." Bash's gaze grew bright, his lips parting, but she pressed on. "I look forward to the nights when it's just us and the world around us vanishes. When you make me laugh and fill my heart with a magic no divinity could. And that reality will be ours. You say you trust me? Trust me on that."

The corners of his mouth lifted into a devious smirk. *There* was her old pirate. Her Bash.

"If that is what you're envisioning, then it's safe to assume your answer?"

She would've smacked his chest if she could. "You truly are the most vexing man I've ever met." Margrete smiled wide, shaking her head at his persistence.

"Now, before you get all sentimental on me, I want to lay down beside you. Midnight approaches, and you know I have a hard time falling asleep without your snoring."

"I do not snore." Bash scoffed in feigned affront. He most assuredly *did* snore.

"Lay down," she commanded, grinning like a fool. The weight of the evening slipped from her shoulders. She was back in his orbit. Back *home*.

"Whatever you wish, my queen," Bash said, easing onto the bed, nearly hovering an inch above the sheets. On his side, he curved his body, watching as she lay beside him, inches apart.

They shared that space for what felt like minutes and hours and an eternity wrapped in one breath. And when the fated hour fell, Bash leaned forward and closed that infuriating distance. He wrapped his arms around her frame and tugged her to his chest. Icy lips pressed against her forehead, and his hands descended to her back, sliding up and down in the calming way she liked.

They'd said everything that they needed to say, so when the quiet continued, Margrete relished it, smiling when she nuzzled into the crook of Bash's neck. She planted kisses on the column of his throat, taking her time, worshiping him. He rumbled his approval with every kiss she bestowed, and by the time she made it to his lips, he was a mess of barely concealed need.

"I want to make love to you, Margrete Wood." He drew back to whisper into her hair. "I want to feel every inch of you." He grasped her chin, running his thumb along her bottom lip. "I want you to feel every inch of *me*. And when we both shatter, I plan on holding you until I physically can't. But soon, there won't be any time limits to how long I can touch you. And you should be oh-so very frightened when that time comes." He laughed into her kiss. "I won't be able to help myself. I never have around you. And I never want to."

Margrete grinned, allowing herself to envision the picture he painted. She thrust herself against him, shivering when she felt his need for her press against her stomach.

"Nice and slow, princess," he warned, moving to her shirt. As he'd promised, Bash removed her clothing with care, with an aching deliberateness that caused her to burn. The anticipation was almost worse than when they ravished one another, and by the time they both lay bare before the other, their limbs entangled, Margrete was already near the edge.

"You'll always have my heart, Margrete," Bash murmured, pressing a kiss to the hollow of her throat. He spoke it like a confession...or a goodbye.

Before she could answer, Bash pushed into her, inch by deliberate inch. Her lips parted, and a strangled sound rumbled up her throat. Gods above *and* below.

"Just like that, pirate." She arched her hips up, meeting his leisurely thrusts, his cock hitting a spot deep within that had her seeing stars. Her lids shuttered, but she managed to keep them open, not wanting to miss the ecstasy etched across Bash's rugged face.

She caused him to unravel, and at the sight of him, heat spiraled into her core. He slid back, drawing himself almost completely out.

"Bash—"

He pushed back in, silencing her protests. He repeated this torturous action many more times until she grabbed hold of his shoulders and kept him in place. So close to his lips, she couldn't resist tasting him, molding her body to his, not an inch of space separating them. Her hands ran across his chiseled frame, over his taut abdomen, up to his chest, his biceps. His scales.

They moved as one, breaking apart only when Margrete lost her breath, but they didn't lose their rhythm. And when he leaned forward to kiss her brow, Margrete felt the potent love he poured into her.

Not too long before the midnight hour ended, Margrete reached her peak, squeezing him as she whispered his name. She clutched both of his cheeks, holding him to her lips, exhaling her bliss into his mouth as she came.

Bash shuddered, her pulsating core undoing him, and he followed after, a look of raw desire painting his dark features in the soft light.

They had minutes before the bell tolled and stole away their touch. Stole the one thing they'd both been deprived of all their lives. But Bash's touch was fire and sunshine, the feeling of being wrapped in a blanket before an open hearth. Her skin tingled as he ran a finger down her bare arm, goosebumps rising in his wake.

She laid her head on his chest, one hand tangled in his black curls. A glint of silver caught her focus, and she lowered her fingers, glancing across a scale. Bash flinched, but he didn't remove her hand. Margrete had made a point to avoid them, knowing how much pain they caused, but he had to realize she considered them stunning. They were marks of what he'd endured, of what he *was*, and she loved everything about him.

Bash's breathing eventually evened out, but she continued to brush her hand up and down his biceps, his torso. She couldn't stop, because she knew she wouldn't be able to hold him in mere minutes.

Calmed by his breathing, soothed by his bare skin, and utterly fixated upon his striking features, Margrete counted herself lucky.

Because even a moment like this was worth a lifetime of misery.

And she was so very grateful she'd gotten to experience a love most searched their entire lives for. Regardless of what their future would bring, she was happy now, enveloped in Bash's tight embrace, and that was enough. It had to be.

CHAPTER THIRTY-ONE

BASH

Bash woke well before Margrete.

Once his eyes had opened and reality settled in like a plague, he couldn't fall back asleep, nor did he desire to. The only part he enjoyed about sleeping in was having Margrete pressed against him, and he could no longer relish in that simple act.

Slipping from bed fully dressed, he peered out the porthole, knowing what today would bring.

They'd reach Rydor by the afternoon, which meant...

Fuck.

He ground his teeth and slipped through the closed door like a cloud of smoke. Perhaps the only positive aspect of his new form was the ability to ignore walls and doors entirely—an act that hadn't gotten easier. Though it would've made sneaking out of the palace a lot easier when he was younger and under Ortum's watch. He missed the man horribly. Ortum had been like a father to him, and he couldn't forget his death was essentially Darius's fault. All of the deaths that had painted his life in shades of gray were the god's fault.

It was odd to think of death the same as he once had, having been to the Underworld himself. While he still seethed at the unnecessary bloodshed, he took a small comfort in knowing his friends lived in their happiest memories for all of time.

Lost in his thoughts, Bash nearly collided with Bay on the steps leading above. His friend let out a high-pitched yelp of surprise, and Bash snorted, smirking at the shrillness of the noise.

"I see you still find it in your heart to laugh at my expense," Bay grumbled, though a smile lifted his lips. "Not all that much has changed."

"Oh, I'll always find it in myself to make fun of you when the opportunity presents itself." Bash poked out his tongue, thinking of all the many ways he would coax that same discordant sound from him in the future.

"So kind, my most generous king." Bay dipped into an exaggerated bow reeking of mockery. Bash would've smacked his shoulder and tousled his hair, but he could do nothing but roll his eyes. When Bay rose, his playful demeanor shifted.

"So..." Bash started out, feeling off-kilter.

"So?" Bay lifted a brow.

"Last night was entertaining."

"And by entertaining, you mean it was the worst dinner party we'd ever been invited to." Bay gave a theatrical shudder. "I swear I didn't even have a chance to sample the main course."

"Lobster *is* your favorite." Bash knew this because Adrian detested lobster, and the two argued over the dinner menu frequently.

"At least Darius didn't allow us to get murdered. Well, *again.*"

Now Bash's smile dipped. "Why do you think he...stopped Calista?"

He hadn't broached the topic with Margrete last night as they had enough to talk about, but now that Bay had brought it up...

His friend scrubbed at his growing stubble and sighed. "Honestly, you're going to hate me for saying this but—"

"Oh, don't you dare start feeling sorry for him."

"No, it's not that," Bay rushed to say. "I'm most definitely not condoning his deeds. I mean, look at you." He waved a hand before Bash's frame, to his dark hair and scales and then down to his black nails. "But maybe his long-lost morality dared to make an appearance. It gives me hope, that's all. Not many people, let alone immortals, are capable of change."

Bash scoffed, recognizing that he sounded like a child. But hell, he had a right to hold a grudge.

"Darius thinks of no one but himself. I wouldn't be surprised if he cut Calista's spell off simply because he wanted to be the one to enchant Margrete himself." The whole night cast him in a good light, and it would be the perfect plan to gain favor.

"That's not the reason at all, king."

Bash whirled around at the sound of the new voice. Darius sauntered into the light, the shadows of the hull still clinging to his body. How long had he been standing there listening?

Feigning indifference he didn't feel, Bash asked, "Then why *did* you stop her?"

The god's blue eyes stormed, steel and gray darkening his usual vibrant turquoise.

"You think I'm evil," Darius stated, and while it wasn't a question, Bash nodded all the same. *Fuck yes, I do.* The god narrowed his stare as if reading Bash's mind before continuing. "But I find I don't believe in the word—evil, that is. Nor do I believe in those who claim to be free of sin." Darius shot him a pointed look—one Bash returned with a searing glower of his own.

Bash had been a malicious creature. He'd tried to kill his love, and he'd felt no remorse at the time. But then again, he'd been under the influence of true darkness. Their situations weren't at all the same, and he cursed the ass for even thinking it.

"You made conscious efforts to hurt people, Darius," Bash said, throwing caution aside. "Your decisions to harm and kill were *purposeful*, and doing one good deed does not even the scales."

He spun around and shot off for the upper decks, leaving Bay alone with the duplicitous god. They murmured behind him, and his envy rose when he heard Bay's voice soften. Whatever they spoke of wasn't full of hatred like Bash would've hoped. His friend should despise Darius, and yet he hadn't left with *him*. He'd stayed behind to chat with the enemy.

Bash clenched his fists, eager to reach Rydor's shores and find Minthe and, hopefully, his corpse. He'd been powerless for far too long, watching the action from the outside, feeling like a bystander in his own story. It wouldn't be long before he took back control.

He just had to make sure he *stayed* in control once he returned.

Winds whooshed in his ears on the upper deck, the ship rocking precariously as the waves picked up. The north wasn't kind to many sailors, but Mila and Dani were manning their course, and Mila was more than adept at steering them safely.

Bash slowed when he spotted Atlas leaning against the rail, her head bent over a tattered map worn from age. She'd shrugged on a coat, the brisk air growing more frigid by the minute.

"How much longer?" he barked, barely able to control his ire. It was a mixture of emotions he experienced then, both anger and fear, and he wasn't sure which one triumphed over the other.

Atlas didn't lift her head at his brusque greeting. "We should be seeing the coast shortly. And then we'll have the gods find Minthe."

"Good." Bash sat beside her, his lips twitching every now and again, his frustration building. He shouldn't feel so damned furious about Darius, especially after he spoke with Margrete last night, but the god got under his skin and made it impossible to work alongside him.

"It is surprising..." Atlas murmured, still scrutinizing the map. "I, too, was curious as to why he stopped Calista. I heard you below. You three speak louder than a gaggle of town gossips."

"Oh no. Not you too." Now his own people were defending the man who murdered their own on the island. Did they suddenly forget the trail of bodies Darius had left in his wake?

"No, not me too. But as Bay was saying, maybe it's a good thing the bastard isn't as malevolent as we assumed. Not that I wouldn't kill him given the first opportunity." She finally lifted her head and met his brooding stare. "But for now, we use his *kindness*, and we exploit it."

Ah. There was the calculating warrior he knew well.

"At least I have you," Bash said, dipping his chin in thanks. Some of the weight in his chest lessened. "The sooner we get this charade over with, the better. And then we can deliver justice to the souls we lost."

Atlas leaned in close, her voice turning to a conspiratorial whisper. "Did you and Margrete ever figure out what that key opened?"

He bristled. "What key?"

"Oh shit. Well, don't get mad at her, she probably just forgot to tell you, given everything." Again, Atlas waved to him like his incorporeal state explained everything. "We found a key in Underworld, and both Margrete and Dani believe the orb affixed to its handle holds a few droplets of Surria's tears."

"Fuck. Yes, that would've been nice to know." Bash exhaled through his nose.

See, they don't even tell you anything anymore. What use was a specter?

"I'll ask her when she wakes, but I wonder why it slipped her mind."

Atlas left Bash to his own mind, which wasn't exactly laden with sunshine and rainbows. He tucked away the information regarding the key, wondering about its significance. As he'd learned thus far, nothing was ever as it seemed.

"Shore!" Atlas shouted from the top of her lungs, causing Dani, directly in front of her at the bow, to cringe. Bash cringed along with her, knowing just how potent Atlas's lungs could be.

But his old friend was right. Rydor popped up on the horizon, and with the winds on their side, they'd reach land in no time.

Bash had the sudden urge to vomit.

Which was entirely impossible. He thought.

"I'm right here, so don't start getting ahead of yourself. I know how that mind works," Margrete chastised to his right, standing close enough that he could reach out and hold her. Hopefully, he'd get that wish soon enough. If he didn't go full-on monster and rip her immortal throat out.

She, too, wore a jacket over her shirt, and while not as worn as Atlas's, it sported a few holes and rips. He couldn't feel a damned thing, so the temperature drop had little effect on him.

He nodded at her in detached agreement. Minutes ago he'd been rearing to get to shore, but now that they were *here*, he thought of all the ways he could end up murdering her. Fuck, he'd blacked out when Minthe had fed him his first human soul. The creature inside of him had assumed command, and all traces of him had been devoured by phantom teeth and an insatiable hunger.

In fact, the hunger was the clearest thing he recalled from the time right before his transition. It devastated him, turning Bash into a true beast without an ounce of humanity or thought.

The only comfort he took was knowing Bay—or Darius, for that matter—would strike him down if, or when, he lost himself to the monster. The god would probably be all too eager.

They sailed in silence for another hour or so, both Bash and Margrete standing by the railing, watching as the rocky, gray land of the North came into view. It certainly was no Azantian. He couldn't understand why anyone would *want* to live here, where the shores would cut your bare soles and the glacial winds stole your air. *This* was how he'd originally pictured the Underworld to look like. Funny that his idea of death was located in the living realm.

"Something's in the water!"

That shout came from above. Bash tilted his chin, taking in Mila, who hung from the main sail, her short, red hair fluttering around her face.

"It looks like a raft," Bay remarked coolly, scrambling to peer over the side. Margrete sprinted next to him, her excitement palpable.

Bash approached them slowly, wary of what Mila had seen. It couldn't be anything good. He wasn't *that* naïve.

"There's something in it," Margrete whispered, squinting. She lifted a hand, magic unfurling and igniting. With a flick of her wrist, the waves surrounding the wooden raft—which was no bigger than ten feet—lifted it forward, bringing the decrepit vessel close to the sides of the *Mare Deus*.

Bash didn't need to look to know what lay within the raft.

He already knew. He *felt* it.

Everyone gasped, Darius included. Surrounded by black reeds that reeked of decay was Bash's body.

He froze at the sight, drinking in the pale skin and dark circles underlining his closed eyes. It was odd, seeing himself there, dead, while he fluttered about, a ghost. Yet he couldn't look away—he was under the spell of the impossible, and it made his phantom form tremble.

"Help me get it out!" Bay cried. He rushed toward the ladder when Margrete grasped his arm.

"Don't touch it," she warned. She scanned the waters through narrowed eyes, seeking out an enemy. "It could be a trap. And I find it far too convenient."

Minthe would never have relinquished his body like this...

Margrete was right. It had to be a trick.

Bash inspected the far shores of Rydor's rocky beaches. There wasn't a sign of movement, but there wouldn't be. Nymeras were extraordinarily stealthy—

Fins pierced the tops of the waves, giving way to an elongated body of the deepest red. Margrete grabbed hold of Bay, dragging him deeper into the vessel, away from the approaching danger. A wave drenched them as the creature breached the surface, only to fall back into the deep with a chilling roar. Seconds later, Bash made out its silhouette beneath the waves, headed toward them at an impossible speed.

Bash had expected his mother to make her entrance, not another of the sea's larger beasts...

To the east, a figure lurched into the air, though this one flashed a bright azure, vicious spikes dotting a bulbous head. Tentacles peeked up, but unlike the Eliam, these tentacles were narrow and tapered into serrated tips. More than a dozen menacing eyes blinked, their irises a haunting shade of silver.

"There's a third one!"

Bash whirred to where Mila pointed, the last shreds of his hope vanishing.

There, fifty feet beyond the first serpent-like creature, rose a *third* monster. He didn't see much more than the top of its hide, but its green scales dazzled in the low light of the overcast day.

"Margrete!" Darius roared. "We need to strike the Tralla now."

The Tralla. Another name for a monster she'd have to fight mere seconds after learning its existence.

Darius didn't wait for her reply as he grasped her hand in his and turned them both to the nearest creature. It was the silver-eyed beast with razor-sharp tentacles and scales of blue. He murmured something in her ear that Bash couldn't make out, and then she was mimicking the god's actions, directing them toward their foe.

"Trust your instincts!" Darius thundered when Margrete's shoulder slumped. "Direct the rush of magic outward, *demand* it to do your bidding. If you are forceful enough, it will listen. And control that breathing of yours!"

Margrete's jaw tensed, but she righted herself, and together, they twisted their wrists and flicked their fingers out in nonsensical patterns. Bash watched in a trance as the waves around the creature curled upward, rising high into the air. They flashed a brilliant blue, and he made out sparks of electricity flashing within the rising waters.

"Release! Now!" Darius ordered, bringing his arms down to his side. Margrete followed suit, and the sea they commanded responded.

In a violent rush, their enchanted waters shot toward the monster, a deep wail sounding as their target was struck. It sank deeper below the surface, likely to recuperate, but Bash suspected it would be back.

"The creepy red one is coming," Mila snapped, drawing their focus to the left.

There was too much to focus on all at once, and Bash was just as useless as he'd been for the majority of this journey. He clenched his fists, wanting to scream, to jump on the rail and send a spear flying through the air and into their enemy's belly.

He couldn't just stand here and *watch* as Margrete saved them—or gave her life trying.

Bash made a rash decision, and one that might end his life for good right then and there. While the rest of the crew was distracted, he crept to the ladder, the boat his body rested upon rocking agitatedly against the stern. Easing down the rungs, he dropped, falling on top of the vessel, his lack of weight making no impact.

He peered down at himself, horrified by the black scales and sharpened claws. In his current form, they were shorter, albeit still black, and his scales not nearly as lethal. But this sickly corpse was him, the horrid body at his feet, and whether he liked it or not, he would have to wear that gruesome face to save the ones he loved.

Bash lurched forward, hovering atop his body, his hand an inch away from his wan and bloodless cheek.

I've been expecting you.

Minthe's voice filtered through his thoughts. He retracted his hand. Slowly. She was a predator after all.

Don't be afraid, son. This was meant to be. The girl might have actually been useful for something. There was a pause and then, *I must admit I'm surprised by the lengths she went to get your soul...*

Hearing his mother speak of Margrete had his hackles rising. Even if the last half of her speech held a tinge of gratefulness.

Tell me what to do, he demanded, searching the waters for a sign of her languid form. He could argue and seethe at her later. Now, he required answers.

Nothing but a chuckle greeted him.

You'll be hungry once you connect, and this time, I expect you to feed. I won't lose you for a third time, son.

The first, he'd been a babe, stolen from her arms by his own father. The second time, death had robbed him. Pity swarmed through Bash at the thought of his mother, before she'd turned into a heartless entity bent on revenge. Revenge that he suddenly considered to be warranted. If anyone had taken away his child, Bash wasn't sure of the permanent damage it would do to his heart.

Come on, Minthe coaxed, pulling him away from a dark past. *Your friends need you.*

That was all she needed to say.

Screams sounded around him, and he scraped his claws into the fleshy part of his palms, focusing instead on his unmoving form. Just when he was about to scream for Minthe's aid, the surface shifted and rippled, and a head of black hair ascended, a pair of midnight eyes glimmering at him in what he swore was adoration.

Minthe had arrived.

Hurry! he said, waving her closer. If she knew how to help reconnect his soul with his body, he'd accept her aid. But she had to move faster. Already Margrete was groaning from the weight of bearing such devastating magic, and her whimpers nearly had him doubling over.

I'm doing this for you. Always for you. Her depthless eyes clouded, her lips tugging down. Bash saw how her elongated arms twitched at her sides, almost as if she desired to reach out for him. She didn't. *Now...dip your hand into your chest cavity,* she instructed, her voice detached. *Once you've wrapped your hand around your heart, squeeze.*

She stared, ten feet from the craft, and while her eyes told him so many truths, there was also mystery in them, and a hint of an emotion he likened to genuine fear. An emotion only a being with a soul could carry.

Bash hesitated, unsure of how her instructions were true. He moved *through* everything else.

Trust me, she urged, and while he *didn't,* Bash plunged his arm into his body's chest and searched around. His fingers buzzed with unfamiliar magic as he found his heart and wrapped himself around the cold, lifeless organ.

While his heart had been injured, he was able to feel it, to hold it between his phantom fingers and squeeze, just as Minthe directed. Sounds of the battle were muffled, growing less clear by the second, and he surrendered to the all-encompassing energy zapping up his hand and arm and into his chest. He shut his eyes.

Images flashed across the backs of his lids, of the time just before Bay had shoved that dagger into his heart back in the arena. He glimpsed himself as he truly was, and he witnessed in horror as he lunged for Margrete, who whispered his name and begged him to break the hold.

Bash drifted in a sea of horrid memories, unable to break free. A current of nightmares whirled around him, and while he no longer felt in control of his own form, Bash pictured Margrete's tear-stained face, gripping it tightly. Hoping it would be enough to keep him from being sucked into the darkness entirely.

Slowly, Bash curled his finger, his eyes still closed. He wiggled his feet, his arms, wrinkled his nose...

Bash's eyes shot open—

And that same hunger that had led to his death now returned.

CHAPTER THIRTY-TWO

MARGRETE

MARGRETE WAS LOSING ENERGY. FAST.

Slow down! Darius screamed into her mind. She strained her neck, using what little strength she had left to angle his way.

While sweat beaded across her brow and her body shook, Darius remained solid and unmoving...though when she looked closer, she noticed how his right hand quivered ever so slightly. That tremor hadn't been there at the beginning.

They'd successfully brought down the Tralla using electrified waters. The electric part belonged to Darius, likely a gift from his mother, but Margrete had used her magic to aid in the wave's lethal force. It had taken all her concentration to aim it at the creature's head where it was most vulnerable, according to Darius. But her thoughts were beginning to wander to Bash and where the hell he'd vanished to.

No doubt, he was doing something foolish—like attempting to rejoin with his physical body so he could help fight.

Yes. She was certain that's what he was doing. While she yearned to seek him and aid his endeavors, she couldn't move her feet. Her legs were rooted, frozen like unyielding stone, and it took great effort to merely shift her hands and guide her magic.

Focus on the Cyros, the red one. It's coming back around, Darius said, his voice beginning to crack. *Use your force to guide my magic to the right side of its underbelly. There's a patch of its hide that's paler. Aim for that.*

His instructions were clear, but as it approached—the beast resembling a snake with wide, stingray-like fins stretching out on either side—the less confident she became.

A massive wave struck the hull, sending the crew tumbling. Shouts sounded, and then the worst sound greeted Margrete's ears...

The sound of someone falling overboard. A splash followed by Atlas's high-pitched screams.

"Dani!" Atlas raced to the side and peered over, frantically searching for Dani. She didn't resurface. There was no sign of her.

Margrete's magic coiled tight, begging for a monster to slay, but the creature they'd sought now hid—in the same waters Dani had fallen into.

"I don't see her!" Bay yelled beside Atlas, both hands gripping the wooden sides.

Atlas cursed before leaping onto the railing, the riotous waves causing her to lose her balance in an instant. She plunged into the sea with a hoarse cry.

"Darius! We need to do something *now.*"

Her friends were down there, likely about to be killed, torn apart, and shredded by the two surviving creatures. As she thought it, a red fin flashed as the muscled nightmare of a beast aimed for their ship, for Dani and Atlas, both of whom had yet to resurface.

You have to let me in again, Darius insisted. *We'll connect our powers and use them as one. Our strikes will be much more potent. We can save them together.*

She faltered, momentarily frozen with fear, but Darius grabbed her hand, his hold firm but gentle.

Trust me, Margrete, he begged. *I will not trick or harm you. That is never what I wanted.*

But you did, she argued. *You've done nothing but trick me. I can't lose them.*

Darius sighed across her mind. *I'll never be a good person, Margrete, but let me do this one good thing. Please...*

He sounded sincere. Then again, he always did.

Margrete shut her eyes and did the only thing she could.

She let down her guard.

CHAPTER THIRTY-THREE

DARIUS

Darius slid past her walls, which had been erected with care, and he dove into her mind. Her thoughts were chaotic, spinning around in a dizzying mess of doubts and fear.

He hadn't believed she'd actually do it after the last time, but Margrete trusted him. Just enough. This was so much more than communicating in their minds—he was presented with her innermost reflections, exposed to all of her vulnerabilities.

Suddenly, he realized the weight of such a gift. It reminded him of how he felt when Bay thanked him, a knowing look in his green eyes. Darius had felt it then too, that faith. And while every inch of him had the desire to explore her mind, he held back...just enough to not corrupt her with his own darkness.

Blue and silver light flared across his vision, and Margrete's hand shook. Together, they buzzed, burning with a joined power the Underworld had never seen before. Not even when he and Malum worked together had they experienced such raw, potent energy.

Hold on to me, he instructed, grasping a tendril of her magic. Her power stemmed from strength, from force, and his magic centered around accuracy.

But as one, they were a foe to fear.

He opened his eyes.

Atlas and Dani had breached the waves, the former keeping Dani's head above water. Her eyes were shut, the woman's black curls slicked across her face. She wasn't conscious.

Atlas did her best to swim to the *Mare Deus*, aiming for the ladder, but she never reached it. The Cyros—the beast with glimmering red scales—was already upon them.

Margrete screamed as the creature dug its mighty jaw into Atlas's forearm, yanking her from Dani and dragging her beneath the depths.

Someone dove in. Darius watched as Bay's blond head poked up. He swam to where Dani was slowly descending, his strong arms wrapping around her a heartbeat before she went fully under.

With Dani safe, Darius turned his focus to where Atlas had been taken. He'd never particularly cared for her, but Margrete did. She was a part of this little family, and Darius's magic sparked when he imagined their grief-stricken faces if they lost her.

He seized Margrete's hand, drawing on her power, her strength, forcing her to lend some of her magic to him. Her knees wobbled, but she must've understood his intentions because she didn't fight him off. She let him take and take and take.

There. A flick of a tail three hundred feet away.

Darius struck without hesitation.

The waters rippled as his might collided with the sea, striking the Cyros's tail. An inhuman shriek pierced the air as black blood saturated the blue waves.

He found he was holding his breath, waiting for Atlas's blonde head to rise. He waited and waited—and nothing. She was likely already dead, and Dani was still unconscious, thankfully unable to watch when Atlas's corpse rose.

"Where is she?" Margrete shouted, losing her grip. Any semblance of control vanished, and he watched her shaking hands, the tears streaming down her face.

Blonde hair.

"She's a hundred feet west!" Darius pointed wildly to where a body floated, red blood flowing freely from some hidden wound.

Before they had a chance to formulate a plan, a boat was being lowered and Mila was rowing out by herself, her strokes firm and unwavering. An unfamiliar rush of anxiety sent Darius's head spinning, and he watched helplessly as Mila made her way to Atlas.

Everyone held their breaths, and even the waves seemed to settle, as if the sea, too, watched.

The second she was near enough, Mila dove into the sea, swimming for Atlas.

"Fuck, it's coming back!" Bay warned. He'd been hovering over Dani as she slowly came to, but he lurched to his feet, scrambling to stand beside Margrete.

Slick, red scales glimmered in the light, the Cyros and its wide fins slicing through the water with ease. It wasn't one to give up its prey, and if Darius and Margrete didn't intervene, it would take both Mila and Atlas.

An image of Mila's cold and bloodied body flew across his mind.

"Focus!" he commanded of Margrete, intertwining their fingers. He gripped her hard enough to bruise, but she merely squeezed back, just as fiercely. "We need to draw it away and kill it before it reaches them."

Their minds collided with a clash.

While he grasped hold of Margrete's power, and she held his, images of the past slammed into him.

It was the worst possible time for such a heavy realization, but so deep in her mind, deeper than ever before, he glimpsed a hint of the woman she used to be—*his* Wryn. But then that woman would vanish and a new sensation would make a home in his chest.

He might've viewed Margrete and Wryn as the same, but...

Wryn was a weak flame in the back of her head, and the new, powerful creature she'd become felt more like a stranger. A stranger he was trying to force to love him.

Wryn was gone. She'd been gone for a thousand years. And Margrete wasn't her, not the same soul he'd fashioned from his own. She'd taken the pieces Darius had given her, and she fashioned them the way she wanted, growing into a person his heart didn't entirely recognize.

This understanding both ruined and energized him. It freed him from a cage of his own making and brought a single tear to his eye. He grieved what he deemed lost, and he loathed himself for allowing himself to play the fool.

You're losing your grip, Margrete whispered, her tone firm. She likely knew every emotion his heart radiated so freely, their bond making it difficult to hide truths from one another. But instead of utilizing cruelty, instead of gloating at his sudden understanding, she gave him a reassuring squeeze.

We're going to flip it. We have twenty feet before it reaches their boat, she said, *and then when it's floundering, we strike. I'm going to need you to be ready when I take aim.*

Hell, she sounded so sure, so focused. And here he was, a mess of a man. He hated himself.

Stop, she pleaded. He twisted to her. *I need you to focus. I can't do this without you.*

Such mighty words. Darius's heart leaped at the sound of them.

It wasn't because the woman he'd loved spoke them, but because the woman who should detest him with every fiber of her being had decided to take a chance on him and allow him inside her mind. To trust him.

Darius's plans fell by the wayside. He didn't ruminate on the past, and for once, he pondered what might happen if he lost her fragile trust. If he lost Bay's trust. How would he feel if he died? If Atlas or Mila died?

Mila had tended to his wounds even though he'd stolen the most precious person in her life. Mila didn't deserve to die, not a woman with such ferocity in her blood and glimmering life in her eyes. None of them did.

They weren't insects to squash. They elicited emotions from Darius that he believed were long dead. While both a gift and a curse, being apathetic, cold, and unfeeling was worse.

Fuck.

Margrete squeezed him harder, forcing him to narrow in on the Cyros. It swam less than two hundred feet away. Mila had brought her and Atlas close to her vessel and was working on hauling Atlas over the side. She rolled to the bottom, the sailor still unconscious...or worse. Mila pushed herself up and plunged beside her friend. They were both onboard. Still, Darius knew they stood no chance on the open waters. It was now or never.

On my mark. Margrete took control, flicking her free hand up and then moving it in circles, the act creating a whirlpool. Darius allowed a surge of his own power to enter her system, and the current grew stronger still. He felt freer than he had in decades, despite his fluctuating emotions, despite bestowing yet another piece of himself to a woman who refused to love him back.

He gave it all, little by little, and Margrete's hold on the whirlpool strengthened. And before long, he watched in wonder as it towered high above, high enough that he had to crane his neck to take in all its lethal splendor.

The waters were dark and churning with flashes of aqua-blue, and when he exhaled, Darius added his own spark to the mix. He concentrated on the motion, on the current, reinforcing it so when they aimed for the Cyros, it would be a deadly strike.

You ready? he asked Margrete.

Whenever you are.

Darius twisted his fingers, as did Margrete, and the spinning waters crashed down upon the red beast, causing Mila's boat to sway precariously to the side, nearly flipping over entirely as she struggled to row them to safety. He couldn't see the details of her face, but he knew it was scrunched in determination, her sharp eyes likely narrowed into slits.

For a heartbeat he worried they'd failed, and that the Cyros had managed to swim beneath and far from his aim. But he caught sight of its rolling body, its underbelly exposed.

Strike him! Margrete commanded, and Darius unleashed himself.

He discharged the rage that emboldened his magic and freed the power that was an extension of himself. The wave he directed at the Cyros's underbelly struck hard and true, piercing it as efficiently as any blade.

Water was a weapon in Darius's hands—one he knew better than anything else in his life—and he held nothing back.

The beast bellowed as its body split open, its rumbling cry music to Darius's ears. Its slick skin curled as the tear grew, ripping it in half, black blood gushing in spurts.

Before he knew what was happening, two arms banded around his waist and he was being...*hugged.*

"We did it!" Margrete screamed, her excitement wafting off of her like the sweetest perfume.

Darius's hands were stiff at his sides, but he slowly returned the embrace, his heart beating faster.

Her eyes were alight when she drew back, but as if she were coming out of a daze, they quickly sharpened when she took him in. She'd forgotten herself, and *him*, and the excitement he'd felt fizzled to nothing.

He felt himself fizzle to nothing.

"They're almost here!" Bay said, elation in his voice. His joy quickly simmered out like a dying flame. Hell, it hadn't even had time to take hold. "Shit. Look to the northeast!" he warned, shattering the precarious moment, and they both spun back into action.

"The Kora. I should've known it was just biding its time," Darius warned.

"The what?" Bay asked, rising from where he'd placed Dani on the deck. She was just now coming to, a dazed look smoothing her features.

Darius pointed to the waves, to the green-scaled monster lurking beneath. "You're about to find out."

Malum had created it, and it was by far the deadliest beast of the lot. Darius was preparing to warn Margrete when a shadow thrust across the tops of the swells.

No. Not a shadow. A *man.*

Margrete cursed and sprinted toward the ladder and the boat that carried the king's corpse. She had to grasp hold of the banister to keep from tumbling over, her knees wobbling.

"His body...Bash is gone."

CHAPTER THIRTY-FOUR

MARGRETE

BASH SHOT BENEATH THE SURFACE WATER LIKE A BIRD IN FLIGHT.

His body glowed, though it was an odd sort of light; dark and silver. Margrete tracked his movements, her pulse racing when she confirmed her suspicions, no matter how obvious they had been.

Bash was going to attack the Kora. By himself.

"Help me!" Mila called out, her boat rocking against the *Mare Deus*. Bay sprang to life, leaping down onto the vessel and aiding Mila as they brought Atlas onboard.

There was so much blood...

Dani released a choked sob, feebly rising on her unsteady limbs to wrap her arms around Atlas the moment she was brought onto the planks. She wasn't moving.

Bay pushed on her chest, trying to rouse life back into her heart. Dani sobbed over her, holding her hand, bringing it to her lips.

"We never even got a chance," Dani rasped, lowering her head.

"She's lost a lot of blood, but there's a pulse!" Bay flipped her onto her side just as Atlas spewed a lungful of saltwater onto the planks. She gasped for air, her skin paler than snow. She'd lost far too much blood, and even if she'd expelled all the water from her lungs, she was far from safe.

"Your king has a death wish!" Darius brought her focus back to Bash. With Atlas alive and breathing, under Bay's care, she wished she could feel joy. But Bash was now in danger, and he'd foolishly taken on one of the sea's children alone.

Margrete opened her mouth and called his name, her grip on the banister hard enough that she swore she heard the wood creaking. Sparks flew from her fingertips, but they'd lost their potency, and the more she spiraled out of control—her panic overtaking everything else—the less her magic spoke to her, and the harder it was to seize it.

"We need to do something!" she said, facing Darius. He watched with a mixture of what she assumed to be wonder and...respect?

Darius opened and closed his mouth. His entire body went rigid.

"There's something approaching," he murmured, eyes narrowing into a squint.

"More beasts?" she cried, scanning the sea. There was no damned way they could defeat—

Her jaw went slack as she faced the latest arrival. *There's no way...*

A ship. A grand ship with a blue flag and a crescent moon.

The flag of Azantian.

"Adrian," she whispered to herself in awe, eyes widening as the Azantian vessel approached. "How on earth did he find us?"

Bay rose from where Dani embraced Atlas. "I told you I sent a missive to him when we were in Maribella, but I have no clue how he found us out here. I'd say it was a gift from the gods, but I now know that not to be true." He eyed her and Darius both.

Margrete was gaping, no longer in control of her facial expressions. Fuck her grief, her anger, her confusion. She yanked Bay into a tight hug, twin tears slipping free. She'd nearly lost Atlas, nearly lost Mila.

She understood how precious time could be.

While she didn't want Adrian or his men in danger, she knew they could help them now when they most needed it. And Bash...

Adrian would know what to do. He was his brother in all the significant ways, and she wanted him to be with her king more than anyone else.

Margrete drew back from Bay, noticing he, too, had tears tracking down his cheeks. He gruffly wiped them away and cleared his throat, unable to meet her stare.

"I love you," she said, swallowing thickly. "I know why—"

"I love you too," he said, cutting off the words that weren't necessary.

The seconds they shared seemed too brief, but a booming crash pulled them back to the fight.

A cannon fired from Adrian's ship, striking the waters near the *Mare Deus* with a thunderous roar. Bay instinctively grabbed hold of her arm, preparing to cover his body with her own, but there was no need. The explosion sent the Kora tumbling to its side, spinning to the right.

She held her breath, frantically searching for signs of Bash. Only when a raven-haired head broke the surface did she exhale.

"Your king better be a good swimmer," Darius murmured. She went still, the statement catching her off-guard. Had the God of the Sea attempted to make a *joke*? A poor one, but still.

"We need to help them," she said to him, grabbing at the god's hands. "Connect with me again. They might not see Bash and could strike him instead."

Darius hesitated, a muscle in his jaw feathering, but then he nodded and promptly shut his eyes.

Margrete opened herself up, just as she had before. But this time... this time there was *nothing*.

No spark. No overwhelming rush of his thoughts. She was on the outside, banging her fists against his mind, and no matter how hard she tried, she couldn't breach his defenses.

"Why aren't you letting me in?" she asked, exasperated.

"I *am*," Darius argued. "Or I'm trying to. There aren't any barriers."

Margrete swore loudly enough to battle the enraged winds whooshing in her ears.

"Fine, then we do this alone." To Bay, she shouted, "Get us closer!"

Her friend shouted in confirmation, adjusting the sails to send them lurching forward. Margrete used her magic to aid their advance, speaking to the current to carry them to the next foe. She held her hands aloft, aiming for the Kora.

A second cannon blast sounded, and she braced herself—and the *Mare Deus*. Adrian, standing on deck and commanding the crew, managed to direct the strike with precision, firing all that gunpowder at the Kora's tail. The waves shook at the impact, and the blue waters turned black with the beast's blood.

It might've been weakened, but the creature was far from done.

It lurched into the sky, its maw opening to reveal four rows of serrated teeth. With half its body midair, she likened it to a sea dragon... the monster she'd seen in her books of myths.

And on his back, holding tight to one of its fins, was Bash.

She turned to Adrian's vessel, noting he'd signaled that they halt. No more cannons fired, and when she peered to the upper decks, she caught sight of his towering figure, one hand held up.

Adrian couldn't know that the man on the back of the Kora was his friend and king, but he recognized the shape of a man, and he wasn't the type to fire on an innocent.

Deep slate clouds roiled across the horizon, and dense fog swept around Bash and the beast. When it lunged downward and back into the sea, her king held on, diving with it.

Margrete shut her eyes and allowed her soul to wander. Instantly, she was beneath the surface, a phantom bystander. The Kora thrashed as it attempted to dislodge the king, but Bash didn't relent. If anything, she noticed that odd glow of his strengthen.

Raising a hand into the air, he roared, his voice carried to her through the dense water. It wasn't muffled as she expected...

Was he breathing underwater?

Margrete's detached mind swam closer. Bash's eyes were the darkest she'd ever seen, and his blackened nails were no longer trimmed and neat, but sharp and long and tapered into perfect points. He climbed up the Kora's back, hardly affected by its struggle. He didn't stop until he'd scaled its back and reached its massive head. There, he clutched both sides of the monster's face, his nails digging into its iridescent hide. Margrete gasped as he unhinged his jaw unnaturally wide, his nymera scales aglow with dark magic.

The creature shrieked now, ramping up its fight, but Bash merely inhaled, and bright crimson tendrils slithered from the creature's gaping mouth.

Bash was...stealing his *soul*.

Of course, he would need to feed once he returned to his body. They knew this was a possibility, but watching him perform the act, even on a monster, sent Margrete spiraling back into her solid body on the *Mare Deus*.

She hissed, opening her eyes to find Darius and Bay gawking at her, the former wearing a solemn look.

"Where did you just go?" Bay asked, clutching her shoulder. His solid presence settled her.

"I-I saw him. Bash is...he's taking the Kora's soul as we speak."

The sea where her king and the creature battled rippled violently, the swells churning, hiding the scuffle taking place below.

Minutes passed, and just when Margrete prepared to dip back into her remaining reserves of magic, the waters ceased their heaving...

She saw his head first, his handsome face contorting with a near feral snarl. Bash rose into the air, his bare torso glimmering with his nymera scales. Gracing the tops of the waves, he advanced, gliding toward the *Mare Deus* with a glazed expression. There was no humanity there, just emptiness, and she stifled the terror rising in her heart.

Just before he reached them, no more than fifty feet away, another nymera showed herself.

Minthe.

She leaped from the sea and circled Bash like a serpent, her flowing hair a blur of midnight. Margrete saw nothing but Minthe, and she acted instinctively when the nymera dug her claws into the man she loved.

Margrete jumped onto the railing and leaped off the side of the ship.

CHAPTER THIRTY-FIVE

BASH

He was eternal.

His body thrummed with energy, the soul of the Kora feeding his adrenaline. So detached from reality, he hardly became aware of the figure encircling him. Could hardly be bothered to stop her from grasping his arm.

You did good, my son. The voice was familiar, and he focused on the woman—the nymera—gazing into his eyes. There was a warm sensation in his chest, but it vanished as she shifted her attention to the side, to where a ship rocked back and forth in the swells.

Rain clouds covered the blue of the skies, and soon, droplets fell. He shut his lids, indulging in the sensation, his every nerve electrified, his skin almost too sensitive.

We need to go, the nymera said again, panic lacing her tone. He frowned, realization striking him.

Minthe.

Yes, she said, clutching him tighter. *Now we must go.*

She tried to yank him below, but he jerked free, uncertainty and fear causing him to pause.

He was missing something...

His name. What was his name again? He thought on it, ignoring the nymera's protests, and wracked his mind for the answer. He found nothing but the lingering traces of magic leftover from the Kora.

What a meal that had been. He felt full of its soul, so very deliciously satisfied. The beast that threatened to eclipse his thoughts seemed to howl in agreement, and he had to work to shove it back.

He had something he needed to do, right? A mission, a goal he had to reach. But with his blood humming and the fog in his mind growing thicker, he couldn't remember.

Movement to his right captured his focus.

A figure swam toward them, a woman by the looks of it. He sniffed the waters, wrinkling his nose when he sensed that she wasn't human. He scented her divinity, the reeking foulness of her floral scent. Lavender.

An image flashed; of a dark-haired beauty staring at him, a smile on her full lips. She vanished in a blink.

Instinct had him rearing back, preparing for a fight, his talons curling together. If she dared attack, he'd be ready.

Listen to me! the nymera yelled, clinging to him. *We need to go!* Her eyes went wide with alarm, a look that confused him. There was no need to be alarmed. They were the predators, the monsters others should fear.

No, he said coolly, *there is an enemy approaching.*

He may not know his name, but he didn't shirk from a fight. Besides, he was strong, his limbs burning with power. His last meal had been a decent one, much larger than any natural soul should be. Its weight sharpened his thoughts to a terrifying degree.

But he wanted more. Always more. That yawning pit in his stomach continued to grow, taunting him until his teeth ground together.

When the stranger slowed twenty feet away, she lifted her head from the surface of the waves. He took in blue eyes and soft skin, and his inner beast snarled in delight. He could feel it claw his insides, yearning, *aching* for him to steal her soul.

But then she raised her palms, and the waves surrounding her began to rise. With only her hands, she brought herself above, hovering like he did, though the water seemed to brush against her almost affectionately.

He stared at her...a sudden pang stabbing him in the chest. Such a sensation gave him pause.

"Bash," she said, a fierceness punctuating the name, turning it into a weapon. "Come here."

Bash? Such an odd name. Yet there wasn't a doubt she meant it for him. He cocked his head, taking in a long inhale.

That scent was overpowering, familiar and warm. It reminded him of summer and sunshine and happiness.

He wanted to devour it.

That's right, Minthe coaxed. *Steal her soul.*

Her soul would be even better than the sea monster's. There wasn't a doubt. Something about her was unique in a way he couldn't pinpoint.

Without thought, he coasted over the top of the sea and toward the woman with the most vibrant blue eyes that rivaled the sea itself.

"You aren't yourself," the stranger said, the muscles in her neck taut. "Come back to me, pirate."

He could sense her fear. It wafted sweetly from her every pore. His grin blossomed.

"We talked about this," she said, her voice rising, "what would happen when you returned to your body. How lost you'd be." Wetness lined her eyes, and while he itched at the sight of the unshed tears, they also made him feel...*wrong.* "But I know you recognize me. I know you're questioning how and why...and I need you to remember. Remember me. Remember *us.*"

He paused, drinking her in. She dared approach him and argue. If he hadn't ravaged the Kora's soul already, he would've attacked by now, yet there was something else holding him back...

Lavender.

That damned scent again.

It clogged his nostrils and overpowered all senses, and then more images flickered by like shooting stars. He glimpsed an island in the sun, a blonde child giggling as she raced across the surf. He saw the woman before him cupping his cheeks, telling him she loved him. Calling him *Bash.* Holding onto him like he was her greatest treasure.

He knew her, his *beast* knew her, had tasted her before. Invisible nails dragged down his back, his vision tunneling.

She was no stranger.

She was...

"M-Margrete?" His voice cracked as he spoke it aloud, sounding deep and hoarse, like he'd been screaming for hours on end. She released a relieved gasp, those tears she'd kept at bay now sliding down her cheeks. He was Bash and he was a king. He...he knew her, *loved* this woman—

A whirl of black lunged.

The nymera—*Minthe*—was the night itself as she propelled herself onto Margrete, who had been too distracted by him to defend herself. His mother wrapped her arms around her and dug her nails into Margrete's smooth skin, eliciting a shriek of pain.

Bash fought against the churning chaos that was his inner beast's thoughts, the sound of Margrete's scream driving him forward.

Before he could grab hold of Minthe, before he could free Margrete from his mother's grip, a man rushed behind her and yanked Minthe into his clutches.

No, he remembered, not just any man. A god.

Darius.

He'd somehow managed to sneak up on them all, and he trapped the thrashing nymera in his arms with ease. Blue light danced around him, the air sparking with magic.

"Kill them!" Minthe shrieked, observing Bash through narrowed eyes. "They'll only betray you in the end. They always do."

He recalled her tale of heartbreak and loss. She'd been betrayed by his father all those years ago. Was imprisoned beneath *rock*. During Darius's trials, Bash had felt pity, but that was before she forced him to become a monster. Even now, the darkness screeched in fury, trying to dig its way back in and assume command. But Bash's hunger wasn't nearly as consuming as it had been on the island, and he clenched his fists, willing away the wicked enchantment.

I'm not that thing anymore, he thought. *And I won't ever become it again.*

His body shook as he slowly made his way to Margrete, careful to keep some semblance of space between them. He didn't trust himself, and he feared his grip on his body would slip, his vision growing darker, the little black spots fluttering over his eyes.

Rigidly, he turned and faced the creature that birthed him, keeping Margrete safely out of his sight. Even still, he felt her stare bore into the side of his face. He could sense her worry, her emotion rolling off her in waves.

A memory came to him, of a time when he'd commanded a mighty ship, the day after he'd stolen his enemy's daughter.

"You can't condemn an entire species simply because evil men live among them," Bash said, repeating Margrete's words from that fateful day. "I'm sorry you've suffered, that you were tossed away by my father. His actions were despicable, I'm not arguing that." No, he realized now just how cruel his father had been. To give his love to Minthe and then lock her away. To keep her from her *child*. Every good thought Bash ever had of him changed the second she'd told her tale. "But this woman right here..." He motioned to Margrete who beamed with pride. "She is my heart. My soul. I gave her my love freely and she's kept it safe, gifting me with her own love in return."

Bash glided forward, mere feet from where Darius still clutched his mother. Minthe's brows were bunched, her teeth on display in a ferocious rage. Her eyes drifted to Margrete and then back to him.

"It won't last," she snarled, yanking fruitlessly against Darius's grip. "She'll see the real you and run away. Just give it time. You're satiated *now*, but what happens when you grow hungry?"

"Then we'll deal with it," Margrete snapped. "We'll find a way for him to survive *without* him losing his humanity." She studied Minthe, pity shining in her eyes. "I see his darkness, just as he sees mine. I'm not pure. I'm flawed and selfish and so very angry most of the time." She took a stuttering inhale and lowered her chin. "I've made choices I am not proud of, possibly condemning thousands of innocents to death because I love your son and couldn't imagine life without him. I'm no hero."

Minthe went still, her lean limbs frozen.

"If your son can find it in his heart to forgive my indefensible actions, then how can you claim I won't forgive his?"

"He's all I have left..." Minthe struggled with the words, a black tear cascading down her hollowed cheek. "I—he was taken from me. And I just found him. You have no idea what it's been like to lose a child, and I loved his father, the same as you love my son. I loved him with every fiber of my being, and he stole my soul when he locked me away." She turned to Bash. "I just wanted *time* with you. Time that was robbed from me."

Something within Bash broke. While his mother cried tears of onyx, her face was more human than he'd ever seen it. She'd been wronged. Hurt. Destroyed.

What he stared at was a broken shell of a woman who was reaching for an ounce of love. *His* love.

"We need to kill her or Halio won't honor his end of the bargain," Darius said sternly. "She has to die."

Margrete went rigid. "But—"

"No." Darius shook his head sadly, and when he loosened his hold on Minthe, she surprisingly didn't use the opportunity to claw her way free. "Halio told you to slay the sea's children. The beasts *I* created. And she, unfortunately, is one of them."

"Azantian..." Margrete choked on a sob. "Halio will wipe it away if we fail. Is he truly so callous that he wouldn't spare her?"

Minthe remained frozen, her black eyes glued to Bash. To her son. Her features softened, and this time when she turned to Margrete, it wasn't with malice or suspicion. Bash saw...hope.

"You love her that much?" Minthe asked of him, her throat working to keep the sobs at bay. "You'd risk *everything* for her?"

Bash nodded without pause. "Everything and more. All of what I am. I risk the island I love for her, whether it's right or wrong."

Minthe shook Darius off, and he allowed it. She drifted toward Bash, searching him for a lie, her stare as potent as her scales.

"I lived a lonely life full of betrayal," she said, reaching for his cheek. He flinched when her icy skin made contact. "But I never want that for you." Another black tear dripped down to her chin. "Can I...can I hold you?" she asked, her lips quivering, her lithe body beginning to tremble.

Bash sucked in a breath. The last time she'd held him, he'd been a baby. Too young to remember what her touch felt like.

When he gave her a curt nod, Minthe wrapped her arms around his shoulders and gripped him tight, her nails cutting into his neck. He didn't mind the bite of pain—she couldn't help but cause it.

"I missed you," she murmured. "This was all I ever wanted. All I needed." Minthe trembled in his hold. "I did all I could to see you whole, to see you happy. I don't want to turn into the man who destroyed my own life. I won't."

Bash swallowed hard, his father's face flashing once more. Gods, his life felt like a lie.

Minthe embraced him for what felt like minutes, and then she drew back, putting distance between them.

"You can fight the darkness," she whispered, "as long as you have something to hold onto." With that, she took one of her long nails and ran its razor-sharp edge along her throat.

Bash screamed her name, and Margrete rushed to grasp the nymera, holding her up as she slumped forward. Black blood poured from the self-inflicted wound, streaming down Minthe's form and covering her in death. And all the while she held Bash's eyes and reached out a hand, one he took.

He shed a tear of his own, mourning his mother. The woman she might have been had circumstances been different. The relationship they might have had one day.

She'd sacrificed herself for *him*. Out of love.

Minthe's eyes fluttered closed, her last breath expelling.

Bash watched in horror as she shattered into a thousand pieces before their eyes...crumbling into the sea and swept away by a single wave.

CHAPTER THIRTY-SIX

DARIUS

HE'D BEEN ABOUT TO KILL HER.

Minthe was the last of the nymeras, and she was one of his own creations. Meaning her death was necessary if they wished to succeed and complete the bargain with Halio. Sure, Darius had hesitated just before the kill, knowing full well the crew would've called him evil for the act. A villain. All the things they already considered him. And maybe they were right.

But the nymera had chosen a different path. One he hadn't expected.

"Bash..." Margrete began, inching closer, though not close enough where she could reach out and grasp him. The apprehension was still there, the uncertainty as to how the half-nymera would react. Darius watched them now, preparing himself to intervene should Bash's darkness take root, which was a possibility he had expected.

Surprisingly, Bash whirled away and plunged into the depths, slicing through the water like an arrow. He swam just below the surface, his silhouette visible from where Darius and Margrete hovered, the waves caressing their sides.

Darius snuck a peek at her now, grimacing at her reaction.

"Give him some time," he said. "He has to process." The words were stiff, he knew this much, and likely of no comfort. But he tried his best to sound soothing.

"She did that for him," Margrete murmured, still in shock. She stared off to where Bash had last been seen, though now even Darius wasn't aware of his movements. He could hunt him down if he desired, but he took his own advice and let the king be.

"Minthe gave up everything for his chance at happiness. Without a single second of hesitation." Margrete's eyes grew fierce as she stared at Darius. "She...she changed, and all because of a single moment in time. A plea from her son."

Because of love. Minthe gave up her son and her chance at reconnecting with him because of *love*.

Darius shut his eyes, understanding Margrete's deeper meaning. He wasn't like Minthe. Not selfless enough to let go of the past. Or the future he envisioned. He claimed he loved her, and yet...

And yet he didn't love her enough to let her go.

Darius opened his eyes.

He was out on the waves—

Alone.

CHAPTER THIRTY-SEVEN

BASH

Bash didn't remember how he got back on the ship. He didn't remember much at all...aside from the look of grief that distorted Minthe's features as she sacrificed herself for him, his island, and his well-being.

After everything she'd done, after all her ambitions and plans, she had made her choice, and it was *him*. She chose him right when he needed her.

How easy it had been for Bash to first look at her and scream *Monster*. He saw her scales, her nails, her teeth, and he'd shut off his compassion like a switch. Perhaps that's what most people did when faced with something they didn't understand—they deemed it an abomination, some demon. But the truth was, a truth he was just now learning, was that they were all monsters, in some form or another in someone else's eyes.

There were no shining heroes, and not one person on this vessel could claim the title, least of all him. Maybe that's why heroes belonged solely in his stories, because real life was messy and gray, and he no longer assumed choosing the *wrong* path made him evil.

Distantly, Bash sensed someone touching him, grazing his jaw. But everything felt surreal, like a dream he couldn't wake from. He felt the softness of a mattress beneath him, cotton sheets pulled over his bare torso, his damp shirt having been removed. He smelled salt and old wood, and a hint of lavender.

"Look up," the voice demanded.

Delicate fingers grasped his chin and forced his eyes up.

Dani hovered above, assessing him in a way that left him feeling even more wretched. Her lips were curved down at the sides, and her eyes were narrowed in either apprehension or disbelief.

"You're...you," she finally uttered. "I mean, I thought it would be harder but...how *did* you reconnect?"

Bash didn't answer. Again, the past few hours were all a blur.

But he felt full. Which was a relief, although the skin around his scales itched incessantly.

"He'll need to feed soon," Dani said, glancing over her shoulder. Bash realized Margrete and Bay were behind her. They were in the cabin he shared with Margrete, the rest of the crew absent. Darius included.

Feed. The word sounded so dirty. Minthe claimed he'd have some time before he'd have to consume another soul, but his pulse raced at the mere thought of losing himself to the darkness once more.

He searched Dani's eyes, startled when they flashed silver, the sapphire-blue masked entirely by hardened steel.

"How long does he have?" Margrete asked.

"He's *half*-nymera, so hopefully the Kora's soul will sustain him, but again, he'll need to feed on souls eventually. He wasn't returned to his body and *cured*. I just thank the gods that the Kora, unlike a human, has a soul that will be much more potent, giving us time to regroup. It's probably the reason he was able to maintain some semblance of himself."

Margrete was asking her a question, but Bash found himself utterly transfixed by Dani's flickering eyes. How unearthly they shone in the low lighting of the cabin. They reminded him of another's...a certain god of death.

She sniffed the air, her hands dropping to her sides. "Seeing as he fed from the beast, I can only assume he can feed from animals, but that would grant us mere hours."

They continued talking about him as if he weren't there, and Bash found he didn't care. He was back on the waters, sucking the life from the Kora. Back in time, watching his mother slice open her own throat. It repeated over and over in a vicious loop. He shut his eyes, as if that would do anything at all to save him from the memory.

Bash mourned her even as residual anger lived in his heart. He wondered if her final moments could outweigh her choices on the island.

The lost child inside of him wanted to believe it just might.

He must've drifted off, because the next time Bash opened his eyes, only Margrete was in the room. He stared back, transfixed by her, his senses slowly heightening the longer he took her in. Everything felt so sharp, clear, and overwhelming.

Bash wasn't sure what had changed since the island. How he'd been able to fend off his inner beast today, even after the Kora's soul.

"Bash, what is it?" Margrete scooted beside him on the bed, careful to leave an inch between them. She was being too cautious around him, and it made him feel off. More so than he already felt.

"I—" He shifted on the bed, itching in his own skin. He grazed a serrated scale at his throat, the edges prickling the pad of his finger. They were larger than they'd been in his phantom form, as were his nails, which were tapered into perfectly honed points.

"This time, I wasn't as...easily overpowered." He'd been full, yes, but his darker side would've still desired a kill, especially one that had smelled as divine as her. "I want to think it was more than the soul I had that made a difference. I held onto you, and while I don't want to place such a burden on your shoulders, I feel your face kept me present."

His voice was barely above a whisper, but she heard him, nodding in contemplation.

"I was thinking the same," she admitted. Her nose wrinkled, and some of the weight lifted from his chest. He loved when she did that. A small quirk that occurred when she was perplexed by some mystery.

Her face went slack, and suddenly, a knowing look softened her features.

"What is it?" he asked.

She ran a hand through her curls, which were tangled and smelled of the sea. "I couldn't reach Darius back there, during the final battle with the Kora. We were fine when the first two attacked, but then something shifted and...I couldn't reach him at all. I only felt you."

Bash pondered her words. He certainly was no expert in souls or gods or immortal bonds, but he had an idea why she'd struggled to reach him on the island. And it had to do with the same god who'd swindled her into an unwanted bargain.

"If Darius didn't have a hold on your soul..."

"Then it could connect with yours," she finished for him.

He sighed. What the hell did that mean then? Was Darius finally finished with her? Or had it merely been a stroke of luck?

Bash was about to voice his thoughts when another one struck him.

"Wait." He took her hand in his cold one, and she let out a relieved sigh, curling her fingers tightly around him. "Did you see how Dani's eyes turned silver just now? Or was I hallucinating?"

That sure as shit seemed important.

But Margrete frowned. "No...when was this?"

"When she was inspecting me. Her eyes flashed silver for a brief moment, but they weren't...human. I don't know how else to describe it." Bash's skin tingled as he dared to lift his free hand to Margrete's cheek. She shut her lids as he let his fingers slide down her smooth skin.

An hour each day hadn't been nearly enough, and it felt like the first time he'd touched her in weeks.

"She...she was below the waters for far too long. She fell overboard. Atlas dove in to rescue her, but then the Cyros attacked." Margrete swallowed thickly. Bash's breathing hitched. He'd been so lost to reclaiming his body that he hadn't known how close he'd come to losing his friends.

"Are they all right?" he asked, his throat constricting.

She nodded, and he released a faltering sigh. "Atlas lost a lot of blood from the wound on her forearm, but she's almost healed and resting now.

And Dani..." Margrete paused, a furrow forming between her brows. "She seems fine but...I sense something in her, or maybe it's something missing. Like the sea..."

"Like the sea took her and returned her soul?" Bash offered, thinking of when he'd lost Margrete. How her eyes had changed when the waters gave her new life.

She jerked her head in affirmation. "She won't speak on it, but it's a sound explanation."

They sat in silence for many long minutes. Bash worried for Dani, for Atlas, for every member of his crew. But he also worried about himself. About what would happen when he grew hungry. It wasn't *his* life he feared.

"How are we going to fix this? Fix *me*?" he eventually asked. "I feel like a bomb about to go off, and I don't want you caught in the aftermath."

Bash wouldn't be able to rest without a plan. Plans made sense, order made him feel slightly in control, and control was safety. It was one of his many rules as king, a way to handle the stress of the crown. It might not always have been healthy, but it was the only way he coped.

Margrete glanced to the far corner of the room, her bottom lip stuck between her teeth as a thousand emotions flashed across her eyes. She rose slowly, walking over to a stool where a small leather satchel rested. Digging through its scarce contents, she then pulled out a key.

A key.

Shit. Yet another thing Bash had forgotten to ask her about. Atlas had told him she'd discovered a key in the Underworld, and while he'd meant to question her, they'd been so overwhelmed by, well, by *everything* else. Fuck, he was still reeling from Minthe's sacrifice.

"This was inside a desk in my chambers. In the Underworld. I meant to tell you sooner, but I was more concerned with your safety." She held it to the light, granting time for Bash to take in the intricate wave details on the handle that rose to encircle an orb. Within the glass, blue-tinged liquid sloshed about, a slight shimmer radiating from the mysterious fluid.

"What do you think it is?" he asked, his chest growing tight. Something about the key had the hair on the back of his neck rising, and the darkness he'd kept shoved down, swam to the surface. It was cold, his magic, his *dark* magic. As before, it had a sentient quality to it, like he shared his body with a separate entity.

Margrete ran a finger across the glass. "We think these are Surria's tears. And they supposedly have the ability to create a new god. She created Darius and Malum with them, after all." She lifted her head, the question she wasn't asking apparent.

Bash scoffed, momentarily stunned. "You want to try and use it on *me*?"

If that worked, if they *were* Surria's tears, then...then Bash could become a god beside her and live out the rest of his life without worrying about killing her. He would possess magic, and hopefully, the ability to squash his darker instincts.

It all felt *too* perfect.

"I wanted to ask Halio about it when we returned, but I'm not sure if I can trust him." She raised a brow as if to say, *Obviously.* "I certainly don't want to expose you to something that could harm you, so we might be forced to ask for his help anyway." She sighed, rubbing her free hand across her face. Margrete was beyond exhausted, and Bash didn't want to add to her concerns. But time was running out, and sooner or later, he'd get hungry again.

He glanced down at his hands, to his sharpened black claws. And then he laughed.

Margrete frowned, looking at him like he'd grown two heads. Hell, at this point nothing would shock him.

"What's so funny, pirate?" she asked, an adorable scowl on her face.

"My nails. I need to trim my damned nails." It wasn't funny, not at all, but Bash lifted them up and twisted his wrists, smiling like a fool. "I legitimately could poke my own damned eye out with one of these."

Bash assumed that people turned to humor when their lives had gone to shit. And he was embracing the nearly hysterical laughter bubbling up his throat. "I swear, one wrong move in my sleep and that's how I'll go. If I die by a *nail*, please lie to my people."

"Gods, Bash. Calm yourself," Margrete said, though she fully failed to suppress a giggle.

When he'd settled, his laughter fading off, Bash leaned his head against her shoulder. He sighed into her curls, gently shaking his head at the absurdity that had become their lives.

"So," he began after many minutes of blissful silence, "we killed all the beasts, right?"

Margrete's shoulder tensed. "I think so? Right after we returned onboard, Darius barked out, "It's done," and then vanished. I might've seen him headed to the waters, but I'm not sure. I haven't thought to look for him."

Bash imagined the god would've taken the time to posture about, rubbing in the fact that soon he'd have everything he wanted. But Darius had vanished, which was odd for the smug bastard, who took any opportunity to gloat.

Then again, maybe he was just as affected by Minthe's sacrifice as Bash was...but where Bash felt a mixture of grief and confusion, Darius might be experiencing envy. His own mother would never have done what Minthe did. Surria would've killed *him* before herself.

And whereas Bash had someone to comfort him when he woke, easing the pain with laughter and sweet touches, Darius had no one.

Don't feel sorry for him, Bash scolded, stunned he'd even felt the damned emotion at all. Maybe when he'd returned to his body, something vital had been altered. That could be the only reason he felt undeserved pity.

Margrete ran her fingers through his hair, her nails scraping against his scalp. He shut his eyes, releasing the first truly relaxed breath since he'd woken. He would cement this moment into his mind, because he knew when he reflected upon his life, these memories would be the ones he thought about; the times that felt insignificant but meant the entire world.

"Can we return to the Underworld tomorrow?" Margrete broke the silence. "I just want one night before we face all of them."

The gods. Halio. *Darius.*

They had yet to figure out a loophole.

"Tonight will be ours," Bash promised, pressing a kiss to her brow.

A knock rattled the wood of the cabin. They both flinched at the same time, jerking to attention.

"It's just me, don't get too worked up."

Bash lurched for the door, swinging it open to reveal the best sight he could've conjured. He'd believed it had been a dream, a hallucination brought about by his state, his weariness, but...

Adrian flung himself at him, his arms steel bands squeezing the life from his lungs. Bash grunted, but gods, did he return that hug, a smile stretching his lips.

"And here I thought you forgot about me after my valiant efforts to save you. Though I'm not sure we did much aside from weaken it. You did the rest," Adrian murmured into his ear, drawing back. He clasped Bash's arms, studying him from head to toe. Finally, he shook his head and rolled his eyes.

And because he was Adrian, he always knew exactly what to say.

"You were always one for the dramatic." Adrian grinned, and warmth flooded into Bash's chest, chasing away the lingering doubts. "Lucky for you, your appearance now matches."

"So kind of you to say," Bash said, snorting. "I take it Bay's message reached you?"

The warmth in Adrian's green eyes flared. "It did. Although it took a while to get into my hands. Our scouts on the nearest human islands had to send a bird to carry it the final distance."

"Remind me to give him a raise," Bash said, knowing he now owed Bay for more than one reason.

"I'm just glad you all are...all right," Adrian whispered, sobering. He glanced at Margrete who remained on the bed, allowing them space for their reunion. By "all right," Adrian meant he was thankful they'd forgiven Bay for his act on the island. Bash was sure his boyfriend had filled him in while he'd slept.

"We are," Bash assured, taking hold of Adrian's shoulder. "And we will continue to be fine. Nothing can change that, and nothing can take away the gratitude I feel for both of you." Bash couldn't help but bring Adrian in for another hug. He held his brother, thankful for his steadying presence, thankful that he'd journeyed to Rydor to assist them when they faced the sea's children. Adrian was his family, and their bond had never been greater.

Adrian was the first to draw back. "Tell me, Bash...aside from your new look, what else have I missed?"

Margrete released a choked laugh.

Adrian probably should sit down for this tale.

CHAPTER THIRTY-EIGHT

DARIUS

DARIUS SAT PERCHED ON A BOULDER OVERLOOKING THE GRAY COAST.

The second he'd returned to the vessel he'd checked on Dani and Atlas. Both women would live. Atlas was recovering, asleep under Dani's watchful eye. When he'd drawn close enough to them both, he'd sensed a change, something calling out to him.

Dani. She'd been reborn by the sea. He felt her now, forever a part of the waters he loved. She'd drowned, her heart surely stopping. But it hadn't been her time to die. Not yet.

Some people could cheat death—only because death had a much greater fate in store for them.

Darius left them alone and marched up the steps and to the bow. He had leaped right off the side of the *Mare Deus* and swam.

He didn't want to suffer the scrutiny of the others. He'd done nothing wrong, and yet he worried he'd earned their distrust. Darius had been *so* close to slaying the nymera. But now, dwelling in silence, he ruminated over the scene again and again until all he felt was emptiness.

To have someone care for you like that...to do the unthinkable? He'd never known such an impossible thing. He probably never would. Darius was alone. Now and forever.

Never in all of his many years had Darius been around a group of people like this before. When he wandered the world, cursed as a mortal, he'd kept to himself, only interacting when required. At that time, he'd done so with the belief that humans were beneath him, and therefore, a waste of time.

But this family of misfits loved each other to a degree that even Darius's callous heart could feel.

So lost in his own dour reflections, he didn't notice the newcomer until they spoke.

"They're wondering where you are, you know."

He jerked his chin up, finding Mila marching up the shore, headed in his direction. Beyond her lithe body, he made out a small skiff hauled onto the sands. Darius was off his game if he missed the sight of her approach.

"Why are you here? Come to deliver insults to make me feel even better?" he grumbled, even though he wanted nothing more than to ask if *she* was all right. Mila had jumped into the waters without pause, putting herself at risk. Ever since she'd leaped into the churning waves, a flicker of anger had burned within him.

Mila huffed, and then she had the audacity to take a seat right beside him. So close, he could feel the heat of her body through his trousers. An undercurrent of electricity sparked before distinguishing.

"How are you?" The words were out of his mouth before he could contain them. He cursed himself.

"I'll live," she replied gruffly, and Darius's ire simmered. She had no regard for her own life. It irked him to no end.

"Why are you out here?" she asked when he didn't reply. "Are you bothered by what Minthe chose?"

Darius shook his head. "I'm...I'm confused by it, if I'm honest, but it's not just that."

An elbow went into his ribs with surprising strength, and he choked out an exhale, whirling to Mila with wide eyes.

"What was that for?"

"I'm trying to be nice to you even though you hardly deserve it, and you're brooding and being all vague. It irritated me. Hence, the elbow to the side." She shrugged as if it were obvious. Darius couldn't believe the nerve of this woman. Fearless. Absolutely fearless.

"*You* being nice?" He scoffed. "That's something I'd pay well to see."

"You're seeing it right now, asshole." Mila shifted in place, a frown creasing her forehead. Her look of rage was incredibly adorable, like a kitten with claws. He hid his blooming smile behind his closed fist.

"You didn't kill her," Mila started after a stretch of them quietly watching the waves. "Why? She was well within your grasp, and you had the opportunity. But you hesitated."

Darius twisted to face her. "I *was* going to kill her. She just finished the job before I had the chance."

"No," Mila snapped. "You had *minutes* to slice her throat or break her neck, but you held her as she talked to her son. As he confessed his love for his queen. You wouldn't have killed her unless she provoked you."

"Why so certain?" he asked, heat boiling his blood. Days before, she'd practically cursed his name, and now she was defending his actions? What was her game?

Mila ran a hand through the dark sands, sifting the grains through her fingers. Darius found himself watching, mesmerized by the gentle motions as he awaited her reply.

When her green eyes met him, his immortal heart skipped several infuriating beats. How had he never realized how bright they were? How vibrant and lush? The rest of her was all sharp angles and harsh lines, but her eyes? They were so warm, Darius's breath hitched when he stared too long into them.

She must have seen something shift in his gaze, because she hardened before him.

"Don't misunderstand me. I still hate you for what you did. I don't think I can ever stop. But you were a victim as well. And while you were never taught how to properly love, I do believe you're learning what it is to feel empathy. Maybe there's hope you can change."

Change. She wanted him to change. Of course she did.

"And what if I don't?" he asked, his voice rising. "Why does it matter to you if I become less of a monster in your eyes? Hmm?"

Her nostrils flared, and she shot to her feet, glaring down at him with all the rage of a gale.

Darius, caught up in his own anger, continued on like a fool. "I practically killed the only father you ever knew. Your friends." Darius whispered the words, gauging her response—which was nothing. Mila's expression hadn't changed. "You shouldn't *pity* me. Or wish for me to be a better man. I am nothing to you but a nightmare."

Mila was thoughtful, her long lashes fanning across her freckled cheeks as she blinked rapidly, considering. "And yet I'm irrational enough to believe you could do better. That you have *already* done better. Grant —my father—would've wanted that. He would've told me to listen to the voice I often shove aside, that small voice that tells me I need to be more open, more understanding, to accept that life isn't black and white." Her eyes glowed red as wetness filled them. Darius felt like he was falling over and spinning the longer she stared at him, like she was truly looking into his rotten soul.

Fuck. He should've kept his damned mouth shut. It was always his greatest enemy.

"I'm...sorry." Two words. Two simple words that he'd never spoken and meant. Two words that he said now, his heart twinging in his chest, an uncomfortable band wrapping around him and squeezing. "I-I don't know what the hell I'm doing anymore. Or saying, for that matter."

He ran a hand through his hair, which was greasy and unkempt and utterly not him.

Something soft and unsure flickered across Mila's face, gone in an instant. "If you're sorry, then continue to do better. Words are useless, sea god. Show me. Show *yourself.*"

Mila turned on her heel and marched down to the shore, to her boat. She was in the water and sailing back to the *Mare Deus* minutes later, never once turning back to peer in his direction.

Darius remained on that boulder until the sun set and the world was stolen by night. He sat there until that skiff returned and another joined it from the larger Azantian vessel moored in the waves.

The Azantians had come to Bash's aid, and now they aimed for the island. Some lit torches in preparation for the night, dusk having just fallen. One woman played a triumphant tune on an old beat-up violin. Faces passed, familiar voices rang out, and all Darius focused on was how small he felt at that moment. Insignificant and easily forgotten.

Not a god. Not an all-powerful entity.

But a man who had nearly torn the world apart searching for the one thing he would never have.

CHAPTER THIRTY-NINE

MARGRETE

"Thank gods Bay sent for my aid," Adrian said as their skiff brushed against Rydor's shores. "Bash would never have asked me for help by himself. Stubborn man."

Bash hopped off the skiff and helped them haul it over land. He shot his oldest friend a look caught somewhere between feigned annoyance and gratitude.

Margrete left them to their teasing, joining Atlas, Dani, and Mila on the sands. Atlas was wan, her arm bandaged, but other than that, she held strong. Dani appeared unchanged, but every now and again when the light hit her face just right, Margrete glimpsed the spark in her eyes that hadn't left her since her rebirth. It had always been there, she realized, hiding just beneath the surface. Now she could no longer hide what fate had chosen for her.

Bash, Adrian, and Bay wandered into their group, her king and Adrian side by side.

"Did Bay tell you what happened on Surria's island?" Mila asked, her gaze wandering to a grouping of boulders, her eyes searching. When she didn't find what she was looking for, she returned to Adrian. Her face was pinched, the dent between her brows more pronounced than usual. Margrete wished her magic allowed her to read minds.

"Yeah, he told me," Adrian said with a groan, glancing at his boots. Red tinged his cheeks. He cast a wary glance to Bash, who met him with a soft, encouraging smile.

"Hey now. We're not moving backward," Bash said firmly. "In fact, we're *celebrating* tonight. I think we're all tired of unending doom on the horizon. We deserve a break, and I know for a fact Adrian brought some Azantian ale with him."

At this, Adrian perked up. "My crew is transporting it here as we speak." Twin dimples popped up on his cheeks. "Just don't drink too much, my king. Remember the time when you drank so much you ended up naked in the gardens, clinging to a statue of—"

"Shush!" Bash chided, rushing to playfully grab Adrian's collar. "They don't want to hear that story."

"Um, I certainly do," Margrete argued, feeling more like herself than she had in weeks. She felt like she was on Azantian again, surrounded by its people. The beach they occupied may not be the same golden shores, but she found the only thing that mattered was who she shared it with. She slipped an arm around Adrian's waist as they walked further up the beach. "Please do tell, Adrian. I love hearing about the oh-so-formidable Bash of Azantian."

As Adrian began a tale of drinks, nakedness, and statues that had apparently *demanded* to cuddle, his crew of around twenty trickled onto the shore. It took three trips for all passengers, and more importantly, the ale, to be brought to land, but Bash was right—they should have *one* night where they laughed and told stories and imbibed in drink.

Tomorrow...well, that was an entirely different unknown.

Margrete glanced at her tattooed forearm while her friends laughed and teased one another. The tattoo appeared the same, not changed since she'd completed the bargain with Halio. And it *was* complete, right?

Maybe she was supposed to return to the Underworld for it to be officially concluded.

"Your mind is elsewhere," Bash leaned in to whisper into her ear. The violin picked up a lively tune as Bay passed out mugs of ale. She caught his eyes as she accepted hers.

Her mind *was* in a thousand places at once, and the grand scene of Azantians dancing and sharing drinks around a roaring fire had lost its effect on her.

"So," Bash pressed, "what are you thinking about?" His voice was raspy and sounded different. Deeper. She wondered if he thought of his mother and her death. He hadn't spoken a word about it after they departed the *Mare Deus*.

"I should be asking how *you* are." She cupped his cheek, enjoying the solidness of him, how his stubble prickled her palms. He gave her one of his too-bright smiles, the ones she'd long ago discovered to be false. The sight was disheartening.

"I'll be fine," he said. "I just..." He paused, and she dropped her hands to his lap and grabbed his free hand. "I didn't even know her. She was a stranger really, and while I realize I *should* feel ruined after her death, all I feel is gratitude. An odd sense of peace? Does that make any sense?"

Margrete knew not everyone processed grief the same, and Bash's reaction wasn't entirely shocking. He was right—he hadn't known Minthe, not really, and she'd forced him to steal his first soul, effectively wiping away his mind. His sense of free will.

While the nymera might've redeemed herself at the end, Bash might still struggle with what she had set into motion. His transformation.

She snuggled into his side. His skin was cold to the touch, but she didn't mind. "I'm sorry things happened the way they did. And I wish she'd have made her choice to relinquish her revenge earlier when there'd been more time. Time for you both to reconnect. Before you were sent to the Underworld."

They each missed out on a reunion. A chance at experiencing the bond that existed between mother and son.

Margrete peered up at Bash, noting how tightly he clenched his jaw. She placed a gentle kiss there. "But in the end, she *did* show her love the only way she knew how, and I think her sacrifice, while horrid, was her way of saving you."

"Maybe you're right," he murmured, scanning the beach, taking in the Azantians he called family. People who would literally go to the ends of the earth for him. Most caught his eye every now and again, dipping their chin in respect, but they had the decent sense to give him space, instead flocking to where Bay was wrapped up in Adrian's arms. Adrian clutched him tight, nuzzling his hair while whispering into his ear. Bay's skin no longer appeared wan, his eyes sharper and more vibrant than they'd been in weeks. Even Atlas and Dani mingled among the others, a few who Margrete recognized and some she didn't. But the theme was the same.

Every single one of them was escaping for the night. It was well deserved.

"I see how they're looking at me," Bash said in a rush, watching the same scene with interest. He lifted the collar of his shirt as if that could help conceal the scales. It didn't.

She didn't know what to say, because he was right.

Yes, his people nodded in respect, but they also lingered on their changed king and his dark appearance, some seeming to force a smile on their lips or hide behind a drink. And whenever a lull would ensue, she noticed how Adrian raised his voice, ensuring the attention of any wandering minds.

They might have laughed and sang and drank, but they weren't fools. Things would never be the same. Even if they *had* won against the beasts.

"Let them look," she finally said, turning in Bash's arms. "You should wear the marks of your trials with pride. You've undergone so much for them, and you're still fighting. They should see that and be proud."

Margrete could tell he didn't agree, but Bash leaned his head atop her curls and sighed. "I'll say this every day until you're sick of me, but I'm incredibly lucky you're mine, princess."

Warmth blossomed in her chest. "Don't worry, pirate. I'll never tire of hearing those words."

Bash ran his hands up and down her arms before sliding them around her waist. "Care for a walk?" he asked, a slight lilt brightening his voice. She nearly died at the sound of it, because it had been ages since she'd heard such lightness. "But no liander blooms this time," he added, doing his best to appear stern.

She turned her head up, widening her eyes in innocence. "I don't know what you mean," she said, grinning impishly.

How could a moment feel so joyful and yet weighed with sorrow? With both love and fear?

Bash lifted to his feet and extended an arm to her. "Such a gentleman." She accepted his hand with a smirk.

"Don't tell anyone."

She nudged into his side, allowing him to lead the path to the coast. They wandered over the boulders, beyond the party and its many sounds. They walked in blissful silence until it was only them and their breathing, playing out like a joyous melody.

"We actually did it," Bash said, breaking the hush. "I can't believe we actually killed the monsters." He scoffed. "I feel like there's a catch, or that it's too good to be true."

She slowed, bringing them to a halt. Above, the moon, nearly full, cast its light upon his face, outlining the prominent edges of his cheekbones. He looked handsome, just the way he was. She found him more attractive now than when she'd first set eyes on him, and her heart had never known such fullness.

"Maybe things actually worked out for us," she mused. "I'd like to think we finally won a battle. Gods know, we deserve a little peace."

They'd been through so much in such a short amount of time. All she wanted to do was go back home to Azantian and spend her days with Bash and Birdie and—

Fuck. She'd forgotten. Or rather, she forced herself to forget the truth. That she wasn't human and wouldn't grow old, and that Bash would eventually die. They might experience peace for a few years, but she knew it wouldn't last. That would be naive to think otherwise.

Margrete reached for Bash before her mind caught up, a desperate fear driving her actions.

He flinched in surprise, but when his lips met hers, he groaned. He wound his hand into her hair and gripped the strands, his tongue slipping into her mouth, moving in time with hers. It was a gentle kiss, slow and sweet and brimming with love.

The waves thrashed against the shore, the scent of salt heavy in the air. It smelled like home, and with Bash in her arms, Margrete vowed she'd pretend—the same as the others—if only for a night.

"I'm done being your adorably handsome pessimist," Bash murmured suddenly as he drew back for air. "I know what you're doing, what you're trying to forget."

Her chest rose and fell unevenly as she panted out, "And what am I forgetting?"

"Things *can* be good. We haven't solved *all* our problems, but we succeeded in this round, the most important one, and I'll be damned to let you give up." He grasped her chin, holding her in place. "When we get back to the Underworld, if Darius refuses to break off your deal, then you'll kill him. Or maybe *I* will. The only reason I haven't is because of you, and it's taken immense strength on my part."

The words sunk into her heart like poison. She wasn't sure why she could hardly breathe. Darius deserved death, right?

So why was she hesitating?

"We'll figure out the rest after he's...dealt with. Immortality or not, you have me, princess. You'll always have me." He kissed her temple, and she shivered. "We'll find a way because we won't stop until we do."

His lips trailed down the side of her face, to her cheeks, her jaw. Her body tingled when he made his way to her throat, sucking the sensitive flesh, likely leaving a mark. She didn't care.

"Fuck. When did you become so optimistic?" she rasped, her lids shuttering. He was working her over now, his tongue circling that delicious spot below her ear. "Not playing fair."

He laughed, a deep, rumbling sound that vibrated up and down her body. "Life has never been fair. Why should I? Besides, I should be *dead* right now, so optimism might be called for."

Bash yanked her back in for a kiss, and gods above and below, Margrete gave in to his fantasy. To what *could be.*

If things went sideways tomorrow, then she'd take what she wanted now.

"Why is it"—he whispered, kissing down her neck—"that I've never made love to you on the beach?" He moved to her chest, his hands cupping her breasts. She arched against his hands, craving his mouth. He didn't make her wait long.

When he drew away, she noticed how dark his irises had grown, the pupils nearly eclipsing the whites of his eyes. A hint of his inner beast was coming out to play, and while apprehension danced down her spine, so did exhilaration.

There was something about his dark side that called to hers. That made her blood boil and her heart pound.

Bash reached for the top of her shirt and fisted the thin material before ripping it down the middle. Buttons fell to the sand, lost forever on the island of Rydor.

He leisurely ran his hands up her ribcage, over the swells of her breasts, a low growl rumbling from deep within his throat. His calloused palms felt delicious against her skin, adding just the right amount of friction, electrifying every nerve.

Bash drove her over the edge with his slow ministrations. He took his time, relearning her, memorizing her every inch. She was trembling, a mess beneath his skilled fingers.

Icy lips lowered to encircle a rosy peak, his wicked tongue worshiping her before his teeth scraped the sensitive flesh. She whimpered, arching into him, pushing her breast deeper, needing more of his teeth. More of him. A great emptiness consumed her, one that expanded the more he toyed with her.

His hands gripped her hips as he worked, moving to her other breast and delivering the same torture. She swore he smiled against her as she clawed at his back, urging him on. Pleading.

Margrete had enough.

"Wicked man," she murmured, pushing him away only to tear open his shirt. His stare seared her alive as buttons flew everywhere, leaving his glorious muscles on display. Her eyes fell to his stomach, to his rippling abdomen, to his strong chest. She wanted to lick every inch of him.

She grabbed for his belt, undoing it slowly, trying to torture him as he'd done her. She never lost eye contact, even as her heart fluttered wildly beneath his dark attention. A muscle in his neck went taut when she tossed the belt aside and undid his trousers.

"Your turn," she whispered, slipping a hand inside, her fingers wrapping around his cock. He groaned, the sound primal. Impatient.

"I planned on making love to you, my sweet, sweet, vexing Margrete, but now..." he hissed when she guided her hand up and down, teasing him while tightening her fist. "Now I'm going to bend you over those rocks and fuck you until you can't move." He grabbed her hand, and with shocking strength—the strength of a nymera—he tore her away from his trousers. She opened her mouth to argue, but Bash leaned down and hauled her over his shoulder.

"Bash!" she shrieked, a smile grazing her lips. She loved it when he was like this, just as much as she adored when he took her tenderly. Hell, she might've liked this side of him more. Because it was him. It was her.

A monster and a god.

He lowered her beside a smoothened boulder overlooking the sea. With hooded eyes, he slipped the rest of her shirt off her shoulders, every muscle in his face taut with control. Her belt came off next, and then he went to his knees, looking up at her as he stripped her of her boots. Gods, the sight of him on his knees always did her in, and he knew it. Bash's smirk was devilish as he eased her trousers down and off, his exploring hands lingering on her curves.

He kissed her ankle, working to the inside of her calf, her thigh. Margrete groaned in frustration.

"Impatient," he scolded, before gently nipping at the inside of her thigh. She whimpered once more, the sting causing her core to throb almost painfully.

Too slowly, Bash ran his tongue to the apex of her legs, lavishing his attention everywhere but where she needed him. She threaded her fingers into his hair, tugging on the strands, urging him closer.

His ensuing laughter only made her tug harder.

Just when she thought she could take no more, Bash licked up her slit and she choked on a sob. The coldness of his lips, his tongue—it was delicious. It was everything.

"So sweet," he murmured, sending vibrations radiating everywhere. "I could taste you for hours."

Yes. She mouthed his name, barely able to move, too lost to the pleasure he was giving her.

"Now be a good girl and come on my tongue."

Bash sucked her into his mouth before plunging a finger into her heated core. She did call out his name then, though it was broken and hoarse. He added another finger before curling them, reaching that delectable spot that had her seeing stars. She lifted to her tiptoes with a cry, nearly losing her balance.

The magic in her blood thrummed to life, and she rode his face, called out his name, cursed and praised him. Margrete lost herself entirely to the sensations he wrought from her body, and when she let go and fell, blue light emanated from her every pore, illuminating the night.

Bash didn't cease until her glow simmered out, until her body went lax and only his tight grip on her thighs kept her upright. She could barely breathe properly.

"I'm not done yet," he threatened, sweeping her up and into his arms again. When he put her down next, it was upon cool, smooth rock. Tingles shot down her spine. "I believe I made you a promise..."

He flipped her onto her stomach, an arm beneath her, protecting her from the stone. With his free hand, he lowered his trousers, the sound of his buckle being loosened heightening her anticipation. Margrete smiled, her power alive and surging, her body floating and satiated. She peered over her shoulder, taking in the magnificent sight of him. His rippling abdomen, his onyx scales, his deep, dark eyes that could look at her with both adoration and sin.

"Don't hold back," she said. "I want *you* tonight, not the king."

She wanted the beast.

And Margrete wanted to unleash all of herself in return.

"No holding back," he promised. And then he plunged into her core in one punishing stroke.

She radiated her power as Bash groaned, the sound better than music. She pushed back against him, urging him to continue, needing him to reach the deepest parts of her. As usual, her pirate obliged.

His hands flew to her hips, digging into her skin as he thrust in deep.

They were completely in sync. Completely one.

She didn't have to hide what she wanted from him. She didn't have to be anything other than herself. Whether a god or a mortal, Margrete was thankful she'd found a partner she never needed to hide from.

"So good," Bash panted, his movements wild, uneven. Frantic. "But I need to see your face, beautiful."

He was out of her before she could argue, and then he repositioned her so she sat upon the stone, facing him. Margrete wrapped her legs around his torso and drew him close. Bash went still at the sight of her, at her wide eyes she knew to be overflowing with hunger.

Only for him.

Bash didn't plunge into her, rather he slid, inch by delectable inch, inside her heat. She whimpered, the fullness almost too much. He never broke contact as he shifted back, merely to ease back inside, making love to her in a way that felt deeper than the emotion itself.

"I can never help myself with you. You ruin me so sweetly, Margrete," he whispered, leaning over her, the muscles in his arms tensing. His mouth skirted across her lips, and whenever she lifted her head to meet them, he shifted back.

"I need this to last. I need to watch your face." One hand wound around the back of her neck, securing her where he desired, and the other gently kneaded her breast, his fingers pinching the sensitive bud, causing her to edge closer and closer to bliss. "Only you can tame whatever monster lies inside of me. And I'll gladly wear the shackles for you, my beautiful, powerful queen."

Margrete came so abruptly, her entire body convulsed.

Every nerve was electrified, and her magic swelled, the soft light that had radiated from her skin now turning into a blaze. She fell so long and deep that she wasn't sure she'd ever return. Hell, she didn't want to.

"That's it," Bash praised, quickening his pace, seeking his own relief. "Fuck, you feel like you were made for me." When she finally came down from her high, she grabbed his hips and yanked him harder, closer, faster.

She squeezed her walls around him, delighting in the nearly pained look on his face. "Show me then," she rasped. "Show me how I own you as well."

Bash hissed out a curse, driving into her mercilessly, hitting the heavenly spot inside of her over and over until she called out his name, spasming around his thick, hard length.

"I love you," he groaned, just before he shuddered and warmth spilled into her core. His cock pulsed, every throb wringing out the lingering pleasure that had wrecked her.

Bash's hands fell beside her, caging her as he caught his breath. She studied him in the moonlight, memorizing his every beautiful feature. When she could physically move, she cupped his jaw and placed a gentle kiss on his lips.

"I love you," she echoed, knowing that nothing would ever be as true. "And—"

Screams pierced the air.

Bash jerked upright at the same time she did, both their heads swiveling in the direction of the party.

The screams grew louder, shriller.

Bash helped ease her down and rushed for her clothes, handing them to her as he searched for his own. She had to tie the loose ends of her shirt together, her midriff exposed. Bash abandoned his ruined shirt entirely, only tugging up his trousers, leaving his scaled chest bare. When they were both ready, he grasped her hand in his. Together they raced toward the sound of mayhem.

CHAPTER FORTY

BASH

BASH'S CHEST STUNG.

The dark magic inside of him flared to life, seeming to react to whatever was happening just up ahead. Margrete sprinted at his side, blue streams of light flying from her palms, her hair alight with its ethereal glow. Bash didn't shine, but he sure as shit felt the great change.

That moment when the gate holding his darkness a prisoner gradually slid back. That barricade had just clashed down when they rounded the bend and came across a scene so horrid, even his inner nymera hissed.

Blood covered the sands where the Azantian sailors had celebrated. Bodies lay unmoving, arms and legs bent unnaturally, throats slit and the final gurgling breaths of life sounding.

Figures comprised of luminous light flickered past, moving too quickly for the few surviving crew members to react. Only around six or so remained from Adrian's small batch of sailors, and Bash grimaced when he saw Atlas, her bandaged arm torn open, her gash bleeding anew. She winced in pain as she wielded her dagger, attempting to catch one of the fleeting attackers. Bash counted around ten of the ethereal creatures.

Margrete didn't wait. She burst to life, lifting her palms toward one of the assailants, and sent out a blast of raw power. But her target was far too quick, and by the time her magic singed the sands, the figure was moving on to their next victim.

"Glad you could join us," Darius grunted, appearing from their right. Bash took to Margrete's left, both he and Darius flanking her.

"We heard the screams and ran as fast as we could," Margrete said just before she managed to nick one of the figures. It slowed its pace, and Darius sent a blast of his power directly into its center. A shrill screech pierced the air, and then the creature dropped to the sands. Bash couldn't make out the details, Darius's magic still shrouding their newest form.

"Good hit," Margrete praised, and Darius dipped his chin, searching for another target.

"What are they?" Bash panted, his claws regrowing. They tore from his nailbeds, and he hissed at the sting. The air was thick with blood, the potency of it causing his stomach to churn in want. He itched to move, to do something to make the growing pit in his core vanish.

Before he answered, Darius shot down one more, and this time a distinctly human-like snarl sounded. Bright red light blazed, and Bash glimpsed the form beneath.

"Shit."

"Shit indeed," Darius concluded. "Charion and Calista both share nymphs. Though some are more loyal to one than the other. Since Calista is no longer with us..."

Charion had to be behind this last-ditch effort. He might've known they succeeded, but they hadn't reached the Underworld just yet, meaning he still had time to deliver what he considered his rightful vengeance.

Mila roared as she dodged one of the nymphs, lunging to the side before it could wrap its hands around her neck. The light radiating off its form was blazing, too bright to distinguish features, making it difficult for Bash's crew to pinpoint its weak spots. But Mila was determined, and she chased after one, her dagger ready, a battle cry on her lips.

Darius sucked in a breath when she managed to slash at its sides, slowing it down just enough for her to drive her dagger directly into its chest. Mila kept slashing, her face speckled with blood, the nymph's life essence coating her hands.

"You're going to need to narrow your scope, Margrete," Darius commanded, tearing his focus from Mila. "Your aim has to be impeccable. Mila got lucky bringing that one down. No mortal has been able to defeat one. Not that I know of." Pride filled his voice, and his focus remained locked on Mila, who snarled as another nymph advanced.

Margrete nodded, the muscles straining in her neck as she raised her palms. A pinprick of power escaped, clipping one of the bastards' on its upper body. It didn't fall but it stumbled, and Bay appeared from between the dense trees, swinging his dagger down to finish the job. His face was streaked with blood, his blond hair covered in red.

Bash scanned the beach.

Adrian.

He sent a spear flying into one of them, but the nymph smiled when she yanked the blade from her chest. She tossed the weapon to the sands, her body slowing enough for Bash to see her muscles tense, her skin gleaming with magic and malice.

In a blink, Bash moved, his speed inhumanly fast as he threw his body before his friend's. The nymph didn't hesitate.

When she took her crude blade and sliced at Bash's bare skin, he bled black ooze, trickling down his abdomen. His inner beast roared. The nymph released a cry of triumph, her full lips pulled up into a malicious grin.

"Bash, no!" Adrian shouted, but he'd already raised a hand, his newly sharpened nails aiming for the nymph's delicate throat. He felt nothing but blissful adrenaline sweep over his entire body when he connected with flesh and muscle, his nails cutting into her pale neck with sickening ease.

She grabbed at the wound, wide-eyed. Bash struck her with his other hand, his nails deepening the wound, carving right through the fingers covering it. He was barely aware of Adrian's worried shouts, his oldest friend's voice cracking with panic.

Bash glimpsed a blur of metal flying past his shoulders, piercing another nymph who he'd spotted from his peripheral. He twisted around. Bay stood directly behind him, his hands now empty—he'd saved him once again. With Bay and Adrian working together, Bash rushed into the frenzy, his claws reaching for any who dared attack.

From the corner of his eye, he glimpsed Margrete and Darius working in tandem, wiping away the glimmering nymphs, their screams shrill in the night air. But Bash wasn't a part of their unit, and the more blood that was spilled, the hungrier he became, and the bigger the gaping hole in his belly grew. He killed, but he hadn't eaten.

When he reached his fourth nymph, Bash slowed. Without gashing her throat and watching her bleed as he'd done the others, he grasped her by the neck and forced her mouth to part. She scrambled in his hold, her hisses unnatural and wicked. Wicked like *him*.

He inhaled...

The nymph screeched.

The world slowed.

Bash stole her vile soul with three swallows, dropping her lifeless husk of a body onto the sands with the others. His dark magic seemed to smile.

The next nymph tasted better, if not older. Her soul reminded Bash of winter days and overcast skies. Not like the other one, who'd tasted too fresh, too much like a fall breeze.

He didn't know how to describe the sensations flooding him, as they likely wouldn't make sense if he tried, but his belly was bursting and full, and his limbs burned with energy. He moved quicker now, more confidently. He shoved an Azantian out of the way just before they were attacked, and he robbed that reckless nymph of her vicious soul as well.

Bash didn't realize he was grinning until his cheeks strained.

When he lunged for his next victim, he was too far gone to care how much he was enjoying himself.

CHAPTER FORTY-ONE

DARIUS

Fᴜᴄᴋɪɴɢ ɴʏᴍᴘʜs.

Darius despised them almost as much as he had his brother. They were evil little gnats, creatures whose supposed loyalty meant less than nothing. He'd just slayed one of the nymphs who'd pledged their fealty to *him* only weeks before, back on the island.

Traitor.

Margrete panted at his side, not used to channeling her magic in such a meticulous way. The nymphs could move with shocking speed, and as quick as her and Darius's magic was, sometimes the nymphs were quicker. But she was a fast learner, and she'd destroyed one of them without his aid.

Darius took a moment to regain his strength, watching as Adrian aimed his dagger, missing a nymph by a half-inch. Fortunately, Bay, hot on his boyfriend's heels, sliced the creature's other side. Blood fell as the nymph shrieked and limped away. Both Adrian and Bay followed, likely to end her once and for all.

Atlas's injury wasn't doing her any favors, but surprisingly, Dani held her own, standing before the blonde with a fierceness in her stare he hadn't seen before. She slashed at the air, daring their enemies to get closer. The sea had changed her after all.

Darius was prepared to track down the remaining nymphs and finish them off when a familiar cry sounded. One of pain. Of pride. Of stubbornness.

Darius whirled around.

"Hello there, handsome."

Shade. She held a blade to Mila's throat, a smile blossoming on her cruelly beautiful face. Her long, red hair was braided behind her, a circlet of crimson thorns at her brow, a crown death. Darius had all but forgotten her, believing she scurried off the island with the rest of her cockroaches.

Mila struggled in her grasp, but her glower was directed at Darius as if this massacre was all his fault. Her eyes were stone, her every muscle clenched. Her original scream was the lone sound she had permitted to escape.

"Let her go," he snarled, abandoning Margrete's side. He felt her gaze on him, but she didn't ask, likely too busy dealing with the few nymphs who refused to die. Bash was making a mess of his own, and Darius suddenly didn't care about upholding the line.

Hell, he cared only for one thing.

Shade scoffed, her blade scraping Mila's neck, drawing more blood. It bubbled to the surface before sliding down Mila's graceful neck. She'd never looked so fragile as she did then, ensnared by pure evil wearing a stunning face.

"Shade, this is between you and me." Darius jerked his chin to Mila, something in his chest squeezing. "Stop your minions and let's settle this."

"I followed you for years, Darius," Shade hissed, "and I never realized just how weak you were. I should've listened to the others, but like a fool, I believed you could rid yourself of the flaws that didn't plague your brother. I bet wrong, and now I'm alone, my mistress gone, and I'm paying the price."

"Paying the price..." he trailed off, realization striking.

"Calista had sent you before she died, didn't she?" he asked, stepping closer. Shade instantly tightened her grip, and Mila whimpered as the blade dug into her freckled skin. Had he never realized her freckles dipped down and across her chest, the pattern akin to tiny constellations?

Focus. Not the time.

"I should've never betrayed her to begin with," Shade said, shaking her head. Her hair shifted back, revealing her old burn, her mark of the goddess—a wilted flower. Darius had charmed it to vanish on her skin for years, but he'd long been distracted by Margrete and her king, so he hadn't thought about Shade much, even after the island.

"Now I'm forced to side with a new master, and he certainly isn't fond of you." Shade tilted her chin triumphantly. "A sentiment we both share."

"Just kill her!" Mila demanded, seeming to grow impatient. Darius almost smiled at her audacity.

"Someone has a death wish," Shade snarled, bringing Mila's ear close to her lips.

The Azantian king roared from somewhere behind Darius, too busy inhaling the souls of the nymphs to notice Mila in Shade's grip. Then again, Darius should be combing the beach to make sure they were free of the threat, not trying to save one measly mortal.

And yet he couldn't move.

"I see how you look at this one," Shade taunted. "She means something to you even if you don't understand it yet. It's not so powerful a look as the one you had for the soon-to-be Azantian queen, but..." Shade paused to draw her blade up, moving the sharpened tip across Mila's reddening cheek, slicing at the skin as she went. It wouldn't scar, but Mila hissed at the sting.

A great heat began to churn in Darius's core. It was the same beginnings of rage he'd experienced when he killed Malum out on the waves of Azantian. Darius had wished to set fire to his corpse after playing with it, after cutting it into pieces and watching him bleed out. Slowly.

Darius felt the same kind of hatred for his brother, his mother, and the other gods as he now did for Shade. Even as a small, unimportant part of him felt pity for her. An emotion he hadn't been familiar with mere months ago.

But watching Mila's face contort in pain...his wrath won out.

Shade was speaking, likely mocking him some more, but he grinned, harnessing that living and breathing flame that seared his insides so deliciously.

All he had to do was release it. Yet he allowed it to build, to grow like a weed, until he physically couldn't handle the pressure anymore.

He locked eyes with Mila. The woman whose family *he* had essentially killed. And yet, while she'd tended to his wounds with hatred radiating off her, she'd shown him more kindness than anyone he'd ever known. All because she believed it to be the right thing. Even for someone as unredeemable as him.

Darius held her stare, which went soft for just a fraction of a heartbeat.

And then he erupted.

CHAPTER FORTY-TWO

MARGRETE

She'd just struck down the last of the nymphs when a blast shook Rydor's shores. Bash, who'd hovered over an unmoving body, his skin softly glowing with a sickly wan light, turned to bring his stare to where Darius released his magic.

Shade. She was back, *here*, and battling Darius. Margrete wanted to rip the nymph's throat out. She wanted to tear her limb from limb if only to satiate her own rage. Shade's betrayal had cost not only Margrete, and Birdie, but Bash and his people as well.

Bash continued to growl, his focus aimed at the sea god. Yet he didn't attack, even as he curled his now elongated nails. She suspected he, too, envisioned ripping out Shade's throat.

Adrenaline shot down her spine as Darius's vicious magic encircled Shade and the woman she held; a hostage, no doubt. But when Margrete squinted and took in the hostage's features, alarm seized her. Mila...it was Mila in Shade's arms being used as a human shield.

She was about to rush forward and send a blast of her own power into Shade, when Darius lifted his hand and clenched it into a white-knuckled fist.

Mila screamed as Shade's knife pushed deeper into her cheek, but Darius's magic wasn't focused on her...

It slid between the sailor's body and the nymph's, a surge of vivid blue and gray steel. Shade hissed out, cursing his name, but Darius didn't relent. He stalked toward her, an unnatural wind blowing in his blond hair. His outstretched hand tightened, and Shade's ensuing scream rocked the island.

Margrete watched in horror as Shade—once the esteemed court treasurer of Azantian, once Bash's supposed friend and confidant—exploded into a thousand pieces of black ash.

Her scream echoed long after that same unnatural wind swept her remains away, the nymph torn apart so brutally, so easily, Margrete couldn't help the fear that grew at the sight of Darius. She'd never seen such a blatant display of power. Didn't know he was capable of it. And judging by the momentary shock crossing his features, neither had he. It was as if the threat to Mila's life had unlocked an entirely new aspect of his magic.

Darius raced to catch Mila before she fell, his hold careful, tender almost. He surrounded her, one large hand supporting her waist, the other pressed to the small of her back.

With the battle all but over, and the blood of nymphs and Azantians alike coating the sands, Darius's focus never wavered from Mila. Her lashes fluttered as she pried open her eyes and stared into his, her lips parting in shock. A second later, she slumped in his arms, passing out from exhaustion, adrenaline, or the aftereffects of being so near his potent magic.

Darius scooped her up with all the care in the world. With the redhead in his grasp, he turned toward Margrete, his blue eyes three shades darker. Bash growled, a blur of gleaming black as he sprinted to stand in front of her. He was a beast guarding her, his mouth gaping, his canines poking out, the tips glinting in warning. It was instinct, and he acted without any other thought than to protect what he deemed his.

"It's all right," Margrete whispered, soft fingers caressing his arm. Back and forth she ran them up and down his arm, coaxing him to still, for his shoulders to gradually loosen. But he never took his attention away from Darius as he stalked past an injured Atlas and a worried Dani, who gripped Atlas's hand as she pressed her head into the woman's side. Bay and Adrian clutched one another as they, too, witnessed the God of the Sea carry Mila in his arms, clouds of blue and white swirling around them both like steam.

He only stopped once he'd reached the shore, the sea gently washing over his boots. Darius stood there as the others regained their balance and assessed their injuries. He didn't move, but he tipped his chin to the sky, to the moon. Margrete couldn't imagine what was going through his head.

"We need to get back to the boats," Adrian croaked, moving to where she watched the god. Margrete jerked back to him, forcing herself from ogling Darius and wondering why she still couldn't sense him as clearly as before.

Now that she thought about it...

She hadn't been plagued with a memory. Not one single memory of her past since...since she failed to connect with him when they fought the Cyros.

Bash sniffed the air, his nostrils flaring. "The nymphs are gone. All of them." His voice was brusque and coated in gravel.

"Bash..." Adrian shook out of Bay's hold and reached for his friend, his hands quivering slightly. Bash startled, his black eyes narrowing. Margrete's heart skipped several beats as Adrian dared to touch his shoulder. "I'm right here, mate," was all he said, though he stepped even closer, boldly cupping Bash's stubbled cheek.

Her king was a statue, the warmth he typically radiated now absent.

She stood beside Adrian, who shifted to allow room. Together, they held onto Bash, calling his name, whispering it over and over.

"I—" He paused, his body jerking uncontrollably. "I feel off."

Adrian grabbed hold of him before he collapsed to his knees. Margrete bowed beneath the pressure, but she, too, held on, keeping him from falling.

"We got you," Adrian murmured, his voice, as always, a lullaby. A soothing timbre that could never be replicated. "We're right here."

They ambled toward the skiff, Bash between them, eyes glazed and unfocused. Margrete and Adrian supported his weight, urging him to get to the boat that would carry him to safety and to a warm bed. He needed to rest, to recover. They all did.

Margrete peered over her shoulder, taking stock of those they'd lost. Over a dozen souls were gone in a blink.

"I'll take care of them," Bay whispered, just behind her. He placed a calming hand on her arm, giving her a reassuring squeeze. "I'll stay and perform the burials."

"I'll help as well," chimed a sailor from Adrian's crew, a young boy who reminded her of Jonah. Her heart panged at the reminder of his loss. Two more offered to stay back and fashion the rafts necessary for the traditional Azantian burial. They set the crafts aflame on the waters, burning the body to ash where the ocean would consume what remained.

"Thank you," Margrete replied, holding Bay's stare. A lot could be said in such a short amount of time, and what they exchanged spoke beyond fragile words. Then again, they'd always had that way about them. She knew then that their bond could never be severed.

"He needs to sleep," Adrian softly reminded her, and she nodded, picking up the pace and easing her king toward the skiff. They managed to slide him into the belly of the vessel, and he lay back with a groan, his scales shining ominously in the night, almost glowing.

Margrete cast a look at Darius, who, surprisingly, was staring her way.

She didn't find animosity or love or lust directed at her. Rather, the god, for once, gazed upon her with what she could mistake as regret.

"I'll send the boat back," she called out to him, nodding toward Mila, still passed out in his arms. The god gave a subtle jerk of his chin in acquiescence. She noticed how he pressed her closer to him, one hand at her temple, brushing aside the tangled red strands.

Adrian, Atlas, Dani, and two of Adrian's crew pushed the boat into the waters.

The second Margrete stepped into the waters, her hands on the wooden craft—the last to jump in—she sensed the sea tremble. Like a relieved sigh. Elated she was back, standing in its embrace.

The current thrust beneath her feet as she leaped, propelling her onto the ship. As they rowed back to the *Mare Deus*, she trailed her finger in the rocking blue waves, her other hand grasping her king's.

Almost, she thought, twirling her fingers beneath the surface.

Tomorrow we will end this all.

BASH WOKE THE NEXT MORNING, GASPING.

Margrete had stayed beside him all night, perched on the edge of the bed. She couldn't sleep, unable to find any semblance of peace. He'd tossed and turned all evening, and she'd soothed his creased brow, hoping to draw him from whatever nightmare that consumed him. Needless to say, it had been a long night.

Her king startled as she reached for him, moving slowly for his face, for his cheek. He shifted out of the way with a pained snarl, his eyes darker than midnight.

"Bash," she whispered, retreating. He scrambled against the mattress and pushed himself back against the wall, his stare wary as he scanned her from her boots to the crown of her head. She swore he ceased to breathe.

"Talk to me..." Margrete understood last night had been different for him, not like it had been when he'd consumed the Kora's soul. She just didn't know why.

Boldly, she inched closer, ignoring his ensuing rumble of disapproval. "Tell me how you're feeling." She wouldn't leave until he spoke to her. Today would be life-altering, and while it was merely one step toward their goal, it would be the biggest one. Bash had to be ready.

"I feel..." He cleared his throat, his voice cracking. "I feel l-like I'm f-frozen."

He'd devoured the souls of nymphs yesterday. Who knew what sort of wickedness thrived inside?

When Margrete went to cup his cheek again, Bash let her, although he tensed, the muscles in his neck straining. She ran a finger across his jaw, her warmth burning his icy skin.

"Today we go back," she said, easing onto his lap. He didn't resist, but he remained on guard, his back still pressed against the wall. His nails were untrimmed, and his canines appeared unnaturally long in the morning light.

"I'm full," he grunted, and she scrunched her brow before understanding.

"Oh," she hummed, nodding stiffly, unsure of the right thing to say. "Then you should be strong if we encounter any...obstacles."

Like they had with Surria and Calista on Zandar. Darius had said the nymphs worked with the love goddess, and the ones who had served him but weeks before—Shade included—owned no sense of loyalty. They now had given their worthless loyalty to Charion.

Bash finally relaxed, and she sighed when he leaned into her palm, shutting his eyes.

"It was bizarre," he began, swallowing thickly. "I felt like myself this time, my thoughts somewhat my own, but..." His lids shot open, and she noticed none of the usual silver flecks dotted his irises. "I had no restraint. If I wanted to slash an enemy, I was suddenly doing it. There was no hesitation beforehand."

He glanced down to his lap, and she dropped her hand, only to grab his. His claws poked at her flesh, but she ignored the slight sting.

"But you protected me," she said, recalling how he'd stood before her when he'd deemed Darius a threat. "You were high from feeding, and still you resisted."

Bash ran a hand through his black locks. "That might've just been luck," he grumbled, clearly frustrated.

"We'll figure it out," she promised, moving to press her forehead against his. "I plan on opening the portal in one hour. And then the deal with Halio will be complete." She'd figure out what to do with Darius afterward, although...

He'd been absent since last night, and Margrete could've sworn she'd seen him enter Mila's cabin. Perhaps his guilt had finally caught up with him. Or maybe he was learning its meaning. Whatever the reason, she was thankful, because it gave her hope there was a moral compass buried within the god. *Somewhere.*

"Now, before we do that"—she said, gently pushing Bash onto the bed—"I want to hold you a little while longer." She curled around him, her hand on his chest, her head resting on his muscled arm. Bash didn't say a word, and neither did she.

They held each other until a knock sounded.

The time to return to the Underworld had come.

CHAPTER FORTY-THREE

BASH

SOMETHING DIDN'T FEEL RIGHT.

They supposedly finished off the beasts. Defeated the bloodthirsty nymphs. And they'd worked with Darius. Who Bash continued to despise with every ounce of his being, regardless of how the others appeared to have softened around him.

Did they so easily forget all he'd done?

Bash walked beside Margrete up to the main deck. His legs wobbled slightly, but the only one who took notice was Adrian, who hastily glanced down at his boots before returning his stare to the waves. He sidled up beside his friend, Margrete on the other side, Darius next to her.

Behind him, Bash made out Bay requesting more blades to replenish the ones lost during the fight with the beasts, but he drowned out the talk of weapons. There was enough going on in his thoughts. Thankfully, Atlas had fully healed after last night's attack, her Azantian blood a blessing. Still, Dani had resided by her side all evening.

And Mila...

Bash searched for the sailor, finding her off to the side, hidden away in the shadows. She sat propped against a barrel, fiddling with a loose scrap of rope, her fingers red from the friction of running it through her hands. She looked everywhere but at Darius.

Bash wondered why the sea god had taken a liking to her. She didn't appear to return the sentiment, although Mila hardly ever showed her true emotions.

"You ready?" Darius asked, seemingly unable to look them in the eyes.

He meant if Margrete was ready to open the portal to the Underworld. To finish the bargain made with the God of Death. A bargain, that if successful, would lead to his own triumph.

"Ready," she said, her jaw impossibly tight. Every inch of her held tension, and Bash noticed how her hands glowed slightly, a gentle blue that reminded him of the sea during summertime. She was nervous, tucking her hair behind her ears every now and again, her bright eyes searching the horizon as if waiting for an enemy to strike.

Bash had never seen her so apprehensive, and it worried him.

As much as he hated to admit it, he needed her to be all right today, because truth be told, *he* wasn't all right. Each breath he took was heavy. Every time he inhaled the sea air, the scent of rot lingered in his nostrils. The world was too bright, too full, and too noisy. And every second he spent in the light, the more his skin prickled, the areas around his scales on fire.

He hadn't allowed Margrete or Adrian to trim his nails in case they encountered trouble today. Adrian had wrinkled his nose in annoyance. Bash knew Adrian wasn't turned off by their color, but rather their length; he was obnoxiously meticulous about certain things, and the jagged edges likely gave Adrian heart palpitations.

As if he knew he was in Bash's thoughts, Adrian slipped a hand into his, carefully avoiding his claws.

"Admit that you needed me, and you're glad I came," he demanded, and even though he was teasing, his words, as always, had a tendency to come across as genuine.

Bash squeezed his hand. They'd grown up together. Of course he was glad Adrian stood at his side. He just didn't want him to get hurt.

"Bay's cockiness must've rubbed off on you," he replied, tightening his grip once more before letting go.

"You never can just say what you mean." Adrian tsked. "So damned stubborn. If I didn't love you, I'd be annoyed."

Warmth chased away some of the icy adrenaline in Bash's chest. But he didn't look at Adrian. He had to build his walls and prepare, not expose himself further.

Margrete stole him from their friends, drawing him back to her side. The feel of her, her welcoming heat, the floral scent of lavender in her hair, it soothed him. Brought him back from suffocating in the stench of dark magic that saturated his lungs.

She leaned up onto her toes, her breath tickling his ear. "I love you, pirate," she whispered, kissing his cheek. Before she could drop to the balls of her feet, Bash gently surrounded her waist and lifted her, bringing her lips to his. He kissed her in front of his crew, his friends, in front of the sea god who wished to destroy their happiness.

Bash kissed her as their fate lay at their feet—all the unknowns and obstacles they'd yet to face.

But he didn't care. He'd have this moment. *They'd* have this moment.

When he finally released her, she was nearly breathless, her lips curling into a subtle smile. Only for him did she smile like that.

The right side of her mouth was slightly higher than the left, her right dimple on full display. Her smile shone in her eyes as she looked at Bash with everything he never thought he deserved.

Again, some of the frost around his dark heart thawed, and this time, he didn't try to replenish it. She could take what was left of him. He'd give her everything.

"Let's go," Darius commanded, and Bash let out a rumble that sounded more beast than man. Maybe he was one now.

Yet as he glared at the god, he found no pleasure. Darius's face was blank—an unfeeling canvas of stone. Not even his eyes sparked with mischief when he turned to Margrete, offering her his hand.

Bash furrowed his brows. Either he was up to something or something had happened *to* Darius. There wasn't time to question it more.

Bash's possessive nymera instincts flared at the sight of her hand in Darius's, but he bit the inside of his cheek, focusing instead on the powerful vibrations now shaking the *Mare Deus*. He had to shove down his need for bloodshed just a little while longer.

The waves became riotous, the winds vengeful, and in a minute's time, gray clouds masked all the blue of the sky.

Bash peered over the side of the ship. There, fifty feet ahead...

The water was *parting*.

It began slowly, so slowly that he had to blink to make sure he trusted his sight. But then Margrete's body illuminated a vivid turquoise that seeped across the ship and brightened the faces of the remaining men and women. Most clutched their weapons, and all held a trace of fear in their eyes. Even Mila, who'd wandered closer, her lips open in awe.

Darius lifted his free hand, and Margrete followed. The water shuddered at their unspoken demand, and when the sea god began to match Margrete's glow, a vibrating rush of magic swept across the waves, separating it further.

Bash hadn't been there when Margrete originally broke into the Underworld by creating her own portal. To his credit, he'd been very much *dead*. But watching the two of them now—working together, lids shut in concentration, bodies aglow with power—Bash couldn't help but feel the same wonder as the others.

He would still throttle Darius if given the chance.

Darius and Margrete spread their hands farther and farther apart, and the *Mare Deus* gave a violent tremble as it perched precariously over what was now a ledge of water.

They'd split the sea in half—or more precisely, they'd crafted more of an oval-shaped hole, the soft sea floor entirely visible from their vessel.

"Now for the hard part," Darius whispered. He flicked a hand, sending a wave cascading over the side of the *Mare Deus*. Bash jumped as water rushed beneath his boots, beneath the boots of his sailors. That same enchanted water Darius had commanded to aid in their escape from Zandar lifted them up, thrusting them forward...over the damned railing.

Bay stifled a horrified screech—Bash knew he wasn't a fan of heights —and Dani hissed, reaching out to clutch Atlas as they were carried over. Adrian, unable to reach Bay in time, called out his name, doing his best to soothe him.

He'd expected Darius to lift the remaining members of Adrian's crew, but they stood on the wooden planks, mouths agape as Mila and Bash joined their friends.

It appeared as if the sea god was playing favorites. Or in his case, he was simply transporting the main players.

Margrete glanced over her shoulder and smiled. Bash relaxed as her power reached for him, seeming to sense his unease. He let out a sigh. Her magic was light and airy and smelled of spring seas. It made him feel warm, and Bash's nerves settled enough for him to keep a leash on his fear.

He may be half a monster, but he felt fear well enough. That was a misconception, he decided then, as they were placed gently upon the spongy sands. People often thought monsters felt nothing, or maybe they only experienced bloodlust. He knew now that wasn't the case.

He turned to Darius before quickly averting his attention.

His boots sank deep into the muck, and it took him great effort to shift and move around. On either side of their party, the waters rose. It reminded him of the sea glass walls of his palace, but if he squinted, he could make out the flash of a scale, the flick of a tail. The animals of the open waters roaming the depths.

It was...breathtaking.

"It'll be easier if we open a portal together," Darius said, still holding Margrete's hand.

Bash couldn't cease looking from their entwined fingers. His jealousy wasn't something he was proud of, but it thrived. He closed his fists, his long nails digging into the meaty part of his palms. He smelled copper in the air seconds later.

Margrete went rigid. She turned his way, her focus dropping to his hands as if she, too, smelled the blood of his anger.

"Let's just get this over with," she murmured, still looking at Bash.

She mouthed those three little words he'd never get enough of, and he loosened his fists...*a little.*

Bash had expected Darius to gloat or say something wicked and taunting, but he just nodded. It was odd, his behavior, and again Bash wondered what on earth had happened to the bastard. He only cared because Darius's presence affected the deal with Halio. A deal that could result in the end of his island home.

Bash studied his face, picking apart every minute detail. *There.* It was so subtle, lasting just a blink, but when Darius peered at Margrete, a deep crease formed.

Darius brushed off the indescribable emotion, smoothing his features. Without warning, he took their entwined hands from the air and plunged them into the soft sands.

Blue light exploded, spreading everywhere. It refracted against the walls of water, sunshine rays and magic combining, blinding them all.

The earth shook, and Bash swayed, held in place by the muck that trapped him. And after the shaking reached its crescendo, the world seemed to sigh in relief, the sea floor parting, breaking apart. It crumbled into nothingness, a gaping hole of midnight.

Bash stumbled forward, instinct propelling him closer to Margrete. He was there the second the magic left her palm, which now hovered over the empty void. Before her knees gave out, her divine form trembling, Bash scooped her into his arms.

Darius had released her without a fight, his attention solely on the yawning abyss they'd created.

"I-I'm all right, Bash," Margrete whispered, gazing up at him. A weak smile played on her lips, but color painted her cheeks, and her breathing had become even and assured. He didn't want to release her, didn't want to put her down. It might make him sound like a bastard, but he desired nothing more than to keep hold of her and run away from it all. He could blame the temptation on his inner beast, but Bash knew the truth.

"It'll be all right," she assured, resting a hand on his stubbled cheek. He leaned into it, holding onto every word as if it were a gift. "We need to do this."

And she very well couldn't go charging into the Underworld with him carrying her. Bash grunted but placed her on her feet. Her gaze lingered on him before Bay coughed pointedly and she was forced to turn back to the mission at hand.

His queen nodded stoically at his crew—Adrian, who bestowed her with a tender smile, and Bay who dipped his chin, still unsure of where they stood. Atlas and Dani had given up the pretense and were now holding onto each other for comfort, Atlas's arm slipped around the young woman's waist, her chin resting against her black curls. And then Mila, who stared at Margrete with a ferocity unmatched by any being they'd encountered.

Mila marched up to Margrete with that confident walk of hers, hips swaying, shoulders back, and she...she yanked her into a tight hug.

It stunned them all.

"I'm glad I was wrong about you," Mila said, drawing back. She gave Margrete a slight bow and then a cunning wink. Bash knew her teasing words were of the highest compliments, and Margrete must've known as well, because she beamed at the sailor with a warmth that rivaled the sun.

Bash reached for her hand. Together, they took the first step back into the Underworld. Together, they would enter, and together, Bash vowed, they'd leave.

CHAPTER FORTY-FOUR

MARGRETE

MARGRETE PEERED INTO THE GAPING VOID BELOW HER FEET.

It all felt like déjà vu. Except this time, she clutched Bash's hand in hers, his steps matching as they descended. The ground sloped, slippery footholds forming before they placed their boots down.

Her magic was buzzing in her veins, and somewhere in the distance she sensed the portal waiting; the silver entrance to the realm of the dead. The key she'd stolen from the Underworld hummed in her trouser pocket, coming alive as if it sensed it was finally on its way back home.

Bash's frozen fingers were clammy, but she held tight, even though his elongated black nails poked into her skin. They certainly made fine weapons, as proven during the nymph attack, but she could tell they bothered him.

Darius quickened his pace, leading the way with inflexible determination. He'd hardly spoken a word to her this morning, and she'd expected a hint of satisfaction from him, *anything*. He was one step closer to his end goal, and yet he almost seemed melancholy.

Dani drifted to her right. She must've finally untangled herself from Atlas's arms. The pair had been inseparable since last night...well, even before last night. But their glances were no longer shy. She was happy for them both.

"I can't help but sense that something is different," Dani murmured into Margrete's ear. "It doesn't feel like last time, and the air smells heavily of decay."

She didn't look at the sailor, but she whispered, "Charion is likely waiting to attack. He's probably itching to kill us before we meet with Halio."

It made sense for the war god to wait until the last minute, when they were all wrangled together in one place. If he didn't have to expel any more energy, then he wouldn't.

Margrete smelled smoke the closer they got to the portal, and she and Bash turned to one another at the same time.

"The gods are waiting," Darius growled, fingers resting on the portal's handle. "And I doubt they're going to be as welcoming as before."

Welcoming. If that was welcoming she hated to think of what lay in store for them.

He gave them no time to prepare. Darius yanked open the door, the multiple suns of the Underworld streaming through the crack between realms.

Bash hissed as the faded crimson light touched his pale flesh, and Margrete squeezed his hand in reassurance. She didn't dare use her words to comfort.

The Underworld was darker than before, the suns a more vibrant shade of red. The rocks held shadows upon their ragged sides, almost as if ghosts flitted across their surfaces, their invisible eyes trained on the unwelcomed newcomers.

Margrete kept her shoulders back as she adjusted to the brightness. This was the defining moment, and she would do everything in her power to fake her confidence.

Darius had been right—the gods were waiting.

Margrete made out Halio's looming form standing at the entrance of the glass bridge, the blood river tumultuous today as it crashed against both banks, red staining the slate rock. She shivered, thinking of the attack on her people just last night, how their life essences had seeped between the grains of sand.

Her shiver turned into a tremor as a ripple of magic pulsated through her. There were no other visible gods at Halio's side, but that didn't mean she couldn't *feel* them.

There were at least two others.

Margrete lifted her chin and forced herself to let go of Bash. He gave her a knowing nod, though it was tight. He didn't wish to release her, and to be honest, she wished she could've held his hand as she walked before the death god.

Marching down the steps, she led her crew, her friends, her *family* into the pits of hell. All the while, Darius's magic flourished, his palms glowing, his features etched in stone. She called forth her own power, allowing it to flood her system, its cold presence like a winter wave. She had to admit, she'd grown rather fond of the feeling.

It made her all but invincible, and to a woman who'd been beaten down most of her life, having such magic made her head dizzy with the possibilities. When the time came would she hesitate to give it up?

Margrete warred with herself the entire walk down. She could do so much good, could possibly change the lives of others for the better. Hadn't she prayed to the God of the Sea less than a year before, desperate for aid? But instead of a callous god answering, Margrete could be the one to deliver miracles. She could be a light in the dark.

The realization nearly robbed her of air.

She slowed her pace when they reached the bottom, attempting an air of nonchalance. Halio's attention honed in on her every movement, and his lips curved upward, his black robes billowing out around him like a shroud.

"We've completed your task," she intoned once they were within speaking distance of the death god. "Our bargain is complete."

She was tempted to turn to Bash but she held firm. *Do not show weakness,* she thought, trying not to wither beneath Halio's steel eyes. His smirk persisted as he assessed her, down to her flickering palms. His stare turned to Darius briefly, and she swore she glimpsed a hint of surprise ignite Halio's cold irises.

"You've returned," he said, studying her and her friends. She heard Adrian clear his throat. Likely nerves. Bay was either jabbing him in the ribs to hush or soothing him. It could go either way.

Halio drifted closer, lifting himself from the ground, his feet dangling in the air. "But I see you have *not* completed our bargain."

Her blood turned to ice.

But her magic...it *boiled.*

"What do you mean I haven't completed the bargain?" she asked, not recognizing the viciousness lacing her tone.

Darius stepped forward. "We've killed the beasts. I sensed no more roaming the oceans."

Halio shook his head, a subtle frown tugging on his lips. "No. There remains one more monster borne from the deep."

"But there isn't—"

No.

He couldn't. He *wouldn't.*

Margrete shook her head as if that would do her any good. Her knees shook as she stumbled back a step, the world tilting precariously to the side as all the blood rushed to her head.

Halio was never going to allow Bash to return with her. He always knew she'd have to...to *kill* him in order to complete a useless agreement. She'd been so easily fooled.

"He is half-nymera," Halio said softly, tilting his chin toward Bash. Her king stared ahead blankly, his body frozen, his chest not seeming to move. "He has the blood of the original nymeras in him, and therefore, he has the dark magic crafted by Darius and his brother. He does not belong to the human world. He never has."

At that, Adrian strode forth, shoving off Bay when he tried to stop him. Bash's oldest friend walked right to the God of Death, his nostrils flaring. She'd never seen him lose his temper before. He was the calm, collected one.

Not anymore.

"He is no monster!" Adrian snarled, shocking them all. Even Atlas exchanged a stunned glance with Bay, who'd slowly eased to his boyfriend's side. "Whatever bargain you made with Margrete, you should honor it," Adrian continued. "Deception is beneath you, God of Death."

Bash's eyes went wide, the first sign of life since Halio declared him a beast.

The Underworld shook, rocks tumbling down on either side of the walls encasing them. "I did not deceive her," Halio thundered, storms clouding his irises. "I told her what I required, and she accepted. It's not my fault she didn't understand the terms."

No. Enough with this.

Margrete shot off a blast of magic before she thought better of it. Electricity sizzled in the air as it struck—an inch away from her target. Her bolt soared beyond Halio, who'd shifted to his right in the blink of an eye. She tried again.

This time when she stormed forward, both palms raised and a pained sound escaping her throat, Halio had to use a shield to block her assault. He grunted as she aimed for his chest, for his immortal heart. Bay grabbed Adrian and shoved him out of the way, the crew scrambling for safety as she screamed her fury. Margrete didn't know where Bash was or where Darius stood. All she saw was Halio, and all she heard were the words he'd spoken. They echoed, and she used her rage as fuel.

"Stop this!" Halio hissed, shoving both hands to the side. Margrete felt a rush of rotten wind. It barreled into her midsection, knocking her off her feet. She didn't stay on the ground for long.

Halio blocked her next advance, but she was so incensed, she'd allowed her magic *complete* control. There was hardly any thought inside her head other than *Kill.*

"Margrete!"

Her name. It sounded from Bash's mouth, and yet she shoved it aside, choosing to focus on Halio's lies. His deceit. She'd gone to the Under-world and back merely to be fooled by yet another crazed god.

Margrete was through with it all.

Clouds eclipsed all three suns as she commanded the only liquid within reach. The blood surrounding the fortress rose, a stream of red spiraling her way. It slipped beneath her feet, lifting her even as the scent of copper clogged her nostrils. It should've been overwhelming, but she inhaled deeply, relishing its potency.

Halio watched from below now, the God of Death seemingly unimpressed by her little display. "Get down, youngling," he commanded, flicking his wrist. The blood beneath her boots wavered, and she almost stumbled. "I did it for your own good. You weren't thinking clearly when you first arrived, and you needed time to discover your power. Time that I gave you."

There was a brittle laugh that sounded from just behind her. Margrete spared a glance.

Darius rose, stealing some of her bloodied wave as his own pedestal. He glowered at Halio, his golden hair whipping at his face in a furious wind. Sea salt and spice permeated the air, overpowering Halio's magic.

"You never even gave her a fair shot," Darius said, his tone taking on a mocking lilt. "You're all alike. All you gods." He nodded to the palace and then to the top of the ravine. "Come on, Charion, I know you're hiding somewhere. Come down and face me, why don't you?"

Darius came to her rescue. He defended her without a mask, without an ulterior motive. She knew then that he'd changed, because he fought against his own wishes. For her.

"Charion!" Darius called out again. "Face me!"

The world shuddered and the suns wavered, their light blinking. She sensed the war god before she saw him, the way his presence could implant terror into her being by simply existing. Then Charion, in all his glory, was floating down from above, his muscled form covered in flames.

He landed gracefully at Halio's side as if they were readying to fight together. In all likelihood, they were.

"Not surprising," Darius said, his laughter cruel. "But I thought you were better than this, Halio. You were supposed to be better than all of them. Even if that's not a hard feat to accomplish."

Margrete sniffed the air.

That smell...that cloying sweetness.

She looked to Darius, and they exchanged a knowing look. "There's one more."

"My mother," he said, observing the palace, his brows scrunched. "I sense her too."

Margrete searched for Bash below her river of red. She'd lost herself for a heartbeat, and because of her carelessness, she'd lost sight of her pirate. He wasn't with the others, not pressed against the walls of the crevice, not fearfully looking at the gods.

He was...gone.

But before she could open her mouth and call his name, the clouds parted and a wind not belonging to her or Darius or Halio swept through her curls. In typical fashion, Surria made a grand entrance, floating like the others, although she descended from the sky on soft clouds the shade of the purest snow.

She didn't land, choosing to stay at eye level with Margrete and her son, who growled low in his throat.

Surria smiled, her pointed canines on full display. No longer did she hide behind a mask of pureness, of reverent innocence. She'd shed her façade and bared her teeth, and she faced them now with a look of fierce resolve.

"I've waited too long for you to become what you were always meant to be," she said, her voice taking on an eerie, tinny quality. "But I realized I could help you in other ways. I could be softer, more...motherly." She scoffed at the last word. "And I will soon give you everything you want." Her gaze drifted to Margrete. "Maybe then you can focus on your potential."

Darius snarled. "You fucking snake! I need nothing from you—"

A flash of black floated past her vision, careening into the Goddess of the Wind and Sky. Sharpened nails glinted in the light of the three suns, and Margrete watched in horror as Bash sliced at the goddess with a viciousness she hadn't seen in all her years.

The goddess didn't scream. No, she didn't make a sound at all.

Surria idly lifted her hands and sent a blast of magic straight into Bash's scaled chest.

Light exploded, momentarily blinding her. She lowered her wave of blood and leaped to the ground, set to race after Bash, but the world tilted and spun.

Surria wrenched Bash into the air, gusts of wind wrapping around his form, making him a prisoner. He struggled and hissed, the noises he released feral in nature.

"A lovely attempt," she sighed theatrically.

Margrete's heart dropped into her stomach, her pulse beating wildly against her ribcage as Bash fought.

"I'll kill you," Bash grated out, his black eyes sparking silver. "All of this is your fault. Your fault your own son despises you. That he spent his life creating monsters and killing others for sport. All because of you!"

Margrete tried to send her magic at the goddess, but she struck a barrier, some invisible wall that had her gifts recoiling. Surria lifted a knowing brow at her.

"Let him go," Margrete demanded, both hands tingling, prickling with unspent power. "You've caused enough damage."

To her sons. To Margrete. To the *world*.

Surria laughed. The shimmering winds encircling the man she loved twisted, growing tighter. He wheezed, and a part of Margrete died.

Charion, who she'd nearly forgotten about after Surria's entrance, began to chuckle. He crossed his arms against his chest and leaned back, enjoying the show. He did nothing to deter the Goddess of the Wind and Sky.

Halio, however, showed a hint of remorse, his face creasing for just the briefest of seconds. He shifted backward, his head slightly cocked in the direction of the palace. She met his eyes, held them, and she saw so much...

If you don't like this fate, then change it, a voice murmured into her mind. It wasn't Darius, because he was too distracted by his soulless mother, his lips curled into a snarl, his fists clenched as his magic sparked. *Don't disappoint me. I knew you'd be the one to change everything. Prove me right.*

Halio spoke to her now, his voice a gentle melody, a vibration against the walls of her thoughts. Margrete didn't understand. Minutes ago, he'd all but admitted he worked to deceive her. And now—

Bash's scream broke her free from Halio's grip.

Surria's winds slithered to his throat, circling his neck, choking and bruising him. All of his nymera strength was useless against the goddess, who easily overpowered him. And Margrete could sense his newly returned life force draining from his body.

She called his name. Once. Twice.

Margrete screamed as she blasted off shot after shot, only to strike that same barricade. Halio was right—she didn't like this fate. And she sure as shit didn't accept it.

Surria held Darius's eyes as she slowly killed the Azantian king. "I'm doing right by you, son. You just never seem to understand it at the time. I may not possess the humanity you relentlessly seek, but I've never needed it. It's a weakness, a mask I shucked years ago when I discovered how very pleasant life could be without its weight."

Darius was speaking, spewing words of hatred in return, but Margrete was distracted. She felt a sudden buzzing in her trouser pocket, the key she'd stolen coming to life. It burned through the linen of her pants, singing its haunting song meant for her ears alone. She was about to grasp the key when Darius sent his magic out.

Then, all hell broke loose.

CHAPTER FORTY-FIVE

DARIUS

Darius wasn't sure when he'd decided to forgo all of his well-laid plans. Wasn't sure of the exact moment when he crassly said, *Fuck it,* and decided to join in on their rebellion.

He. Was. Done.

And the worst of it all? Darius wasn't sure what he was even fighting for anymore.

He'd wanted Margrete and the love he'd shared with her a thousand years before, but he'd been a fool. More than a fool. So deluded was he, that Darius assumed he could bend and shape her will any way he pleased, forcing her to accept him.

Just like Surria had done to *him.*

Charion sent a burst of fire his way, the ancient god roaring. Darius slid to the left, effortlessly blocking the attack without a trace of magic. He was being reckless, but again, he simply didn't care.

The war god raced forward, rising on the smoke of his flames, meeting Darius at eye level. Margrete sent some of her magic into his torso; an attack he surprisingly didn't block, all his focus having been on Darius. Her magic struck his shoulder, blue blood trickling from the wound. He didn't flinch, continuing to sprint ahead, his attention fixated on Darius, his true target.

Waiting until Charion was ten feet away, Darius finally thrust into action. This close, his magic would have more of an impact. He lifted his hands—

"Fuck you!" Margrete roared, an electric wave of blue and white encircling Charion. His attention dropped from Darius, who lowered his arms as Margrete approached, the swells of blood lifting at her back. The might of her aim might be set on Charion, but she stared at Bash, who continued to struggle in Surria's thorns. Of course, his mother watched it all play out with a smirk on her face, amused by the spilled blood. It further cemented that there was no humanity inside of her, that there never had been.

"I'm so sick and tired"—Margrete shot another round at Charion, who fashioned a shield—"of you gods fucking up my life." Another blast. "I won't let you win. Not again. Not *ever* again." Her power was a sentient being that reacted to her whims without a thought. It radiated from her body, spirals of it discharging, cords of furious power rushing to shatter Charion's shield.

Darius paused, uncertain. He'd always imagined he'd be the one to kill the war god, but watching Margrete take charge, watching her become consumed with the same fire that had burned within his gut for centuries, had him standing back.

She...she wasn't the same. Or she wasn't who he had always imagined.

Margrete wore two faces. One, the loving, warm, and stubborn woman whose heart couldn't help but hope. And the second one—which Darius believed to be her true face—the immortal who'd do *anything*, destroy anything, for those she cherished.

And of course, because Darius was only now understanding he didn't truly know this woman at all, he came upon the harsh realization that she wasn't Wryn.

A soul could change, he imagined, just like a heart.

Margrete, unaware of his inner turmoil, continued to battle the God of War with fervor. Charion managed a decent assault, and she screamed as flames wrapped around her leg. The bottom of her trousers singed to nothing, her skin blistering.

Still, she pushed on, even as she grimaced in pain.

"You don't deserve this power!" she shouted. "You need a heart in order to share it with your people. With those who worship you." Margrete took a fumbling step forward, her cheeks ablaze with rage. "You. Are. Not. Worthy."

Margrete Wood of Prias shrieked, the sound so ear-splitting, that Darius nearly covered his ears. Her magic seemed to scream with her, and just when he thought he couldn't take any more, she opened her palms and sent out another strike.

This one fatal.

Charion's stomach had turned into a gaping hole, Margrete's power having shot straight through him. He peered at his wound in shock before bringing his focus to her.

"This is the end of your reign." Margrete's magic encircled his form, consuming the remaining flesh and bone. Charion's legs snapped off first, turning to a liquid, transforming into nothing more than puddles of saltwater. The god screamed, frantically attempting to cast his magic and save himself, but it was too late.

Across the way, Surria's smile finally dipped, Bash still frozen in her arms. Yet no fear flashed across his eyes when he beheld the woman he loved. Darius sensed his pride.

Charion's head slid from his neck, bits of his torso slipping to the ground like falling rain. Margrete's eyes were silver, the metallic sheen brightening when the last piece of flesh disintegrated.

Then she turned those silver eyes to Darius's mother.

He would have found joy at the blatant fear twisting Surria's features, but he knew her better than to believe she wasn't scheming. Already a step ahead.

"Let him go!" Margrete held up her hands in warning, her bloodied wave and her blue light mingling together. It was grotesque, sickly, and unquestionably terrifying.

Surria's lips turned down, and she chose the final weapon in her arsenal.

With a sickening *snap*, her winds broke Bash's ribs, his spine, his every limb. His scream echoed in the cavern, the agonized noise the most horrid sound Darius had ever heard. Time seemed to stop, the world ceased to turn, and every thought that had occupied his mind disintegrated. All he felt was pain.

Surria released his broken body, which collided gracelessly with the hard earth. He didn't move, but Darius heard his pained gasp. He'd be dead soon, *again*. Darius studied Margrete, who didn't shatter at the gruesome sight like Surria had anticipated.

No.

She fucking attacked.

Her brilliant light turned sapphire, her eyes rivaling the Underworld's suns. Surria countered her attack with surprising effort, but she managed to elude the worst of it.

Darius looked away from the battle between his mother and Margrete. The king was forced to watch as Margrete fought an ancient deity. His eyes were struggling to remain open, and wetness filled them.

Surria made sure he'd stay alive to witness his love dying.

Darius reflected upon all the years he'd spent alone, wishing to find the missing half of himself. He created Wryn to fill that void, but as he realized earlier, while Margrete might be her soul reborn—a part of *his* soul—it was the heart that mattered.

And in this life, Margrete had found Bash.

Darius hadn't admitted how jealous he'd been until that moment. And not simply of Margrete. But rather, what she'd found.

Help him, a small voice whispered into his mind. It was familiar. He whirled around, finding Dani staring at him, a knowing look on her face. She was speaking to him as immortals often did, although her voice was muffled, so soft he'd barely made it out. But her words...

She had already been unusual, a soul possessing the rare ability of Sight. It appeared that after the sea had chosen her, Dani's once dormant strength had increased tenfold. A strength that Darius now forced himself to feel.

He spun back around, knowing what he had to do. Marching to the unmoving king, he knelt.

Bash stared at him through half-lidded eyes, his breaths uneven and hoarse. Any second now death would claim him. Hell, he hardly had one foot in this world as it was.

Halio.

At the reminder of death, Darius searched for Halio, finding only Margrete and Surria engaging in a vicious fight to the end. Yet as he leaned forward, inches from the king, he found himself glancing over his shoulder one last time.

A pair of green eyes held his, begging him, imploring Darius without words to act. To do something selfless. She lifted her stubborn chin, her short, red hair sliding back from her face. In all the chaos, Mila stood still, an unmovable force of will.

Right the past, Dani whispered again, growing louder. *Do it not for her, but for yourself.*

He gritted his teeth, hating that he knew the *her* the voice spoke of— and it wasn't Margrete. Why he cared, or why his heart fluttered wildly whenever he beheld Mila's smirking mouth, was beyond him.

But maybe he longed to find out.

Mila started to blink, to lose eye contact. Losing hope. She didn't think he'd do anything, and as her chin slowly began to dip, Darius acted. Bracing both hands on Bash's chest, he warily scanned the king and his many injuries.

"Don't worry," Darius muttered when the king peeled open his eyes, which widened in fear. "I don't kill mortals so close to death. That would be no fun at all."

His lids fluttered shut, his hands pressing into Bash's icy skin, his nymera scales poking into Darius's fingers, his palms. He delved deeper than he'd ever gone, past years of listless traveling, years of Surria and Malum and their sneers and disappointment. Darius slipped beyond the barriers he'd erected and broke them apart with his own magic, watching as the walls crumbled and fell.

He still loved Margrete. He always would. But Darius wanted to find a love that would choose him in return. To choose *only* him.

And that wasn't her.

After all the horrid things Darius had done to Margrete over the course of a few weeks, he decided to offer the only apology he could give. One that would cost him *everything*.

What was immortality if he had no one to share it with?

Slipping free from his own mind, Darius delved into the king's. He rearranged his thoughts, his organs, his very blood, and the parts of him that belonged to his nymera half. He released his magic into his veins and hissed when his power protested.

He became aware that he was glowing, that they both were. He didn't hear the roars of battle or see Margrete or his mother. He didn't see the crew, but he felt Mila still, her penetrating green eyes that sometimes softened when she looked at him.

Below him, the king shifted, an anguished groan slipping from his mouth. Darius persisted, pouring all that he was into the mortal's half-dead body.

Every. Single. Thing.

Minutes or hours or days passed before the final spark of magic left him. When the last ounce of what made him a god vanished, Darius collapsed, his vision speckled with black, his heartbeat too fast and too loud in his ears. He slumped to the side, his head hitting the ground with enough force that he bit his lip.

With the last of his energy, Darius lifted a finger to his mouth, touching the broken skin. When he brought his hand before his face, he saw red coating his fingertip.

Not blue.

Not the blood of a god.

The blood of a mortal.

Darius lost consciousness just as an explosion rocked the Underworld.

CHAPTER FORTY-SIX

MARGRETE

MARGRETE SCREAMED AS PAIN SHOT DOWN HER TORSO, SPREADING to her legs, her toes. She screamed as black spots clouded out reality and she could no longer see Bash's mutilated body from the corner of her eye.

She'd lost every rational thought when Surria had broken him. She lost herself. Gave it away, in fact. Margrete *became* the power, rather than a woman possessing it. And how it had worked well in her favor. Until now.

Surria laughed, the sound grating. Margrete whirled around seeking the noise, unable to make out much of anything besides smoke and jagged stone. She heard footsteps, sensed the goddess hovering nearby.

She was taking her time. Enjoying the kill.

But Margrete wasn't going to make it easy on Surria. The gods had taken *everything*, and she was left with the curse of consuming rage. Such a powerful yet dangerous emotion. It could fuel a person to seek revenge and complete it. Or it could destroy the bearer entirely.

Margrete would rather go up in flames than surrender.

Without her vision, she was back in time. Back in the box her father built her once upon a time. She was used to the dark, accustomed to being without all of her senses. Her heart thudded in her ears.

Margrete smiled.

"What's so funny?" Surria asked, her voice coming from every angle. "You're about to die along with—"

She was cut off by a roar Margrete recognized. It belonged to a god she'd hated for so long yet didn't understand. A god who had been vindictive and cruel and cunning.

Darius screamed, his voice soon joined by more voices.

An arrow whooshed by her ear.

Margrete blinked, taking advantage of the distraction to clear her vision. Slowly, the blackness dissipated, though it didn't wholly vanish. Still, she saw enough.

Adrian. He released another arrow aimed at the Goddess of the Wind and Sky, and at the same moment, Bay threw a silver spear through the air, the lethally honed tip soaring toward the goddess. Both weapons pinged harmlessly off her invisible shield, her arms raised in protection. A gust of wind lifted the fallen arrow and spear and turned them around.

Back toward her friends.

She screamed as they were released, as the spear made contact with Bay's right shoulder, the arrow slicing into Adrian's leg. Both fell, both hissed in pain.

With Surria's attention on them, Margrete caught movement to her right.

Darius. And he wasn't alone.

She would've cried with joy had the danger receded. But the vision of Bash striding—not limping—toward her didn't bring joy. Only fear blossomed. It meant she could still lose him, even if she didn't understand *how* he stood to begin with.

Pieces of herself shifted back into place, her bloodthirst abating. Her pocket began to vibrate once more, the key trembling. It was asking something of her, directing her to salvation. Begging her to follow fate's path—

Fate. That was it. She suddenly knew exactly where the key desired her to go.

It was time to relocate. To not only finish this and end the corrupt immortal once and for all, but to distract Surria from her king.

Thankfully, she didn't have to act alone.

The next time an arrow soared through the air it vibrated with magic, striking inches from Surria's unfeeling heart. The goddess growled as she grabbed the arrow and pulled, blue blood gushing from her wound.

Margrete whirled around.

Brielle stood proud and tall behind her, bow in hand, a somber smile on her harsh face. Leather encased her body, daggers and bows and arrows and all manner of weapons strapped to her muscular frame. She glared at Darius, but then turned her attention to Surria.

"Too long," Brielle whispered, "have we cowered beneath your power. Too long have we allowed you to speak for us all."

Surria sneered. "You're all weak. Someone had to stand up and make decisions."

Brielle began to respond, but Margrete took her chance.

She sprinted to Bash, a light blue haze haloing his body. Something had changed, and she tasted the potency of old magic, of divinity. It didn't make sense.

Hurry, she mouthed as they locked eyes, Bash running to close the distance. She waved toward the river of blood, urging her feet to move faster.

As if it knew her intent, the key buzzed painfully against her thigh, eager. Her boots struck the glass bridge with force, and seconds later, another pair thudded along with hers. Bash was right behind her, nearly on her heels.

There was a whirl of arrows and a rushing breeze. Lighting cracked the sky, and steel clouds blocked the light, forcing Margrete to peer over a shoulder. Brielle and Surria continued to clash, the Goddess of the Deep Woods and the Hunt painted with as many cuts as her opponent.

Margrete had just made it to the other side when Bash reached her. Before she could inspect him for injuries or hold him in her arms, more footsteps pounded the glass. Again she turned, but instead of ruthless gods, Mila, Dani, Atlas, Bay, Adrian, and Darius raced to keep up, all on the bridge, determined looks hardening their faces. Although both Bay and Adrian were injured, their Azantian blood worked quickly, knotting torn flesh together just enough so they could continue the fight.

They scrambled her way, breathless. Even Darius appeared surprisingly winded.

Warm fingers slid into hers, and she jerked her chin up, momentarily stunned. Bash's skin lost some of its ethereal glow, but his dark eyes flickered with silver now.

"What happened to—"

"There will be time later," Darius said, panting as he and the others surrounded her. He clutched at his sides as if he had difficulty breathing. Margrete didn't understand.

"The book," Dani urged, her eyes encased entirely by silver; barely any white shone in her gaze. Copper exploded on Margrete's tongue as she looked at her friend, but it wasn't blood. Whatever Dani emitted, it made her insides feel frozen, her head fuzzy.

"We don't have long," Dani pressed. The haziness vanished, and Margrete shook her head, hoping there was time later to question her. She spun to Bay, Atlas, Adrian, and Mila, and to them, she asked, "Do you have my back?"

All nodded, and Bay's lips curved slightly, both dimples on display. "Always, Margrete."

CHAPTER FORTY-SEVEN

MARGRETE

MARGRETE ENTERED THE THRONE ROOM, HER FAMILY AT HER SIDE, Bash's hand in hers. Darius may not have said the words, but she knew what he'd done. Done for Bash.

Even with time running out—Brielle's distraction granting them only a few minutes—Margrete paused and cupped Bash's rosy cheeks, her eyes sliding down to his throat.

His scales...

"They're gone. How..." she murmured to herself. His nails were trimmed, no longer lethal weapons. But his hair remained black as midnight, the strands falling into his dark eyes.

He was a god. Immortal. As if in confirmation, his magic reached out to graze hers. Unlike Darius's, he smelled of his signature sea and pine scent, its familiarity like a welcome embrace.

With the divinity in his veins, he was freed from the shackles of his nymera blood. Yet she knew he'd never be the same as he once was, and that he would wear those changes for the rest of his life. A reminder of all they'd been through.

Before Bash had a chance to open his mouth, Darius hobbled over, sweat dampening his brow. "As much as I'd enjoy this saccharine reunion, there simply isn't the time to explain the intricacies of gifting a mortal with your divinity." He grunted, limping to the center of the room where the emerald book was raised on its pedestal. "I can feel your confusion from here, and it's giving me a headache."

"Is he saying what I think he is?" Again, she *knew*, but fuck if she needed to hear the words out loud.

One corner of Bash's mouth quirked, and a spark of the man she loved resurfaced, the shock fading away. "I think you know," he said softly, leaning down to brush a kiss atop her temple. He briefly turned to Darius, the pair sharing a look. Bash dipped his chin, and Margrete felt his gratitude pour out of him in waves.

Bash was alive and healthy before her, and Darius could hardly stand—

"Yes, yes," Darius snapped, tired of waiting. "I realize now I made a horrible mistake. Being mortal fucking *hurts*."

"Good. Now you'll feel my punches better." Mila stepped forward, and Margrete couldn't help but see how long Darius held her stare. He swallowed thickly before forcing his focus back to the book, though his cheeks were tinged in red.

He was *blushing*.

"This hasn't been opened for centuries," Darius said, clearing his throat. "Since the dawn of time, it has been in our care, the Book of Fate. Somewhere along the way, the key was stolen and then lost, likely due to power-hungry gods battling over it." His focus drifted to the palace doors, where the clashing of powers sounded. "I think Malum found it, and it was the sacrifice he made on the island during the trials."

How he'd managed to deceive Surria would remain a mystery, but she thanked the dead god for secreting it away, regardless of whether he'd originally planned to use it for ill intent. The key was more precious than anything in this world—and just as dangerous, if not more so, if it fell into the wrong hands.

Margrete peeked up at Bash one final time. She inhaled, noting how his scent now held traces of smoke. It reminded her of Darius.

He truly gave up his divinity. For her. Or maybe he'd done it for himself.

"Finish this," Bash whispered, running his index finger down the side of her cheek and to her chin. He lifted her head. "I knew you'd be the one to change my life, Margrete Wood. The one to change all of our lives."

"Enough!" Darius cut in, exhausted by their display. "You must hurry."

"I love you," Margrete said to Bash before she turned and ran for the pedestal. The sounds of the fight grew near, and she didn't have a doubt that Surria was making her way to them now. She prayed nothing had happened to Brielle, who'd come to their aid. She, too, had been fed up with Surria's reign of terror.

Margrete reached the ancient tome, which appeared nothing more than a regular book. Nothing special. And yet the lock that encased its thick, leather cover shone, the gold glittering with magic.

The key was screaming at her now, violently pulsating. She reached for it, and when her fingers curled around its smooth handle, the doors to the throne room slammed open.

A gust of wind shot toward her, knocking her to the side, the key flying through the air.

She couldn't see anything as she tumbled, only the white robes of the Goddess of the Wind and Sky as she marched into the chamber. Margrete heard the key, its melody, its haunting song. It sang to her even as it soared...

And then the music stopped.

When she came to a halt, her body aching and her mind clouded with fear, she looked up.

Dani.

She stood before the goddess, the key in her hands, the orb crushed in her fist. Shards of glass lay at Dani's feet, her hand cut and bloodied. Margrete surged forward as the palace rattled and shook, the young sailor flung high into the air by some otherworldly gust.

Dani's body shone with light, the shade neither blue nor red. Rather, it was a combination of the two, a deep violet color. She spun around and around, her transformation illuminating the entire throne room. Margrete's mouth gaped in shock as Dani finally dropped to the stones seconds later, falling to her feet gracefully. Too gracefully for any mortal.

Surria's screech rang in Margrete's head.

"You idiots!" The goddess set her sights on Dani, striding closer, her dress torn and dirtied. It matched her insides.

But Dani didn't shy away.

Power erupted from her slight frame as Surria neared, and it was brilliant, so impossibly electric, that it knocked Surria off her feet. It was the power of a god.

Surria's tears, combined with whatever the hell Dani was—seer or *other*—resulted in an eruption greater than any magic Margrete had ever seen.

Dani's eyes glowed as she marched to the fallen goddess, looming over her like a vengeful angel. "I hold you responsible for the actions leading to my brother's death," she hissed, her voice echoing. "And I request your life in return."

Bash grabbed a staggering Darius, hauling him to the side of the chamber and out of the way. The others followed suit, lunging for safety when Dani closed her eyes and sent all of her new magic barreling into Surria.

Somewhere, Margrete heard the broken key clatter to the floor, but she was too focused on Surria as she held up her arms, which were the shade of slate. Her hands began to char and wither away, breaking apart inch by inch. Dani radiated triumph as the goddess's form disintegrated, turning to soot.

Margrete spared a peek at Darius, who made a low sound in his throat. He didn't defend his mother, but he also didn't appear elated at her demise. Margrete supposed no child delighted in the death of a parent, no matter how cruel they'd been to them in life. She understood this well, as screwed up as it was. When she'd killed her father, she didn't feel happiness, merely justice.

They all watched as Surria crumbled and fell, turning into a pile of ash at Dani's feet.

Margrete held her breath, the Book of Fate before her, the key some-where in the chambers. Not all was fixed, she realized. Not until they repaired the past to save the future.

Dani turned toward Atlas, who'd taken a few shaky steps toward her, her blue eyes trained on the newly fashioned goddess. Dani didn't hesi-tate to close the distance.

They were blurs as they both raced into each other, colliding, Atlas's hands moving to Dani's cheeks, whose body began to flare with light. Dani perched on her tiptoes as she pressed her mouth to Atlas's lips, her hand winding into the warrior's loose braid. Margrete's heart squeezed as she watched the pair, pure joy emanating from them both.

Dani finally drew back, panting for air. "I've wanted to do that for ages, and not while under a goddess's spell," she whispered against Atlas, who had yet to release her. "You took far too long."

Atlas smiled, her face alight with radiant happiness, even as the ashes of a goddess were swept away by a phantom breeze. "I won't wait so long again," she promised, a tear slipping free. Margrete had never seen such emotion coming from Atlas—it seemed she reserved such a look only for Dani.

As they embraced, Margrete felt a prickling race across her arm.

Her tattoos. She watched as Halio's ink began to fade, leaving only the marks that had appeared when she'd first opened the portal to the Underworld. She grasped her forearm, her lips parting when that, too, slowly vanished.

A bargain made with a god was fulfilled with blood and ink. Some-thing Halio had taught her. And Margrete had the suspicion that the swirling flames tattoo that had decorated her skin on the island was a bargain she made with *herself*. To get her king back.

There was one last tattoo.

A prickling sensation worked down her spine, and she knew if she looked into a mirror she'd see that Darius's lilies were gone. Ripped from her skin just as his divinity had been taken from him.

Instantly, her stare narrowed in on Darius, who gazed at her in a knowing sort of way. He dipped his chin, motioning to his now mortal frame.

Their bargain...

It was null and void. And he must've known this when he chose to save Bash. Her lips parted. She'd never thanked him.

She did so then, mouthing two words across the space. He'd made the hard choice in the end. His life, she suspected, hadn't been full of love, and while his past deeds were unforgivable, this one act would be the beginning of his new story.

Margrete decided she wouldn't stand in his way.

The man who'd once been a god gifted her a smile that appeared more genuine than any she'd seen him wear. She sensed no regret on his part, but she noted how his eyes creased in a way that spoke volumes.

Darius's attention shifted as the King of Azantian strode to the corner of the room, where he picked up a shining sliver of metal. Her heart ceased to beat when he began walking her way, pride illuminating his eyes when he took her in.

He was her heart, her friend. Her partner. And he was *alive*. She was alive. And Margrete allowed her tears to fall then, allowed them to cascade down her cheeks and slip to the stones.

"Don't cry, princess," Bash said, a foot away. He lifted the key, offering it to her. "It breaks me when you cry."

She grabbed at his collar and hauled him in for a kiss, her tears slipping into her mouth. She tasted salt as she devoured him, sobbing as he gripped her waist. If she could stand there and kiss him for eternity, she would, but Bash knew she had to finish what she'd begun, and he reluctantly pulled away. Though he took her hand in his and entwined their fingers. He cocked his head to the book.

Margrete sucked in a breath. Together they walked over to the Book of Fate, the key in her grip. Even with the glass orb shattered, it hummed in approval when she placed it in the lock and twisted, the leather strap that bound it together breaking. The severed ends fell to the table with a thud.

The cover sprang open, and Margrete's eyes went wide at the sight of all the many names scrawled onto the endless pages. They seemed to never cease turning, and she realized with a start what they were.

The names of all the living and the dead.

The pages continued to turn, a brilliant gold seeping from the parchment. Her mind whirled as every name blurred—all the souls that had graced this earth. Souls who'd held fear and felt love. Had families and friends and hopes. She took them all in with a reverent sigh.

A deep voice brought her out of her reverie.

"You'll be needing this."

She and Bash turned at the same time.

Halio materialized before them, a simple black quill in his hand. Behind him stood the God of Justice, Themis, his stark white hair fluttering in his emotionless eyes. The god unnerved her, but he appeared on their side, on Halio's. Brielle limped behind them, a cut across her chest. She'd recover, but Margrete suspected she was weakened from holding Surria back for as long as she had.

Margrete startled when Halio continued closer, her magic jumping to life, preparing to fight if need be. "But...but you—"

"I told you not to disappoint me," Halio said, smiling. "All of the events had to unfold the way they did in order to get to where we are standing now." He eyed the book.

"But you threatened Azantian. You made such a horrid deal..." She didn't understand.

"I never planned on destroying Azantian," he said with a sigh. "Themis here wouldn't have allowed it anyway." The God of Justice remained apathetic, though he bestowed her a barely perceptible nod. "Besides," Halio continued, "Themis believed Darius could be saved, and if it's one thing he hates most, it's wasted potential."

"So I was an *experiment*?" Darius asked, frowning. Without his magic swirling around him, all he could do was clench his fists.

"An experiment that won me Themis's support should this day come. And Brielle's."

"Brielle and Themis wanted me to live?" Darius ran a hand through his hair, disbelief making him seem years younger.

"Apparently, she also thought you could be redeemed."

"Shocking, I know," Brielle muttered, brushing at the blood stains coating her leathers. "Don't disappoint me, Darius. I'd hate to have to kill you when it would be so easy."

Without an ounce of mockery, Darius bent at his waist, bowing to Brielle. When he lifted, his stare was brimming with gratitude. Margrete understood that not many people in his life had believed in him in such a way. Brielle's faith probably meant more than she could ever know.

Halio looked to Margrete, his knowing stare seeping through her skin. "We needed you to be the one to rewrite fate, Margrete Wood." He lifted the quill, offering it to her. "A creature made from flesh and bone, gifted with a power you never wanted. That's what makes you special. You could've taken your new gifts and ravaged the world. Made the people bow down to you. Or perhaps you could've merely enjoyed the luxury the Underworld had to offer. But you didn't, and you never would have. You've lived your life fighting for those who couldn't defend themselves, and while you were selfish risking Azantian for your king, at your core you are still human and flawed. But good, nonetheless."

Margrete swallowed thickly. She didn't feel as if her actions warranted such praise. She was ashamed at the lengths she would've gone to for her own greed.

As if reading her mind, Halio added, "The lines between right and wrong are blurry, young goddess. There is no good and evil, merely the *will*, the desire, to try and do the righteous thing. And while you've stumbled, you've always tried, and I admire you for that act alone. Now, you must prove me right." He motioned to the open pages. "Three gods have been killed and one born." He studied Dani, who still had Mila in her arms. "Now, two more gods must be chosen."

Select wisely, Halio whispered across her thoughts.

Two gods. Two lives.

Bash met her gaze as she released his hand. He nodded, seeming to relay everything he felt in one moment of connection. Such adoration, it drowned her in a way that had her wishing to never come back up for air.

When Margrete took the quill from Halio's hands, the pages belonging to the Book of Fate came to an abrupt stop. The very first page.

Halio's name was written beside hers, followed by Themis, Brielle's, Dani's, and...

"Bash." She pointed to the page. "Look."

His name was scrawled next to hers. The ink fresh.

"He's your missing half, Margrete. Now that Darius bestowed him with his immortality, you may rule together as one." Halio answered her unspoken question, confirming her greatest desire. Bash had *wanted* to be with her, however he could, but now she had to pick others, and they might not desire this destiny.

"I can't pick someone who doesn't want this life," she said, her words echoing in the too-quiet chamber.

"You must," Halio insisted. "The balance is off."

It might've seemed silly, to think that some would refuse such a *gift*, but immortality came with its own consequences. It was a weight the chosen would have to carry for eternity.

"I'll assume Surria's role," Dani asserted, stepping from Atlas's hold. Themis cocked his head at her, and Margrete could've sworn she saw a hint of a smile.

"And I'll go wherever she will," Atlas said in a rush. "If you'll have me, that is." She asked this last part of Dani, suddenly shy, her cheeks blazing.

"You really are terrible at reading people," Dani muttered playfully. Atlas's smile widened.

"I'd accept the war god's position," Atlas said, chin lifted proudly. "I would be much better at it than him anyway."

"That leaves one more space." Themis scanned the room, his cold eyes lingering on those present. He paused on Adrian the longest.

"No!" Bash shouted at the same time Adrian stepped forward. "Don't even open your mouth."

Bay grabbed his boyfriend's arm, refusing to let him continue. Adrian would offer himself without pause because he was the best of them. "You can't!" Bay pleaded. "I can't live my life without you." Because if Adrian became a god, he'd be immortal, and one day Bay would turn old and gray, and his body would wither away.

"His heart is true," Themis whispered with certainty. "He is the best option."

Margrete held Bash's hand, even as he yanked on her grip, trying to get to his friend. She knew Adrian would be a righteous and just immortal, but he'd have to leave his island and Bay, behind.

"I have to do this, Bay," Adrian said sadly, curving his body toward his boyfriend's and grasping his face between his hands. "The world is at stake and..." he choked on a sob, "I can't be the reason you're not in it. *That* would kill me."

"You don't have to leave me. You won't," Bay said firmly. He whirled to Halio. "Darius ruled with Malum. I will rule beside Adrian." He met his boyfriend's eyes, wet with unshed tears.

Halio regarded them both, a dent forming on his brow. Slowly, he brought one hand to Adrian's chest, the other to Bay's.

"Is this your true wish?" he asked. "To not be parted?"

They both nodded. Was there ever really a doubt? One could merely look at them and see the love they had for one another. They were bonded, their souls one.

"Then so be it." The air crackled with energy, the ground vibrating below their feet. From Halio's palms came his magic, and Bay and Adrian both bowed from the force of it.

It was over as soon as it began.

Both of her friends crumbled to the ground, panting. "What did you do?" Margrete asked, breathless. Hopeful.

Halio turned his kind eyes on her. "They were already of one heart in their mind," he said. "I merely made that true. They share one heart now, and so they'll share one role here in the Underworld. Together."

Bay lunged across the floor and into Adrian's arms, wrapping him tight and squeezing. He kissed his lips, his cheeks, his neck, anywhere he could reach, his face glowing with hope.

"We still need someone to rule Azantian." All eyes shot to Bash. "I will not assume the throne, given my attention will not remain on my people."

He was a god now, and as such, Azantian wasn't his only domain. Bash wasn't selfish enough to rule Azantian *and* help Margrete rule the seas. He loved his people far too much for that.

Margrete could only think of one other worthy of the crown. Someone who wasn't standing in this room.

"Nerissa," she said, confident. "She would make an honorable queen. A wise one." She thought of the seer, how much she cared for Azantian's people, how she devoted her life to the island. If anyone else should sit on the throne, it should be her.

Bash nodded somberly, though his eyes sparkled with faith.

"Then it's settled." Themis motioned to the Book of Life. "Write the names."

Margrete inhaled sharply, and Bash squeezed her hand, forever her support, her foundation when she felt as if the entire world threatened to tilt.

"Only the blood of a god can bind fate," Halio added softly, nodding to her hand. "Perhaps that is why the key was 'lost' for many years." The last part was added lightly, a whisper. Malum...had he purposefully hidden the key in his chambers, away from Surria, knowing what she'd do with such a weapon. He'd concealed it to protect them all.

Nothing is good or evil. That was the lesson learned. She could say the same for herself.

Margrete lifted the quill, piercing its tip against her index finger with a grimace. She watched as blue blood blossomed into a perfect drop.

She dipped the quill and hesitantly turned to the page. She paused.

"Can you permit three others into the Sea Court?" she said, looking to Halio.

"I was waiting for you to ask," he replied. "Their souls are pure, and their hearts belonged to the waters they loved. Only this once will I go against Death. Find their names and rewrite their afterlife."

Mila's choked gasp rang throughout, and even Dani released a pent-up sob. Jonah, Grant, and Jace would be given a new life here, and that was a gift those brave men deserved.

She lowered the pen and scribbled two more names onto the page before searching for the friends she'd lost. With a few strokes, she rewrote destiny.

"It's done," she said, allowing the quill to drop from her hands.

Halio laughed. "Oh, Margrete Wood, I'm afraid it's all just beginning."

EPILOGUE
MARGRETE

TEN YEARS LATER

THE WORLD WAS THEIR HOME, AND IT WAS SO VERY LARGE.

"Come on! Help me out," Margrete shouted, the wave she commanded to carry them forward slowly dying. "Don't just sit there brooding."

A scoff, and then, "I'm not brooding, princess, I'm looking at you." Bash's strong arms snaked around her middle, his weight pressing her stomach against the wooden rails of their modest vessel. It had been crafted from Azantian wood, a small piece of the island with them wherever their powers called them.

"Well, stop it," she teased, reaching around to flick his nose. "I would've thought you'd be sick of me after all these years." Indeed, traveling across the realm on a tiny ship big enough for two might cause some to feel desperate for space. Just not her. Margrete thoroughly enjoyed the lack of room, using it as an excuse to lean against him, to feel his arms surround her after a long day.

Bash squeezed, resting his chin on the top of her head. "You know I'll never tire of you." He pressed a kiss into her hair. "Besides, after all the places you've dragged me, I prefer when we're alone at sea. Just the two of us."

Their first adventure had been to track down a ship known to deal in the slave trade. After imprisoning the crew, they'd freed those below, using their gifts to guide the ship to a safe haven. Right after that, they'd been called to the North Sea, where a mystical compass had been located in an old shipwreck. With the power to show its owner the location of their heart's desire, it was a dangerous weapon to have. They'd brought that particular item back to Azantian on one of their visits to Nerissa.

There'd been so many more adventures in the years that followed.

"I miss them," Margrete whispered, thinking of Nerissa and her sister, who she'd been forced to leave in her friend's care. Life at sea, amid their divine power, would be dangerous. They journeyed to the island as often as they could, but Birdie begged them to take her with them, regard-less of the risks. Margrete had merely told her that she would have her own adventures to go on. One day, and soon, she imagined she would.

Bash lifted a stray curl that had dipped into her eyes. Carefully, he tucked it behind her ear. With his other hand, he raised another wave, urging the ship closer to their destination. Land would appear on the horizon any moment now.

"I miss them too," he admitted, spinning her in his arms. She peered up at him from beneath her lashes, the midday sun blazing. "But they understand why you chose the burden. Why *we* chose it."

To devote their lives to the sea and protecting it. To protect the people who journeyed across its surface.

"You ever regret joining me?" she asked, for what was likely the thou-sandth time. Bash scowled, his handsome features turning hard.

"How could I want anything more?" He tugged on her waist, his fingers digging into her hips. "I spend my days on the waters that have called to me since my birth. And to have you at my side? Regardless of the duties, of the horrors we've seen, being at your side has been the greatest blessing of my life."

She rolled her eyes. "So sappy, pirate."

Bash lowered his head, his lips skimming the sensitive skin below her ear.

"Let's see if you call me that afterward..."

"After what—"

Her words died in her throat as Bash scooped her into his arms. She giggled, her hands encircling his neck. "You're absolutely incorrigible."

They had an hour before they reached Azantian. They should be preparing instead of headed below deck. For the *third* time this morning. She swore Bash's need for her grew when he became a god, and the man was insatiable. Not that she complained.

Bash stumbled below and brought her to their bed, pillows and linens from markets around the world covering the mattress. Evidence of their travels lay everywhere, from woven tapestries to gems, from coins to rare shells.

She let out a sigh when her back met the soft sheets. Bash hovered above, his dark hair falling into his eyes, the color a reminder of what he'd endured. He appeared the same as he had the day he became immortal, as had she. Their youth had been trapped in time, but an unnamable wisdom had hardened his features.

Bash unbuckled his belt, whipping it off and tossing it to the side. It clattered against the floor. Margrete leaned back on her elbows, watching her king undress, her lips curling into a devious grin.

"Enjoying yourself?" he asked, arrogance sure in his tone. Bash lowered his trousers to the ground, standing before her bare. Shimmering scales covered his upper chest and wound around his neck, though they'd grown lighter after his transformation. In the sun, Margrete swore they glimmered like crushed diamonds.

This man was all hers. This cocky, stubborn, and beautifully kind man.

"I'd enjoy myself more if you were *slightly* closer."

Outside, the waves turned frenzied, Bash's eyes a storm of need. He sucked in a breath, his stare never once wavering from her as he moved down her form and back up to her face. Sparks flickered at his fingertips, and Margrete blushed, knowing just how *skilled* those fingers would be.

They'd quickly discovered how their magic...heightened certain sensations.

Growing impatient, Margrete lifted up and snatched his arm, yanking him on top of her as she laughed.

"I caught you." She grabbed at the back of his neck, holding him in place, his lips inches away. Margrete did enjoy teasing him.

Bash reached between them, undoing the button of her trousers. She went completely still, trapped by his sensuous perusal, his hands making quick work of removing her clothing. In truth, *she* was the one caught, and as if he read her thoughts, Bash flashed her a crooked grin.

"Catch me anytime you wish, princess," he murmured against her skin, his mouth drifting to her stomach, her hips, her ribs, his lips leaving tender kisses in his wake. She arched into him, seeking out his touch. It had always been like this between them, like a flint to stone.

As Bash shifted to rest between her thighs, Margrete leaned up and stole another kiss. This one was deeper, longer, and unhurried.

They had all the time in the world.

"I love you," he rasped as he entered her. "My beautiful queen."

She may not have gotten the chance to rule Azantian, but Bash had continued to use the title. He claimed she would always be his queen.

"I love you," she echoed, gasping when he languidly slid out. Their eyes locked, the depths of their emotion shining through.

Margrete kissed her pirate until they reached the shores of Azantian.

They'd finally come back home.

Bash

SAILORS SHOUTED UPON THEIR ARRIVAL, THE PEOPLE OF THE ISLAND flocking to the docks to greet them.

After making themselves decent, Bash and Margrete set to work, coaxing the waves to rush them to the coast, their friends all waiting for them.

Nerissa stood front and center, her black hair tangled in the breeze. His friend smiled, but she didn't wave like the rest. Since she became queen, Nerissa had taken her position seriously, placing all of her attention on the people she served.

But the days when the newly fashioned gods returned were the days Bash remembered the most—all of them together again. Even if Nerissa appeared slightly older each visit. It was a reminder of the time slipping by. On a few occasions over the years, Dani and Atlas had met with them as well, but they were often busy, a war having broken out between two kingdoms in the south. As the Goddess of War, Atlas's presence had been required, and Dani had followed.

And Bay and Adrian...they ruled over Calista's old court. One of eternal love. They spent their days imparting the greatest gift the world could know, and they did it together, traveling across the realm to spread their power, filling the hearts of the people with joy.

Today, however, they'd all be in one place.

The second he could, Bash jumped from the ship and onto the docks, racing toward Nerissa and scooping her up in a hug. She gave an indignant scoff but hugged him back just as fiercely.

"You're suffocating me," she complained, but there was laughter in her voice.

Margrete hopped off the ship, closing the distance. Bash released his friend only for her to be captured by *his* queen. The pair closed their eyes, and Margrete whispered something Bash couldn't make out into Nerissa's ear. When she pulled back, Nerissa was grinning.

"I see you've missed me as well, sister."

Margrete jerked away from the queen, peering over her shoulder to the new voice.

Birdie had certainly grown up. Although she insisted they call her Bridget now. Youth's innocence had left her, and she'd become a capable young woman, trained by the best warriors Azantian had to offer in the art of combat.

Margrete snatched her up right away, and Bridget huffed out a groan. "I've missed you so much!" she said, drawing away to peer into her sister's eyes. "You've gotten so big!"

"Time doesn't stand still for the rest of us," Bridget said quietly, stepping back. Bash sensed that she missed Margrete, and while they couldn't visit as often as they might've liked, he hoped Bridget understood. The young woman stood tall as a gust of wind drove her long braid over her shoulder, brushing against the leathers of her training clothes. Various knives and blades were strapped to her petite form. Bridget may not have been born on these shores, but she was an Azantian, without a doubt.

"Ah! And there she is!" Bridget shouted. Bash knew who he'd find before he turned.

"This time, I want to leave with her," Bridget said, cocking her head to Margrete in challenge. "She gets to see the world, and she's made quite the name for herself." Envy shone in Bridget's eyes, her gaze on an approaching ship decked with red sails and Azantian's crescent moon and star emblazoned on the main mast.

Mila certainly had gained a reputation. Specializing in magical items, she could track down anything if given a lone clue, and she wasn't the only one...

Sure enough, when Bash squinted, he made out a head of bright blond hair. Darius leaned against the bow, Azantian in his sights. This far out, Bash couldn't discern his features.

"She brought company," Margrete said, shaking her head. "I'd have suspected Mila would've killed him by now—"

She was cut off yet again.

Figures appeared above the waters, silhouettes taking shape. Four to be exact.

Bash turned to Nerissa. A tear slipped down her cheek, wrinkles crinkling at the corners of her eyes.

They were all bonded. And not just by magic and destiny.

While the others shouted at Mila's ship and the four gods floating to shore, Margrete reached up and cupped his cheek. Bash drowned in her beauty, in the warmth she radiated like the sun.

"You ready to see our friends, pirate?" Margrete asked, grinning wickedly.

"I'm ready for anything," he replied, and holding his entire world in his arms, he meant it.

Margrete Wood had cursed fate long ago, not knowing she'd one day be its master. Yet she had no idea she'd give *him* the greatest gift of all.

Her.

Today, like all the days to come, would belong to them... And there was so much magic in the possibility of forever.

Thank you for reading! Did you enjoy? Please add your review because nothing helps an author more and encourages readers to take a chance on a book than a review.

Find more of from Katherine Quinn at www.katherinequinnauthor.com

And discover THE LAIRD OF DUNCAIRN, by City Owl Author, Craig Comer. Turn the page for a sneak peek!

You can also sign up for the City Owl Press newsletter to receive notice of all book releases!

SNEAK PEEK OF THE LAIRD OF DUNCAIRN

BY CRAIG COMER

Effie exposed her hand to the growling bear. Her fingers found Rorie's head and gave him a few soothing strokes behind the ears. A rumble came from deep in his gullet, as fierce as his wee body could muster. Frigid wind blasted them as they hid behind a large boulder atop the crown of Ben Nevis, the highest peak in the Highlands. A stranger had come to speak with her employer, Thomas Stevenson. Not an odd occurrence, but for a fortnight Rorie had groaned and whined, pawing for her attention as if disturbed by dark thoughts, trying to plead with her that something was amiss. And now that the stranger had come, Rorie's discomfort had turned into malice.

"If only I could peer into that head of yours and see what the fuss is about," she said, planting her hands firmly on her hips.

Rorie squatted on his haunches with a big huff, turning his head away. Though preferring the wild of the forest, he behaved himself around others when she asked. And only because it was she who asked. The bond had something to do with her Sithling blood, but Effie couldn't explain how it worked. It was as much a mystery to her as any of the uncanny bonds she'd made with woodland creatures, lazy housecats, and goofy hounds over the years. As much a mystery as why the queen and all the lords of London abhorred her kind, though she'd done nothing to warrant their wrath.

Rorie had been loyal to her ever since she'd convinced Stuart Graham to rescue him from a carnival the prior year, saving him from a brutal—and probably short—life of baiting. But he'd never acted so ill-tempered. Had the stranger come to take him away? Or was it she who should be fearful? By sight alone, the stranger wouldn't know her for a Sithling. Short of stature, with a young woman's curves and chestnut locks clipped about the shoulders, she lived her life amongst the Scots all but unnoticed, the truth of her mixed fey blood hidden.

Yet such reliance on appearance was a false safety.

Her hair whipped about her face, blinding her until she swept it back. The lodge of the Scottish Meteorological Society perched only a short distance away, a cozy, timbered house well-weathered from years of driving gales. Its chimney puffed white smoke, teasing her with thoughts of hot tea and honeyed biscuits. But that was where Mr. Stevenson had taken the stranger, and he'd instructed her not to return until he bade her. She blew into her hands for warmth, vexed by the riddle of the strange visitor, unable to contain her curiosity any longer.

"I'm going for a closer look," she said to Rorie. "Wait here." Hoarfrost crunched as she shifted her weight and slunk forward. The frozen dew crusted the fern and bracken around the lodge, radiating a cold that sank into her bones. Her olive-colored dress and drab woolen coat were serviceable enough, but they did little against the cutting winds atop the mountain, winds that drove in the damp air as if she wore nothing as all.

She understood why Mr. Stevenson wished her to hide. He was a man who believed in prudence. He would not jeopardize one of his great works, nor his reputation nor her safety, on the off chance a stranger would find her out. There were some who could recognize her fey nature if they stood close enough. The scientists of the day, many of whom had their pockets lined by London's coin, said fey blood corrupted the flesh, giving off an odor that some could smell. Catholics and Protestants alike said it was the sins of the fey that radiated a cloud of evil around them, allowing those pure of heart to perceive them. Other tales held that a fey's eyes glowed in the dark or that they would burst into flame if they touched iron. All of it seemed foolish to Effie. She drank her tea and let it pass the same way as anyone she'd ever met, regardless of their blood. How some knew her for a Sithling while most did not was as random as why some seeds took root and others wilted.

A whistle shrieked, drawing her attention. Next to the lodge, Mr.

Stevenson's plans for a great observatory were coming to fruition. Steel beams braced half-raised walls as masons slathered on stone and concrete by the ton. The pipes of a steam crane shuddered, and a burst of gas exhaled as another beam was lifted into place, soaring thrice the height of a man to the workers waiting above. The construction was what had brought them to Ben Nevis, and Effie guessed the stranger would not have come if he weren't involved with the great project in some manner.

She stalked forward, half-crouched so the wind wouldn't stagger her, and reached the sill of one of the lodge's thick windows. Grabbing the smooth, lacquered wood for support, she peered through the glass into the lodge's main room. It held several tables of a dark and sturdy teak, and a stone hearth large enough for a royal estate.

The stranger stood with his back toward her. His coat and polished shoes bespoke a city, but not the odd leather cap with its flaps that clung tight around his ears. She didn't recognize the tartan on his trousers: blues, greens, and purples all jumbled together as if shouting at her. She recalled he'd driven his own steam carriage up the winding road, working the levers and knobs as if he were used to the task, an odd thing for a wealthy man.

"I will take your concerns into account, Mr. Crofter," said Stevenson. The window's frame had warped over the years, allowing her to hear him clearly. He stood by the hearth. A dark coat fit snugly around his stout frame, its wool threadbare from years of rugged service. His balding head held tufts of hair around the ears, yet they served to dignify his face rather than embarrass it.

"They are not just my concerns, Mr. Stevenson. They carry the weight of the Society. It is time to distance ourselves from such relations. Lord Granville will have his way, and you must choose where your loyalties lie—with the Society or with your fey friends."

Stevenson's face darkened. "We have pushed back these threats before and should not wilt so easily to tactics of hatemongering. Parliament has no grounds, and Lord Granville not enough allies."

A shadow moved from the corner of the room, and Stuart Graham's stocky frame came into view from where she crouched outside. The man's knee-length boots were coated in mud, a workman's badge he wore proudly, and his white locks curled in ringlets atop a face as cheery as it was round. "Bah, let us speak plain, Mr. Crofter. You knew of Mr. Stevenson's associations before you funded the observatory. It was his name alone which brought in enough benefactors to ensure the completion of construction."

Mr. Crofter grunted. "Do you think any of these benefactors will stand against the threat of an Inquiry? No, Mr. Graham, they will scatter like rats." The stranger turned to Stevenson. "You will do as we ask, or we will sever ties and throw you to the wolves. One noted engineer is easily replaced by another. Now I bid you good day." He slapped his gloves together and strode for the door.

Effie recoiled. The news from London must be dire for Mr. Crofter to speak to Stevenson as he had. She crept to the front corner of the lodge and watched the small yard of trampled grass where the stranger's carriage sat. Graham emerged from the lodge's main door. He pulled a worn and battered watch from his pocket and studied it before casting his gaze to the skies. Mr. Crofter came out on Graham's heels, walking cane thumping the dirt as he ambled. The pair exchanged a cordial nod, similar to one shared by passing gentlemen in a city street. Effie didn't understand such manners. It was clear Graham was in a foul mood and Mr. Crofter the cause of it, but they pretended like nothing cross had occurred between them.

Rorie wasn't as polite. A low growl came from behind the boulder where she'd left him, and the bruin's head popped into view, teeth bared. She waved at him to stay back, but the noise had already drawn Mr. Crofter's attention. He peered at the boulder, his eyes growing wide. He muttered something, a scowl on his face, before clambering into the waiting steam carriage. Graham stood stiffly while the other man brought the boiler into action. The carriage's engine was a monster of steel and wood, with copper tubes lashed in a lattice across its flank and a charred snout thrusting upward from its roof. With a parting nod, Mr. Crofter threw open the valve, and the carriage sputtered forth with a burst of burnt coal perfuming the air. Only when the squeaking of the carriage's axles had faded down the mountain road did Graham turn to stare right at Effie.

As he beckoned her, brooding clouds rolled over the surrounding hills, darkening the sky. The wind gusted, flapping his leather coat about his legs. Neither were good omens. She stood and crossed to him, her cheeks flushed in embarrassment. He greeted her with a grin forced from pursed lips, and he spoke in a rushed manner, barely taking a breath.

"Och, lass," he said. "You took a risk. If my waistcoat weren't as round as an ox, ye'd surely been seen. It's like to piss down any moment. Let's get into the warmth before it does. Mr. Stevenson wants a word."

Effie nodded sheepishly as the steam crane's whistle shrilled again. Black smoke belched from its boiler, the engine fighting the strain of the wind. But she needn't watch the work progress to know the shape of the observatory. Its structure had long been affixed in her head from the drawings she'd rendered of the project. That was her place in the endeavor. Stevenson had discovered her talent for depicting his designs years before when she was just a lost girl sheltering under his protection. She'd sought him out after the death of her mother, the famous lighthouse engineer who designed edifices powered by stardust—the glowing azure silt, forged by Fey Craft, that burned hotter than oil and slower than coal. Her eyes grew glassy. The time was a blurred memory that still haunted her dreams. She'd come close to starvation and almost succumbed to exposure. Worse, she'd been captured and beaten by the queen's Sniffers, those who hunted fey, and only managed to escape by sheer luck. Yet none of those trials compared to the sorrow of isolation, the sense that all her warmth and cheer had fled. That she was alone, the last of her family, nearly the last of the Sithlings.

Alone and yet not alone. She glanced at the dark shadows of forest sprouting from the hills ranging beneath the peak of Ben Nevis. How many of the other fey races hid there watching them? Pixies and brownies, gnomes and hogboons all still dwelt within the Highlands. The remnants of a Seily Court existed, yet her mother had taught her to be as wary of it as of the Scots. She could count on a single hand the number of fey she'd ever met, and none were likely to take her in if the need arose.

Such was the way for many Sithlings. Despite their appearance, they lived between races, not quite human and not quite fey. Their blood derived from a sect of the Daoine Sith interbred with the Votadini, an ancient human clan whose might had receded under an onslaught of Scoti tribesmen. What remained centuries later could claim neither as kinsfolk.

Effie followed the man she considered an uncle into the lodge. Heat from the hearth enveloped her the moment she stepped inside, soothing away the bite the cold wind had left. Laid out on one of the tables were Thomas Stevenson's plans of the observatory, his lines and notes as formal and stiff as he was. On another perched the casing for one of his famous screens, a protective box for meteorological instruments. Its sides were angled slats designed to keep moisture from the instruments contained within, allowing them to collect data for weeks on end unattended. Her own worktable rested in a corner. A collection of colored charcoals, neatly arranged within a tin, sat atop a rendering of the observatory. Her drawings always held more flora than the bleak locations Stevenson chose to build on, and the observatory was no exception. Ben Nevis' crown boasted none of the hearty pines and spring flowers her depiction held, but that never seemed to bother her employer.

Stevenson greeted her with a curt nod and gestured to a chair by the hearth. He didn't make her wait long, once settled. "Our caller was Mr. James Crofter, a noted engineer whose father worked with Thomas Telford on the Great Canal." Effie's lips tugged at a smile. To Stevenson, names were always linked to matters of accomplishment. His own noted a long family line of engineers. "He came to us in haste with news from the coast. Murder has been done in the village of Duncairn."

Effie started. If given a dozen guesses, it was not the news she'd expected to hear. She read Stevenson's face, but it remained a stone mask. "Was it someone you knew?"

"A fisherman," answered Graham, bringing her a cup of tea, "An Ewan Ross. His boat capsized in the Bay of Lunan."

She took the cup, piping hot and full of sugar the way she liked, and breathed in its sweetness.

"The importance is not whom but the how," said Stevenson. "Fishermen in the area swear a host of rabid seals tipped Mr. Ross' boat, accosting it in unison. Not normal behavior to say the least."

She stifled a laugh. The poor fisherman deserved better, but the image of a group of seals harassing his vessel, barking and slapping the water with their flippers, was comical to her. "Surely these fishermen are mistaken in what they saw, or perhaps Mr. Ross agitated the seals in some manner. Perhaps they were trying to help the man." She glanced between the two men, wondering if they were jesting with her. "Yet I fail to see how one could call it murder."

"That's what I did say," said Graham. "The Scottish folk are long known for tales of fancy. Any dark bed of kelp becomes the Kraken in their minds."

Stevenson cleared his throat. "Putting Mr. Ross aside, there is a second account Mr. Crofter related. A week ago, a young lass was accosted on the road to Montrose, just outside of Duncairn. She suffered woefully and is much delirious, but describes her attackers as hairy imps slight of stature, with sharp ears and wicked fangs. They battered her as she fled. She recovers now from a fractured skull and other wounds." Stepping to the table, Stevenson rested his fingertips on it. "Short, devilish imps with pointed ears. These creatures have a name. The Shetland folk call them trows."

"Bah, bollocks," spat Graham.

Effie blinked, taken aback by the certainty in Stevenson's gaze. "I had not believed trows real." Her cheeks flushed at the admission. Her knowledge of the fey races, and of Fey Craft, were scarce at best. Much that she knew had come from Stevenson.

"Real enough," said Stevenson, "though not seen in the Highlands for centuries. They are fell creatures not of the Seily Court."

She frowned. "I thought all fey were bound to the Seily Court, before the Leaving at least. The binding is what gave Fey Craft power in this world." That power had dwindled ever since the Daoine Sith abandoned Sidh Chailleann, their ancestral home.

"There are some fey the Seily Court cannot control. They form their own covenants, Unseily Courts they are called, though decades have gone since the last rumors of one's appearance."

"Oh," she said. She stared into her cup, feeling a bit lost. It seemed, every time matters of fey lore arose, she understood the least.

Graham read her expression. "Don't fret, lass. You still ken more of your blood than all of us together. Mr. Stevenson's just got more years of hearing tales than you." He winked. "Many more, by the top of his head."

She forced a smile. Graham often reminded her how young she still was. For all her curves, she was still recent to adulthood by human standards, let alone fey. Thinking on the accounts of Duncairn, she drew the simple connection. "You believe the two attacks are linked, and if these trow creatures did the one, then the seals were really—"

"Selkies," affirmed Stevenson.

"But that doesn't make any sense. Selkies are not wicked creatures. They shed their sealskins in favor of human form to lure men and women into loving them. They don't work in packs, nor accost fishermen at sea."

"I have never heard tale of such a thing either," said Stevenson. "Just the same, fey sightings have grown in past weeks across the Highlands, enough to reach the ears of Her Majesty's Fey Finders, and now with these attacks it is almost certain there will be an Inquiry."

Effie blanched. There hadn't been an Inquiry by the Sniffers in almost fifty years. Most in London called the fey hunters relics, the funds used to support them better used elsewhere. Yet as dire as the news was, it did not follow why Mr. Crofter had spoken of such immediate threats. There was more to the stranger's visit Stevenson wasn't telling her, something she hadn't overheard. She studied his face. Her foot tapped impatiently. Cheeks growing red, she forced herself to still and sip her tea. She could be more stubborn than a stone when it fancied her, but secrets foiled her patience. As much as anything else, curiosity had driven her into the world of man after the passing of her mother, the need to explore the enigma of their society. Yet even as a girl she had always quested after knowledge. Her mother had often scolded her, reminding her life wasn't a puzzle to be solved but a great riddle to be savored.

The lesson had rarely stuck.

She would need to pull the truth out of the man. "Rorie is in a foul temper," she said. "He wants to warn me of something, but I can't understand what. I thought it might be Mr. Crofter."

Graham traded a glance with Stevenson. "She's a woman more than twenty years grown. There's no sense as treating her like the girl she was."

Running a hand over his chin, Stevenson worked at the muscles of his jaw. "Parliament pushes for legislation to formally outlaw any association with the fey. That would include the use of Fey Craft—stardust, precisely —and the harboring of those with fey blood."

"Bah!" Graham cursed. "That kind of nonsense comes up every odd year. They'll make no ground with it. We've still friends enough in London."

Pain flashed in Stevenson's eyes. "That is not the worst of it, you well know, Mr. Graham." He turned to Effie. "The Society feels a sacrifice is in order, something to appease the crown and end talk of an Inquiry. They instructed I draw up a document listing the fey I am in contact with and hand it over to the crown."

Stevenson drew up his weight into a rigid posture, clasping his hands behind his back before speaking. "That is why Mr. Crofter came to us— to demand I betray dear friends."

Effie's blood ran cold, and she had to swallow hard to keep the tea in her stomach from surging upward. So that was it—the missing piece. To protect their investments, the Society wished to send her and Stevenson's other fey allies to the gallows. It was not strictly illegal to harbor pro-fey sympathies, but neither was it fashionable, and those who did often found themselves in prison or their fortunes waning. She sensed Rorie's seething hatred for Mr. Crofter and felt a fury of her own spring to life.

"Do they all know of me, then?" she asked.

"Not directly," answered Stevenson. "But they know I have enough involvement with the fey that I could perhaps influence the crown's good graces."

"You wouldn't!" Effie exclaimed.

"Of course not," Stevenson snapped. He turned from her to cool his temper, yet she thought nothing of his outburst. His benefactors had placed him in a horrible position. They would not let their investments fail; they had too much money at stake. Either he sacrificed the fey known to him, or they would find an engineer to run their projects who would. She had heard Mr. Crofter threaten as much, she now understood.

"It's a fool plan," spat Graham. "I should've skinned the man alive for suggesting such a cowardly thing. The Fey Finders would hang the fey and still seek an Inquiry in Duncairn. Better if this observatory falls to ruin."

Stevenson shook his head. "The Society will not allow that. But they do underestimate the devastation of an Inquiry; they see only what it would mean in London. Her Majesty's Fey Finders care naught whether a fey is good or fell, peaceful or sinister of purpose. Their aim is to demonstrate their own worth. Without check, they'll scour the coast and put to the question all they find, as they did during the Potato Famines a few decades ago. They'll use the Inquiry as a grand stage and propel these legislations through. From there, their wrath would spiral out of control." He pressed his palms against the table, though it appeared he would rather knock it over. "We cannot let that happen. We must strive to show the world that fey and human can coexist."

"What will you do?" Effie asked, eager to hear his thoughts. Part of what drew her to Stevenson was his work, always seeking to blend science with nature. He was a pure naturalist who used stardust to power his famous lighthouses, promoted harmony with the fey, and sought to canonize their lore.

"We must sap the hatemongers of their advantage," said Stevenson. "I will stall them as best I can, but we must find the true motive and intent of these attacks before their Inquiry can come to bear. If the truth is known, there's a chance the Fey Finders will find no allies north of Edinburgh. The Scots have no fondness for London's authority."

Effie considered his words. She had no stomach for politics. Large crowds and public debate went against every fiber of her nature. But that did not mean she would wither away like some English violet. She could not let innocent fey fall victim to such a scheme as the Society planned. If Stevenson meant to unravel the truth of the attacks rather than appease his benefactors, it would take all his resources to hinder their enemies in Parliament, leaving nothing for Duncairn.

So to there she must go.

She rose, her mind settled. "If an Unseily Court exists in Duncairn, we must know of it before the Inquiry. It may be our best chance of gaining leverage, and our only chance to forestall Mr. Crofter's designs." Her words were heavy, but she stiffened her back against them. "I will go there and uncover the truth of the matter."

"What!" Graham barked. "You can't mean to go near that village. The queen's bastards will be crawling over it before the fortnight is through."

Effie swallowed to keep her voice from trembling. "There is danger, but to do nothing is to guarantee more fey will suffer." She faced Graham. "I can do nothing here to help; my presence might even bring greater danger if Mr. Crofter returns."

"You can do less against an Unseily Court!"

"If one exists," she reminded him. She tried to keep herself steady despite the knot forming in her gut. Graham and Stevenson had risked their lives and the fortunes of their families to let her in and give her a sheltered life. She would not balk at doing the same for them. "You are both needed here. At the least you cannot be seen in Duncairn. The scandal would link your names to whatever judgment the Inquiry handed down."

"There are others," huffed Graham. "I ken a man near Montrose who often trades with the fishermen of Duncairn." His tone was more tired than she had ever heard. "He knows much of the fey and has befriended a few in the area. I would have him handle this."

"If you could reach him," said Stevenson. "The man is a drunkard and hasn't responded to your missives in weeks."

"I'll speak with the fishermen and the girl's family," said Effie, "and if an Unseily Court exists, we will throw them to your benefactors and limit the crown's hand. It is the least either party deserves. Please, Mr.

Graham, I must do something to protect the lives of the fey. I will not run and hide when I can offer aid instead."

"Bah!" Graham stammered, but his shoulders sagged in defeat. He spun on a heel and stormed out, slamming the door behind him.

The cold gust that rushed in made Effie shiver. She smoothed her coat and stepped closer to the hearth. Stevenson's face fell as blank as unmarked parchment, and he bent to scour over the observatory's designs. Effie knew Stevenson well enough to leave him be. Silent brooding was his nature, and she didn't take offense. To others it might seem he didn't care, but she knew he cared perhaps too much.

"Mr. Graham left his coat," she said. "I'll go after him."

She found Graham watching as the workmen set the observatory's giant lens in place. It was a moment they had planned for weeks. She knew a few of Graham's crew by name, but they all recognized her, giving her a cheery nod or word of greeting. Mr. Stevenson thought it a risk, yet she took that sentiment with a grain of salt. Where Stevenson placed prudence above mirth, Graham naturally exuded an honest warmth. He treated the crew like family and didn't employ a man he didn't trust.

"He should be seeing this." Graham had his arms folded across his chest. His cheeks and nose were rose-colored, as if he'd been nipping a few drams, but it was only from the wind.

"He has more pressing matters on his mind," said Effie, handing Graham his coat. She was not in a mood to speak in circles. "How dangerous are these creatures?"

Graham raised his eyebrow and stared at her askance. "If they're real? Dangerous enough you shouldn't go messing with them. It's a thick lad who pokes at a badger and doesn't expect to get bit."

"But you doubt trows exist?"

Graham stomped his boots for warmth. "I think Stevenson's nose has sniffed after funding for so long that it doesn't know a fart from a flower." Her eyes narrowed, and he held up a hand for her pardon. "This observatory is funded by landowners hoping its weather data will lead to better crop growing. They don't give a cuss about Acts of Parliament or the stars or the fey or any other bit of science that doesn't put more money in their pockets."

He pointed down the road. "That man, Crofter, is from Newcastle where the Hostmen lord over the coal trade for the entire empire. They aren't the type of men one should meddle with, and I wouldn't doubt the bugger is afoul of them."

"And Mr. Stevenson has been led down this path before." Effie finished Graham's thought. The affair with the lighthouse engineer, John Wigham, had left Stevenson accused of reckless slander, his name tarnished forever in the eyes of many in the scientific world.

"He's blinded by his own interests," said Graham.

"It is the fey's interest too," said Effie. "We are also his benefactors and have no other voice. The constabularies will not defend us. The magistrates of Edinburgh are bought and paid for by men who proclaim us the offspring of Black Donald." She stopped short of mentioning Graham's own interests, those of the French merchants who stocked his warehouses full of goods.

Graham gave her a cheery smile, but she saw the doubt and fear behind it. "We have enemies, lass. Too right. Some we know of, some we don't. I can't say as I understand what's going on myself, and that's what frightens me most. There's a strange feeling to this whole ordeal." The smile dropped from his face. "Robert Ramsey is a good man and no drunkard."

She rested a hand on his arm. "I will inquire after him."

He squirmed in frustration. "The tale of this Mr. Ross being killed by selkies is foolishness, and no doubt the other attack was carried out by some drunken rogue. The lass is just mistaken in what she saw or embellishing the tale for some reason." His skepticism made her love him more. It was the concern of a father not believing night had fallen, if only so his child could play in the sun a little longer.

"I've lived a happy life these past years, sheltered from those who would do me harm. That was your doing, yours and Mr. Stevenson's. It's time I repaid you the favor."

Graham's eyes grew moist. "Be careful, lass. The queen's appointed a new Fey Finder General, the man called Edmund Glover. I fear you know him, and he knows you."

Effie's stomach dropped to her toes. The name made her skin crawl. The last time she had heard it, she'd almost died.

Don't stop now. Keep reading with your copy of THE LAIRD OF DUNCAIRN, by City Owl Author, Craig Comer.

And find more from Katherine Quinn at
www.katherinequinnauthor.com

A war is brewing between the worlds of fey and man . . . but only one can prevail. Find out which in this fantasy featuring nefarious plots, dashing knaves, and militant gnomes.

When Sir Walter Conrad discovers a new energy source, one that could topple nations and revolutionize society, the race to dominate its ownership begins.

But the excavation of this energy will have dire consequences for both humans and fey. For an ancient enemy stirs, awakened by Sir Walter's discovery.

Outcast half-fey Effie of Glen Coe is the empire's only hope at averting the oncoming disaster. But she finds herself embroiled in the conflict, investigating the eldritch evil spreading throughout the Highlands.

As she struggles against the greed of mighty lords and to escape the clutches of the queen's minions, her comfortable world is shattered.

Racing to thwart the growing menace, she realizes the only thing that can save them all is a truce no one wants.

Please sign up for the City Owl Press newsletter for chances to win special subscriber-only contests and giveaways as well as receiving information on upcoming releases and special excerpts.

All reviews are **welcome** and **appreciated**. Please consider leaving one on your favorite social media and book buying sites.

ACKNOWLEDGMENTS

I want to thank every single reader who has come on this adventure with me. I started writing this story years ago when I was struggling to find my place in life. My pen and paper had always been my outlet, and in Margrete's story, I discovered a piece of myself.

To my husband, Joshua, my greatest friend and supporter. To my mother, Nancy, and to my children, who are always insisting I add prettier mermaids. And to Ashley R. King, who was my rock throughout this book. I love all of you so very much.

Thank you to Charissa, and the team at City Owl for publishing this story about love, loss, and finding your true self.

And once more, to you, dear reader, for allowing me to do what makes my heart so full.

ABOUT THE AUTHOR

KATHERINE QUINN is a fantasy romance author and poet. She graduated from the University of Central Florida with a degree in psychology. She resides in Houston, Texas with her husband and three children.

Her love for writing began at age nine after she read her first fantasy series, *Song of the Lioness*, by Tamora Pierce. After that, she wanted nothing more than to be a dagger-wielding heroine. Unfortunately, it's frowned upon to give a child a dagger, so she settled on writing about daring adventures instead.

Coffee is her true love, and she believes everything can be fixed with Starbucks and dark humor.

www.katherinequinnauthor.com

instagram.com/Katherinequinnwrites

ABOUT THE PUBLISHER

City Owl Press is a cutting edge indie publishing company, bringing the world of romance and speculative fiction to discerning readers.

Escape Your World. Get Lost in Ours!

www.cityowlpress.com

facebook.com/YourCityOwlPress

twitter.com/cityowlpress

instagram.com/cityowlbooks

pinterest.com/cityowlpress

Made in the USA
Las Vegas, NV
20 December 2023